The Sequel to "*A Sparrow Alone*"

~ a novel by Mim Eichmann

This book is a work of fiction. Any references to historical events, real people, or real places are used fictitiously. Other names, characters, places and events are products of the author's imagination, and any resemblance to actual events, places or persons, living or dead, is entirely coincidental.

Copyright 2021

Paperback ISBN: 978-1-7344593-7-1
eBook ISBN: 978-1-7344593-8-8

Library of Congress Control Number: 2020949143

All rights reserved including the right of reproduction in whole or in part in any form without written permission from the publisher

WWW.LivingSpringsPublishers.com

Cover model: Julia Franzen Richards
Cover photo: by Don Box, Elm Photography, Downers Grove, IL – all rights reserved.
Cover design: by Frank Wegloski, Maximum Printing, Downers Grove, IL
Background cover photo: by the author

Dedicated to my grandmother, Janie Owens

# Author's Note

*"Nobody ever became a writer just by wanting to be one.
Nothing any good isn't hard."*
– F. Scott Fitzgerald

With the above quote in mind and while trying desperately to find an agency interested in representing my first novel, I began researching *"Muskrat Ramble"* only a month or so after having finished writing *"A Sparrow Alone"*. Although this sequel moves through six decades, the story continues to be told in first person through the eyes of my original lead fictional character, Hannah Owens Barrington.

I knew that I wanted my main fictional characters to head down to New Orleans and for young Emma, now age 12 or 13, to aspire to a career as an early New Orleans style jazz singer. I had to slightly alter my original timeline to accommodate Emma's joining Sissieretta Jones' Black Pattis vaudeville group just prior to that group's unfortunate demise.

Having choreographed various suites using Ferdinand "Jelly Roll" Morton's music over the years, I was very familiar with Jelly Roll, but as much as I adore his music, the man himself was far too flamboyant a figure for my story's lead historic figure. I started looking into the lives of the early Creole jazz musicians who recorded on Jelly Roll's albums in the mid-1920s and almost immediately stumbled onto trombonist Edward "Kid" Ory, about whom I knew nothing whatsoever.

A wealth of internet searches quickly followed and in no time, I knew that Ory was my man! Ory's actual chronological timeline dovetailed so perfectly with everything I'd sketched out for my fictional characters that it was almost uncanny, including his performing career during Prohibition in Chicago throughout the Al Capone years, his resurgence as a leading musician in the 1940s when New Orleans jazz suddenly resurged as a hot music trend, and even his European venture in 1956.

In addition to Kid Ory, Louis Armstrong and Jelly Roll Morton, most of the musicians mentioned were historic figures including, among many others: Sissieretta Jones (The Black Patti), King Oliver, Scott Joplin, Bix Beiderbecke, Buddy Bolden, Tony Jackson, Johnny Dodds, Ed Garland, Wellman Braud, Mutt Carey, Luis Russell, Adelina Patti, Ma Rainey, Lil Hardin, Original Dixieland Jazz Band, Hot Fives, Dixie Syncopators, Bill & Louise Hegamin, Bessie Smith, Minor Hall and John Robichaux.

To that end, Hannah Owens Barrington, Emma Jackson, Octavie (Tayvie) Jackson, Alma & Frank Collier, Helen Mason Campbell, Deirdre Campbell, Margaret Hughes, Alice Barrington Hughes, Zuma Jackson, Joe Peterson, among many others, are all entirely fictional and are not based on any persons whatsoever, living or dead. Although Kid Ory had a reputation as a womanizer (as did Winfield Scott Stratton in "*A Sparrow Alone*"), Ory's only child was by his second wife.

### Various historical clarifications and disclaimers

** All of the quotes attributed to Kid Ory, Jelly Roll Morton and Louis Armstrong listed at the beginning of each chapter were taken verbatim from reprints of magazine and newspaper articles, radio interviews, and one movie.

** There are several versions speculating how Ory's tune "*Muskrat Ramble*" came to be named; my explanation, however, is a complete fabrication. The tune "*Black and Blue*", to which Hannah and Ory dance on New Year's Eve, 1923, actually has a 1929 copyright date by Fats Waller.

** The Alcion boarding house, where Hannah and Alice first live in New Orleans in 1913, was not opened as a boarding house until about three years later.

** The little treats that I've called pie-wheels that appear in both "*A Sparrow Alone*" and "*Muskrat Ramble*" are not specifically a Creole dessert. Women were determined to make every crumb count and would roll out leftover pie crust dough, sprinkle with various ground nuts, spices and sugars, roll up, cut into small rounds and then bake for a fun snack. Regional preferences undoubtedly played a part.

** Kate Chopin's novel *"The Awakening"* was so poorly received, that it was never reprinted after its very limited first edition in 1899, until it mysteriously reappeared in 1968. Chopin was well known for her short stories, but no publications that included her stories ever even mentioned *"The Awakening"* when crediting her works, since it was considered such a monumental blot to her character and her writing career. She died in 1904.

** Many of the discoveries I've noted in the medical texts where Hannah reads about *encephalitis lethargica* were actually found in footnotes from Dr. Sacks' observations in his non-fiction work *"Awakenings"* and sometimes allude to clinical observations by Dr. Sacks and other medical professionals that were documented after the 1920s.

** The Dunning Institute had been officially renamed Chicago State Hospital in 1917, however, almost everyone continued to refer to the asylum as Dunning for many decades thereafter. Treatments mentioned could have been used on the asylum's inmates at that time.

** The Myron Stratton Home continues as a refuge for poverty-level, Colorado Springs' senior citizens to this day – a tribute to the remarkable foresight of Winfield Scott Stratton -- now lasting over one hundred years.

# Acknowledgements

Jon Ball, Don Box, Kathy Carrus, Elm Photography, Colorado Springs Pioneers Museum, Odette Cortopassi, Rose Daniels, Doug Dapogny, James Dapogny, Todd Eichmann, Friends of the Colorado Springs Pioneers Museum, Dylan Goodrich, Charlie Halloran, Michelle Ledonne, Michael Levin, Cherie Little, Living Springs Publishers, Doug Lofstrom, Louisiana Music Factory (New Orleans), Maximum Printing, John McCusker, Myron Stratton Home, Elizabeth Daniels Nicholson, Stephen Charles Nicholson, Jacqueline Peavler, Julia Franzen Richards, SGV Book Club, The Aunties, Frank Wegloski, Richard White

# Table of Contents

Chapter 1: Kansas City, Missouri – 1913 ............................................. 1
Chapter 2: New Orleans 1913 ............................................................ 12
Chapter 3: La Petite Musquette ......................................................... 35
Chapter 4: Tremé 1914 ....................................................................... 47
Chapter 5: The Grunewald, 1914 ....................................................... 62
Chapter 6: Sissieretta Jones ................................................................ 75
Chapter 7: The Muskrat Ramble ........................................................ 90
Chapter 8: Margaux's Wedding ....................................................... 106
Chapter 9: New Orleans 1915-1917 ................................................. 120
Chapter 10: New Orleans 1917-1918 ............................................... 131
Chapter 11: Joe's Barroom – February 1918 ................................... 142
Chapter 12: New Orleans 1918-1919 ............................................... 147
Chapter 13: New Orleans - early 1919 ............................................ 168
Chapter 14: Octavie Edouard Jackson – 1919 ................................ 175
Chapter 15: New Orleans 1920-21 ................................................... 186
Chapter 16: Tayvie's Coat – Chicago, December 1923 ................. 200
Chapter 17: The Dunning Institute, Chicago 1923-24 .................. 209
Chapter 18: Chicago 1923-24 ............................................................ 225
Chapter 19: Emma – Chicago State Hospital – 1924-26 ............... 236
Chapter 20: "La Piaf Perdu" – 1925 ................................................ 251
Chapter 21: Chicago 1925 ................................................................. 265
Chapter 22: Chicago 1925-26 ............................................................ 278
Chapter 23: "Alice made the train ok." .......................................... 299
Chapter 24: Fall 1929 ......................................................................... 315
Chapter 25: The Depression 1929-1944 .......................................... 327
Chapter 26: Helen Mason Campbell - Paris, 1956 ........................ 338
Chapter 27: The Road Home ............................................................ 349
About the Author ............................................................................... 361
Source Materials ................................................................................. 362

*One's life is not at all like a book I reasoned.
Things are never fully resolved, never fully wrapped up
in nice, tidy little stacks
and neatly placed in the corner awaiting
our leisurely perusal and analysis.
We simply do our best to glue together
the often shredded pages of our fragmented chapters
and arrange them in some kind of meaningful sequence.*
Hannah Owens Barrington

## Chapter 1: Kansas City, Missouri – 1913

The splintering explosion of glass jolted me from a deep sleep followed by the inevitable screams of my neighbor's newborn child penetrating the paper-thin walls that separated our apartments. A large rock, shrouded in brown paper and loosely tied with coarse string, was nestled within the shards that had been my tiny front window. I called out to my daughter Alice that everything was all right, and then methodically began sweeping the glass into my dustpan, the full moon glistening over the shattered remains. I knew what the message undoubtedly stated although I did not know which group had resorted to so violent a nocturnal delivery.

As I carefully unwound the hemp from the note Alice appeared, tightly wrapping her faded blue flannel robe around herself against the chilled night air that now invaded the room. Exhaling loudly, she propped herself against the fireplace.

"Now what? My God it's cold in here!"

My neighbors had succeeded in cajoling their little one back to sleep I realized. Other than a trio of dogs still faintly barking in the distance, the night was finally quiet once again. As I had expected the note was almost illegible, scrawled in thick pencil by a scarcely literate hand. I read it aloud to Alice. *Lady techer: if*

2

*you don stop tech them nig—s youll be <u>varie varie sorry</u>*. Well, for what it was worth, I now knew which group had most likely delivered the note. The grown men from the town certainly wouldn't have felt a need to abridge the word and without question it was one they would have known how to spell.

My thoughts drifted momentarily back to this morning's exceedingly monotonous sermon. "A man needs to put down deep roots, yes, deep, deep roots, in his community. And with those deep roots, he needs to work hard to flourish my good friends. Send his branches out far and wide, regardless of where and in what capacity, whether he's a rich man or a poor man. For we can all flourish in whatever place God has chosen for us to send down those deep roots. God always has a plan for our place both in this life and for the one beyond," the pastor had droned. An older, exceptionally well-dressed woman wearing an immense, slightly out-of-style, dark green velvet Edwardian hat, complete with sprouting feathers, yards of bunched tulle and topped by a fluffy yellow bird, who was sitting in the pew in front of me, had remarked quite audibly to no one in particular: "Pfft. Roots indeed. Utter poppycock."

"Well," yawned Alice, then continuing with a smirk, "obviously they'll be delighted to know that you've already been fired and that Thursday is your last day at that awful place."

"I wasn't fired, Alice," I replied, glancing at her. "I wish you wouldn't say that."

I had started carefully stuffing newspaper into the hole, trying to avoid dislodging any of the few larger pieces that still held fast to the window frame. I would have to find a board to nail over it in the morning and then look into having it replaced as inexpensively as possible.

"Three old paunchy men from the town council show up at our door last Friday telling you that your services are no longer required for this 'school' you've been trying to make work for the last five years and that they are closing it down. I would consider that fired, Mother," she retorted, twirling one of her long blond curls around her finger.

"I'm sorry that you see it that way, Alice. It's only been within the last year or so … so much suspicion, unclear rules, parents afraid … I just don't …"

"And besides, now that your little pet student Emma has moved away you really didn't have much interest in teaching there anyway, did you? I notice she sent you another letter. She's written what, at least three times since they had to move down there. So that's almost a letter a month. I'm surprised the ink didn't melt right off the envelope from all that heat she constantly chatters on about."

"I think the window should hold until I can board it over in the morning," I said, clearing my throat in an effort to sidestep any unnecessary confrontation with Alice. "We should try to get some sleep now. You have a full day of classes tomorrow. And a mathematics exam. I almost forgot."

Alice took a few steps into the narrow hallway and then stopped, turning back towards me, her head slightly tilted.

"Did I tell you there was a new boy in my class on Friday? His mother just died over in Jefferson City and now he's living with his solicitor's family here. He bragged that he'll be going to a very fancy boarding school out in Massachusetts next term so he won't be around much. He told me that he's the one who shot Father and that he's actually some kind of brother to Johnnie and me. I told him he certainly didn't know very much because Johnnie had died a couple years ago. His name is Dannie Barrington. Same as ours."

I swallowed. I felt as though another rock had just shattered the fragile crystal prism I had so cautiously grown around myself almost since Alice's birth. Her grey blue eyes unwavering, Alice stared at me, arms rigidly folded. Even as a toddler she had always chosen her moments. Usually I attempted freely and pleasantly to give in to these dark questioning tempers of my daughter, for she was well-rehearsed in said overly dramatic style. But this time I needed distance. My roots were simply not deep enough. The woman with the yellow bird hat had been right.

"It's too much to discuss now. We'll go into it tomorrow when you get home from school, Alice," I stated, knowing full well that she would not budge from where planted in the hallway. Indeed she maintained the same pose glowering at me. Brushing against the wall I squeezed past her, ignoring her stare.

"I'm going to bed," I added tersely. "I'm exhausted. If you want to stand here shivering in the cold until morning, have it as you wish. Good night."

I arrived the following morning at the pitifully-maintained former post office building that had served as my teaching establishment only to find it padlocked, windows newly boarded over, with a hastily scribbled sign nailed to the door stating simply "School Closed until Further Notice." There would of course be no further notice. The few remaining colored children in this district whose parents felt the necessity of any education would have to seek it elsewhere. Most of those families had been less-than-subtly encouraged to leave town. And of the few that remained, typically small business owners who were reluctant to abandon their shops, they were quietly being thinned out as well. There would be no reason to establish or attempt to maintain such services, schools or restaurants for a group of people who didn't live here anyway in the eyes of the town councilmen. I knew better than to attempt to seek out those few families, to possibly hand over some reading materials for their children until they could once again sit in a classroom. It would be dangerous for them as well as for Alice and me. All this was a part of the high court ruling established well over a decade ago that seemed every year to become an even more malicious, voracious mongrel of a hound, eagerly displaying its huge white fangs throughout Missouri and elsewhere. Sadly, from what little I had read about our new president Woodrow Wilson, scarcely in office a few months, Mr. Wilson was quite eagerly aligning himself towards the justification of this schism having recently installed 'whites only' bathrooms and drinking fountains on the White House grounds.

After finding a thin board and nailing it lightly over my home's window as well as making arrangements for the glass to be replaced mid-week, I continued my walk into town circumventing the worst of the snarl of streetcar tracks, nervous horses hitched to small delivery wagons and the newest unpredictable menace maddeningly raging over the already clogged streets: the motor. The only advantage I could discern about the invasion of the motor, truly a wealthy man's toy if ever there was one, was at least there were slightly fewer horse piles (and accompanying swarms of biting green flies) steaming along one's route.

My destination was Andrew Reedy and Associates, the law firm that had represented my late husband's estate. Or at least, the late John Barrington's estate as it turned out. For I had learned just after my husband's murder that he was in fact still married to Dannie Barrington's mother, Vanya, and therefore a bigamist. I could have contested Vanya Barrington's claim to practically everything we owned but, expertly played like a splendid hand of poker, Vanya held scandalizing proof about me, my daughter Alice, my good friend Zuma, who was a Creole of color, and Zuma's daughter Emma, that would have permanently ruined all of our reputations. And without question my interference would have resulted in the retrial of a prison escape and resulting deaths in which Zuma may have been directly involved.

Mr. Reedy was also one of those 'three old paunchy men from the town council' as Alice had less than eloquently referred to them, who had shown up last week to inform me of my school's impending closure. His secretary explained to me that

Mr. Reedy was in a meeting with another client but should be available within the next half hour. Perhaps madam would like to find a café down the street and order a coffee rather than sitting in the dismal waiting area, the young man behind the desk so eloquently offered. I elected to just wait.

"Ah, Mrs. Barrington!" exclaimed Mr. Reedy as he walked his other client to the door. "Please, come in, come in. I only have a few moments before I must leave for an appointment at city hall, I'm so sorry." And to his departing client: "make sure you follow up with them quickly, George. He's quite the slippery one as you know."

Once inside his closed office he began hastily apologizing for the recent seemingly severe actions that his committee had been required to take in closing the school. "We just really had no choice, Hannah. No choice whatsoever. The enrollment had been falling off as you know and we just couldn't continue to pay your salary, admittedly as small a pittance as it was I realize, and the rent, utilities, books, supplies. The whole of it. Well, you understand, I'm sure."

"Yes," I replied quietly. "I know you're only following orders from farther up."

"Exactly," he said with a grateful nod. "I'm so glad you completely understand."

Well, I didn't completely understand and I never would, but questioning the committee's motives was not even remotely the reason for my visit. Since Mr. Reedy had another pressing appointment I moved quickly forward with my question.

"I'm assuming that you had been made aware that Vanya Barrington has passed away and that her son Dannie is now living here, apparently with his solicitor's family in Kansas City."

A quick, slightly guilty trace of a smile accompanied Mr. Reedy's furrowing brow. "Ah, yes. I had just learned of that, er, change in circumstances, from her lawyer in fact. I had just received a letter quite recently."

Change in circumstances? That was certainly an odd way of expressing the woman's demise I thought.

"But you didn't think it necessary to let me know that he was moving here?" I asked.

"Well, Hannah," Reedy replied, a brief look of amusement quickly passing over his haggard face, "the young man is only here temporarily. He leaves for, um, I believe the name of the school is Sheffield Academy somewhere in New England when the next term begins. Since he was only eight years old when the accident happened over in Jefferson City, no one here would even recognize him or really remember the circumstances surrounding the unfortunate incident, I'm quite certain. You'll forgive me if I offend you, but I honestly cannot imagine any reason why he would want to contact you. His mother invested, er, Mr. Barrington's assets quite successfully so I wouldn't be concerned that he would be looking to you for any kind of, well, forgive me if I sound condescending, Hannah, any kind of handout or anything."

"Right. Of course not." I nodded in terse acknowledgement. "He just turned up in my daughter Alice's school last week and mentioned that he was her 'brother or something' which upset her."

"Ah yes, well, children will be children teasing one another, of course, Mrs. Barrington," he laughed. Dannie seemed to have shrunk in stature from a wealthy young man heading off to an expensive boarding school to a silly child rendering nursery rhymes. "I'm sure as a teacher you're more than aware of that fact. Now, if you'll excuse me I really must be collecting myself for my meeting over at the Hall."

"Actually, Mr. Reedy, the reason for my visit, since my teaching post has now been permanently terminated here, is to obtain a letter of introduction and recommendation outlining my teaching skills and personal reliability of character so that I'm able to obtain employment in another state."

"Of course, of course! My legal assistant, Allan James, who you undoubtedly met in my outer office, has all the necessary paperwork and can even affix my signature and stamp to it. Just talk with Allan now before you leave and he'll have all the introductory information you require. And where exactly do you think you might be heading?"

I realized suddenly that our entire conversation had transpired while standing in front of his desk like two wooden actors rehearsing a poorly staged scene from some hideously written play.

"New Orleans," I replied evenly, walking toward the door and then turning briefly to address him face to face. "New Orleans, Mr. Reedy."

***

"New Orleans? What?! You mean as in down in Louisiana? *That* New Orleans?" shrieked my daughter that evening as we ate our meager supper of yet another tasteless, thinned out stew and coarse bread. "Where it's at least one million degrees all year and if the mosquitoes don't completely eat you alive the alligators will finish off the job?"

"Yes," I sighed, settling back in my chair, hopefully resilient enough for what I knew was going to be a nasty confrontation. Not surprisingly, she had apparently been paying attention during her geography lessons. "Exactly that very same New Orleans. Well, even last night you were complaining that you were too cold, so …"

"And just how far is that from this Reserve place?" she countered suspiciously, arms folded on the table. "Isn't that where this plantation is that Zuma and the annoying pet pupil ended up?"

"Yes, you know they're in Reserve. The Dawsons bought a plantation called Godchaux at auction and they wanted to take all of their house staff down with them. And actually, that's where Zuma's from originally. She was hoping many years ago to move there before we all ended up in Kansas City when you and Emma were just babies. It's about thirty miles or so west of New Orleans."

"So why didn't she just go then? I certainly wouldn't have missed the pet pupil all of these years."

I made no reply.

"I honestly can't believe that you're doing this to me! So we have to go trailing after a couple of ni ..." she stopped short realizing that she was just on the verge of pushing too far and changed her tactic. "What about my school? We're not even halfway through fall term, Mother! I have excellents in all of my subjects! Do you know how hard I have to work for those grades? Any idea at all?"

Actually, I did know. She was an extremely bright, very pretty and quite popular girl, and really didn't have to put forth much effort whatsoever for her studies, friends or anything else. Alice's wealthier friends even gave her their beautiful clothes after only a couple of wearings. How she managed that I never did discover. But I declined to mention this at present since it would hardly have contributed in any positive fashion.

"Does this have anything to do with this boy Dannie Barrington showing up all of a sudden?" she interjected suspiciously, her eyes narrowing. "Is he really my brother?"

I exhaled then resolutely plodded on.

"When your father died he was apparently still married to Dannie Barrington's mother and not to me, Alice," I said, surprised at how evenly I was able to answer her. "But I wasn't aware of that situation until his death. In fact I didn't know that they had ever been married at all, although I did know that they ... had a child, Dannie, together. Then when Dannie was just a little boy, playing around with a gun, he accidentally shot ..."

"So he *is* my brother, then," she interrupted. "Or, half brother at least. There's another girl in my class who has half brothers and sisters because her mother was actually divorced and then got married again. A nasty, low business to be sure. No one wants to have anything to do with her, of course. That's just terrific for me to find out now."

Alice was far better informed about these kinds of matters at the tender young age of thirteen than I certainly had been at that age. I held my breath wondering just how far she might go with this, however. Despite my husband's duplicity, I had managed to keep my married name and my daughter's and my honor due to the fact that the court proceedings at the time of the reading of John's will had backed up the fact that during the entire time of our marriage I had indeed believed I was his legal wife.

"Why didn't you ever tell me about any of this before? About Dannie Barrington, I mean, not about your stupid idea to move down to the loony land of alligators," she scowled.

"I don't know, Alice," I replied, the exasperation I usually managed to hide from her pushing through. "I can't answer that question. Maybe I just hoped that you would never have to know about any of it. As for moving to New Orleans now, it just seems like a good place for us to pick up and sort of start over. I'm hoping maybe to work towards getting a position at the French Opera House."

"Doing what, for heaven's sake? I think you're a little old to suddenly become an *étoile* at the opera even though you and the prize pupil were always dueting about like crazy shrieking magpies," she stated, morosely slumping down even further in her chair.

"I've heard that they're actively looking to hire seamstresses for costume construction and alterations, as well as women to tutor children who are in the casts or minding young children whose parents are in the casts," I replied evenly. "The pay can be erratic at the start, but I hope I can manage to make enough for us to live on if they'll hire me. I think that I'm qualified at any rate." Actually, this information had been in a small article I had seen in a year-old fashion magazine even before Zuma and Emma had left for Reserve. I really had no idea how extensive the need or how overwhelming the qualifications for any of these services might actually be. "And, if that doesn't work out, I should be able to find something else with Zuma's help."

"Well, it's too bad you can't cook like her," Alice sighed. "This stew tastes like old boots."

*"Musicians never made much there [New Orleans]; didn't need to; living was cheap and they could get by."*
Edward "Kid" Ory

## Chapter 2: New Orleans 1913

We agreed to stay an additional six weeks so that Alice would at least have a mid-term grade to transfer to whatever school we could find in New Orleans. How could I claim to be any kind of teacher and not realize just how important that was, she insisted. During that time I scrambled to find mending and alterations work within the town, hating myself for deliberately undercutting the prices of the women who were more established in those trades so that I could have their work. The newest elegant evening fashions now had beaded and embellished short-sleeved bodices as well as elaborate drop waist beaded sashes, silk hand-embroidered lace coats and smaller, yet still ornate, feathered hats underneath of which were piled many thick rolls of a woman's hair. Unlike the dresses of a decade ago which had detachable sections that could be laundered separately, these gowns needed to be washed after every wearing, after which the beading and embroidery often needed to be reworked. For the first time I also forced myself to work with a sewing machine, and, although I never fully mastered the devilish black device, I could at least manage the basics of the contraption. At first, however, I spent so much time untwisting badly snagged and miss-threaded bobbins I almost gave up on the entire frustrating enterprise. If I was going to rely on my abilities as a seamstress, I knew that I would have to accomplish this task, however. Sewing machines were far more prevalent – and admittedly, far more useful in my own opinion -- than those despicable motorcars. Desperately I saved every penny towards our train excursion, also selling anything we would not be taking with us.

A series of phone calls down to the French Opera House went mysteriously unanswered during what would surely have been their business hours. I even had the operator ring two or three separate times with each attempt. I had also written them at their Bourbon Street address and was horrified when my letter was returned only two weeks before our intended departure date. I frantically made another visit to Mr. Reedy's offices to see if he was able to find out why I was unable to reach them. After several days he let me know that he had placed a call to another attorney in New Orleans and had been informed that the Opera House had been closed earlier in the year due to financial problems. This stemmed from an apparent overextension to creditors as well as a huge downturn in opera box subscriptions. So many people in the area had suffered losses from the recent hurricanes, especially back in 1909, that they were no longer able to afford the luxury of procuring a box at the opera for the full season. And, as everyone knew, that was the only way one might attend. There were numerous futile attempts to get the well-known concert hall running once again, but there just seemed to be an enormous black hole of debt swallowing all efforts.

Closer to home, Dannie Barrington was definitely becoming more of a threat to the uneasy balance created by his sudden arrival on the scene. Alice remembered living in our beautiful home, with Zuma as our live-in cook, and had been seven years old when her father was shot by Dannie. She never could understand why suddenly, along with her father's death we had no money, why we had to move to several disgusting homes, each one less desirable than the last, or why I had started a school for poor black children unless it was just an excuse to teach Emma, whom she had always regarded as a complete nuisance. Dannie had recently started a rumor that actually, she wasn't his half sister at all, because John Barrington wasn't even her father. Nor was I her mother. Luckily, this was so far adrift in reality for my daughter she informed him he was a raving lunatic.

I had written Emma and told her that Alice and I would be moving down to New Orleans in a couple of months and looked forward to seeing all of the amazing sights she had described in her earlier letters. There was a phone at the Dawson's house but Emma had mentioned in her first letter to me that they were not ever allowed to use it. There was also one in the Godchaux's plantation store on the property, but that was only to be used for emergencies. This surprised me because it seemed very different from the Dawson household when they had still lived here in Kansas City. In my most recent letter I had urged Emma to please write back quickly as it seemed the mail was typically picked up from Reserve only once each week. It was then sequestered briefly in New Orleans before being loaded on some kind of mail train to St. Louis, finally finding its way to yet another train and out to us in Kansas City. I hadn't received a letter for almost six weeks, however, which left me quite uneasy.

With no place to work or live and scarcely enough money saved to pay for such a trip, this whole endeavor was rapidly turning into a nightmare. How different from our fully orchestrated, luxurious trip that John Barrington had planned for all of us from Colorado Springs to Kansas City when Alice and Emma were babies. I had loved my beautiful home and also loved having Zuma and Emma living with us, but hated the lifestyle of deceit that John's political forays stamped upon us for those six years before Dannie Barrington had picked up his father's pistol that fateful afternoon.

Alice knew we hadn't received any mail from Emma (not that she was necessarily disappointed about that fact, admittedly). I informed her that the Opera House was closed indefinitely, but that I was certain I would be able to find some kind of teaching or tutoring position since I had an excellent letter of introduction from Mr. Reedy. In typical Alice fashion, she'd countered that since it was undoubtably halfway through the first semester, she rather doubted that new teaching positions were just popping up anticipating my arrival. Alice was more than willing to move elsewhere to get away from the pesky Dannie, but remained in hostile opposition to my New Orleans plans.

Completely by surprise I received a note from Mr. Reedy informing me of a small compensation that I was due based on my years of teaching that the town council had apparently overlooked. This provided the financial cushion I desperately needed for us to live for several weeks once we had arrived. He had also negotiated an excellent discount at a newly-opened boarding house, originally built by one of his firm's former clients, a Mr. Hernsheim. Sadly, Mr. Hernsheim had taken his own life a few years back after having lost both his wife and sister to lengthy illnesses along with suffering through several business downturns. The house had just been opened as The Alcion, a boarding establishment which included one hot meal each evening, supposedly available only to good working members of society, he added, although it was only a few blocks away from a somewhat rougher area of town. The home was right on St. Charles Avenue exactly in the middle of everything Mr. Reedy had been informed. The streetcar ran right smack in front of it and we would be able to take it anywhere, with transfers of course, to get to practically everywhere in the city.

For some reason I thought back on that woman at the church two months ago with her yellow bird hat. Maybe I didn't have roots that were deep enough, but I definitely had wings that were wide enough I thought to myself. And I fully intended to use them.

I had told Alice that we could each pack one medium-sized steamer trunk as well as whatever we could comfortably carry on board for the two connecting trains. My trunk contained only a few items. I included several framed photos of my son Johnnie, who had fought valiantly against so many illnesses and finally succumbed to a diphtheria outbreak two years ago. Alice's birth certificate was included, along with a few very small items from what I now thought of as my prior life, including a letter posted from London by Colorado's gold mining Croesus, Win Stratton, who was in my life before John Barrington, and a judges' tally sheet from an opera competition twelve years ago in which the judges applauded my novice capabilities and strongly recommended I continue my operatic studies in Europe.

And then, curiously, there was a very slender, cloth-bound book with a light green linen binding, encircled by delicate dark red and green vines twining throughout its deep red lettering entitled *"The Awakening"* by an author named Kate Chopin. Win was terminally ill when the little book had arrived for him in the mail and I had simply kept it, truly enthralled with Mrs. Chopin's writings about New Orleans and Grand Isle and the dearth of choices in women's lives. I was never sure if I loved or despised her main character Edna Pontellier and repeated readings over the years never helped to clarify my initial confusion. I had no idea where Win and Mrs. Chopin had met since he had never spoken about her, although I was well aware that he was tremendously supportive of women in their artistic passions and pursuits. In a beautifully expressive hand her inscription read:

*"To my dearest Win ~ so much of me has poured itself into this creation, but I fear the bounds of propriety will soon stopper the bottle. I wanted you to have a copy before it disappears from the face of the earth*

*~ fondly as always, Katie O'Flaherty Chopin."*

Our connecting train in St. Louis included a half day layover and I intended to restock our small basket of food during the wait. Purchasing anything on board was out of the question since even a cup of tea was outrageously expensive – a cube of sugar was priced at 15¢ I'd been informed! The nation's economic balance so often seemed to be teetering on the vicissitudes of the weather, particularly among the sugarcane plantations in Louisiana. The fields had been ruined with three years of back-to-back flooding involving hundreds of thousands of acres that had been completely wiped out before any crop was ready to harvest. Practically all of the country's sugarcane was grown in Louisiana which had exorbitant implications on market pricing. Rice growers in the South had suffered much the same disastrous outcome. Cotton fared little better. And since everyone had borrowed at record high interest rates to continue farming after the first disastrous year, the economic strain was felt by all throughout the state and ultimately throughout the entire country, exponentially compounded by other farming, manufacturing and trade woes.

Despite Alice's surly disposition throughout the entire trip she seemed to enjoy watching the trees changing from almost leafless to their array of late autumnal colors to full green yet again, as well as observing the gently rolling hills, streams that gradually meandered along into thrashing rivers and waist high fields of corn, grains and grasses awaiting harvest. We both found it amusing to count the surprising number of church steeples as the train clattered through one small town after another.

But as we continued further south the humidity gradually increased, closing in around us with a suffocating choke hold. We both rolled our sleeves as high as possible, dramatically loosening the top buttons on our blouses further than either of us had ever dared in public. Alice somehow managed to shimmy out of most of her undergarments without attracting any unwanted notice. When we finally emerged into the late afternoon sun in New Orleans, the heat had intensified to that of a blast furnace. We found an open-air café just outside the station with a pair of large paddle fans uselessly whirling the humidity over our heads and ordered what we hoped was a cool lime ice drink and small basket of soda biscuits. Most of the menu appeared to be in some abbreviated form of a French patois or dialect. The young girl who waited on us looked the same age as Alice and spoke very little English.

Although ours was a very small room perched on the top floor above an exceptionally noisy street, The Alcion offered up a clean four floor residence with an enormous, ornately carved front porch thrusting out under huge live oak trees, that were draped by majestic lacy valances of something called Spanish moss, where the evening meal was to be served. A pair of fragrant orange trees behind the home provided all with plump juicy fruit. One's morning coffee could be purchased along with a *beignet*, a small, square French donut, while watching the street cars loudly clattering along the tracks in front of the residence. Since everyone's rooms were so unbearably hot, most of the residents spent their time out on the porch when at home. There were no closets or wardrobes in our room, so we lived out of our steamer trunks and felt very fortunate that we only had to share the bathroom down the hall with four other women. There was almost never even tepid water for a bath, but no one really seemed to notice. At night we learned to quickly lower the mosquito netting bar whether we were getting into or out of our beds, determined to keep the insects' frenzied snacking attempts to a minimum.

The discount that Mr. Reedy had negotiated was indeed a remarkably deep one. I overheard several other boarders complaining of the excessively high rates they were being charged, contrary to the original published accounts. The manager, Mme. Laballiere, and her three young teenage daughters lived on the second floor of the residence. The women boarders were housed on the third and fourth floors and the first floor by men. The younger men typically sported straw skimmers, wide canvas suspenders over their open-collared light blue shirts and quite tight-fitting button-up trousers – some trousers were so tight in fact, that the man had to leave undone the top button! The older men tended towards flaxen-colored linen coats, shirts buttoned high at their sweating necks, and far roomier, beige cotton trousers. The young men rolled their long thin cigarettes in assorted dark papers outside – it was far too hot to smoke inside – making a great show of shaking the sweet-smelling tobacco from their beaded, embroidered cut leather pouches. The older men would often be seen with one leg crossed over the other, perhaps revealing a bright red garter holding up a darned sock, enjoying the cooler air under the undulating bamboo fans on the enormous porch, while sipping incredibly hot, dark coffees and smoking their huge, surprisingly fragrant cigars.

The morning following our arrival was shrouded in a dense fog. As the sun finally began to burn through the thick haze, Alice and I took the streetcar back towards the French Quarter or *Vieux Carre*, which meant 'old square', and wandered through the long open markets, partially tented overhead to deflect both the heat and heavy rains. Countless small shops dotted the way, doors flung invitingly wide, beckoning one to explore the wares within. The air was alive with music. Some groups played voluptuous melodies in unusually pulsing, minor modes, others performed a wild mix of ragtime tunes, usually on instruments such as a cornet, violin and banjo, and still others featured guitarists languidly singing in French, Spanish or English, often meandering from one language to another within the same song. Each style of music I found to be more fascinating than the one that had preceded it. How could a musician not find fertile ground for his art!

Many of the darker-skinned women creatively knotted fancy scarves around their heads, and were attired in snugglyfitting calico wrappers of various lengths. The white women seemed to favor more diaphanous loosely-woven cottons, small, white straw hats adorned with a single large fresh flower, and the essential parasol and fan. However, I also observed a number of lighter-skinned women adorned with the knotted scarves and tight-fitting wrappers as well as dark women with flowing muslin gowns and small straw hats, delicately holding their parasols and brightly-painted large fans. Everyone roamed the streets congenially together, sitting adjacent to one another at the tables in the prolific outdoor cafés which seated people of all hues and dress next to one another without a second thought. Divisions typically seemed more by what cuisine one might desire rather than by one's European or non-European ancestry, although I highly doubted this held true in the more expensive restaurants.

We had reluctantly passed up Mme. Laballiere's coffee and *beignet*, although we had brought along several tantalizing oranges we'd found gleaming in a bowl on the porch that morning. Our first purchase was a pair of white hats we had seen so many of the women wearing, along with a small walking map which we studied as we devoured our breakfast. I had never seen coffee served so dark and so hot. Those around us began sipping as soon as the steaming beverage was placed in front of them, whereas Alice and I spent at least fifteen minutes blowing across the surface madly attempting to cool the scalding black liquid and placate it with cream and sugar.

An incredible laziness permeated the hot heavy air, almost like a huge bumblebee leisurely droning along a rambling row of fragrant rose bushes. After a few hours however, Alice looked miserably hot, tired, extremely bored and did nothing to disguise her overall disgust with me for having dragged her to this place. Adding to her displeasure we had discovered that no good schools were located anywhere near where we might have afforded to live.

The following day we had again retraced our steps to what was called the Garden District and I enrolled her in that District's white school. Just out of curiosity I inquired where the black pupils were educated and the secretary shrugged, gesturing vaguely, and said she really wasn't certain, but somewhere out there in Central City there were one or two schools she'd been told. Those children were required to be in session for only four months whereas the white schools required the full six months, she'd nodded with a wide smile. In Missouri the requirement had been for nine months for the white schools and six months for the black schools. Alice was truly livid.

I dropped her off at the school the next day and immediately continued on the streetcar to the long blocks of extraordinary homes along St. Charles Avenue in the upper Arts District. I had several samples of my tatting, embroidery, and beading skills, as well as Mr. Reedy's character reference letter in a leather satchel and attempted to speak with anyone who answered the backdoor at any of these splendid homes. No one needed additional mending or dress construction services and those households with small children who wished to engage a tutor or governess for them had already done so. I did find one household that had recently been informed by their current governess that she would be getting married in six months and had submitted her resignation to take effect at that time. If I wished to be scheduled for an interview for the position, I should leave my letters of reference and current contact information and they would be reviewed by Mr. and Mrs. D'Arcy, I was informed. However, I should be aware that there were already at least two dozen young women who had applied and were on the books to be interviewed within the next month or so. Since I could not possibly leave my one letter, I carefully wrote out what I hoped was an acceptable application, furnishing my address at The Alcion.

Mme. Laballiere had suggested that I apply at La Belle Creole Cigar Factory which was the factory that the late Mr. Hernsheim had built. They almost always had openings and the work paid very well, she insisted. La Belle Creole employed well over one thousand people, mostly women, both black and white, if I didn't mind that, she'd interjected. There were close to a hundred cigar makers in New Orleans, but La Belle Creole was without question the most outstanding and definitely paid the best, attested Mme. Laballiere. Desperate, my small savings rapidly depleting, I applied at the factory and was told to report at 7 a.m. the following Monday to determine if I would be suitable in this line of work. It was a job I told myself.

Rashly, I purchased two local train tickets to get out to Reserve for Sunday. It seemed like five years instead of only five months since I'd last seen Zuma and Emma. Now that we were this close to finally being with them again, I had to justify this extra expense and closed my ears to all of Alice's complaints about another nauseatingly hot train trip, even though it would take less than an hour. The tracks ran along what was known as The Great River Road with fields of rice, cotton and sugarcane in the various throes of harvesting. Sundays, however, were always a day off from everyone's daybreak to full dark workday during harvest, so there were very few workers in any fields. By luck I flagged down a wagon at the train stop that was heading out towards the Godchaux plantation, although it was a fairly short ride.

The plantation was obviously in serious disrepair. Precious little had been done for well over a decade I surmised. Although we passed huge orchards brimming with succulent orange and lemon trees, massive live oaks with hefty branches running so close to the ground one could sit on them as though on a bench, graceful magnolia trees and endless fragrant gardens of wildly tangled rose bushes, everything was thick with dead, ropey vines. Rusting hulks of machinery overgrown with weeds as large as trees in many fields, countless rotting outbuildings, and an overall impression of being down at the heel sadly prevailed.

The plantation house was up quite high, perched upon many columns of brick stilts, and built so that the Mississippi River, which typically flooded several times every summer, wouldn't reach the actual first floor of the dwelling's true living space. The floods brought rich soil down from the northern states to fertilize the crops, so the plantations had to be within easy access of the river. Small levees were built along the way to help deflect the flooding from the plantation house although one could never depend on such flimsy earthen devices.

We climbed a flight of crumbling steps, seriously splintering along the edges yet curving gracefully up towards the front door. A young black woman ushered us from the front entry to the drawing room and then went to locate Mrs. Dawson. Alice immediately wandered across the hallway into the library which I hoped was not a breach of good manners. Mrs. Dawson appeared, fluttering in a diaphanous blue and green chiffon dressing gown, obviously very close to giving birth to yet another child. I had lost count. Would this be her fourth? Fifth? She swooped in to give me a large hug, far more gracious than she'd ever been on our rare encounters when we both had lived in Kansas City. It was quite obvious she was desperate for company, any company whatsoever. Even mine.

"Oh, my dear Mrs. Barrington!" she exclaimed, brushing an unruly wad of light brown curls back into a large, tortoise shell comb. "It's always so wonderful to see someone from up home! Please have a seat, have a seat! Here, over here by the veranda. At least there's some cooler air moving through the jib windows right now. I've asked Felicité to bring us some iced lemonade and *friandises*. I had no idea you were here in New Orleans! And I apologize for my appearance. Naturally, I'm not out in public at all right now since I'm *gros bien souffrante* as they say," she laughed. "It's always so lovely to have another woman to speak with!"

"You're doing well I assume?" I asked. I realized that in my limited correspondence with Emma I had failed to inquire about any of the Dawsons at all. And Emma, not surprisingly, since she was only a child, had not taken it upon herself to fill me in either.

"Oh," she sighed heavily, rubbing her stomach. "Every time it gets more difficult, you know? I feel as though I'm the size of one of those monstrous threshing machines and I still have at least six weeks or possibly even longer to go. Can you believe it? The doctor has given me some pills to help with my swelling ankles and feet ...." She thrust her slippered feet out in front of her chair. "But so far, the pills have done very little to bring it down. These are my last slippers that I can even begin to get on these old poor feet! I just don't know what I will do when I can't even fit into them. We really don't have the money to just throw it away on such silly items as silk house slippers! My husband is quite right about that." She sat staring at her feet for a few moments and then slowly tucked them under her chair.

"So how long are you staying here in New Orleans?" she finally continued, since I had tactfully refrained from commentary regarding her badly swollen feet.

"Actually, my daughter Alice and I have just moved to New Orleans. I thought maybe either Zuma or Emma would have mentioned something about our plans. You might remember Emma was one of my students for many years at the Mary Stratton School, which is why I wanted to see how they were doing and ... thought we would stop by," I said cautiously. What if the reason I hadn't gotten any letters from Emma in the last two months was because something had happened? Could they have left the plantation?

"Oh, yes," replied Mrs. Dawson, with a slightly perplexed frown, leaning heavily back into her chair. "No, neither of them had mentioned anything about it as I remember. They actually do live in the house rather than the cabins since Zuma's our main cook, but even so, I very rarely see her. And I almost never see that girl Emma since she's usually assigned elsewhere."

I relaxed.

"It's a much more difficult life than I might have expected down here, Mrs. Barrington," she began with a deep sigh.

"Please call me Hannah," I replied. I suspected she couldn't remember my first name. Conversely, the name Barrington had been one in Kansas City, in fact, undoubtedly throughout the entire state of Missouri that had carried with it a reputation one rarely forgot.

"Yes, of course, Hannah," she replied, flashing a quick smile, although she did not offer up my using her Christian name. I certainly was not of her social class I inwardly mused. She looked carefully in the direction of the open windows before continuing. "All of these workers, you know, these ... darkies ... as they used to say, complain about their cabins and everything else. We do the absolute best we can for them. They're all sharecroppers, you know, not even poor tenant farmers like on so many other farms, so they have it far, far better. And certainly far better than back in those horrid slave days, let me tell you!"

She looked at me for affirmation and I nodded my head slightly. Felicité brought in a tray containing two glasses of lemonade and a small plate of sugared fruits and cake slices, setting the tray on a side table. Mrs. Dawson waited until she had left before continuing.

"And I don't know what other work we're going to have for some of these people on the house staff after we finish the harvest in the next week or so. I'm certainly not doing any entertaining here until this next child is born and even then, let me tell you, Mr. Dawson has insisted that our entertaining be kept at bare minimum, at the absolute barest minimum you understand. Not at all like our status back up in Kansas City! I hesitate to admit that we're going to have to let several of the house staff go ..." her voice just drifted off as she shook her head.

"I recall Zuma's mentioning that you were bringing everyone from Kansas City with you. I should think with so much more work here you would have needed them all," I replied cautiously.

"Well we do need them!" she exclaimed. "And we certainly need all of the sharecropping farmers to work the land they've been assigned! But they just don't always work out. Actually much of the time they just don't want to put in the work, period!"

"Ah," I replied, nodding my head, feigning agreement. "I see."

"Free of charge their families get clothing and food of good quality, sufficient quarters and medical attention. We treat them so kindly and even give them a patch for their own gardens as well!"

I nodded again.

"All we ask is that they work for us during the year! I mean they don't own the house, mules or tools or anything, but they get to rent all of that from us at a most reasonable rate, I assure you. I don't believe they have any idea just how much all of these things actually cost out there in the world! And then we also give them ten acres to farm in exchange for only one third of their crop. Only a third for heaven's sake! For use of a mule, the seeds and tools they pay us another third, of course, which is most reasonable. And of course, we do have to guide them as to what needs to be planted obviously. Otherwise, *entre nous*, like little children, they certainly wouldn't have a clue!"

"No, I suppose not," I murmured.

"Or how to obtain the best market advantage," she continued with what I was now quite certain was a regular, well-rehearsed rant delivered to anyone visiting. "We do all that for them as well and pay them their share. We always want a money crop such as sugar cane or sometimes rice planted for sale so they do have to plant what we tell them. They get so much practically for free, but really they don't seem to have much incentive at all to work very hard. It's quite difficult to deal with. But, well, you know," she sighed, shaking her head. She took a long sip of her lemonade and bit into one of the sugared delicacies.

I really didn't have any idea how far sharecropping had helped to pull up those who had been enslaved or had lived in squalid poverty over the last fifty years. But from the little I had seen upon arriving at Godchaux, as well as most of the plantations we had passed on the train, living conditions for these workers looked to have scarcely improved. A series of dismal squalid cabins festered low to the ground, shored up by several short columns of bricks, with a single layer of boards for a floor and one window hole, buffered by a shutter, but no glass. Roofs looked to be quite erratically patched and undoubtedly leaked like a sieve. I learned later that huge cracks zigzagged along those bare walls, without paper or plaster or any other adornment. Most of the cabins had an open fireplace, no stove, and the garden that Mrs. Dawson had spoken of was only a very tiny plot of three or possibly four very short rows since the crop of sugarcane or rice was planted practically up to each cabin door. Unlike the plantation house, flooding would have easily breached the cabin floor I strongly suspected. I shuddered.

Not feeling at all comfortable discussing the lack of incentive among the Godchaux workers, I was grateful that Alice chose that moment to walk back into the drawing room with a couple of books in her hand.

"You remember my daughter, Alice," I remarked, praying that the girl would at least be somewhat civil after her uninvited tour of the Dawson's library.

"Of course!" replied Mrs. Dawson, relishing another of the cookies. "How are you my dear? I don't think I've actually seen you for the last couple of years quite honestly!"

"Well, truth to tell," Alice said, glancing darkly at me, "rather hot in this place. But I do like your library, ma'am. It's quite lovely."

Mrs. Dawson laughed and patted Alice lightly on the cheek, a gesture which I knew the girl utterly despised.

"Well, I'm glad you like our books and I guess if you're going to be down here for awhile, you'll have to try to get a bit used to the heat!" she laughed heartily. Then, furrowing her brow, she tilted her head to the side, almost squinting at Alice, her hand moving lightly until under Alice's chin. "You know, I absolutely must tell you, you look almost exactly like Alice Claytor's youngest daughter. They live just a little further down in Vacherie at Laura Plantation. My goodness! You girls could be sisters, practically twins in fact, the resemblance is that uncanny! What's that girl's name again? Oh yes, Margaux, although I think that's short for something else. You know how girls these days like to re-arrange their names as hastily as their hem lengths! I'm sure that Mrs. Claytor mentioned that Margaux was named after some distant older relative – maybe somewhere out in Nebraska or possibly Colorado. Margaux's probably at least five years older than you are, to be sure, but quite remarkably has that same lovely blonde hair and unusual porcelain skin as you. Even the same mouth and those pretty, grayish-blue eyes. What an uncanny resemblance! And your name is even Alice, same as Mrs. Claytor!"

Alice looked over at me with a strange expression that I wasn't able to interpret. "That's actually quite interesting, Mrs. Dawson," she remarked smiling, pulling back slightly so that Mrs. Dawson's hand moved away from her chin. "Actually, my parents originally came to Kansas City from Colorado," she replied coolly. "In fact, I was born in Colorado, right Mother?"

I nodded, smiling slightly. The embers of a memory long ago forgotten suddenly emitted a wraith-like glow.

"Now that is an amazing coincidence!" replied Mrs. Dawson. "I'll have to remember to mention you the next time we're down in Vacherie, although who knows when that might be!" she sighed, again rubbing her stomach.

"We really can't expect to take up any more of your time," I said hastily, perhaps more quickly than I intended. "We wanted to have a chance to visit with Zuma and Emma."

"Yes, so you mentioned," Mrs. Dawson replied, still studying Alice's face. "Would you like a sweet, Alice? Let me ring Felicité for another glass for you. I'm sure you could use some lemonade in this dreadful heat. Although we should finally start seeing things beginning to get a bit cooler any day now they say. You can keep reading while you're here, of course. I'm so sorry though, I can't let you borrow either of those books, unfortunately. Mr. Dawson simply wouldn't hear of it, you know."

"Thank you," she nodded, helping herself to one of the remaining delicacies as Mrs. Dawson rang a small bell. Alice then sat down in a chair in front of another jib window several feet away from us. "One doesn't want one's books to get dingy with overuse, of course. I certainly wouldn't expect you to have a lending library available just for a visitor's disposal."

She meant the remark as a rebuke, but fortunately Mrs. Dawson failed to recognize it as such and lightly laughed.

"We've had to be most frugal since acquiring this estate," she remarked, looking first at Alice and then back at me. "It already had almost a decade of severe debts borrowed against it that were attached when my husband and his investors bought it in 1910. The great flood the year before had absolutely wiped out everything down here and forced the original owners into foreclosure. They lost everything they owned you know. Oh, here's Felicité with your lemonade. Another cookie, Alice?"

Alice shook her head and returned to her reading after retrieving the glass from the tray. As Felicité left Mrs. Dawson continued speaking.

"Yes, well. All of the investors lived up by us in Missouri as you know, Jefferson City for the most part. They just had a couple of overseers in charge down here. Well, let me tell you, even though those overseers were white, it's as though the doors were flung wide open on this entire place – open season! Come at it, free for all! Almost all of the furnishings disappeared from this house, certainly every scrap of value including wall hangings, even the built-ins were chiseled out from the walls! Built-ins for heaven sake! Can you imagine? All of the sugarcane machinery from the sugar house was either dismantled and stolen and sold for scrap or simply left to rust out in the constantly flooded fields. You can't tell me that all of that was managed in the middle of the night without anyone's knowledge. Heavens! Those overseers just let it all happen. Then, of course, they just disappeared as well which certainly didn't surprise any of us."

"You know," she suddenly cut into her own story, "I was always quite mystified that you actually wanted to try to teach those dark little pickaninnies and other assorted ragamuffins back in Kansas City. Always seemed so odd to the rest of us, Mrs. Barring ... er Hannah."

I took a small sip of my lemonade hoping she would just continue without my making a reply, which she did after a brief pause.

"My husband, who was the largest investor, was down here as much as possible to try to get things under, you know, some kind of control. But he realized very early on that the only way to have any success was for our family to simply move here once the house was at least made somewhat livable. To make matters worse he's also suffered some quite dramatic reverses of late on Wall Street so things are in a bit of a pinch, as they say. No new slippers or new books!" she shrugged.

I replied by murmuring something unintelligible even to

me.

"As I'm sure you know, practically all of the white plantation owners, including most of the old French Creole families, actually have townhouses located in the French Quarter and only come out here on the weekends. But," she sighed, "we're out here all the time so far. We had hoped to acquire some kind of affordable residence by The Season, which starts around Christmas, you know, but thus far, it's certainly not looking very good. I'll be so ready to get back out in good society after …" she glanced down at her expansive front, "the newest Dawson has made his or her entrance into the world." She smiled over at Alice who was either truly absorbed in her book or, more than likely, rudely simply ignoring the woman.

"But you've arrived here today on our harvest party Sunday, did you know? We do feel the need to provide the one-day celebration," Mrs. Dawson sighed. I suppose it was obvious to her that I wasn't thoroughly captivated by her complaints and she was most likely now tired and more than eager to have us move along.

"No," I replied, quite surprised. Since their economic situation was so dire, any kind of party seemed rather shockingly out of character.

"Oh yes, I imagine that all of the children, even my own, are probably down by the ditches or creeks, anywhere there's water, with their butterfly nets and other assorted screen traps flailing about trying to catch enough crawfish for the boil this afternoon. Alice, maybe you would like to join them?"

"No ma'am, but thank you," Alice replied, eyes still riveted on her book. Then a moment later she looked up. "But if you would please let me just finish this one chapter in your library I would certainly appreciate your kindness," she said, then adding "I will be certain to shelve the books back in their exact spots."

"Certainly Alice, no problem at all. I'm going to ask Felicité for a bucket of cold water and then pillows to prop up my poor legs, so I'm going to have to retire. She's one I'm going to have to let go I'm afraid. She does excellent needlework, but I just can't afford to keep her on. She's made no effort whatsoever to learn English either, so communicating with her has been nonexistent. You had asked about Zuma before, Hannah. You'll find her in the summer kitchen behind the main house, probably with several huge pots of water already on the boil."

And indeed, that's exactly where I found her. A fairly tall, strong, exotically attractive Creole of color with a contagious smile and an even more contagious laugh, she swept me into her long arms and I instantly felt like a child once again. Even though she was only about ten years older than I, she had always been something of a mother to me – certainly more than my own mother had ever been so long ago.

"Well, I knew dat mebbe you be comin' down here, Miss Hannah," she smiled, wiping off sweat beading on her forehead. "An' I was kinda hopin' dat you wouldn', but now's I sees ya, it's sure a mighty fine sight, yes ma'am, jes mighty fine!"

She was surrounded by several mountains of cut corn, potatoes, sausage and onions, along with two wicker baskets brimming with oranges and lemons that she was in the process of halving. There were four enormous pots of water at a near boil on the huge open fireplace.

"So you did get my last letter then," I smiled. "When I didn't hear back from Emma I thought maybe it had gotten lost. Or, worse, that maybe the two of you had gotten lost!"

She shrugged and started cutting more lemons. "Emma got in trouble fer writin', y'know. Dey dock her pay."

"What! Why?" I replied in disbelief. "What harm was there in taking a few minutes to write me a letter after finishing her day's work?"

"Well, y'know they gots her workin' in that plantation store a coupla days a week, at least during the harvest, 'cause her arithmatic's real good an' so, dat's why she's there. Help 'em figure out accounts an' such, y'know? But she gots in trouble cause she stole some stationery an' stamps. She thought nobody'd see dat they was short, but dey did. So's I tol' her, no more writin' no letters tuh nobody."

"But I had given her a tablet so she could tear out writing paper and quite a few stamps," I stammered, and the letters that I had received had indeed been written on that paper.

"Yeah, well, mebbe dat all got wet or sumpin'. Or mebbe she writin' somebody else too. Dunno," she shrugged. "She's gettin' good pay at dat store even if it's only a coupla days a week durin' harvest. Don' wan' her gettin' fired. Dunno where dey gonna put her after, though I do know what she wants."

"So, she's not in school," I said slowly.

"Uh, no ma'am. She's twelve now an' had all duh schoolin' she gonna git down here or anywheres. No cause fer you tryin' tuh make her intuh a white girl, y'know. No cause fo' dat, ma'am."

"I could still work with her occasionally," I offered quickly. "You know I would love to continue working with her."

Zuma slightly cleared her throat, then looked over at me silently and slowly moved a pile of lemons over to the side. "Yeah, I knows you'd love it an' we both knows *why* you'd love it. But, she's workin' in dat store an' learnin' there's all she needs fer now an' dat's jes' real fine. Some other work'll turn up when dey done wid her at dat store. Always do."

She continued halving the lemons, their refreshing, pungent scent filling the air. I tried to think of some different way to broach the subject. Suddenly a young man stepped up behind me and tossed a small square package over Zuma's shoulder that landed on the cut lemons.

"*Ma foi!*" exclaimed Zuma, momentarily stepping back and throwing her hands in the air. "*Qu'est-ce que tu fais? Eh?*"

He kissed her on the cheek. "Smoked spices, thyme and

cayenne pepper, jes like I tol' you. Can't have no crawfish boil without! *Merde*! Tastes like a Yankee pot roast otherwise!"

Zuma gave a hearty laugh and shook her head.

"An' I brought you my own hot pepper sauce too. You add that at the end, *non*? Don't you go forgettin' now! But you go spare with it, yes? Don' want no tongues burnin' off!"

He was dressed like many of the young men who lolled about on the Alcion's porch. Same open-collared blue shirt, although his had wide blue stripes, along with very tight-fitting buttoned pants, with one suspender hanging jauntily down off his shoulder. His slightly wavy, extremely thick reddish-brown hair was brushed back from his forehead offsetting expressive brown eyes and a wide mouth set into his very handsome, light nutmeg complexion.

"Yeah, yeah, I'll 'member! Don' you worry none. Sure ain' makin' no Yankee pot roast!"

He laughed at her, gave me a kind of funny little salute and then ran past me.

"Yankee pot roast?"

"Well if you don' gots duh good spices in da boil it jes' tastes like dat nasty stuff dey eats in all uh dem so-called fancy dinin' places up North, y'know?" she replied with a wink.

"So was that man some kind of chef or something?" I asked.

"Naw, naw, dat's Kid Ory," she chuckled as she started measuring some of the contents of the package into the boiling water. "Him an' his Creole band are playin' for da party dis afternoon. Dem boys play everywhere these days. If you is havin' a party anywheres ya gotta git Kid Ory's group else yo' music jes ain' happenin', y'know? White people parties ovuh on St. Charles, black uns down on Rampart, picnics eve'where out 'long Lake Pontchartrain. But I tells ya, dat man is one great cook if he ever 'cides tuh stop makin' all dat wild crazy music an' gets serious 'bout life!"

*"Picnics – they usually had all kinds of seafood. Boiled crabs, shrimps, crayfish or crawfish, fried fish, fried oysters, gumbo and barrels of beer. I can sure fix up that kind of food, too!"*
Edward "Kid" Ory

## Chapter 3: La Petite Musquette

Three other women walked into the open kitchen, one holding a wide apron full of what appeared to be small dried sticks and leaves. Zuma lapsed into a volley of patois that I couldn't begin to decipher; it seemed so completely removed from any French with which I was even vaguely familiar. My eyes followed "Kid" Ory as he waved to a group of men on a slightly raised pier close to the stream and began moving towards them. I wondered why on earth a grown man would be called Kid and assumed that it must be an abbreviation for his first name, but nothing came to mind.

I became aware of children's voices shrieking with laughter in the distance and then moments later at least two dozen children of all ages raced out of a dense thicket of live oaks draped in Spanish moss. Several lean older boys were in front, two of them carrying a large tin tub between them, and three others were hugging either tall cylindrical screen traps or rounded mesh jugs as they ran towards us. I spotted Emma sprinting with what looked like a deep butterfly net held steadily in front of her chest, her wild golden curls floating in a tangled cloud. As she got closer I realized she was sopping wet and that her thin white muslin sheath clung to her now rather shockingly-developed light brown body. Five months had brought about far more changes for her than for Alice, even though she was well over a year younger. She handed her net, filled more than halfway with crawfish, over to one of the younger children and ran faster, not towards me, but towards Kid Ory. He knelt as she jumped into his arms, wrapping her long brown legs around his waist and her thin arms around his neck. Rather unsteadily, I started to move down towards them.

"You're all wet *ma petite musquette*," he laughed loudly as he stood up, her legs still straddling his body. "Hey you, my wife she jus' iron this shirt! What she gonna say when it comes home all wrinkled wi' dem mudbugs you been catchin'? *Ma foi*! What, you fall in?"

"No, no," she gasped, breathing hard after her long run as he set her back down on her feet. "No, it just happened. It ain' no mud, though. A couple of those older boys just jumped on me and pushed me under the water. Said they wanted to see my hair all wet. You know, they're just being mean!"

I had almost caught up to the two of them. "Emma!" I called. "Emma!"

"Miss Hannah!" she shrieked. "What are you doing here? What an amazing surprise!"

She ran over to me and gave me a huge hug as I kissed the top of her head which was wet and salty from running. "It's so good to finally see you!" I replied, truly reluctant to let her move away from me. "I was so worried when I didn't get any letters over the last couple of months."

"Yes, I suppose that's true," she said with a huge grin, walking me over towards Ory. "Edward this is my schoolteacher from back in Missouri I was telling you about, Mrs. Hannah Barrington. Oh, and Miss Hannah, this is the one, the *only*, the magnificent, Mr. Edward Kid Ory!"

"Ah, *la grande chanteuse* herself!" he said with a charming slight flourish of a bow and rather rakish smile. His eyebrows lifted in a curious inverted "V" as he smiled. "Emma tells me that her big voice comes from echoing all of those eh, classic opera refrains she learned from you up North."

I extended my hand and he grasped it firmly with yet another slight bow. "And, Miss Hannah," he continued, "you'll have a chance to hear Emma singing this afternoon – *eh, la grande opera ... non, malheureusement – mais les grandes chansons Creole, n'est-ce pas?*"

"And you said I could also sing '*Home, Sweet Home*' this time Edward," Emma added, with a very bold, flirtatious pout, her unusually bright blue eyes flashing at him. "You promised! If I'm going to audition for Mme. Jones any time soon I have to practice and that's her favorite song they say! And please don't forget it has to be really, really slow just like on that record you played for me!"

Ory laughed, throwing his head back in what seemed like genuine mirth. "*Oui, ma musquette, je sais, je sais! Mme. Jones ici de matin ... Mme. Jones la bas de minuit ... toujours, toujours, Mme. Jones!* I promise you! *Je tu promets*! I have to remember to give the band the chords and place out the form for 'em, though. None of 'em know it."

The little girl with whom Emma had left her net had caught up with us. "Here, Emma," she said crossly, thrusting the handle at Emma. "Your net's too heavy. You carry it over to dat boilin' pot."

As the two girls moved away, I followed them with my eyes.

"Who is this Mme. Jones anyway," I asked with genuine curiosity, finally looking back at Ory. "Is she an opera coach out here?"

He looked at me for a second then squinted back over towards the departing Emma. "Mme. Sissieretta Jones. The Black Patti. Eh, you never heard of her, my guess, *non*?"

I shook my head slowly. "No, I'm sorry, the name isn't familiar," I replied.

"Ever heard of Adelina Patti?"

"Well, of course!" I remarked, wondering if he was joking with me. "She's one of the most phenomenal opera singers ever! Who doesn't know about Adelina Patti for heaven's sake? She's on all of the society pages both here and in Europe! I don't think I've ever picked up a newspaper that didn't have some article about her latest gambit. Why even now that she's rather on in years she still has an absolutely magnificent voice they say!"

"Well," Ory smiled, his warm brown eyes looking directly into mine for a moment then off towards Emma again, "Mme. Sissieretta Jones is known as 'The Black Patti'. She got that name 'cause they say her voice is identical to Adelina Patti's. That record Emma's talkin' 'bout just now? That's Adelina Patti singin' that tune she likes."

I frowned at him, confused. Ory hesitated, looking at the ground for a moment and then continued.

"Well, 'cept that Sissieretta Jones' is a Negro opera star y'see," he shrugged, scratching his ear. "And, 'course, Negroes can't be opera stars 'cause there ain' any opera companies wantin' to hire 'em, y'know? Which is why you've never heard of her. Uh, no offense meant, of course, Miss Hannah," he added quickly. "Since you was Emma's teacher before I'm guessin' you know all 'bout those ... well, those ... uh, things, y'know?"

I truly doubted that his remark was meant to offend, just inform. "So, if Mme. Jones isn't an opera star or voice teacher here why is Emma planning to audition for her?"

"She has a vaudeville group called the 'Black Pattis'. They tour everywhere an' been together now for, I dunno, somethin' like sixteen years? Maybe even longer come to think of it. I've worked with 'em a coupla times when they needed someone to fill in when they played here in New Orleans or over in Baton Rouge. Mostly one-night engagements, so's gotta be a rough life, but they's still playin' a full nine month's season far's I know. Sometimes they even have white musicians from Europe workin' with 'em in fact. They're that good. Or at least they used to be. Not sure that's still the case, but very high level of vaudeville entertainment, y'know? They play to both white and black audiences, mixed even some places ... uh, not down here uh course," he chuckled, then winked slightly. "All high-quality performers in her troupe. High comedy, clean skits, good writin.' None of that nasty black Storyville stuff, but all kinds of music on the bill y'know? Mme. Jones insists on her performers' singin' so's they sounds like white singin' an' Emma sounds like a white girl anyway. Guess that's your fault, huh? Anyways, she sure gets teased a lot for that 'round here."

I had never even considered that this would be a problem for the girl. Was I wrong?

"But, point is," Ory continued, "Emma'd be perfect in that chorus – learn a lot. She's been writin' Mme. Jones' agent out in New York, but ain' heard nothin' back as yet. I told her to give 'em my name as a referral an' so forth an' so on. No reason they shouldn' accept her."

This undoubtedly would explain the stolen stamps and stationery, I thought. Emma wouldn't have wanted to simply rip out rough sheets from the cheap notebook that I had given her trying to arrange something as important as an audition.

"But she's just barely twelve," I replied slowly. "That just seems so young to be working away from home if she doesn't have to be."

"Twelve ain' too young!" snorted Ory, coughing slightly as he lit a cigarette. "I was already the bandleader of my own band and we was playin' all kinds of engagements when I was only ten, all up and down here, y'know? Edgard, Reserve, Vacherie, LaPlace, you name it -- even over in Algiers an' a few hefty engagements like Mardi Gras in New Orleans back in them days. I mean, we needed a lotta work – hell, we was rougher'n pig iron playin' -- a little group of no nothins let me tell you! Oh man, did we ever play rough back then! Our tone was *worse* than gutbucket if you can imagine. But you see that's how you learn.

You gotta play music to learn to play music. That's what I tell Emma all the time, y'know?"

I stared at him. "But don't you feel that you would have done better if you'd had more time in school or ..." my voice drifted off. Very few people in my life knew that I had only managed a year or so of any school attendance. And by age thirteen I was also completely on my own, working as a maid in the Hughes' household which was where I had first met Zuma. However, desperate to expand my limited formal education, I had scrambled to read practically every book in the Kansas City lending library as an adult. Nonetheless, I had always felt uninformed, always thirsted for more.

"Nah," he exhaled, blowing a puff of smoke away from me. "If there's sumpin' I can' figure out I just ask. Like the other day, I had to ask Emma to add up some stuff for me tuh pay everybody right 'cause I couldn' figure out how to divide it all up. See a coupla the guys came in late and one left early and the booking ran overtime, but didn' pay the same for overtime, so the money was real odd to figure. She's real good with the numbers, y'know? I guess she got all that kind of learnin' from you, eh?"

I nodded slightly. "Well, I was her teacher for six years, so yes ... I suppose so," I said cautiously, smiling at him. Then, not exactly certain why I asked the question I remarked, "is your wife here with you? I heard you scolding Emma that your wife would be upset if she found that your shirt had gotten muddy."

"My wife? Nah. She ain' so much into music. Well, she is sometimes, but not all the time, y'know? She ain' here anyways," he replied, looking down for a moment, then looked sideways at me grinning as he took another drag on his cigarette. "Well, enjoy the crawdad boil. And the beer – I saw 'em rollin' in several barrels of the good stuff for a change! *Quelle surprise pour alles, oui?* The Dawsons don' usually haul out any good beer for their own workers. But this is a record great harvest for everybody aroun' here, y'know? Finally after all these years of mucked up disasters! *Merde*! Hope you enjoy our music, too. Got some new hot stuff we're playin' tonight."

He sauntered down towards the small pier where I realized the other musicians, similarly attired, were setting up chairs and music stands, taking instruments out of cases. A banjo player was picking through a line of music, trying different variations. A couple of other musicians stood along the pier smoking cigarettes and talking. Large striped flannel blankets were scattered in front of the pier along the hard sun-baked ground, well shaded by trees from the afternoon sun and ringed by tall renegade stalks of sugarcane down towards the water's edge. Dragonflies hovered in the sizzling air above and then quickly darted out downstream.

"Who was that man you were talking with?"

I hadn't noticed that Alice had walked up behind me.

"Kid Ory," I replied, shading my eyes as I looked towards her. "That's his band that's going to play. Emma's singing a few songs with them actually. Isn't that nice?"

"Oh yeah. I'm thrilled beyond the pale," she replied, hands on her hips. "What train are we taking back? I still have to wash out my dress for tomorrow. I couldn't even get near the washtub all weekend with Mme. Lard and her dear doughy daughters Mlle. Lard the Older and Mlle. Lard the Younger in there every time I tried."

"There's one at six. If we start walking back over by five thirty we should make it."

Alice held out her hand for my watch chain necklace which I eased over my head and handed to her.

"Did you see what they're making in there by the way?" she grimaced, motioning towards the kitchen which was now absolutely teaming with women along with several children. We saw Félicité walking back towards the house with a tray piled high with corn, potatoes and sausage. A large half of an orange rolled off the tray and bounced once in the dust before disappearing into a small thatch of weeds.

"Good idea, that," gestured Alice at the tray. "The white folks – except us, of course – don't have to eat those nasty bug-eyed crawfish cooked in with *their* meal."

"How do you know they're nasty, Alice?" I asked trying not to overreact. I certainly had nothing to gain by getting into any kind of disagreement with her. Something about my whole conversation with Edward Ory was very unsettling, but it was worthless to let that spike an argument with the girl. "They're supposed to taste like lobster I've heard." Not that I really knew what a lobster tasted like, but then neither did Alice. I remembered catching small crawfish in the streams in Colorado when I was a child, but we never ate them, just used their tails for bait. However, I thought it prudent not to mention that to Alice. "Let's find a blanket to sit close in so we're able to hear Emma."

"Oh yeah, like we wouldn't hear Emma anywhere on the planet," snorted Alice reluctantly following me. "I just saw her with Zuma, by the way. I guess helping dish that stuff out. Who knows? Luckily she didn't see me. Stupid girl was soaking wet. You could see everything, and I mean *everything*, straight through her dress! Talk about disgusting! If she'd tried to hug me or anything ... absolute ugh! When Zuma saw her she yelled at her to go and change at least."

Thank goodness for mothers, I thought.

Many women were starting to walk down towards the blankets, almost all with large trays piled as high as possible with food, along with additional baskets of fruits and breads that they would be sharing with friends. Two barrels of the beer had been tapped open and several small groups of men and a few women, all with mugs and glasses in hand, were chatting nearby. Everyone had brought their own trays, mugs and platters I realized, and I hoped that we would be able to ask Zuma for tin ware. The warm, spicy aroma drifted over us in the afternoon air. Maybe Alice had no interest in eating, but I for one was ravenous.

As we sat down on one of the blankets I realized that Felicité and another young woman were following us, each holding a plate of steaming food and a mug of beer. Although I shook my head self consciously, trying to politely object, the two women didn't understand me and we graciously took the plates from them, nodding our thanks. I wanted to think that we were being served simply because we were visitors to the plantation that afternoon, but deep within I cringed knowing that we were being served only because we were white and it was simply assumed that we would have been expecting it.

I watched those around me pinch the shell off the crawfish tail then peel away the shell over the body and found the meat quite delicious. A little boy seated just past Alice's shoulder seemed to be squeezing juice from the head of each crawfish into his mouth which made me feel a little queasy. I was glad Alice's back was towards him. The heady mix of cayenne, garlic, onion powders and red peppers, along with the lemon and orange citrus juices created flavors I'd never experienced. If Zuma had ever cooked anything with this dizzying twist of tangy, subtly burning spices for any of us in years past I definitely did not remember. Alice nibbled on a few pieces of corn and maybe a couple small bites of sausage, then set her plate aside and leaned back on her elbows. The little boy touched her shoulder gently, gesturing for her plate, and without a second thought she handed it over to him, undoubtedly eager to have it out of her sight.

I glanced at the platform just as Kid Ory's group began playing. Ory played trombone which surprised me. I had assumed that as a band leader he would play cornet like bands up in Kansas City. The rest of his group was comprised of a banjo, clarinet, cornet, violin and string bass. There was also a drummer playing several small drums, although not the kind you would see in a marching band. I recognized their first tune as one we'd had on a piano roll many years ago, but couldn't remember the title until Ory announced afterwards that it was *'The Wolverines'*. Among other very danceable selections (and in fact most of the young people had gotten up almost immediately and started dancing) the band played *'Elite Syncopations'*, one of my favorite Scott Joplin ragtime tunes. Ory was introducing everything in patois so most of what he said I didn't understand other than occasionally catching some of the names of the pieces. Hearing this kind of piano music arranged for several instruments truly reinvented the music, I thought. Some of it seemed far too bawdy at times, however – in fact, many of the rather lurid interpretations that Ory himself performed on trombone were not particularly to my liking. But I appeared to be almost alone in that opinion. Alice sat completely stone-faced, except for rudely muttering something about the trombone sounding like a moose in heat.

Just before the band was going to take a break Ory motioned for Emma to come up on the stage. She had banded back her tangled curls with a long knotted blue scarf and exchanged the soaked muslin sheath for a short, faded calico wrapper.

"*Eh, ma petite musquette! Qu'est-ce que tu vas chanter pour nous aujourd'hui?*"

Standing on tiptoe she whispered something in his ear then kissed his cheek, her hands laced over his shoulder as he bent slightly forward. He was not a particularly tall man.

"*Ah, mais oui, mais oui! Quel choix formidable! C'est l'autre Can-can!*" exclaimed Ory. The audience applauded in approval as Ory then stomped off the count with his foot.

I knew this tune as well since I had learned it from Zuma many years ago when we had worked together. But the version I had sung had been a very simple, quite childish little song about which I'm sure I had no clue whatsoever as to the meaning. In fact, I had always assumed it was some kind of nursery rhyme! From Emma's expressions, along with Ory's, since he and two other musicians echoed her on the chorus each time, Emma left no question regarding the song's Creole interpretation. Her clear voice was expressive, articulate and she was unquestionably completely at ease being on stage with all of these men. One line included something about *"l'aimez vous"* and the flirtatious look on her face, in fact throughout her whole body, was frighteningly seductive. My once shy little student Emma Winfield Jackson had completely disappeared in less than half a year. Although Ory was glancing at her to give her cues after long instrumental sections, several of which actually contained completely different melodies, she never faltered on an entrance. I was thoroughly astounded at the girl's ease in her performance. I remembered many years ago my terror of performing in front of an audience after endless, completely repetitive hours of rehearsal accompanied just by a piano!

As the audience applauded Ory yelled out: *"Eh, la bas! Eh, la bas, cherie! Comment ça va, eh? L'aimez vous la cuisine? Eh?"* He then blew several kisses over towards Zuma and the other women standing just outside the kitchen area and they waved and blew kisses back at him. Then the audience started shouting *"Eh, la bas! Eh, la bas!"* another song, as the band started into it.

Alice dangled my watch in front of my face. "Time to go. Finally," she stated loudly right in my ear so that I could hear her above the band. As we stood up I waved goodbye to Emma, but she wasn't looking in our direction. Zuma had moved down towards the band and was too far away to hear us, so I guiltily left our plates and mugs on a rattan mat in the kitchen house.

That evening just after we got back to the Alcion, thunder crackled into snakes of lightning and hail mercilessly pinged off the clay-tiled roof followed by several hours of driving rains. The storms provided a good excuse for my sleepless night, but I well knew that it was just that – an excuse.

*"We all do 'do, re, mi' but you have got to find the other notes yourself."*
Louis "Satchmo" Armstrong

## Chapter 4: Tremé 1914

I lasted exactly one and a half days working at La Creole cigar factory. I could easily understand why they always had openings for the thousand workers they needed. I had been assigned the seemingly mundane task of sorting the dry tobacco leaves in a warehouse filled with huge piles that were stacked well past my shoulders. Long leaves were carefully designated as wrappers, other shorter leaves were tagged as fillers, and even shorter leaves and pieces were specified for use in cigarettes. This sent up so much of a rusty brown dust that I was continually coughing not only while at the warehouse, but for many hours afterwards. The other women worked silently without any obvious distress, occasionally humming a few tunes. The afternoon of my second day, however, I coughed so hard I actually started retching and was finally dismissed, most gracious to receive the scant pay for the few hours that I had managed to work.

On an impulse I walked up to Carondelet Street and took the streetcar east, hoping that the slightly cooler air would finally ease my breathing. On my walking map I had found that Bourbon Street where the French Opera House was located was an extension of Carondelet. The fact that the Opera House remained indefinitely closed had been confirmed by others at the boarding house, but simply out of curiosity, I still wished to see it.

As I neared the building I noticed that a man and woman were standing on a loading dock ramp behind the edifice engaged in a heated conversation. The woman was holding a magnificently beaded costume over one arm, the jeweled trim a prism refracting the sunlight into a riot of colors, as she angrily gestured with her free hand. I will never know exactly what prompted me to walk through the narrow badly-pitted concrete back alley to approach them. Perhaps like a moth to the flame I was so drawn to the costume that I simply wished to closely examine the workmanship.

"Yes, miss?" asked the man curtly, staring down at me. "Can we help you with something?"

"I saw the costume," I replied, sounding extremely foolish even to myself, "and I wondered if I could see it a bit closer. It's so sad that the Opera is closed and we're deprived of these beautiful gowns."

"Yes, quite beautiful gowns and also quite hideously rotting themselves to an expensive regal death upon their own hangers," scoffed the woman.

And she was quite right. As I got closer I could see that there were thin ribbons of green mold along the jeweled bodice front, and badly discolored, shredded gussets under the arms as well as serious rends, gaping holes and drooping flounces unraveling over the entire garment.

"How incredibly sad," I remarked, then added in a more positive light. "But possibly a good cleaning to start and the ..."

The man glowered at me. "And your vast experience in these matters comes from?" he inquired, continuing to stare at me, one eyebrow arched quite theatrically.

"Oh for heaven's sake, Allan, put a sock on it," sighed the woman, rolling her eyes. "Have you ever worked in costuming?"

"No," I replied. "But I've done beading, some other fancy work and alterations." Then as an afterthought I added, "and finer laundry, although all of that was a long time ago. I'm not a true seamstress, however," I added quickly.

"Where did you work?" demanded the man.

"In Colorado some years back, but also alterations and repairs more recently in Missouri," I replied slowly. The tobacco dust must have thoroughly infected my brain. Why was I even talking about any of this?

"We've hired three different highly recommended seamstresses in town to work on these to piece the better parts of different costumes together so that we can sell them to several houses in Europe that have expressed an interest," the man sighed. "The investment group is desperately attempting to pay off part of their debts and reopen the Opera House sometime in the next year or so. Selling off as much of our inventory and other assets has been mentioned on many occasions as a possible way to make that happen. We've already sold many of our wing and drop canvasses that only required very slight restoration. Some beautiful backgrounds. So sad to see those absolutely irreplaceable treasures go, let me tell you. Singers, actors, musicians – eh, they come and go. Bah! Who the hell cares? But the element which breathes the life, truly breathes the magic, the fantasy, into each opera season, season after season, year after year ... so horribly tragic to have it simply vanish beneath our very fingertips."

"And, as you can see from the garment at hand," added the woman, "none of these so-called seamstresses for all of their promises and supposed talent have even begun to scratch the surface."

"Well, maybe they simply overlooked or neglected to fix this one costume ..." I offered.

"Hah, neglected!" shrieked the man, crimson-faced in the late morning heat. "Look at this!"

He grabbed my elbow and pulled me just inside the scarcely lit loading dock's huge receiving room. As my eyes adjusted to the gloom I could see rack after double hanging rack of costumes, along with piles of additional materials stacked on the floor underneath. Long wooden tables bowed under the merciless weight of thousands of accessories, a magnificent hammered, black-glass mirrored tin coach had collapsed on one side, disintegrating into black shards in the corner, and an enormous clay head had toppled onto the coach and appeared to be sprouting chives. Around the perimeter of the room were dozens of immense wooden shipping containers, usually in stacks of three, one end pried off exposing additional costumes bursting from within.

I was speechless. How could anyone possibly deal with all of this? Horrific visions of Rumplestiltskin spinning straw into gold swam before me.

"I think you would need quite an army of very good women to tackle all of this, you're absolutely right," I stammered. "I can't even imagine how one would begin!"

The woman had followed us into the dock's receiving area. "I've actually hired two young women to start working on this mess tomorrow as an absolute last-ditch effort," she said, looking me over critically. "If you can start then too, you're also hired. I'm assuming you're looking for work?"

I frowned slightly, but nodded affirmatively.

"I'll fix your wage once we've seen the quality of your work, but count on it being reasonably decent if your work bears that out. We'll be in daily to evaluate your progress. If it's too slow we'll have to just let the whole thing go. What have we got to lose at this point, Allan?" she stated, turning towards the man who was now just muttering to himself looking at the stained wood ceiling.

She turned back towards me saying, "and if you have anyone else in mind …"

My immediate thought was Emma of course. She was quite good at maintaining a quick, even stitch even at age twelve, was a tireless worker and had always enjoyed tackling impossible tasks. I also thought of Felicité since Mrs. Dawson had mentioned the young woman's sewing capabilities and stated outright that she would really have no use for either of the girls in very short order. They would make good money, possibly even better than on the plantation I conjectured. They would be able to live with Alice and me in town during the week and then take the train out to Godchaux on weekends. Alice would be livid about the entire plan, but I refused to let that dissuade me.

"Yes, I would like the job," I responded quickly before common sense had a chance to intervene. "And I do have two capable young women in mind, although they might not be able to start until next week or so."

"Evelyn, are you completely off your nut? You don't even know this woman's name much less if she knows warp from weft!" fumed Allan, stomping down the loading dock ramp still muttering to himself and disappearing through the concrete alleyway. "And don't forget to lock up or we'll find snakes, muskrats and God only knows what else in there tomorrow!" he yelled back to her.

I extended my hand. "Hannah Barrington," I said to the woman.

"Miss DeWitt," she answered warmly. "Let me guess, you tried to work in one of the cigar factories, which explains why you're covered with brown tobacco dust," she added, quizzically raising one eyebrow. "How long did you last?"

"Less than a day and a half," I replied with a rather embarrassed half smile.

"I've never known a white woman who could manage to work in those places. Those Black Creole and Indian women must be made of far sterner stuff than are we."

Alice's complaints of her classmates or of anything remotely worthwhile imparted by her inadequately educated teachers made no impact on me that evening. She finally realized that my thoughts were elsewhere and stopped talking. I had a job. And right now, that was all that mattered. What's more, with any luck whatsoever, I might actually be able to make something decent out of it. Just how quickly those costumes might be refurbished was anyone's guess. Even given seven or eight months I had no idea how many could possibly be rescued and if that would be early enough for the investment group's needs, but I was determined to do my best.

I told Alice that I had been fired from the cigar factory, but mentioned nothing about the costume venture. There were far too many pieces of this puzzle that had to fit perfectly. I had already decided to start work tomorrow, hoping that the other two women were skilled hard workers and then contact Mrs. Dawson to ask if Emma and Felicité might begin the following week. I would also have to find other housing for all of us, since it was more than obvious that Mme. Laballiere would never allow two black girls to live under her roof even for one day. Her definition of "good working society" translated rather obviously to "whites only society". I hoped that the woman would be gracious enough to refund our weeks not used, particularly since she could certainly let our room for far more money than Mr. Reedy's slim negotiated amount. And I could only hope that Zuma would approve of this entire venture for Emma.

The two young women hired by Miss DeWitt were white Creole sisters in their late teens. Even though their native language was French they actually were more than eager to converse in English since that's what all of the young French Creoles did now they told me. They introduced themselves as Adele and Aline although I sometimes wondered if these were their real names. They giggled constantly about seemingly trivial matters, but all that was really important was that they were very fast, creative, and surprisingly quite well-disciplined seamstresses.

The three of us had re-made a dozen very respectable, almost completely matching chorus dresses from a disparate pile of sixteen light teal, lavender and black costumes by late afternoon. Adele had the strongest hands I'd ever seen in a woman and could rip out and then re-stitch row after row of huge fastening metal hooks and eyes. Aline was amazingly adept at finding totally mismatched accessories, tearing them apart and creating startlingly beautiful new motifs which we could then use to unify each bodice. Before her departure that morning, Miss DeWitt had shown where we would find several enormous wash tubs, soap and bleach. Adele and I dragged the tubs out into the loading dock, filling them with clean water from the cistern mounted above, undoubtedly originally installed for that very purpose. Anticipating our continued work tomorrow, I set to bleaching about five dozen dingy white cotton shirts and blouses as well as white sleeves, collars and lace trim that we'd hacked off various other garments. We had unearthed three rugged, but serviceable, sewing machines and all of us energetically tackled the work. When Miss DeWitt came by late that afternoon she was quite pleased: we were officially hired.

That evening I called Mrs. Dawson and told her that if Emma and Felicité wanted steady paying jobs for the next several months, possibly even through early next summer, that I could offer them good work. Felicité was already sixteen, Mrs. Dawson felt it prudent to inform me, and, truth be known, since the young woman's mother was just a prostitute over in black Storyville, she didn't hold out much hope for the girl. She had only taken her in as a sort of Christian outreach advocated by her church, but it had proven to be a very dubious experiment at best. However, she was certain that Zuma would have no problem with allowing Emma to stay with me in New Orleans for the week and then return to Godchaux for the weekends. Since I had been Emma's teacher all of those years that seemed a very natural step.

I signed a six-month lease and we moved to a double shotgun house in Tremé later that week despite Alice's non-stop tirades. The community in Tremé was mixed race, comprised of many nationalities of all shades. All that they really had in common was being poor, but almost all of them were scrambling for an honest day's wage. Although there were occasionally problems in the district, they were quite infrequent our Italian neighbors occupying the other side of the double informed us. They also loaned us a couple of pallets to sleep on the floor; there was an icebox, stove, a table and two chairs, but no other furniture in the house. For the next six months, I rationalized, it was affordable, reasonably clean and most importantly, it was ours.

The term shotgun was simply a name for a house that had no hallways, meaning that each room connected straight through front to back with a door in the same place in each room. A shot fired through the front door which opened directly onto the parlor, would thus theoretically go straight through the one or two bedrooms and out the kitchen door, possibly whistling through the back stoop directly to the privy. Most homes were on concrete stilts to avoid flooding, and were built with very high ceilings making them surprisingly quite cool during the blistering summer months. In addition to the kitchen stove, a bedroom fireplace warmed the home in the cooler winters.

Zuma's response to my taking Emma to live in the city and work during the week at the Opera House was reserved. Also, she wasn't at all certain that hiring Felicité was a wise choice. In Zuma's opinion the girl was "downright sneaky, dishonest and a liar" and only possessed very average sewing skills, despite Mrs. Dawson's more positive assessment of that skill. But more chilling was Zuma's quietly whispered parting remark to me regarding Emma as I left Godchaux with the two girls that first weekend: "I gots her this far 'long, Miss Hannah Owens. Don' you go messin' it up now."

Over the next six months we accomplished what I felt was nothing short of a miraculous overhaul of the costumes. Keeping Felicité on task was indeed challenging, but having Adele, Aline and Emma on board to yell at her in her native patois proved to be essential, since the girl responded to no English whatsoever. I relished having the opportunity to work with Emma for three nights each week, much to Alice's ire, and accomplished this by simply using Alice's text books in the evenings. If Alice was working on mathematics, Emma and I were reading history or geography or vice versa. Felicité was usually out somewhere during all of this and I never questioned her regarding her whereabouts. I only required that she be home a half hour after dusk since I locked our doors for the night by that time. She was surprisingly good about getting home on time each night.

I was not aware at the time of our move, however, that Kid Ory had been booking the Economy Society's main hall on Ursulines Street, only a few blocks away, on Monday nights for over a year. The large meeting hall served as a community center and public dances were held there practically every night with different bands each night. Mondays, Ory's night, always drew the Economy's biggest crowds and without fail, Adele, Aline, Emma and Felicité were among the earliest arrivals within that crowd heading out straight from work each Monday. Occasionally, Ory would call Emma up on stage to sing a couple of tunes, but not always. She had continued to write Mme. Jones every few weeks about auditioning, but thus far had heard nothing in the way of a reply.

Emma was anxious to work with Kid Ory's band on whatever terms he might offer up to her. His group was a hot playin' band, a dancin' band, he'd told her, not a backin' band for female singers. If he had her up there to sing too often every black woman who thought she could sing the blues in Tremé would be annoyin' him. That's what vaudeville was for, y'know? In his view audiences tended to drift away once the lady singers started into their stuff because the people were there to dance, y'know? He continually assured her, however, that he truly loved her voice. On many occasions Ory and one or two of his band mates stopped at our house after the dance, bottles of beer in hand, for an hour or so, chatting with Felicité and Emma in the front room. Since the conversation was almost entirely in dialect, I rarely knew what was being discussed. Alice slept on a pallet in front of the stove in the kitchen on Monday nights, attempting to avoid all the noise. We seemed to have settled into a frozen truce of sorts with only the barest of communication as was needed, although her sharp, critical tongue was always at the ready.

Christmas, followed by an unusually frigid new year and Easter, came and went with scarcely a change in our routine, other than loading more wood into the fireplace to keep warm in the coldest of the winter chill, while listening to an occasional display of fireworks or a brass band leading a funeral procession. Whether you were rich, poor, black or white, every corpse received a brass band funeral procession to the cemetery.

Kid Ory and his bass player, Ed Garland, were now stopping by almost every Monday night after the dance. I insisted that the two men leave within an hour since both girls needed to be at work early the next morning and I was never comfortable with these two men stopping by at all. Ory also had a brass band that played for funerals. Fortunately, however, they only worked on weekends when the girls were at Reserve and during the week earlier in the day when we were all at the opera house. Emma was an entirely different person when Edward Ory was around ... not one I particularly liked.

On one of the first warmer days of April, however, a knock at our front door forever destroyed whatever fragile equilibrium might have existed within my tiny household. On the threshold stood Margaret Hughes, a woman I had last seen over fifteen years ago and had hoped to never encounter again. Although now slightly wrinkled, her pale oval face was still quite attractive, her dark brown hair reflected traces of light silver strands, and her tiny figure, perfectly outfitted in a stylish deep purple matching dress and coat, was as pert as it had always been. And equally amazing, as usual, her boots were perfectly blacked without even the tiniest hint of dust.

"Mrs. Hughes! This is indeed ... an unexpected surprise!" I uttered, stepping back from the door.

"Indeed, as I'm certain it is Hannah," she replied stiffly, taking in my thin cotton dress and disheveled hair as she brushed past me into the small parlor. "I'm sure you were assuming that I would never locate you at all."

Without invitation, methodically removing her gloves, she sat down on our one decent chair and I carefully sat on an adjacent ladder-back chair in the corner.

"I'm sure you know why I'm here."

"No ma'am," I answered. "I really have no idea. I could put some coffee or tea on if you have time. I may also still have some chocolate on the stove if you would prefer."

She stared at me for several moments undoubtedly assuming I would be able to guess why she was sitting in my front room.

"You didn't remember that my family, the Claytor side that is, is from Vacherie? That my father's fortune was made and almost completely lost on his plantation in Vacherie?"

Zuma had originally worked for Mrs. Hughes and her husband in New Orleans prior to their moving up to Colorado Springs many years ago. Undoubtedly, Mrs. Hughes' parents had brought her up in a palatial home among the wealthy families along St. Charles Avenue in New Orleans, for no decent family actually lived on one's plantation as Mrs. Dawson had lamented! However, I'd never heard of a town called Vacherie until Alice and I had moved down here.

"No ma'am. Until my arrival a few months back I don't believe that I'd ever heard of Vacherie, Mrs. Hughes."

"Where is she?"

"Where is who?"

"Don't try my patience woman! Abigail's daughter, what

do you mean 'who'?" she retorted with a barely strangled shriek, almost jumping out of the chair. "I've gone mad with worry all of these years, but I'll have you know that I'm still lucid enough!"

I sat quietly looking at her. I considered making another offer of tea, but thought the better of it.

"Perhaps you weren't aware that my husband, Dr. Hughes, just passed away a few months ago in Colorado Springs," she bristled.

"No, I hadn't heard. I'm so sorry."

"We had been, um, 'estranged' I guess is the expression they use for it these days, for quite some time, as you may remember, but in the end he positively insisted that I be at his bedside for his every waking moment. He was terrified of dying. And I was there with him for all of those last horribly painful weeks. He died of cancer, you know."

"I'm glad you were there with him," I replied evenly. "I'm sure that was a wonderful comfort for him."

She glowered at me not certain if my reply was genuine. And with good reason I'll admit: it wasn't.

"Albert talked to me about many different things that were troubling him – a religious cleansing perhaps. I'm not entirely certain what prompted all of it. But he became very religious during those last months as people so often do. He had been a doctor for his entire life as I'm sure you remember. Tears rolled down his face when he told me that fourteen years ago he'd been called to identify the bodies of several people who'd been blown up in a terrible mine shaft dynamiting. Our only daughter Abigail was one of those people he identified. She had on a gold necklace that he had given her, so there was absolutely no chance of any mistake you understand."

I frowned, but made no reply.

"But even more importantly, he told me that he was certain that she had given birth to the child she had been carrying, because there were no ... well, remains of that child ... to be found with Abigail."

"Ah," I whispered, taking a deep breath.

"In Albert's last words he insisted that I find you to see what happened to Abigail's child," she stated. "He said that you'd been living with Abigail out in Cripple Creek at the time when her baby would have been born. She had run away from home – from me. I was indeed ... upset when she'd told me she was expecting a baby and that ... it would probably be awhile before she and the baby's father would be getting married. But I certainly didn't expect her to simply, well, completely *disappear* from my life!"

"Abigail had told me that you had thrown her out, beaten her in fact," I replied steadily. "She tried to move in with Dr. Hughes, but the hotel in which he was living wouldn't allow it. They didn't believe she was actually his daughter."

"Well, that certainly sounds like my Abigail's overactive imagination! My, oh my! Always the fairy tales that girl!" Mrs. Hughes replied with a constrained chuckle.

I made no reply. White-knuckled, my fingers gripped the edges of my chair.

"So imagine my total surprise when my second cousin Alice Claytor writes me last month about a conversation she had with another plantation owner's wife, Ursula Dawson, over in Reserve, about a young woman also named Alice who is the spitting image of my cousin's daughter Margaux, although a number of years younger. Probably about thirteen years old or so. And furthermore, that this child, who even claims that she was born in Colorado, is supposedly your daughter!"

I remained quiet and remarkably, so did Mrs. Hughes. She continued to stare at me for several moments then cleared her throat.

"And you're certain that Dr. Hughes remembered all of this ... correctly," I stated as evenly as possible. "You had said he was quite ill with cancer when he'd spoken to you about these details. People do sometimes forget things, memories become ... scrambled ..."

"His mind was razor sharp practically to the very end, Hannah. Only his body was tragically wasting away," she snapped.

"I had assumed that Abigail was still pregnant and had died in the fires back in Cripple Creek, Mrs. Hughes. That was the information made available within the town back then. And those fires were several months before any mines were dynamited during the mining union protests as I remember."

Mrs. Hughes slightly pursed her lips, tilting her head sideways and narrowing her eyes.

"And just how do you know then to which mine explosion I'm referring?" she demanded.

"Well, obviously meaning that I had no idea what had happened to her, ma'am. I assumed she had died in the fires. Everyone was terribly scattered for days afterwards and information was limited," I responded, meeting her stare, my heart thundering within my chest.

Mrs. Hughes' eyes narrowed even further. In a frighteningly quiet voice, she continued speaking. "You're lying. Years ago I threw you out when I caught you red-handed stealing money out of my strong box. Now you're trying to steal my only grandchild. I demand to see this girl Alice that you claim is your daughter."

"She's out with friends this afternoon. I don't know when she'll be returning. Probably quite late," I replied, standing up, hoping that would serve as some kind of signal for the woman's exit. This was a lie. Alice was actually at the library; she had made no effort whatsoever to acquire any friends since we'd moved here.

Mrs. Hughes slowly stood as well, carefully drawing up her gloves and moving to the door. Her hand on the knob, she turned around to face me again. "I'm staying at the Grunewald, Mrs. Barrington. They do a magnificent brunch on Sundays, I've been informed. I'll expect to see you and Alice there tomorrow morning at 11. As my guests of course." She opened the door and stepped out.

*"Get up from that piano. You hurtin' its feelings."*
Ferdinand "Jelly Roll" Morton

## Chapter 5: The Grunewald, 1914

The trolley transfer lines had suffered some kind of electrical misfiring and we were late arriving at the Grunewald Hotel the next morning. I had considered not going at all, but realized the complete folly of said action. Almost all of the tables in the hotel's restaurant were lavishly set for parties of four, although there were a handful of smaller tables for two. Doubled thick white tablecloths graced each setting with napkins folded into complex pyramids, along with hefty water glasses, delicate champagne flutes and a full complement of spotless sterling silver. A luscious red, long-stemmed rose in a delicately spiraled crystal vase graced each table as well, completing the classic ambience of entitled wealth, thoroughly underscoring everything luxurious that I was unable to offer my child.

Mrs. Hughes sat near the far wall, sipping a glass of water as she looked over her menu. I had told Alice that a woman visiting from Colorado Springs wanted to meet us for lunch. Alice had never once mentioned that conversation with Mrs. Dawson from several months ago, although I was certain she wouldn't have forgotten it. As we approached her table Mrs. Hughes stood up slowly, dropping her menu to the floor, one hand on her throat, her eyes fixed on Alice.

One of the waiters moved in quickly to retrieve the menu from the floor. *"Eh, Madame ... s'il vous plaît, votre carte ..."* he said softly, holding it out to her.

But Mrs. Hughes was walking over to Alice as if in a trance. "My God, my God," she whispered. "It's you! You're really alive! A Claytor as I walk and breathe! I can't believe that kind of beauty was hiding somewhere within Abigail all those years!" She fiercely pulled the girl into her arms, holding her for several moments before finally releasing her. Alice remained motionless, her arms straight down by her sides. "Here, sit down my dear. Please, please sit down!"

The waiter who had retrieved the menu held out the chair for Mrs. Hughes and then for Alice. Another young man moved in quickly to hold out a chair for me. Additional menus appeared as well, although all of us simply set them aside. This entire scene unraveled in less than two minutes. Like a statue, Alice sat in her chair staring at Mrs. Hughes. Neither of us had yet to utter even so much as a greeting.

Quite surprisingly Alice spoke first, eyes wide, calmly addressing Mrs. Hughes. "I read about a dessert recently called *Pêches à la Melba*. Might I order that for breakfast?"

Mrs. Hughes fired the question to our waiter in rapid French to which he nodded affirmatively. *"Oui, madame, oui! Avec la sauce framboise chaude, n'est-ce pas?"*

"With warm raspberry sauce, Alice?" asked Mrs. Hughes smiling.

"Yes ma'am," she replied. "And vanilla ice, of course."

"Would you like something else first though, my dear?" Mrs. Hughes continued sweetly. "Perhaps a poached egg? A croissant or maybe a muffin? And a coffee, I assume?"

"Yes, that sounds quite lovely." Alice nodded with a smile, handing her menu back to the waiter.

"And you?" Mrs. Hughes directed coolly at me.

"A poached egg and muffin also," I replied quickly. "Thank you."

She gave the rest of the order, again in French, and the waiter collected our menus, bowed slightly and had just begun to walk away when Mrs. Hughes added, *"et trois jus d'orange du jour aussi."* I had never heard Mrs. Hughes speak French in all the years that I had known her, but since she had grown up here obviously she would have been completely immersed in it. Certainly not for the first time in my life I wondered how on earth she and Dr. Hughes had ever gotten together at all.

"I've also ordered all of us a glass of orange juice. They serve it over slivered ice here with frozen slices of mango and banana. It's quite tasty."

Alice nodded seemingly in appreciation. Now that the waiter had retreated from our table I knew that Mrs. Hughes would get right down to business. And after a few moments of idle chit chat, including actually introducing herself to Alice, she finally did so.

"So Alice, your last name is Barrington, correct?"

"Yes, ma'am," she replied.

"And your middle name?"

"Elizabeth."

"Indeed? How *very* interesting. And your father was a man named John Barrington, who met with an unfortunate end, according to my ... sources at any rate, about six or seven years ago, correct?"

"Yes, ma'am. He was shot."

"I actually knew Mr. Barrington, although not particularly well, back in Colorado Springs. He was a friend and something of an investment partner with my late husband, Dr. Albert Hughes. But, I rather doubt that your father would have ever mentioned Albert to you since you were so young."

"No ma'am."

"And I'm going to assume that your mother never mentioned anything about me or my daughter Abigail Hughes either."

"No ma'am," Alice answered yet again, glancing darkly in my direction and then back at Mrs. Hughes.

"Well, here's what I think happened. Feel free to try to correct my, um, shall we say hypothesis, if I am wrong," began Mrs. Hughes, momentarily flashing a brittle smile towards me.

I tried to keep my breathing steady. Mrs. Hughes cleared her throat.

"My daughter Abigail was unmarried, but had unfortunately found herself … um, well, in a family way, as they say. It's my belief that the child's father was John Barrington, although Abigail never actually gave me a name. Mr. Barrington had been on a business venture, but then briefly disappeared without explanation apparently. My daughter was understandably frantic since she had indicated that they were supposed to be getting married as soon as possible."

Alice said nothing. Nor did I. The waiter appeared with our glasses of orange juice.

"Abigail and I had a misunderstanding of sorts … you know how those things can be, my dear! And I'm sorry to say that she ran away from home as a result of our argument. I fully believe that she was looking for Mr. Barrington during that time and they finally located one another. This was up in Cripple Creek, Colorado. Has your mother ever mentioned that town to you?"

"No ma'am."

Mrs. Hughes took a long swallow of her orange juice. Alice did the same and then pulled a chunk of mango off the rim of the tall glass.

"Delicious, yes?"

Alice nodded.

"Well, at the time, I never knew if Abigail had her child or not. There were two dreadful fires that swept through Cripple Creek killing a number of people and she was listed among the fatalities."

"Ah, I see," murmured Alice.

"But as I believe I mentioned before, my late husband was a doctor. And a couple of months after those fires there was a terrible mine shaft dynamiting and Abigail's … um … remains were identified by my husband at that time. He didn't want to tell me then because he didn't want to upset me yet again since, well, I had already assumed the worst from the fires, you understand."

Mrs. Hughes shot a black glance in my direction.

"Of course," agreed Alice, taking another sip of her juice.

"My dear Albert passed away about six months ago, Alice. Of cancer. It was a slow, horribly agonizing death. You just can't imagine. I was with him practically every hour of every day. He had become very religious those last few months. He felt it important to tell me then about having identified Abigail in that mine explosion fourteen years ago. But more importantly, his dying words were to find Abigail's child because she had indeed given birth he discovered and there were no signs of that baby's remains in the mine shaft. And he also told me that John Barrington had rented a house out to Abigail and … Hannah … during the time that the child would have been born. Albert had even talked with Abigail in that place, so he was quite certain that she was indeed living there. He begged me to find Hannah to see what might have happened to our grandchild."

"And obviously you believe that I'm Abigail's child," Alice replied without any emotion.

"Well, yes!" smiled Mrs. Hughes, giving one of her irritating shrugs that had faded from my memory so long ago. "I'm sure at the time when Abigail was killed in that explosion it made sense for John Barrington to just marry Hannah and the two of them to simply, well, claim you as their own. I really can't blame either of them for their actions at that time I suppose. It makes a certain sense."

No one spoke.

"Well, then I guess everybody got skunked all the way around," replied Alice with light sarcasm.

"What do you mean?" asked Mrs. Hughes, frowning.

"Because John Barrington was already married and apparently had been for quite some time," she stated simply with a small laugh. "They even had a son named Dannie. I met him last year. He ended up in my class for awhile back in Kansas City when his mother died."

Mrs. Hughes' frown deepened. This obviously wasn't part of her semi-fabricated tale.

"Hannah?" inquired Mrs. Hughes brusquely, turning towards me, "you mean to say that you were married to a man who you knew was already married?

Fortunately our meal was served at that very moment as I attempted to collect my thoughts. I really had no idea what direction my explanation should take. Eyes lowered, Alice took several bites of her egg and quietly buttered one of her muffins.

"I wasn't aware that John Barrington had ever been married at the time of our wedding," I replied evenly. "I was informed about it just after his death."

"But you *do* agree that Alice is indeed Abigail's daughter and not your own," stated Mrs. Hughes firmly. "She looks absolutely nothing like you anyway. She has "Claytor" written into every single pore of her being. In fact, to be honest with you, she doesn't really resemble Mr. Barrington either as best I remember the man. He had that rather swarthy foreign look your type of woman seems to go after. But we'll have to trust my poor departed Abigail's integrity on that."

Several moments passed in silence. Mrs. Hughes took a small bite of her breakfast, then paused looking at me. I had yet to even pick up my fork. I sat fingering the napkin in my lap.

"Well?" demanded Mrs. Hughes. "If you're not willing to admit this now, Hannah Owens, I will take up the matter with the courts. Given what I know of your sordid history in Cripple Creek, I'm quite certain that they'll provide a most willing ear. And believe me you'll be most distressed once I've done that!"

"Yes," I finally admitted weakly, sinking back listlessly into the chair, tears beginning to course down my face. "Yes, she's Abigail's daughter, Mrs. Hughes. I delivered her into the world.

I was the first one to hold her, the first one to look into those unusual grey eyes, the first to bathe and swaddle her. And I've always felt that I was truly her mother ever since Abigail's disappearance. I never knew what had happened to Abigail. I only knew that if she were still alive there was never a question in my mind that she would have returned to be with her baby!"

Alice stared at me, her face completely blurred through my curtain of tears.

"So what happens now?" said Alice crisply, frighteningly dry-eyed, showing almost no emotion whatsoever. "What difference does any of this make now?"

"It's my hope that you'll agree to come back with me to Colorado Springs, Alice," said Mrs. Hughes, gently, placing her hand very lightly over Alice's. After a moment Alice carefully slid her own hand away. "We'll call it a long visit to see how everything works out for you. That only makes sense of course, my dear. We'll be coming back to New Orleans in a few months for my cousin's daughter Margaux Claytor's wedding, in Vacherie, in early autumn and will certainly make time for you to visit with everyone here. Assuming that all goes well, we'll plan on doing that at least twice each year since that only seems the fair thing to do. I certainly don't expect you to give up all of your friends here."

Alice glanced over at me, eyes narrowing slightly, but said nothing.

"Also, you should know that I have a beautiful older home up in Colorado Springs my dear, one of the most desirable estates you could ever hope to find in the entire country! It was built by one of Colorado's most prominent architects several decades ago; in fact, a Stratton-designed home these days demands peak top dollar up there. It's quite the rare find to discover anything of his for sale, let me tell you. Mr. Stratton was a multi-millionaire and one of my husband's longtime friends actually, although he died a number of years ago. A huge retirement establishment and orphaned children's home in Colorado Springs was just recently opened as bequeathed in Mr. Stratton's will. I was invited to attend the marvelously extravagant opening gala just last year and signed on temporarily as part of their social committee. You know, sponsor teas, small programs and other modest, social afternoon events for the older residents of the home."

"Funny that," replied Alice, coolly staring at me then back at Mrs. Hughes. "Mother attempted to run a school in Kansas City she called the 'Mary Stratton' School. Stratton's hardly a common name like Adams or Jones or Smith."

Mrs. Hughes simply shrugged, slightly frowning, but no one spoke. Trembling, I attempted to whisk the tears from my face with both hands.

"And speaking of school what happens with that?" inquired Alice. "I have hopes of going to college in a few years Mrs. Hughes. I want to be a scientist or a chemist like Marie Pasteur or Mme. Curie."

This came as a shock. I had never heard Alice say anything whatsoever about her future.

"Well, I must say, just what kind of schooling can you be getting out in that miserable little place where you're living now – Tremé? For heaven's sake! What a filthy spot to bring up a young white girl, Hannah! My parents sent me to private schools throughout my entire school life and we even lived in New Orleans proper." Mrs. Hughes shook her head vigorously, shuddering as well. "Don't worry, Alice. I'll make absolutely certain that your dreams of getting into an excellent women's college and becoming a scientist are realized without any question or delay! I worked very hard to give my daughter Abigail the best education possible and there's certainly no reason I can't provide the same or even better for you my dear child."

A small cut glass bowl of *Pêches à la Melba*, the aroma of

warm raspberry sauce deliciously hanging in the air, was set in front of a faintly smiling Alice. At that moment I knew she was forever lost to me.

Alice and I had moved her few belongings to Mrs. Hughes' hotel room later in the afternoon. She had given me a brief hug and promised to write, but not surprisingly there were no tears on her part. The entire transition seemed completely effortless for her I realized. From what I had observed of Mrs. Hughes while working for her all of those years, there was much more than just the Claytor looks that Alice had evidently inherited.

When Emma and Felicité returned from Godchaux later that evening I offered the simple explanation that at a very last minute invitation, Alice was visiting her grandmother back in Colorado for a few months. As Emma translated Alice's departure to Felicité both girls started snickering and then walked back out to the front stoop, taking along a small basket filled with blackberries and nuts they had brought back from the plantation. Emma handed me a note she'd found outside on the window sill that our six months lease was up and I either needed to sign for another six months or vacate in two weeks.

****

A dozen people along with Miss DeWitt greeted us at the opera house's loading dock the following morning. They looked around inspecting the garments, whispering to one another and occasionally shaking their heads or gesturing at certain fixtures, wandering about the room for a good half hour as we set into that day's work. Without any word to us they left quite abruptly. We had recently torn open and attempted to reorganize the remainder of the shipping crates' holdings so that all of the double hung garment racks were once again completely filled with costumes, desperately in need of tedious miraculous refurbishment. All of our prior work had been shipped elsewhere. I could only surmise that it was met with at least limited satisfaction by both buyer and seller. The massive piles of accessories, slightly diminished, still needed weeks of categorizing, although Adele had actually done a fair start at that job. It was obvious that in the six months we had been working only a relatively small amount of the work had been completed. I was now completely numb, ambivalent as to whether I wanted the project to continue or end. I just needed an answer by Friday before I had to sign another lease.

As always on Monday nights the four girls headed off for Kid Ory's concert at Economy Hall. I couldn't face going home to that empty dark house without Alice. I was trying to convince myself that her leaving with Mrs. Hughes would offer her the education and experiences that I would never have been able to provide -- that I had taken her growth as far as I was able and should just accept that fact. Somehow in my feeble attempt to do everything possible, I had forgotten that children grow up with their own version of themselves. A version that we adults are all too often only allowed the slightest glimpse and even less control.

Although I was not particularly hungry, I stopped at a small café. It was early yet, but the restaurant was already fairly crowded. Seated at a small table in the corner, I accepted the waiter's suggested glass of red wine and crusty loaf of bread. The words on the menu swam in front of me, however.

"Such an enchanting woman, so deeply absorbed in mysterious thought," said a man's voice. "Perhaps she might entertain the thought of a companion at her table this evening."

I looked up to see a pleasant-looking, middle-aged man, slightly thinning hair grayed at the temples, attired in the typical business dress of the day with linen coat and tightly buttoned cotton shirt. He held his white skimmer in one hand and the back of the other chair at my table with the other. "Might I join you madam? There appear to be no other tables at the moment," he remarked as he pulled out the chair.

"Oh," I replied, glancing around the café, "why yes, of

course."

"Popular place this evening it seems. But they serve an excellent seafood gumbo on Mondays and Thursdays I'm told, which is probably why all these people are electing to dine here this evening. My name's Joe, by the way, Joe Peterson," he said extending his hand to me. "I was over this way trying to negotiate on some fixtures for my new place and was told this café had great gumbo, so I just had to meander over and try it out, of course."

"Hannah Barrington," I replied, shaking his hand. "I hadn't really thought about what to order. Thank you for the suggestion."

He signaled the waiter over and ordered a glass of wine for himself and a small cheese tray. "For us to share, of course," he nodded at me. "Least I can do since you're allowing me to share your table."

"So are these fixtures for your home?" I asked. I hadn't particularly wanted any company this evening, but the man, at least on the surface, seemed to be a decent sort I had to admit.

"No, no," he replied, shaking his head as the waiter delivered the glass of wine. "For my new saloon. Over on Iberville. It's just a little bitty place, almost a hole in the wall, nothing like Tom Anderson's huge concern or Pete Lala's of course, but decent, you know? Right on the outskirts of Storyville so real good positioning of course," he continued with a friendly wink, then toasting "to your health!"

"When are you planning to open?"

"Well, soon's I can take delivery of a large ice box, a few of them newer-styled mirrors and more tables to match the ones I already got. See they shorted me when I ordered them. Men can stand and drink all night long, and of course, they will. No problem there! But if you wanna have the ladies comin' in to order drinks, well, you gotta have a place for 'em to sit down and be proper, you know."

"Ladies?" I questioned. "I guess I didn't know that ... well, decent women ... frequented saloons in New Orleans, Mr. Peterson!" The world had changed so much since the turn of the century that I doubted I would ever catch up with the current acceptable measures of propriety.

"Please! I've dropped in on your sweet hospitality sharing your table. I'm just plain ole Joe!"

"Ok, Joe," I nodded. "I'm Hannah."

"Lovely name for a very lovely lady."

"Um, thank you," I replied rather uncomfortably, which I'm certain he sensed immediately. The cheese tray was delivered to the table and he offered me the first choice.

"Anyway, getting back to my saloon, we're not talking about those places actually in Storyville itself you understand," he laughed. "Now those places are pretty raw! Even I don't like goin' in there as a rule unless I have to!"

I refrained from asking why he might 'have to' of course. He sampled another one of the cheeses and thickly buttered a hunk of the bread.

"So, here you are dining alone, Miss Hannah," he said after taking a few bites, leaning back slightly in his chair. "I'm going to make a not-so-long stretch of a theory that you're either newly divorced or a widow and that you were just coming home from work and stopped in here. Am I correct?"

"I'm a widow," I replied.

"Somehow I kinda guessed that as well. You don' look like the divorcin' type, you know? But, well, I'm a divorced man myself. Coupla years now. Married for over eight years. Felt more like eighty though. Miss her cookin' but sure as hell don' miss her carpin'! My oh my!"

I laughed slightly. He was fairly charming I had to admit. After John's death my position as a schoolteacher at a school for poor, dark-skinned children had certainly kept any available men skirting the widest possible path, quite reluctant to make my acquaintance. And I really had no particular reason to have wished it otherwise.

"Children?" he inquired. "None for me, thank goodness!"

"Yes, one," I replied quickly. Then, since I was certain his next question would be inquiring why I wasn't home feeding my child dinner I added: "she's having dinner at a friend's tonight, but will be home by the time I've finished here. She's almost fourteen so she's very good on her own."

"Fourteen? Why you don' look like you could have a daughter that's almost fourteen!"

"I was very young when I got married," I answered smoothly. And that's certainly all that you need to know for the time being I said quietly to myself.

We both ordered the gumbo, which was indeed some of the best I had ever eaten, and despite my protests he insisted on paying for my meal. I agreed to meet him at the open air festival at *La Place Congo* the following Saturday afternoon. When I got back to the house Emma and Felicité had just arrived, but thankfully, without any additional company for once. Most importantly, Emma had finally gotten a letter from Mme. Jones. They were currently casting for their newest show, "*Lucky Sam from Alabam*" and auditions were being held in St. Louis next week. Based on Mr. Edward "Kid" Ory's fine assessment, they wanted Emma to audition.

*"Well, I tell you ... the first chorus I plays the melody. The second chorus, I plays the melody round the melody, and the third chorus, I routines."*
**Louis "Satchmo" Armstrong**

## Chapter 6: Sissieretta Jones

Emma and Felicité left for Reserve after working on Friday. I knew that Emma was planning on taking an early train to St. Louis on Sunday. She said that Zuma would be going with her and they would be back late in the week. The thought of living just with Felicité for most of the coming week was daunting – the girl still spoke almost no English and somehow my limited French rarely seemed to connect with her patois vocabulary. I knew we would be fine working at the opera house with Adele and Aline keeping her directed, but dealing with her at home would be extremely difficult. And I still missed Alice, of course. I had written her two very lengthy letters in as many days, although I had visions of the envelopes languishing unopened for several weeks atop Mrs. Hughes' antique marble hall table.

I truly looked forward to meeting Joe Peterson at the festival. Thinking back on it afterwards, our dinner had been most enjoyable I now realized. And after a sleepless night in my empty house last night, I knew that I would definitely welcome his company for a few hours today. When I arrived at *La Place Congo* I found it wonderfully alive with countless merchants displaying colorful clothing and rugs, small tented structures over temporary ovens where one might sample delicious-smelling foods of Creole, Cajun, Indian and Spanish origins, long pavilion tables laden with pottery and metal crafts, jewelry, unusual sun parasols, fanciful kites and all manner of children's wooden drums, whistles and other toys. Several brightly costumed young Spanish men with guitars and mandolins were performing on a raised platform, the crowd around them clapping along in wild rhythm. The bright throng of people undulated in the warm sunshine. I wondered how on earth I would ever find Joe within this huge crowd as I worked my way over to one of the food vendors.

Suddenly I felt a hand lightly touch my shoulder followed by a voice whispering in my ear "try the red beans 'n rice or the catfish plate, very good stuff, y'know?"

I turned expecting to find Joe, but instead was surprised to see Kid Ory.

"Oh, hello," I replied, the disappointment undoubtedly obvious in my greeting. "I guess one should expect to find you here."

"Yeah, we're not on for another hour or so, but I had a second line engagement early so just came on over after that. You, uh, waitin' for someone?"

"Yes, a friend. He should be here any minute." Then, feeling that I should at least make an attempt at brief conversation while waiting for Joe I added, "I guess I don't know what a second line is truth to tell."

"Brass band that plays for a funeral procession, y'know."

"Ah. So your band does that as well. I see."

"Well, yes, and no. It's a different band, y'see. See what you do is you sign up as a leader for a second line, then you just head over to a couple of saloons and grab the players that are around an' looking for some work. You know, need the money and so forth. There's free beer -- barrels of the stuff in fact -- and lotsa good sandwiches with plenny o' mustard -- every several blocks along the route. And the pay? It ain' bad either for an hour's or so work. You make double if you're the leader, so that's why I do it. Don' make no difference to me who I bring on for that kinda stuff, long as they're at least decent musicians, y'know? You've heard of Jelly Roll Morton, right?"

I shook my head.

"No? Probably the best ragtime piano player in New Orleans ... eh, well, other than maybe Tony Jackson, y'know? Great musician. Writes amazin' stuff too. You probably know his stuff, but you jes' don' know him by name. Left here an' went out to California a few years back. Yeah, well, anyway, Jelly Roll, he's the one that got that way of bookin' fer them second lines around here ages ago."

"Yes, I see," I replied, nodding my head and hoping that Joe would appear quickly. I had already learned from Ory's visits to the house after his concerts on Monday evenings that more often than not his stories were extremely long-winded and rarely resolved quickly to an ending. Fortunately his music didn't seem to suffer from the same affliction.

"Now my string band, however, that's a way different story. That playing matters, y'know? And it matters a helluva lot!"

"So you also have a string band? Is that different from your, um, dance band that I saw out in Reserve last year?"

"Well, no, no. See you just call a sittin' down band for a dance a string band even though you got yer trombone, trumpet and so forth and so on. Sometimes there's as much brass as actual strings in a string band," he laughed.

I found all of this pretty confusing, but it really wasn't particularly important that I understand any of what he was talking about.

"Oh, I should thank you for your help in getting Emma's audition," I suddenly remembered. "She's really excited as I'm sure you can imagine."

"Yeah, we'll be leavin' on the earliest train heading up to St. Louis on Sunday," he replied, scratching his ear. "It'll be a long coupla days for her, but she's gonna do real fine, I just know it. In fact I wouldn't be surprised that back when Mrs. Jones started out, before all that fancy opera stuff she's doing now, that her singing voice was just like Emma's, y'know?"

"She told me that her mother was going to travel with her!" My voice was undoubtedly harsher than I intended. Just what exactly did this grown man want with this young girl anyway?

"*Non, non, jamais, jamais,* Miss Hannah!" he avowed, stepping back from me, both hands stretched out in front of himself. "I ain' messin' with no thirteen-year-old girl! Hell no! Well, less she's a workin' girl over on the street, y'know, but that's a way different story, y'know? I gotta say, she's been a might too friendly maybe at times, but I don' just keep company with some young girl who ain' a workin' girl!"

I folded my arms, glowering at him.

"Well, actually *seein'* a young girl's nothin' but trouble, Miss Hannah!" he declared. "An' the last thing I need is some young girl who's gonna make trouble in my life, y'know? I wanna find a woman I just head over to Rampart and Perdido streets, y'know? Helluva lot safer there!"

"And that's all you have to say about it? How do you think those young working girls become young working girls in the first place, Mr. Ory?"

"Um, well, most times it's 'cause that's all they ever known growin' up or maybe they just find the work easy money or interesting or … some of 'em even enjoy it, y'know?"

"Interesting? Enjoy it?" I guffawed, which came out as a loud, distorted snort.

"A lotta times their mamas an' even their grandmamas was just walkin' them streets too. If they're smart they saves up their money and moves on, new town and such, even gets married if they's still pretty enough, y'know? Now the ones that are your chronic alcoholics or your opium dippers and such, well, now those are your real unfortunates, I admit. I ain' never been so broke that I had to head that far past town. Those women scare me."

I stared at him shaking my head in disbelief over his incredibly narrow-minded perception. "But you really think that any of these women are able to find their way back into … acceptable society, Mr. Ory?"

"Well your friend Zuma did all right by that. But she was never a drunk or dope fiend, of course," he added quickly.

Inadvertently I stepped back from him and could feel the color drain from my face. Zuma had been a prostitute at one time? She had never mentioned this to me. But then I had never known anything about her life in New Orleans prior to her having been hired by the Hughes family as their cook. This was after her husband and two-year-old daughter had died in a diphtheria epidemic and Dr. Hughes had hired her to work for his family, several years before they had moved out to Colorado Springs where I had met all of them.

"I'm sorry, Miss Hannah," Ory continued. "Maybe she didn't want you to know that 'bout her. But I ain' tellin' tales or nothin'. I knew her brother Paul and her husband Ben, too. Most important though, she's done ok for herself, y'see? Things can sometimes turn out real good for people."

"Yes, she's done well," I replied slowly, looking past Ory into the crowd and inadvertently thinking out loud. "All of those years we worked together in Colorado she was so adamant … so worried about my reputation, my singing at Pearl's place …"

"Pearl's? What's Pearl's Place? Sounds like some kinda brothel. You were a white lady singin' in a brothel? Where in the hell was this?" whistled Ory, eyebrows arching.

"No, nothing like that, Mr. Ory," I replied firmly.

I needed to find out more about his trip with Emma. That was certainly far more important than my own ancient history.

"And your wife … she's fine with your taking the train to St. Louis for several days … with a thirteen-year-old girl?"

"My wife? Well yeah, sure, she's still around, y'know? An' what she don' know she jes' don' need to know, ma'am," he shrugged. "Emma and me, we'll be stayin' with my older sister an' her husband up in St. Louis."

I looked at him without reply, my arms still rigidly crossed.

"I'll be sleepin' on a pallet out in the front hallway like I always do when I go up there to visit 'em. An' Emma, she'll be in with my younger sister who lives with 'em. Annie, that's my little sister, she sleeps in the bedroom right next to 'em in the back. Y'know, if I didn' know you was just Emma's teacher, I'd think you was so bossy 'bout her that you were more like her mama, Miss Hannah."

"I just don't want her to lose out on what she wants from life. Times have changed maybe, but all a girl really ever has in this life is her reputation," I stated brusquely.

"Well, Miss Hannah, a white girl that is," replied Ory with a wry smile. Then he added after a pause, "A black girl though, she don' even have that most times, y'know?"

We were both silent as he gave me a moment to let that statement sink in.

"Emma told me at the Economy last Monday night 'bout Alice's trip to Colorado Springs," he remarked, then adding, "said she's visiting some grandma or other that nobody's ever even mentioned before. She an' that Felicité assumed well, y'know," he shrugged.

"Assumed what?"

"Well, y'know when a white girl her age gets sent away for several months to visit some unknown relative kinda outta the blue, you pretty much figure she's sorta along … in the, uh, you know … in the family way."

"No!" I replied indignantly. "That's not it at all, Mr. Ory! I can't believe Emma would have twisted it around that way!"

"I didn't say I agreed! And quite honestly? Your girl Alice don't exactly look the type anyways … she's, eh, mighty uppity if you'll excuse a black man makin' that kind of remark 'bout a white girl. But take it up with Emma when she gets back next week, y'know? An' hey, just one more thing, Miss Hannah before you go stompin' away from me like a mad mud wasp, 'cause I can see yer fixin' to do jes that. If you don' like calling me 'Kid' I'm just 'Ed' or 'Edward', please. I ain't Mr. Ory," he said, his brown eyes smiling into mine. "Or then there's 'Dutt', but pretty much only my family or my really old friends calls me 'Dutt' these days. Means 'dude' in Creole."

Still disgusted about Emma and Felicité's misunderstanding about Alice, I was indeed ready to just stomp away without any further conversation when Joe walked up, out of breath and red-faced, fanning himself with his skimmer.

"Uh oh, looks like maybe I'm too late!" he panted, looking first at me and then at Ory. "Here I'm only ten minutes late while circumnavigating the park looking for my beautiful date and she's already found a much younger and far more handsome replacement!"

"Hi Joe. No, nothing like that. This is Edward Ory," I said, limp of any emotion. "Edward, Joe Peterson."

"Edward Ory as in Edward "Kid" Ory?" exclaimed Joe, firmly grasping Ory's hand with both of his own. "Why Miss Hannah I had no idea that you were acquainted with Kid Ory! I've been hoping to engage your boys for opening night at my saloon, Ory! I mean, an opening night like that would be sure to put my place in everyone's book!"

Ory nodded his head and smiled. "Sure thing, Mr. Peterson. Friend of Miss Hannah's always a friend of mine. When you thinkin' you'll be openin'?"

"Hopin' to make the grade by middle or end of next month," replied Joe, shaking his head. "Still got a few things to get in line, but I'm gettin' mighty close, mighty close, y'know?"

Ory nodded then took off his hat momentarily, pushing his hair back from his face.

"Y'know, you should advertise it on one of them motor-pulled, furniture haulin' wagons. If you want I can work a good deal for you where we'll advertise playin' on that wagon all over town and then play the next night at your place. Have done that several times recently for 'em over at Pete Lala's saloon an' Betsy Cole's lawn soirees when they're havin' some big fancy bash an' they wanna spread the word. People have said it brought in a lotta good payin' folks. Yessir."

Ory wiped his arm over his forehead and then replaced his skimmer.

"Hey that sounds really great, Ory! I'll definitely take you up on that score!" replied Joe, smiling broadly and obviously elated. "But, I do have to mention just one little thing."

"Sure. Hey, I'm good with just a very small percentage up front if that's your worry."

"Well, that's terrific, I must say! Thank you! I certainly appreciate knowing that! Actually, what I was going to mention is that I'm not real big on them, uh, buckin' contests you boys have with other bands on those wagons sometimes. Just seems, well, kinda uncivilized in my mind. Maybe I'm just too old to appreciate those kind of well ... shenanigans. You know to do that with all of that great hot music you guys play and such, well ..."

"No problem. I can always avoid gettin' into them loud freak competitions! Heck, usually I'm the one that starts 'em in the first place! And they ain' really meant to attract a white audience like you're lookin' for anyways!" Ory laughed. "Just let me know when you're ready for us an' I'll put it on the book. What's the name of your place gonna be?"

"Uh, well, I'm thinkin' probably just Joe's Barroom. It's just a little bitty place, you gotta understand. Nothing like those big-time fancy concerns running over there, like Anderson's place or Lala's 25. But I've been kinda warned that it's best if I stay out of the way of those bigger concerns anyway ... you probably know exactly what I mean."

Ory nodded with a soft whistle. "Yes sir, I sure do. In fact, that's probably some of the best advice around, y'know?"

"And you think just callin' it Joe's Barroom is a good idea?"

"Hell yeah!"

I stood silently, on the surface attempting to appreciate the business arrangement the two men were conducting. But my thoughts were far away dwelling on Alice and Emma … and also Zuma truth be told.

"That's terrific! Thank you!" said Joe, pumping Ory's hand in an enthusiastic handshake. "Hey, you still got that new kid playin' cornet with you occasionally, Ory? He was truly amazing on those coupla tunes he sat in on with your guys down at the Iroquois Theater last month." Joe then turned to me. "This kid was still in short trousers, can you imagine? An' man oh man, could he blow a note! What's his name again?"

"That's Little Louis," nodded Ory, smiling. "Louis Armstrong. And, yep, I'll wager we'll all be hearin' a lot more notes that Little Louis has to blow for many years to come, sir! Boy's got tremendous talent. An' you know where he learned to play?"

Joe shook his head. "Uh, well, Buddy Bolden or Freddie Keppard most likely, right?"

"Nope, not even close. Ya see, Little Louis was arrested a coupla years back for shootin' off a gun in front of his grandma's house, right over near the Iroquois, in fact. On New Year's Eve of all things. Hell, everybody's shootin' off guns on New Year's Eve y'know? Anyway, he gets himself sent to that Colored Waifs Home out there and next thing ya know, gets put in the waif home's band for no particular reason other than it's just something for the kid to do. If he hadn' been shuffled off there I doubt anyone would've ever thought to give that boy a horn to blow! Lord works in amazin' ways sometimes, ya gotta admit."

Ory then glanced sideways momentarily at me. "An' amazin' too, his mama's just a prostitute over in black Storyville. Has been since she was maybe nine years old, same as her own mama they say."

*****

When Emma returned late Thursday evening, she was glowing with a tired excitement, but I also sensed an odd manifestation of discouragement welling up within her. She had been hired. Mrs. Jones and the music director, Mr. Pond, were both concerned that she wouldn't even be fourteen for a few months yet, but Ed Ory had apparently assured them that she could carry it all off without any problem. Rehearsals on the new show were scheduled to begin in New York in less than two months and set to open there in mid-August. Mr. Pond did acknowledge the fact that they were still experiencing some trouble with the music, lyrics and overall presentation, but everyone had been assured that all would be smoothed out very shortly. Was the discouragement due to Emma's sudden concern about being away from home for several months at a time? Or, being away from working even occasionally with Ory's band ... or was it just about being away from Ory himself?

"So what was Mme. Jones like," I asked, eager for information. Emma had placed this woman very high up on a pedestal, although she certainly seemed deserving of those accolades.

"She's absolutely beautiful, sophisticated, so poised and just, well, graceful, I guess you might say," smiled Emma wistfully, settling back against the wall on one of the stools in our tiny kitchen, her hair drifting down well past her shoulders like an exploded deep-yellow milkweed pod. "Inside and out."

"Did you have an opportunity to hear her sing?"

"No, I didn't. She's been ill supposedly. Actually, she hasn't been able to work with her troupe at all the last six months or so. Some kind of vocal problem they say. But, I'm really not sure that was the truth."

"But she liked your work. Well, I guess that's obvious since she hired you!"

Emma nodded quietly then began rolling a tiny marble of hardened glue, undoubtedly left from my latest letter to Alice, on the rough table. I placed my hand carefully over hers for a brief moment. "So then, what's wrong exactly, Emma? Something's definitely bothering you."

"Have you ever heard of arsenic wafers? They're available in the Sears catalog."

I shook my head, frowning. Something to poison rats maybe?

"Well, you see, Mrs. Jones asked me about my parents. I told her that my mother was a black Creole and that my father was a white man, but that I don't know nothin'… sorry ma'am … I mean, anything … about him."

"That seems like a rather unusual question," I replied cautiously.

Emma concentrated on rolling the glue marble from one finger to the next in small circles.

"She said that if she was as light-skinned as I am, with my blue eyes and this dirty lint hair, she would have taken those arsenic wafers to make her skin even lighter and tried to pass. She's pretty dark, you see. She said that I should do everything possible to make myself white because that was the only way anybody white would ever recognize me as being anything important in life at all, let alone as a singer. Nobody ever expects anything of quality coming from a colored singer she told me. She also said I should thank you for my speaking and singing voice at least sounding decent already."

"What else?" I replied softly, quite uncomfortable that Ory had made the same thinly-disguised assessment as a disparaging remark when I had first met him.

"Well, for one thing, she really hates this whole Black Patti thing."

"The group itself or just the name?"

"Both actually," Emma replied, her shoulders slumping. "She says that she actually thinks her voice was much better than Adelina Patti's in the first place and has always found the comparison very demeaning. But, she went along with her managers at the time to call her troupe the Black Pattis. They felt that was a great idea and promised her that the performances would be the best way to provide a showcase for her classical singing and make the white folks in America sit up and take notice of her immense talent the way so many audiences had done in parts of South America and the West Indies."

"Well," I said cautiously, "and maybe they were right."

"Mme. Jones complains that the show is really little more than a minstrel show and does practically nothing for her serious Opera Kaleidoscope as she calls it. They do full out scenes from operas like *La Boheme* and *Carmen* with costumes and scenery for the Kaleidoscope, but she says that she always feels as though she's being trotted out like some kind of highly-trained trick monkey in front of all these white audiences. And most of the places they play are all white. In some places there's an upper balcony with some cheap seats for the colored crowd, but not too often."

"That seems pretty harsh, but you mentioned that she hadn't been feeling well …"

"Do you know that she's actually sung at the White House for four different presidents?"

"That's amazing! Certainly she has to feel honored about that!"

"The first time was for President Harrison, she told me. She sang for a private luncheon for him and a couple of ambassadors before an important world events meeting."

"That's really impressive, Emma! Extraordinary in fact! I had no idea she had that far-reaching a reputation!"

Emma looked down at her hands.

"But of course, she had to use the back door at the White House. In fact she was expected to use the back door for three of those four presidents. First time she was invited to use the front door was when she sang for President Roosevelt. But even then I don't think she was asked to sit down and stay for a meal or meet his guests like any of the white performers."

I swallowed and stayed silent. Given President Wilson's harsh segregationist moves since taking office I thoroughly doubted that Sissieretta Jones would ever be invited to perform at the White House again, even with a back-door entry. Separate was definitely separate, but certainly never equal. I had nothing even remotely constructive to offer as encouragement.

"And she also mentioned that divas in opera companies in Europe and in America always get bouquets on stage after they've performed."

"Yes, that's true, they usually do," I nodded. "Or at least they used to. I remember seeing that many times at the opera back in Kansas City when Mr. Barrington was still alive."

"Well, she said that she finally received a bouquet on stage about five years ago. And she thought that it was really just sort of an appeasement – at least I'm fairly certain that's the word she used – because the Metropolitan Opera, you know, that big one in New York City, had offered her a leading role in one of their operas and then told her that they had changed their minds because they'd decided that America just isn't ready for a colored woman to be the focus on their main stage. One of the girls who'd been in the troupe back then, said that as soon as Mme. Jones was in the wings, she'd ripped the heads off those flowers and just flung the whole mess into the garbage can."

"So did she say what she would have done differently?"

"Just been born white," answered Emma darkly, flattening out the ball of glue on the table. "Otherwise you're just nobody and you have no chance in this life."

I remained quiet for several moments hoping that something encouraging would come to me, but my mind was absolutely blank. I also wondered how on earth Ed Ory's band had managed to get past that color blockade. Or had they?

"Mme. Jones also said their attendance has been down the

last couple of seasons, so they've had to make the troupe much smaller and she's not even sure it'll continue. It's only about half the size as when they started out. That's mostly because people are tired of minstrel shows and more people, especially in the bigger cities, are just going to the moving picture shows these days she says. That's now the biggest attraction," Emma said, rolling the glue marble again.

"Did you talk about any of this with Ed Ory?" I finally asked. "Surely he's encountered some of these problems as a … musician."

"Sure he does, but then he's also a man," shrugged Emma, tossing the little ball of glue over into the corner. "And he's a hot, young black musician playing great music that the young crazy white crowd has suddenly latched onto and wants to dance to. Puts him smack down on the map for sure. Ain't the same."

I knew that now was certainly not the time to correct her grammar.

"A black man only has to deal with a white man you see. But a black woman? She's got to deal with 'em both according to Mme. Jones. If she hadn't been married to this guy who was gambling away all of her money almost faster than she could earn it, she said that she would have gone to Europe permanently and could have probably been a real *étoile* performing in real operas. 'A performer's skin color's irrelevant to their reception by an audience over there' were the exact words she said to me. I wrote those words down in this journal I've started keeping so I wouldn't forget that."

Emma paused looking out the back window and then continued.

"She finally got a divorce a few years back, but that doesn't help with her reputation either, of course. And now with her mother being real sick, she needs to stay in America to be close to her anyway. Even so, a woman will go to almost any length to stay with a man rather than face getting divorced she told me.

That's always your absolutely last resort."

"Well, I would have to agree, although that's true for any woman. Skin color really has no bearing on that problem."

Emma shrugged her shoulders.

"However, it sounds as though Mme. Jones has experienced a lot of hard knocks in her life," I continued slowly. "Your experiences will be entirely different, Emma. I hope that you won't let her, well, her disappointments, squash your own dreams."

I hugged her lightly. Unlike Alice she actually hugged me back for a few moments.

"Edward's not living with his wife these days by the way," added Emma, as she quietly pulled away from me. "He's living over at Papa Mutt's. His wife keeps threatening a divorce, but he's not concerned because he knows she'll never go through with it."

"And who is Papa Mutt?" I replied, rather unsettled as to what prompted this shift from her future as a performer to Ed Ory's present living situation.

"Mutt Carey. I think his real name might be Thomas, but he's always just been Papa Mutt. He's Edward's cornet player that was over here on Mondays for awhile. He was the one seeing Felicité, but that's all over now," she replied.

"I see."

"Oh also, sorry, I almost forgot. Mrs. Dawson says they need me back working at their plantation store for the next couple of months before I leave for those rehearsals. I'll do the sewing work with you tomorrow, but then I can't come back after that. And Felicité won't be coming back either. She didn't give me a reason just that she'll be working someplace else."

*"The melody is important.
Listen to those Louis Armstrong records.
He played melody with the band,
then made up something different by himself."*
Edward "Kid" Ory

## Chapter 7: The Muskrat Ramble

Miss DeWitt paid us on Friday afternoon as always and announced that the overseeing committee had been pleased with the progress; sales had been tepid but at least steady and they planned to keep us on. The opera house currently was on the market and there were several potentially interested buyers. The more debt the current owners could pay down the better for all concerned of course. They had also been authorized to hire several professional seamstresses in an attempt to finish all of the sewing work within the next two months. Losing Emma and Felicité was of no concern to Miss DeWitt.

I gave notice to the landlord and all three of us moved out of the shotgun that weekend, heading in different directions. Through Joe, who also helped me move, I was extremely fortunate to get into the Christian Women's Exchange's inexpensive boarding house at South and Camp streets in the Garden district. I was well aware that as an unmarried white woman in a mixed-race town, it was far too risky for me to even consider living anywhere on my own. And the CWE offered help and training for single women, surprisingly of all ages, all races, and even those with young children, to find employment. The exchange provided a quite reasonably priced cafeteria, lending library, large laundry facility and many other amenities available on a bartered services basis. It was a very unique approach, well ahead of its time. I would not be allowed to live here indefinitely, but for the time being it was the perfect solution.

The work at the opera house now pushed ahead at an exceptionally breakneck pace. The oldest of the newly-hired seamstresses was obviously far more experienced than any of the rest of us and immediately took to directing the entire operation much to my relief. I held back a set of five brightly-striped full skirts and off-the-shoulder embroidered peasant blouses, apparently deemed too ethnic for consideration and headed for the incinerator, thinking that Mme. Jones might possibly be interested in the rather unique creations.

On most Saturdays I helped Joe with the many last minute details in getting his saloon ready to open for business, usually followed by an early dinner at one of his many favorite inexpensive restaurants, and on Sundays I boarded the train to visit Zuma and Emma for a few hours in Reserve. Emma asked me if she could sing for the opening, but Joe told me that was out of the question since she was underage. Ory seconded that concern. Joe didn't want to get closed up the same night he had opened, for heaven's sake, he appealed to me. Emma still hadn't met Joe, but she felt that this was a very shallow excuse even though Ory had concurred with him.

Joe stated many times that if he could just manage financially through the next few months or so he would be quite comfortable. Rumors abounded that horse racing was destined to be reinstated as legal once again in New Orleans by the beginning of the following year. Once riverboats and trains jammed with eager, thirsty gamblers from up north stopped by his place when the Season was in full swing after Christmas, Joe could be well-assured of turning a handsome profit. Horse racing had been illegal since 1908 in New Orleans and the loss of revenue coupled with the hurricane in 1909 were truly staggering blows for small and large businesses alike.

I was finding myself slightly more drawn to this quiet,

seemingly very docile, gentleman. He was tall, thin to the point of being gaunt, and his skin seemed to give off an odd grey cast at times. He was very different from the kind of man one would expect to own a saloon in my opinion. I had been compelled early on to tell him the truth about Alice's history and he seemed genuinely upset by the entire unfolding of circumstances. There was much more from my past, but I was unable to visit those places with him as of yet, and very possibly, might never be willing to do so. I countenanced this evasiveness since I knew very little of his past as well.

Joe's grand opening was indeed exceptional. As Ory had promised, his band's performance from the advertising wagon the night prior had created exactly the desired promotional hysteria. The place was filled shortly after the doors swung open to a crowd wild to hear more of Kid Ory's music and take up Joe's generous offer of a free small bottle of champagne for couples while supplies held out. Joe insisted that he didn't want my assistance, but nonetheless I found myself clearing tables, wiping off glassware and finally, even serving a few drinks to patrons seated at the tables, all of which I found enjoyable while listening to Ory's band.

Similar to when I'd heard his group at the plantation, Ory started out his program with a few ragtime selections and then several of what I now knew were called blues tunes, rather subdued both in tempo and volume. The audience was listening yet still carrying on their conversations, greeting friends as they walked in the door. Only one or two couples were dancing. Within the first half hour or so however, Ory masterfully seemed to know exactly when to begin the transition of this easy style to his hotter music. At times he would bring the entire band down to practically a whisper, which the crowd adored and then fire everything back up once again. More and more couples crowded onto the very tight dance space, with every chair at the tables and bar seating filled. I was very surprised that many women, drinks in hand, were willing to stand alongside their escorts and watch the band once all the available seats were occupied. A few darker men showed up and found seats at the bar, quietly sipping a few beers. Joe had told me earlier that if that situation arose there would be no problem as long as the black men didn't try to dance or hold extended conversations with any white women. If I saw that happening I needed to notify him at once so that he could tell those men to leave or face arrest.

The last couple of weeks had been so busy on the weekends prior to Joe's opening that I hadn't gotten out to see Zuma and Emma. Ory informed me during one of the band's early breaks however, that they had played another crawfish boil the prior Sunday for the Godchaux's planting season party.

"She's leaving this Tuesday, actually," replied Ory to my question about Emma's departure for New York City, as he thirstly downed a beer. "She sang a few tunes with us out there last Sunday – sounds as good as always, that girl! Love that great big sweet voice! So exquisite compared to that Ma Rainey rough kinda stuff, y'know?"

"Did she ever mention her conversation with Mrs. Jones to you?" I asked.

He smiled as he lit a cigarette.

"You mean about the arsenic wafers?" he replied, signaling the bartender for a refill.

"Well, yes, that's part of it. Mme. Jones seemed to be quite impressed by her ability, but very discouraging about being…" my voice trailed off since I really didn't know how to finish that sentence.

"About bein' a black girl tryin' to sing anything worthwhile at all, eh?"

"Well, yes," I admitted uncomfortably.

"Well, what d'you think?"

I stared at him for several moments.

"What do you mean, what do I think?" I replied, frowning.

I found that to be a pretty ridiculous question. Who cared what I thought for heaven's sake!

"Eh, colored women been lightenin' up tryin' to pass as white for centuries," shrugged Ory, sipping his new beer. "She's got them bright flashy blue eyes an' that crazy old corn-yellow hair, so ..."

"Meaning?"

He took a couple of drags on his cigarette, slowly blowing out the smoke.

"Meanin' it's pretty obvious she should do what she can if she wants to pass."

"You're serious," I replied, shaken. "What does that mean exactly?"

"Means just what it sounds like, Miss Hannah," said Ory, his brown eyes dancing in the light reflecting from the bar's mirror. "She changes her name, invents some story where she came from. Y'know, some little town nobody's ever heard of in, say, Indiana for instance. Hell, that's a state with lots of towns nobody'd ever wanna go to! Maybe invents that she's an orphan, both her parents been dead since she was three or four years old, y'know, an', she was raised by different charities an' so forth and so on. So, she was never in any big towns and doesn't know nothin' about where she's from, y'know? Does all that and then heads out to a big town like maybe, say, Chicago. *Et voila! Une petite fille blanche est nee!*"

I was finding all of this unsettling and found it difficult to breathe. I needed to change the subject. "Why do you call her '*petite musquette*,' by the way? I've never quite understood that one."

Ory took a long draw on his cigarette, then stabbed it out with a slight cough, smiling. "Ever seen a baby muskrat swimmin' upstream?"

"No, I don't think so," I replied, shaking my head.

"Well, y'see, they've got that squiggly little brown body

surrounded by this huge swirl of reddish yellow hair floatin' in all directions when they's paddlin' in the water," he laughed. "Fact I even named a new tune after her last week at the Godchaux boil."

"*Ma petite musquette*?" I said, smiling in spite of myself.

"No, no. Called it the '*Muskrat Ramble*' 'cause she was dancin' with some kinda new combination of steps she probably learned over at Economy Hall or some place. Everybody started imitatin' what she was doin' so we kinda just all followed along, y'know and I decided to give the tune that name. The tune's kinda like this old Creole song actually called "*The Old Cow Died*." Let's hope I remember that's what I called it the next time we play it!"

Being part of Joe's excitement over the initial success of his saloon's opening, along with the renewed push to finish the costuming refurbishments at the Opera House and my self-imposed task to become acquainted with the many women and expansive opportunities at the Christian Women's Exchange, all helped to slightly allay my concern at not having received any communication from either Alice or Mrs. Hughes after more than two months had now elapsed. My first letters from both Alice and Emma arrived on exactly the same day in fact. Joe and I had intended to have dinner that evening at one of his favorite cafés, but I begged off saying I wanted to savor each of the letters alone, with just a cup of tea and a couple of lemon biscuits. He held my face gently in his hands, kissing me very lightly on the lips as was his custom. "Enjoy your evening with your girls," he smiled. "I'm always here for you tomorrow as well as the day after my dear one." I was truly grateful for his compassion.

I opened Alice's envelope first.

Dear "Mother"~

*I've received your letters, but I have been very busy as I'm sure you can imagine, with no time available to post an answer. I'm now enrolled in a private school in the Springs, but we've also had to engage a personal tutor for math and science since, no surprise there, I'm more than a year behind in those important subjects according to the school's entrance evaluations.*

*Grandmama has taken me round to meet everyone after rushing about to get something of a decent wardrobe constructed. How I love having the same stylish clothes as all the girls at my school and not having to beg for last year's castoffs like back in Kansas City. I'm also now on the tennis, archery and golf teams at the school. Even though I've never had a chance to play any sports before, it seems that I'm just naturally quite good and enjoy very much participating. I'm up for president of the archery club in fact.*

*Grandmama had said that we would be traveling back to New Orleans for Margaux C's wedding in a few months, but it's now going to be delayed until November. This has something to do with her fiancé's family coming over from Europe. Winters can be quite troublesome up here my friends say, but Grandmama assures me that no matter, ultimately the trains will get through.*

*My tutor, Mr. Evans, will be here in a few moments and I must review my science homework before he arrives. Yours truly ~ Alice*

I slowly read the letter through twice, shaking, so grateful that she had even written me at all, then folded it carefully and settled it back into its envelope. I picked up Emma's letter and pressed it to my chest with both hands for a moment before finally slitting open the envelope.

*My dearest sweet Mama & Miss Hannah (please read this letter to her as soon as you can, Miss Hannah!) – hope you're both well!*

*It's very late & I'm so tired, but I know you're anxious how everything is going up here. My train was a day late arriving although the reason was unclear. I'm sharing a room at a boarding house with 3 older girls & it's very tight, but we're all used to that & no one complains. It's only a short trolley stop to the hall for rehearsals every morning. We just throw a little water on our faces, drink a quick coffee & are on our way.*

*On our first day of rehearsal we had to sing & also dance --*

another audition. The only dancing that I know is from Edward's shows so that's what I did. Everyone seemed impressed which surprised me since that kind of dancing is quite easy. Happy to say I ended up in two of the most important Opera Kaleidoscope scenes with Mme. Jones & several regular vaudeville pieces.

The work is very tiring. We start early in the morning, have a short break for lunch & continue until dark. Often we have to repeat singing the same few phrases of music over and over and <u>OVER</u> until the music director finally grunts approval. Best of all is listening to Mme. Jones sing in the Kaleidoscope rehearsals. I've managed to imitate her singing voice & my roommates are always urging me to do so, sometimes in appreciation of her talent, but other times in dismissal of the same. She brings out a wide range of sentiments from the cast from one day to the next, but she has always been very kind to me.

There are a lot of problems with the 'libretto' for the main musical, "Lucky Sam from Alabam'."  Mme. Jones says it might as well be 'Shufflin' Sam from Alabam' because it's so hokey & she wants the title changed. She also no longer wants anything performed in black face, which I must agree -- I don't quite understand why they want us to put cork on our faces either! The organizers argue that it's way too late for any changes since posters have already been printed for the various venues. I overheard Mme. Jones say that their excuses are "simply hogwash," so I guess you can see why there's a problem! My one roommate, Mattie, says the smartest thing to do is just do what they tell you & stay shut up about everything else. I'm thinking that's pretty good advice.

We'll be off for two weeks around Thanksgiving & I can't wait to see everyone. I miss your cooking, Mama! My clothes just droop down on this poor scarecrow body these days! No one up here can even begin to cook up a decent gumbo like yours or Edward's! Edward always says that when you bite into a good gumbo, it should bite back. I think that's his favorite expression! Makes me hungry just writing about it! Sending along all of my love & I promise to write again very soon

~ always your Emma

****

I enjoyed the time spent with Joe Peterson although I was uncomfortably aware of the fact that his feelings towards me were far stronger than mine, which remained only lukewarm. He was an incredibly sweet gentleman even asking permission to thread my hand over his arm when we walked at dusk along Lake Ponchartrain or to smooth back a lock of my hair behind my ear or to almost whisper his goodnight kiss. Our conversations were almost always about our work, particularly the often amusing personalities we interacted with each day. In answer to his questions about my employment plans after the Opera House project I was truthfully unclear, although I had been fiercely saving as much of my salary as possible. My thoughts centered entirely on getting to see both Alice and Emma once again in November. Beyond that was a blur.

We had both evaded any detail about our parents and respective childhoods. On the two month anniversary of our first meeting, celebrated as a rather soggy picnic after one of my return trips from Reserve to visit Zuma, he finally went more in depth when I inquired once again about his earlier years.

"Well, there's not much to tell, Hannah," he laughed rather self-consciously. "Pretty uninteresting fodder if you ask me!"

"All I really know is that you're originally from southern Illinois and your father was a farmer," I replied. "Surely there's a bit more to the story."

"Well, yes he was, uh, a tenant farmer actually. Rented about sixty or so acres from a Mr. McCoy I believe was the man's name. I don't know which is a worse situation tell you the truth, being a tenant farmer or working under a sharecropping agreement. My father always worked so hard, it truly beat him down. I worked in the fields as well from the time I was probably about eight years old or so. Well, you're younger, of course, but even so I'm sure you were laboring might hard yourself by that age, Hannah."

"Not many kids anywhere manage to sidestep hard work, Joe."

"You know I was talking about the very same thing with Ed Ory the other night. He grew up on the Woodland Plantation in LaPlace, you know, right out there near Reserve. Even as a little tyke they had him sorting and hauling out rice and cane harvests before he was deemed finally old enough to work as a cutter. And he's kind of a little runt of a feller as you know, so he decided early on he had to get out of that backbreaking type work. Said that's probably what really pushed him into making his music a 'viable business' as he calls it."

"What about brothers and sisters? Did your parents have many children?" I asked, not particularly wanting to get sidetracked by a discussion on what may have prompted Ory's early music ambitions.

"Well, my parents kinda had two families. They had several children -- I think there were five in fact -- that had all died from a diphtheria epidemic, so my folks were pretty old by the time the rest of us came along. There was just me and my two sisters, and then like I mentioned to you once before, my older sister drowned when I was just a few years old. So she's pretty much just kind of a dim memory for me. And my younger sister ... did I tell you about her before?"

I shook my head.

"Well, my younger sister was born with something terribly wrong with her back. It was all kind of twisted so one hip was jutted out in front of the other rather than straight across, you see. The local doc made some kind of leather and metal brace thing, heavy as a western saddle if you can imagine, trying to straighten it out, but it didn't do much good. In fact, I don't know that it did any good at all -- just made the poor kid suffer something awful. She was always in a heap of constant pain."

He stopped and cleared his throat, looking down. I put my hand lightly on his arm, waiting for him to continue.

"Our folks passed within a couple months of one another so I then had full responsibility of Mary Anna, you see," he said. "I was already in my 20s by then, but still living at home because my folks, well, they obviously really needed my help, being so up in years by then, you know. Well, so I got married a short time after that to a very pretty young woman named Maudie Spencer. Now Maudie was a mighty fine lady at first, Hannah. I don't want you thinkin' otherwise even though we ended up gettin' a divorce. After everything that happened, it was just too hard to turn around and go back, you see. And, that wouldn't be fair, because there's too much that we don't know and then there's those things that I just couldn't reconcile."

"So, can you tell me what happened, Joe?"

He stood up, which I did as well. We shook out the blanket on which we'd been seated and placed the few items we hadn't eaten back into the picnic basket. As we started walking on the fairly short trek back towards the streetcar stop he finally began speaking again.

"Maudie was kinda well, high-spirited you might say. She didn't like having to do housework all day while I was gone – I had gotten a job as a clerk for the electric company in Peoria by then, so at least the money was real steady. Had a nice little house not too far outside of town. Quiet little neighborhood. She had no cause to complain about any of that. But Maudie especially didn't like having to take care of Mary Anna's needs, see, which were might plentiful I confess. She couldn't walk or set straight enough to feed herself most times, both hands shook real bad, you know, and sometimes she had a hard time swallowing so food would sometimes just ooze down her chin. And she couldn't tell when she might mess, so's it was like mindin' a baby. Pa had made her a special chair she could kind of spread out on, but she had got more and more crippled over and it didn't fit her right anymore. She just preferred to lie on the floor on a pallet in front of the fireplace. She was always cold, too, even in the summer, so Maudie had to keep the fireplace stoked blazing hot even when it was hot enough to fry an egg out on our front stoop."

He stopped walking and sat wearily on a tree stump. We were less than a block from the trolley.

"So one very hot day, late in the summer, I get home from my clerk job and there's a note from Maudie tacked up on the front door that she's walked into town to pick up a jar of pickles. See, she hadn't put any up yet from our garden that year and we had gone through all from the prior year. And with what she had fixed for our dinner, a kind of salted beef affair that held up well in that kind of heat, she said she really wanted that exact pickle to go with it. And she was mad at herself that she hadn't looked first to see we'd eaten all our own supply before she'd fixed that salted beef."

I put my arm around his shoulders. "And?"

"So as I said, I got home and found that note and when I went in the house, the fire had broken through the grate sometime hours earlier, 'cause it was almost plumb cold, and there was Mary Anna almost completely charred to death on her pallet. And the pallet was much closer to the fireplace than I had ever seen it placed. No way Mary Anna could've moved it herself, but if she was still feelin' cold, I imagine that Maudie could have moved it closer, not thinking of any consequences."

"My God!" I whispered, my eyes tearing over. "How long had Maudie been gone?"

Joe exhaled and looked up at me, circling my waist with his arm. "That's what the police chief wanted to know, because obviously with something happening like that, there was an investigation. Maudie said that she walked down to the market for the pickles and then she was so hot she stopped at the drug store for a couple of ice-cold dopes which she drank down real fast. She also said she was certain that she was pregnant and was so tired that she fell asleep in the swing behind the general store.

There was a nice breeze and she just slept the afternoon away. She wasn't pregnant as it turned out, just overcome by the heat perhaps, but several people did see her asleep in that swing. So everyone deemed it a terrible accident."

"But you weren't convinced," I said quietly.

"No, I wasn't convinced."

There were fireflies flickering near us, but the mosquitoes were also beginning to bite. We knew the streetcar would be arriving at any moment.

"Let's stop somewhere for a glass of wine," I suggested. "Maybe Ida's. It should be fairly quiet by now so we can finish talking."

Neither of us spoke during the short streetcar ride.

"The rest of the story gets ... even uglier," Joe said, holding my hand atop the table after we'd been seated in the café and ordered our wine.

I waited for him to continue.

"Maudie tried real hard to make me believe that it was an accident, which was understandable, but she insisted on constantly remarking on how much better we were without Mary Anna around through what I perceived as just completely fake tears. And then she kept doing all kinds of sweet things for me. Fixing up my favorite meals and even desserts every night, for example. I didn't even know the woman knew how to make a blueberry pie for God's sake! Then making certain that my shirts were lightly starched and ironed just exactly the way I liked, and sitting in my lap almost every night stroking my hair and kissing me, trying to get me to well ... you know. You were a married woman. And then when I showed no interest she must have talked to some girlfriends or read some filthy book or something, because she tried a few moves that a nice woman shouldn't know about let alone attempt, even on her husband!" he snorted.

"Those, um ... kinds of books, are around, Joe," I replied

carefully. "I was quite shocked to find what was considered perfectly acceptable when a friend recommended such reading to me early in my own marriage."

He shook his head and sat back abruptly in his chair, downing the rest of his glass of wine and ordering another.

"Sorry if I offend you, Hannah, but I thoroughly disagree," said Joe darkly. "That's why men frequent brothels if I may be so blunt. They don't want their wives to act like wanton …"

"Sluts?" I suggested quietly, frowning.

He surprised me by banging his fist on the table, both of our glasses of wine slopping slightly over the top. His voice remained at a low level, however, and surprisingly quite controlled.

"Yes. Exactly. Sluts. If I'm in need of a woman like that, I'll seek her out. Pay for her and then leave. Like a transaction of any service. But in my own home? My own wife? The woman I've chosen for my very own sweet children's mother? Oh, no. No, no. That cannot be. I simply will not have it! I told her that and do you know what she did?"

Warily, I shook my head.

"She laughed at me, Hannah. She laughed!"

I carefully took a sip of my wine wondering if he was going to elaborate. The conversation had moved far past what I had originally hoped to learn about this man. I thoroughly doubted that he would have wanted to obtain a divorce simply because she had laughed at him. Obviously there was more to this story.

"So I moved out of the house the very next day, left town, traveled around taking odd jobs here and there until I finally came down to New Orleans. It's harder to track people down here. I refused to make any rent payments or pay for any of her bills or upkeep any more, so she was finally bounced out. And I never spent another night with her or even saw her again. Took her a couple years to finally file for desertion, but I was more than ready to accept that claim let me tell you."

*****

    The older seamstress who had taken over the Opera House costuming reins had commented after Joe's numerous appearances that I would be an utter fool at my age if I didn't accept that charming gentleman's marriage proposal should he offer such. As a woman staring down age 30, I was well aware that I was far beyond any storybook or idle girlish dreams of matrimony. The only man I had ever really been in love with was a fading memory, a red rose crumbling between yellowed pages. I had been grateful that Joe hadn't ever asked for anything more permanent since my feelings for him were quite diluted, like a tea bag squeezed one too many times in one's cup. After this evening's disturbing conversation, however, I honestly didn't know how I would respond.

    A trip to the post office the following evening after an extremely hot, frustrating afternoon's work at the theater rewarded me with another of Emma's letters, although its contents were quite disheartening.

    *Dearest sweet Mama & Miss Hannah ~*

    *I'm writing this quickly & sorry will be short. We opened here in New York last week, but the reviews are* **very** *bad so far. Mme. Jones is furious & says if the managers had just listened to her the show wouldn't be on such shaky ground. We're now rehearsing many, many changes to songs, dances & completely new lines for dialog we're supposed to remember for that same night. It's horrible. We're all being yelled at constantly & tempers are very short. My roommate Mattie was crying so hard today because she just couldn't sing a line the way Mr. Pond wanted & he threw a clipboard at her that hit her so hard on her cheek it's now badly swollen & he called her a 'hopeless, stupid nigger.'*

    *We have 5-8 shows every week -- mostly one nighters. We finish, pack up fast, head over to someplace that will serve us for our only meal, & then it's back on the train. We're on our own train, with a bunk that we have to pay for in a sleeping car. We're 10 in each car - girls in one*

*& boys in another. We're supposed to have a day to do our wash & such, but everything now is just more rehearsals. The managers say that the show must go on no matter what, but some places have cancelled 'cause they've heard the show's a flop I overheard Mr. Pond say today. I'm very tired & I love & miss you.*

   *~ always your Emma*

> "Jazz music is to be played sweet, soft, plenty rhythm.
> When you have your plenty of rhythm
> with your plenty swing
> it becomes beautiful."
> Ferdinand "Jelly Roll" Morton

## Chapter 8: Margaux's Wedding

I had now been out of work for several weeks, the opera house having finally dismissed all of the costume crew. The project was far from being completed, but no one mentioned what was planned for the remaining items and certainly none of us cared to ask. Although nothing as rigorous as my very short-lived trial at La Creole Cigar, the opera house back rooms' gloomily lit work areas, incessant heat, oozing molds, algae clinging along the walls and decades of choking dust had created a suffocating workplace at times. Finally I felt as though I could straighten my back once again and the constant sharp pains in my hands and wrists had begun to subside. My vision had been getting rather blurred as well, but thankfully that was gradually improving. Since I desperately wanted to spend as much time as possible with the two girls, I was delaying a search for other work until after Alice's and Emma's visits in a few more weeks. I had received only one slightly informative letter, even shorter than the first, from Alice, and several progressively unsettling ones from Emma.

Most of the time Joe hired a piano player to pare down expenses rather than hire Ory's band, but on one of his group's rare appearances, Ory mentioned that he had also received several letters from Emma and even a desperate, expensive phone call late one night. He had managed to get her calmed down and coerce her back on the train to continue with the tour to the next town. She was homesick, exhausted and mighty unhappy, that was for certain. He was unwilling to speak any further of their conversation, but he mentioned having lined up a few engagements for her to sing with his band while she was back in New Orleans on her break. One of them was for Margaux Claytor's wedding reception.

Joe was doing very well even on the nights that he didn't offer a full band like Ory's. He typically insisted on taking me to dinner several evenings each week and, after a quick kiss on my forehead, he would return to the saloon. I didn't expect anything else. I honestly didn't *want* anything else. Occasionally on a Friday evening I would accompany him to the saloon for an hour or so. Unless Ory's Creole Band or another hot group called the Eagle Band was playing, Joe's bar was typically filled with a fairly sedate, slightly older crowd, primarily men, but also a surprising number of nicely-dressed, sophisticated women who evidently deemed his place respectable. I couldn't help comparing his saloon to the raucous Cripple Creek establishments I remembered from less than two decades ago, where no decent woman would have ever set foot in such a place. In fact to have done so automatically labeled one as being thoroughly depraved of character.

For those men who were looking for more exclusive entertainment in their evening, they had only to venture a couple of blocks over on Basin Street to Miss Lulu White's place, locally known as Mahogany Hall. Like all bars, Joe had many copies of the Blue Book (as well as matchbooks and ash trays) on tables throughout the saloon, printed out by Miss Lulu and many other Storyville madams, poetically advertising the best of their girls' attributes and services. Joe's establishment was just a saloon he would wink, but he could definitely recommend "full service" institutions when out-of-town male customers frequently inquired about the little blue address books.

Although Joe had never actually come forward and asked

me to be his wife, he had ended many a sentence over the last several months alluding to the possibility with lines such as "well, we can certainly talk about looking at a house over in Algiers another day, my sweet" or "hmmmm, who knows what next summer will bring us, right?" or "ah, that extra couple hundred I cleared from tonight's take goes straight into our special wish fund, right my dear?"

November's cool breezes finally washed over what had been a horribly unrelenting, fiery summer and autumn even for New Orleans. I forced myself to wait for three days after Emma's arrival to take the train out to Reserve. She would need time to talk with Zuma, see her friends from Godchaux and just become little Emma Jackson once again I realized. Although difficult to restrain myself, I knew I had to give her some time to readjust.

But the horribly thin, tense skeleton of the girl I hugged those few days later was not even remotely a shadow of that same Emma Jackson. She seemed like a terrified jack rabbit cowering at the merciless jaws of a rabid fox. Despite the constant rewrites of the libretto the show continued receiving abysmal reviews playing to less than half-filled houses and had now been slammed with additional cancellations of major bookings originally slated for early spring. Emma's friend Mattie and another girl in the show had been jumped by two white men and brutally raped when walking back to the train late one night from the only restaurant willing to serve the cast in one town. There was no way they could even think of making any kind of complaint, however. Not in that town. Those things just didn't happen around those parts they were advised. In fact, if those girls weren't careful, they could just as easily be fined for soliciting as prostitutes they were told by the authorities. Mattie's boyfriend had insisted that she quit the tour and come home, but Mattie had refused, terrified of the consequences from the show's managers if she did so.

Emma and several other girls had walked past those same

two men just minutes beforehand she admitted dully. Less than a week later in another town, three of the show's young musicians had gotten into a knife fight with several drunken townsmen and one of the young men had been so badly cut up they had left him behind at a prison hospital. He hadn't started the fight and was actually not guilty since he had never even used a knife, but the only way he would be able to get any kind of medical treatment was to confess that he had initiated the brawl and go to jail.

Ory was planning to stop by later that afternoon, Emma said. There was a wedding reception and one or two outdoor engagements that he had booked and wanted her to sing a few tunes. She was looking forward to working with him during her break she admitted. I told her that Alice would be attending that wedding, that the girl getting married was some kind of cousin. I was fairly certain that the information failed to even remotely register with Emma, however, even though she uttered "ah, well, isn't that nice. I'm sure you'll be happy to see Alice again." Her expressionless blue eyes seemed to have sunk back frighteningly deep in her skull. Emma had never asked anything further about Alice's move to Colorado Springs and I had said nothing in the desperate hope that just maybe, Mrs. Hughes' unpredictably vicious temper might press the girl to return to me.

Kid Ory had talked one of the wait staff -- a banjo player hoping to sit in for a few tunes with Ory's band some night -- into inconspicuously seating me at one of the guest tables for the Claytors' extravagant outdoor wedding reception, which was being held at the groom's parents' immense mansion on St. Charles Avenue. Sparkling like dew off the leaves of the live oaks, magnolias and orange trees, long strings of lights crisscrossed over an enormous terra cotta-tiled open pavilion. Lush, perfumed gardens surrounded the pavilion on three sides and the fourth was graced by a glistening, sugary-white marble gazebo large enough to hold at least twenty people, I surmised.

The men were attired in white tie and black tails, the ladies in exquisite pastel, lightly-beaded gowns which flowed about them like a ballerina's long tulle skirt, their hair adorned with tufts of little feathers and tiny sparkling jewels. Gone forever, thank goodness, were the massive female headdresses from a few years back upon which one might easily have consumed a four course meal!

Several lace-draped tables were nestled against the largest of the live oaks displaying the couple's lavish panoply of gifts. Magnificent gilt silver services, gleaming black marble sculptures, three breathtakingly beautiful oil paintings by John William Godward — an English artist fighting to maintain his classic traditional style against the wildly more popular works of Pablo Picasso -- hefty heirloom jewelry begging to be reset into modern tastes, exquisitely hand-detailed French porcelain, and an 18th century intricately-carved solid oak chest brimming with silver and gold coins, all fought for attention while being examined by the wedding guests, Mrs. Hughes and Alice among them.

Alice looked absolutely stunning. Her long blonde hair had been pressed tightly back into waves of soft curls on her head under a new style hat that I had read was called a *cloche*. Her light lavender matching dress draped flawlessly over her trim figure. I waited for a moment to gather my nerve before I finally walked over to say hello. Alice spied me first, however.

"Ah, well, hullo! This is a bit of a surprise," she said giving me a very light, superficial hug. "Look who has turned up, Grandmama."

Mrs. Hughes looked me up and down with a lorgnette, a new acquisition which could easily have been originally designed with her in mind I thought. "How did you manage to get an invitation?" she inquired brusquely. "Bribe the busboy?"

"Yes, something like that," I replied, smiling. She obviously meant it as a cut, but of course, it was quite close to the truth.

"It's so good to see both of you. Your letters didn't really go into much detail, but I assumed that everything has been going well with school and all of your sports interests. I've ... I've missed you a great deal, Alice."

"Yes," she answered, smoothing back a loose curl with a small shake of her head. "So you mentioned at least three or four times in every letter you wrote."

"I would have loved to have been able to give you all of those things, Alice," I blurted out. "I know Abigail would have wanted for me to do so. I wish somehow you ..." I began, but was interrupted by Mrs. Hughes.

"Yes, yes, we all know how that tune goes. If wishes were horses, beggars would ride," Mrs. Hughes recited in a singsong fashion, looking past me through her lorgnette.

"I don't know if you were aware that Emma is singing with Kid Ory's band for the reception tonight," I added cheerfully, refusing to let Mrs. Hughes' typical ill humor drag me down right now. "I wrote you that she's been touring with a vaudeville act for the last several months, a very famous one actually known as The Black Patti Troubadours. It's been a quite grueling series of concerts, but she's learned a lot."

"Kid Ory?" scoffed Mrs. Hughes. "What, do they have toddlers leading the bands down here these days?"

"Actually that's just a name like "King" or "Buddy" or "Professor" that musicians give one another, Grandmama," Alice replied gently. "I agree that it's quite a bit of nonsense, but all of the men in these hot bands you hear about these days refer to themselves by these incredibly silly nicknames for some reason."

Just then Margaux Claytor, now Mrs. Thomas Addams, and her new husband appeared bringing on cheers and applause as all of the guests stood during the couple's breathtaking entrance. Everyone had been right. Margaux and Alice looked so much like one another they could easily have passed for identical twins. I felt that if Alice had donned Margaux's shimmering light pink, off-one-shoulder wedding dress and dashed off with Mr. Addams later this evening, he might well have never known that his bride was a different young woman. Although I had carefully refitted and augmented my own dress with some tasteful beading, I felt myself a terribly moth-eaten house sparrow in this pavilion of extraordinarily brilliant and expensively decorated peacocks.

Ory's band had set up much earlier and gone elsewhere as the guests were gathering, but now they almost miraculously reappeared, quietly picking up their instruments. Very softly they began playing a slow waltz followed by several schottisches and foxtrots as the young couple greeted their guests while moving towards the expansive head table.

Alice had begun to move back towards their table which was on the other side of the pavilion from my own, but Mrs. Hughes signaled that she would join her in a moment.

"Just so we're completely clear on this issue, Alice has no intention of returning to live with you now or ever, Hannah," stated Mrs. Hughes dryly. "She's almost fully caught up finally in her studies at school, about which she's most proud, and as I believe she wrote you, she's quite extensively involved in her sports activities and fulfilling social engagements. We may come down here to visit my cousin again next year, but I don't know that for certain. Alice has said she has absolutely no pressing desire to return since she has no friends here or, for that matter, any back in Kansas City either. Ah, there's the little bell that they're going to begin serving our dinners in a few minutes, so I need to rejoin Alice now. Our train leaves day after tomorrow, but we've quite a jammed schedule of parties and sightseeing that my cousin has engaged for us. Frankly, it's quite doubtful that we'll have any additional time to see you again this weekend, Hannah." She followed Alice over to their table.

At that moment Emma walked up on the stage to join Ory's

band. I pushed Mrs. Hughes' exasperating voice out of my mind and found my way back to my own seat. Emma still looked quite depleted. She was wearing a dark blue and silver printed, tightly-wrapped sheath with a large matching scarf wound loosely in her maize-colored hair and long glistening earrings, all of which somehow gave her an older, almost ethereal appearance. I was quite certain it was a costume from the show that she had somehow clandestinely borrowed; I couldn't imagine the managers allowing members of the cast to waltz off with some of their costumes during the show's break! For many years afterwards, whenever I thought of Emma, I almost always envisioned her in that dress.

Emma introduced the first song as a favorite ballad from "*Lucky Sam from Alabam'.*" This was followed by a song entitled "*By the Beautiful Sea*" which was also relatively new and apparently one that the bride and groom had requested. She then performed Sissieretta Jones' favorite song, "*Home Sweet Home.*" Despite her exhaustion her voice was more powerful than ever, articulate and energetic, yet still beautifully light, sweet and passionate when necessary. I thought back on Edward Ory's encouragement of Little Louis' cornet-playing abilities and realized that the man had an incredible ear for these talented youngsters. I was ashamed of myself for having once thought his interest in Emma was only towards a vile end.

During a break I saw Ory introducing Emma to the new Mrs. Addams while Alice and Mrs. Hughes lingered nearby. After a couple of moments Margaux moved on towards several other guests, Ory headed in the direction of the bar, and Emma walked over towards Alice. Even though I heard nothing of their conversation, from Emma's frown I knew she had found the shocking physical comparison of the two young women to be as unfathomable as had everyone else. Somewhere during this conversation as well, Alice must have also introduced Emma to Mrs. Hughes. Emma slowly turned, frowning, her hand at her throat, looking out through the crowd in my direction and then turned back towards Alice. Having finished their brief meeting, she then just walked away.

When Emma was called up again by Kid Ory during the second set, she sang the British music hall favorite *"It's a Long Way to Tipperary"* that had everyone joyously clapping in rhythm and then sang and danced a lively little tune called *"Ballin' the Jack"* which the younger crowd asked her to repeat several more times so that they could learn the dance routine. But although her performance was flawless and extremely enthusiastically received, there was a reserve, a depression almost like a dark cocoon, enveloping her during her entire appearance. I decided that I would go out to Godchaux tomorrow afternoon to talk alone with Zuma, since I was fairly certain that Emma had another engagement with Ory for a harvesting party over in Edgard.

Zuma was explaining to two very young girls how to boil jars when I arrived. She actually seemed to have been expecting me, however, and motioned for me to follow her just outside the open kitchen area to the side path. For some reason I remembered last autumn seeing half of an orange topple off a tray that Felicité had been carrying into the house. I hadn't thought to ask if the girl was working again at Godchaux; I hadn't seen her on any of my recent visits.

"Well, Miss Hannah," Zuma exhaled, frowning, her strong arms crossed. "So's I hopes you is happy now."

"I just wanted to talk with you about Emma," I said shaking my head slightly, attempting a smile. "I'm not quite sure what you mean by 'happy'."

"So, let's talk," she shrugged. "It'll take dem two girls a couple hours tuh boil up all dem jars an' slice up all dem gherkins tuh git ready for puttin' up dem pickles. Them girls' is slower den molasses in January."

"I'm sure you're concerned as well that she's been so upset

about everything that's been happening on this tour. When we've read her letters …"

"Oh, wait, wait, wait now, jes' wait now," interrupted Zuma, holding up her hand. "When we've read her letters, huh? As I recollect, *you* is the one doin' all the readin' an' I is jes' listenin' an' sittin' back like the dumbes' fool of fools."

"I don't understand."

"You don' understan'. Ain' no reason why Emma couldn' jes send dem letters tuh me. There's plenny people aroun' dis place tha' kin read, even tho's as you well know, I cain't."

"Zuma, what exactly are you talking about?" I frowned. "Every time I've gotten one of her letters I've come out here as soon as I possibly could!"

"Yeah, but you'd already read it, if I ain' mistaken," stated Zuma firmly.

"Well, yes, I confess that I had always read them, Zuma. I'm sorry. They were written to both of us but … I should have waited, you're absolutely right," I replied, shaking my head even though I fully agreed with her. "I'm so sorry that I didn't see it that way, but I … I certainly should have. It was very rude on my part. Please forgive me! It won't happen again!"

Zuma just stared at me, arms still crossed. Although she had to be close to forty, she'd lost absolutely none of her powerful presence over the years.

"I promise to do better when she rejoins the tour and will open them here, Zuma. But right now, can we please talk about what's going on with her? She's not at all herself. She's lost so much weight! And she seems, well … so distracted, listless or depressed … or something … and so … well, actually pale," I stated emphatically.

"Yeah, pale like dat white gal you's been tryin' tuh git her tuh be her whole life," retorted Zuma.

I let this remark go past me. Zuma had made small accusations to this end before, but I refused to be sidelined at present.

"She had mentioned something after her audition about these arsenic wafers that Mrs. Jones talked about, to make herself, well ... lighter. Ingesting poison to make her skin lighter, for heaven's sake! I'm hoping she's not doing anything so crazy! Do you know if she's taking them? Or ... anything crazy like that?"

"No, she ain' on no kinda drugs. No arsenic wafers. No nothin'. She don' drink neither so don' be goin' down tha' road. Figures you'd be thinkin' hard things 'bout her when you ain' aroun' to oversee, y'know? She gots a lotta talent, tha' girl. But she slammin' up hard agin somethin' she mebbe cain't ever git aroun'. An' tha' somthin's you!"

Speechless, I stepped back, shaking my head in confusion.

"See here's jes' what I sees, Miss Hannah Owens," Zuma continued. "I done keeps ma mouth shut all dese years 'bout all dis an' you nevuh thought 'bout my side in it. But then, y'see, like mos' white folks, you thinks might high of yo'self an' your own opinions. But y'know what? We don't."

"Zuma, I ..." I tried to interject, but she continued speaking.

"Y'see, I sees a white girl who has everthin' goin' fer herself aimin' fer a singin' career after all I done tuh help keep her name unsullied despite her makin' a lot o' plumb foolhardy moves. An' then fourteen years ago she goes an' gits herself pregnant up in some minin' camp in Colorado while I's down here'n jail waitin' out some kinda trump up charge 'gainst my brother's mess. An' tha' white girl, she then tries tuh pass off her black baby as some famous white man's baby, but everybod' knows tha' sure's hell ain' gonna fly! Fly 'bout as far as an anvil floatin' upstream as da sayin' goes! So's I gits set up agin an' have tuh claim tha' black baby's mine or dey threatens tuh send me back tuh jail down here 'cause of some kinda new charges 'bout my hand in my po' dead brother's prison break an' killin' off dem white guards. I shoulda jes' agreed tuh go back tuh jail rather than sittin' aroun' in all dis mess dealin' wid you all of these years."

"Zuma!" I cried, swallowing hard. "No! Please!"

"Emma don' fit in nowhere, don' you git that? She a black girl, but she's talkin' an' thinkin' an' walkin' aroun' jes' like some uppity white girl. An' who done that tuh her? Not me! No way! You's always pushin' an' pushin' her tuh be white. Be as good as you is. Bein' black is bad, bein' white is good. Subtle ways sometimes, but not always so subtle neither. Even her name's a white girl's name! Emma! *Merde!*"

She paused for a minute, breathing hard, and then continued, hands now on her hips.

"When Mr. Barrington got hisself murdered an' you lose dat big fancy house, know what I thought? Good riddance! Praise the Lord! An' den I find a real good live-in cookin' job over at the Dawson's in Kansas City an' I's so happy for Emma an' me tuh move away from you an' dat nasty brat Alice. But no, you still can' let go, can' you, so you starts a color'd school. Dat so's you kin still be 'round Emma every day an' always makin' me looks like I's some kinda ole dumb nigguh 'cause I cain' write or read or do my numbers or care tuh speak all elegant like you fancy white folks does. An' then what happens when I moves down here with her? Six months later surprise, surprise! You followin' after her down here like a blind tomcat in heat! An' den you even manage to find her a job, get her tuh live wid you agin' so's you kin keep on stuffin' up her head wid all dat useless educatin'. Jes' cain' leave off yo' grip even then!"

"Zuma, please," I tried to interject, tears streaming down my face, but she waived me off.

"I ain' done yet. An' teachin' her all dat fancy opera singin' like you learned back in Colorado! Since you nevuh made it as a singer, you is bound an' determine tuh make her intuh one. Well honey, guess what? Nigguhs don' sing dem kinda songs. Tha' crazy Miz Jones thinkin' she could manage it? Another anvil sinkin' down in dat stream way I sees it! Least I taught Emma some ole Creole tunes same's I sang tuh you years back dat she's singin' all aroun' down here! In fact, dat's how Kid Ory first heard her. She was singin' 'Creole Bobo' to the little ones one night. Den when he heard Emma talk an' gettin' teased an'such, he say she should try tuh git work wid dat Mrs. Jones. Thought tha' might be a good place for her since she's sumpin' of a misfit. But course he didn' know dat Mrs. Jones' also a misfit in her own way. Dat woman's so bad heaped up wid her own problems, tryin' tuh git whitey tuh recognize her as bein' worth anythin'! An' it jes' closin' in on my po' girl on all sides."

Finally I found my voice, small as I could muster. "Zuma, yes, you're right. Almost everything you've said is true. I couldn't just let her go out of my sight. I just couldn't. I confess. It was impossible. She's my daughter and I'll always love her! With that sweet disposition and constant love of life – who wouldn't have loved her when she was a little girl growing up?"

I gulped for air as I fought to continue speaking at all.

"But her father was Winfield Stratton, there's no mistake to that. Win told me that his mother, Mary Stratton, was darker skinned, probably an escaped slave who died when she was still very young. When Win's father died there wasn't even mention of ... his ... first wife in his obituary."

"Dat's da same anywhere," snorted Zuma with a shrug. "Ain' nobody recognize a white man's half-caste wife. In fact mos' places it ain' even a legal marriage. She jes trash dat's all, same's always. A white man kin go an' marry a white gal an' leave dat black girl an' fam'ly he gots wid her behind, smack down in da dirt, no questions put."

I shook my head and plunged on.

"When I realized that I was pregnant with Win's child I was terrified of my future, but so happy, Zuma! He was so sick that I never had a chance to tell him before his death that I was expecting our child. You were there! You saw how ill he was! But then when Emma was born I was more than terrified.

Because I knew no one would believe that she was his daughter. And both you and John convinced me that I couldn't possibly raise her with any hope of success. That she would ultimately hate me as well as herself. Don't you remember telling me that?"

"And it looks as though that's been a self-fulfilling destiny," said a girl's voice as she emerged from inside the kitchen.

Emma walked slowly out onto the path and looked at Zuma and then over at me. I had no idea how much of our conversation she had overheard. But I knew at that instant that I was forever damned in my daughter's eyes.

> *"They claim Buddy Bolden went crazy because he really blew his brains through the trumpet. He was the blowingest man that ever lived since Gabriel."*
> Ferdinand "Jelly Roll" Morton

# Chapter 9: New Orleans 1915-1917

About a month later I accepted Joe Peterson's proposal and shortly thereafter we were married in a small chapel on a very dreary Friday evening. Two of Joe's business friends served as our witnesses. Our ceremony that night coincided with the upsetting news in *The Indianapolis Freeman*, a nationally distributed colored publication, about the abrupt disbanding of Sissieretta Jones' Black Patti vaudeville act. According to *The Freeman* dated January 1915, *"the troupe had arrived at the Robert R. Church Auditorium in Memphis, Tennessee and it was stated that some of the company's members filling minor roles were disgustingly intoxicated and gave a shocking, horrible performance. Over and above that, the performance itself was a sad disappointment – comedy and songs substandard and a dismal failure when compared to prior years – all a loss except for the Black Patti herself. As always her incredible talent remained truly excellent."*

Based on these outraged reviews immediate cancellations for the remainder of the tour were wired to the manager resulting in the dissolution of the entire company. Theater managers stated they refused to book drunken colored shows in their venues, especially since most houses played exclusively to innocent young white theatergoers.

Joe had booked us for a couple of nights into the very beautiful Hotel Monteleone on Royal Street, but I scarcely remember anything of our first nights together or the hotel itself having just read about the demise of Mrs. Jones' tour a few hours prior to our marriage ceremony. I couldn't help wonder if Emma had been a participant, or worse, an instigator of the drunken melee which had caused the show's dreadful, abrupt end. On the one engagement that Ory's band had played at Joe's saloon I had attempted to talk with him about Emma, but was thwarted by a huge crush of The Kid's -- as he was now known -- female admirers.

    I had now resolved to keep everything about Emma from Joe. He already knew about Alice from our earlier conversations. I had also told him about my son Johnnie, who had struggled with one illness after another from the moment of his birth and died just after he had turned three. I was not quite thirty years old and boldly looked forward to having other children with my new husband. I attempted to convince myself that this was not my only reason for having initially accepted his proposal, but deep within, I knew otherwise. The stark reality of facing the years ahead without any family at all absolutely paralyzed me. Although Joe's explanation for having turned away from and ultimately divorcing his first wife still didn't sit well with me, I tried to keep those emotions aside. I made every attempt to convince myself that our marriage was a solid one. But somehow, in so many ways similar to my marriage with John Barrington, I felt that we were merely playing at our expected roles and not even remotely involved with one another's lives. Also, for some reason I had assumed that his divorce had been fairly recent, but was surprised to learn when obtaining our license that it had occurred over fifteen years ago.

    I continued to write Alice at least one or two letters every month. I told her about my marriage, briefly describing our tiny, but pleasant Creole-style cottage in the Garden District with its sunlit kitchen and fairy-tale like courtyard, magnificently alive with the beating of ruby-throated hummingbird wings, adding that I hoped that she would be able to visit some day. The only mail I had received, however, was a stamped Christmas card, although foolishly I cherished even that small token.

Kid Ory had now started working with a very well-known cornet player named "King" Joe Oliver – or maybe King Oliver had actually started working with Kid Ory, no one seemed to be entirely certain. But the hot music of the Ory-Oliver Creole Band, now typically referred to as "jass", more regularly spelled "jazz", a slang baseball term, was the most sought-after group in New Orleans and becoming widely copied elsewhere. They were completely booked out many months in advance and Ory's high salary requests were far beyond Joe's modest means. Ory graciously did still play for a far smaller fee for the plantation dances and picnics in gratitude to those folks who had helped him when he was starting out, however. I knew Joe could not possibly be hiring Ory any time soon, meaning there was no hope whatsoever for me to speak with him at the saloon. Desperate for news about Emma after many months following the Black Patti debacle, I looked in Joe's small address book one day and extracted Ory's phone number. I had already decided to give a fictitious name inquiring about booking his band for a large party on St. Charles Avenue should his wife answer, which she did. Ory was still asleep she told me pleasantly, but she would have him call me back sometime later in the day. When the phone finally rang some four hours later I tried to remain calm as I answered.

"Uh, yeah, hi, this Mrs. Williams?" said Ory, clearing his throat. "This is Edward Ory, uh Kid Ory. My wife took this number down a couple hours ago. Said you're lookin' to book some music for a party?"

"Hi Ed," I said quickly, swallowing. "It's … it's Hannah Barrington, um, Peterson. I just wondered if there's a chance you would be willing to talk with me about Emma. Somewhere when … when you might have time. I know you're very busy, but … I …" My voice trailed off. There was silence for several moments on the other end of the phone. My heart beat loudly in my throat.

"Um, yeah, we could probably fit that in, uh, Mrs … Williams," he finally stated. "How 'bout I meet up with you an' your husband at his office say, early tomorrow afternoon? Oh, wait … wait a minute." He put his hand over the mouthpiece of the phone and I could hear muffled voices as he apparently discussed something with his wife. "Ok, so I forgot I can't meet then. How's 'bout the followin' day in the afternoon? Uh, what day's that?"

I heard his wife's voice say calmly, "that would be Thursday, Ed."

For some reason that made me smile.

"That's fine, but not at Joe's office," I said. "There's a very public coffee stand near the cathedral. So 1 p.m. on Thursday? Is that all right?"

"Yeah, thanks. That'll work fine. So long then." And he hung up.

I had almost given up on Ory when he finally arrived well over an hour late. I had no idea what Emma might have said, but I was absolutely certain she would have confided in him.

"Hey," he said with a kind of sleepy smile spreading over his face as he sauntered up. "Good to see you an' uh, congratulations on gettin' hitched to Ole Joe Pete. Nice guy, I guess. A little too intense for my tastes, y'know, but seems like a nice guy all the same. Marriage looks to be treatin' you well if I might be allowed to say. Let me grab a coffee and I'll be over. D'you need anything else, Miss Hannah?"

I shook my head.

"So what's on yer mind," he said, straddling a chair, sitting down opposite me at the table after looking around for a quick minute before setting down his coffee.

"I just need to know if Emma's all right," I began, my voice choking up despite my having fiercely willed myself to remain calm. "After what I read about the younger cast members on that tour being ... intoxicated and destroying the entire show beyond imagination several months back ..."

"So you wanna know if she was one of those stupid drunk kids that tore everythin' up, right?"

"No, no! That's not it at all, Ed! I just want to know where she is and if she's all right. If she was involved with any of that ... mess, it's over and done with. That's truly not any of my concern. Honest. Please just tell me -- do you know where she is?"

He exhaled and took a long drink of his coffee, then turned the chair around and settled back in it. "Yes, Miss Hannah, I do," he replied slowly. "She didn' want me tellin' you anythin', but she's ok."

"She's spoken with you then about ... about everything that happened out at Godchaux though."

"Yes, ma'am, she did," he nodded. "Everything. An' truth to tell you, I think I knew all along you wasn't just her teacher. Teachers don't follow their students somethin' like eight hundred miles downriver to New Orleans, y'know?"

"I don't expect you to betray her confidence," I smiled somehow, "but I just need to know what's happening with her. Where she's living. If she's safe. If she's healthy. She looked so horrible, so utterly defeated and thin the last time that I saw her! I can't just let her disappear completely from my life. Do you understand, Ed?"

He nodded and coughed very slightly.

"Is she going to be singing with you again anytime soon? I could maybe just ..."

"Just happen to show up in the audience not knowin' she was goin' to be there?" he rubbed his hand over one eye, concealing something of a wink as he sipped his coffee. A black man could never be too casual in public with a white woman. In fact even his sitting at my table for longer than a few moments might easily be suspiciously misinterpreted these days. "Not a good plan. She'd never trust me again, y'know?"

I looked down at the cold dregs lining the bottom of my own coffee cup and said nothing. He was absolutely right. I had nothing to gain and everything to lose by trying to see her.

"I'm tryin' to get her into another tourin' vaudeville show," he finally said after a few moments had passed. "Certainly ain' near as good a performin' group as the Black Pattis was, but it's not bad either. More blackface and slapstick kinda low comedy stuff, which I ain' always so keen on myself, but … well. Anyway, that's all I'm goin' to tell you. I ain' tellin' you where she's livin' or anythin' else."

"I assume that she's not out at Reserve anymore."

"No, she's cut herself off from Zuma too," he said gently. "But I guess you kinda expected that, right?"

"How could I have made such a mess out of all our lives, Ed? By loving Emma so much I've now completely lost her."

"I can't answer that," he replied with a warm, rather lopsided smile. "But I'm willin' to let you know every once an' a while how she's doin'. That's the best I can offer. Don' know if that's gonna be enough for you, but like I said, that's the best I can offer."

The group that Emma had joined was called Mack & Mack, a husband and wife team comprised of Billy McBride and Mary Thacker along with a troupe of about a dozen other singers, actors and comedians. Reviews of the act claimed that it was pleasing to patrons, free from vulgarity and had the ability to make an audience laugh without offending refined tastes. They toured throughout the South and East although, unlike The Black Pattis, they played almost exclusively to black audiences. Occasionally I found Emma's name mentioned in a review of the tour in *The Indianapolis Freeman*. Her most well-known act was mimicking the operatic singing style of the real Black Patti, Sissieretta Jones, who had now completely ceased performing, which apparently set the audiences howling. Her rendition was so good that the few black patrons who had actually ever heard Mrs. Jones sing claimed that Emma Jackson's voice was indeed identical. She also excelled at a ragtime rendition of a popular tune called *"The Cakewalk in the Sky"* in which she both sang and danced. Her sky-high kicks in the cakewalk, a popular dance performed back during the antebellum era, rarely seen these days except in minstrel acts like the Mack's, were complimented by many reviewers.

Ory kept his promise and roughly every two months he furnished at least a small update to me about Emma. Occasionally he failed to call for more than a couple of months, but eventually I would hear from him. He was so busy I was quite certain that he had just simply forgotten all about it. I already suspected that his wife was quite instrumental in keeping his engagement calendar up to date and, needless to say, our conversations, although certainly innocent in every respect, would not have been noted on such a calendar.

Life continued fairly seamlessly for Joe and me until late September that year when the hurricane later dubbed The Great Storm hit New Orleans, thoroughly crippling the entire city. According to *The Times Picayune* the Gulf welled up with twenty-foot-high waves and Lake Ponchartrain rose by over five feet, its water bursting through the meager lakefront levees. *The Picayune* stated that there were *"curtains of lightning like fire coming out of the mouths of serpents"* which destroyed most church steeples and leveled all of the French Market pavilions. Countless buildings were destroyed beyond repair either from multiple lightning strikes from above or several feet of rat-infested flood waters surging in from below. The French Opera House, which had been undergoing major improvements by its new owners with aspirations to open within the following month, was severely damaged with all of the remaining stored costumes and sets destroyed beyond redemption. Many hotels and other large edifices were so badly battered that they had to be torn down and rebuilt from the ground up. Ironically, Storyville, the well known prostitution district of New Orleans, suffered very little damage much to the scorn of the churchgoing faithful.

Fortunately our house was not seriously damaged being raised quite solidly on its chunky four-foot high brick posts, suffering only minor roof and window leaks. But Joe's saloon incurred such an extensive structural blow from a series of lightning strikes that it was deemed unsafe and had to be completely razed and rebuilt. Like most small business owners, Joe was swallowed up into enormous debt stemming from such devastating financial losses and had to obtain higher interest loans from less legitimate sources than what was available through the badly overextended banks.

Until the hurricane completely altered the course of my concerns, I admittedly had begun to despair that I would ever manage to become pregnant again. What had seemed so effortless when I was a younger woman now seemed to elude me completely. Even after the hurricane's devastation of his saloon, Joe refused to let me work to help out with finances other than taking in some sewing alterations for a few wealthy women. I also became involved again with the Christian Women's Exchange, volunteering to teach the many children who were housed there for any length of time while their mothers recovered from illness, desertion or simply utter destitution. The hurricane had financially wiped out many hundreds of families from all walks of life. Often I found comfort just singing with the children, making up little rhymes and silly anecdotes to help them through some of their darkest days ... and some of my own as well I confess.

Emma toured with Mack & Mack for almost two years and then early in 1917 the Macks signed on as the resident entertainers at Pete Lala's huge, brand new First Class Theatre in New Orleans, with Kid Ory and King Joe Oliver's group serving as the house band. The curtain would rise four nights every week to a sold-out house opening with the Ory-Oliver Creole Jazz Band on stage rather than down in the pit, certainly a new elevation of live music's place in music hall entertainments, and also featured an array of highly-amusing comedic skits and some of the loveliest new voices in vaudeville according to advertising flyers.

I realized that, like practically everyone else in New Orleans, I now found Ory himself extremely charming on stage and enjoyed the entire ensemble's performance, especially Ory's tailgate trombone style as it had become known. Every note the band played seemed to be perfectly calculated for such an astonishing fugue of different melodies at the end of their tunes – which I learned was called the "out" chorus – so tightly knit that I assumed everything was completely memorized. But after listening to them perform the same tunes on many occasions, I became aware that the musicians were actually adding different rhythmic patterns and alternative melodies, playfully working and reworking around one another in incredible precision, able to sense each other's nuanced contributions every night. It was always an extraordinary, original experience. As Ory typically said as an opening to the audiences, "we're just up here havin' fun y'all! Enjoy the show tonight!"

It was certainly easier to find Emma now, even though I knew better than to try to actually speak with her. Her yellow hair was a cotton halo that framed her small light brown face, with large, extravagantly made-up, kohl-rimmed blue eyes and a red, pencil-slim lined mouth. I had gone to the show several times at the First Class Theatre which surprisingly maintained a very civil, completely mixed house that I could only assume was allowed to continue due to Lala's huge political connections, both legitimate and illegitimate, in the town. Emma's voice was still truly exquisite. Her operatic spoofs of the magnificent Black Patti were well publicized as a major, hysterical part of the show, but I couldn't help but imagine how beautiful her voice would have been in a classical opera setting. And indeed, as she had often been praised, her dancing was incredibly lithe, sultry and actually seemed rather too promiscuous in origin for the rest of the production at times I thought. I wondered that no one had mentioned this to her and weighed whether to mention my concerns to Ory.

But when Ory finally called me our conversation was very short.

"Hello, Hannah?" he said when I picked up. This greeting by itself was highly unusual since he had always called me "Miss" Hannah, although unlike most women, I certainly didn't feel that the title was necessary. "I only got a coupla minutes to talk. But I know you've been down to Lala's place several times so you've seen her and you know she's doin' ok."

"Yes," I replied, although I wondered how he would have known since he was playing in the orchestra on stage. I always bought seats at the very back of the theater and left immediately afterwards.

"She seems to be quite happy, Ed. In fact, even kind of glowing and her voice sounds as amazing as before. I don't care too much for that horrible dark eye make-up and some of her dancing is well, rather … risqué. Do they really want her … slithering around like that?"

He laughed slightly and then took what seemed like a nervous puff on his cigarette.

"Yeah, well, I'm glad you've seen her so you know she's doin' ok. She's makin' some very good money too, y'know. Especially for a young kid like her. Real good money. An' that's real important. I'm tryin' to teach her to be kinda frugal. Save up. Never know when them lean days are gonna be barkin' 'round the corner in the music industry, y'know?"

"I imagine she knows about that actually," I replied, smiling to myself. "Money's never exactly been falling like leaves off a tree for her."

"An' she's eatin' real good. Can' get enough of my red beans 'n rice or spicy shrimp gumbo, y'know?"

I smiled. I had forgotten that Ory had the reputation of being such a good cook.

"Yeah, well, so I uh, wanted to tell you that I'm, uh, livin' back at Mutt Carey's place again, since Mutt's moved up to Chicago to work for awhile. He hates the cold up there though so who knows how long he'll stay, but for now, y'know, he's got some good-payin' work there."

"I'm glad for him, but sorry to hear about your … um, living … situation," I said quietly. I was rather surprised that Ory felt compelled to tell me this. He had always contacted me so I honestly wouldn't have ever known that he and his wife had separated yet again.

"And, I, uh, also wanted to tell you that, um, Emma and me, we've been livin' together for the last several months. Pretty much since Mack & Mack signed on here at the First Class with Lala."

> *"Man, if you have to ask what jazz is,*
> *you'll never know."*
> Louis "Satchmo" Armstrong

## Chapter 10: New Orleans 1917-1918

Joe had finally managed to rebuild his saloon and had reopened about six months after the hurricane. However, he was now seriously indebted to a small network of unpleasant men who very uncomfortably reminded me of the rough, unscrupulous pimps and extortionists with whom my deceased husband John Barrington had curried allegiance back in Kansas City. Work hours had now completely taken over Joe's life. The harsh ring of the telephone late at night often resulted in Joe's quickly getting dressed and disappearing for the next few days without any explanation whatsoever. If I asked about any of these men or their activities he nervously flashed a quick false smile, patted my hand, and avowed that all was just fine. But I knew he was lying. Occasionally, while in bed, I found him staring at the ceiling, whispering feverishly for hours.

I continued working as a volunteer at the Christian Women's Exchange. There were so many young women and their youngsters, abandoned by their men, whether husbands, long time boyfriends, or casual liaisons and I prayed Emma would not soon be among their number. I could only assume that Ory would know how to prevent her from becoming pregnant, but I wasn't so naïve as to presume this a particularly pressing concern on any man's mind.

And then on April 6, 1917, our insulated world flipped upside down overnight. The United States declared war on Germany and entered The Great War as it was known throughout Europe. All men between ages twenty-one to thirty-one were required by law to register for the draft. Joe was far too old of course, but Ory was only thirty, and possibly even younger, since questions remained about his actual year of birth. A married man could claim a deferment if he was actually residing with his wife and in early June Ory moved back in with his wife Elizabeth, or Dort, as she was commonly known, over on Jackson Avenue.

I had bought a ticket to Mack & Mack's newest advertised show that opened mid-June only to discover when I arrived that some of Emma Jackson's roles were now to be performed by another young lady and that Ms. Jackson's Black Patti numbers would, unfortunately, no longer be offered as part of the show's extensive repertoire. I managed to squeeze into the throng surrounding Ory outside the theater after that evening's performance. After almost half an hour I finally was close enough to speak with him, although certainly not without a few others nearby.

"I don' know where she's ended up," he said, after informing me that he had moved back with his wife. He'd closed his eyes wearily for a moment, deeply inhaling on his cigarette. "We had a huge fight over all of this. She just don' understand that I had to go back to Dort y'know? Otherwise I'll be drafted. She actually thinks I should wanna go over there! To fight! Me? Hah! Them romantic dreams of wartime by these crazy young girls are somethin' else, y'know? No way, I told her! I just ain't mean enough to go over there and fight them Germans. Those guys scare me – hell, even all of the German guys who are actually Americans livin' around New Orleans scare me! An' y'know, there's a lot of 'em! You'd be surprised. They're so intense. Quiet. An' a lotta muscles. Big guys some of 'em, too. An' they're real, *real* smart too, y'know?"

"Did she give you any hints at all, Ed?" I pleaded. I knew that there was nothing that I could do, but clung irrationally to some scant idea of a trail.

Ory had to stop talking and sign several more autographs

for three giggling young white girls, innocently flirting with them and their chaperone, undoubtedly one of the girl's mothers, who eagerly informed him that she had just purchased the brand new record of *"Livery Stable Blues"* and the *"Dixieland Jass Band One-Step"* and that Ory's band sounded just like them playing those tunes. I somehow doubted that he particularly embraced that as a compliment. The recording had just been released by the Original Dixieland Jass Band, a white band from New Orleans. Many of the leading black jazz musicians claimed the ODJB had simply stolen a lot of their material and headed up to New York earlier that year. That record, the first jazz recording ever made however, was selling like crazy all over the United States, war or no war. I had heard Ory denounce it as a lot of tinny noise fighting for a melody rather than anything resembling decent jazz music. It certainly seemed reasonable that he would resent that band's jump on what he claimed as his, King Oliver's and Freddie Keppard's personal territory.

After the woman and the girls left he turned to me, snuffing out his cigarette under his shoe.

"I'm worried she's gone over to Miss Lulu's," he confided in me finally.

"Miss Lulu's …" I replied, trying to place that name.

"Mahogany Hall. Y'know that fancy octoroon place over on Basin Street," he continued.

I caught my breath.

"She'll make a killin' over there. Jes' what fat ol' Lulu's lookin' for y'know? Talented sweet l'il black girl with such nice light 'n tight flesh …" he remarked darkly.

Before I realized what I was doing, I slapped him hard across the face.

"If that's where she is it's only because that's what you've done to her!" I hissed, tears instantly blurring my vision.

He roughly grabbed both of my shoulders which shocked us both. "Oh no, don' you go layin' all that blame on me, Miss

Hannah!" he retorted, shaking his head, tears in his eyes as well. "Yeah it's my doin' right now. I'll claim that. But there's a helluva lot leadin' up to it, an' I sure as hell ain' guilty of it all!"

Both of us stunned by his actions, he then let go of my shoulders, his arms falling limply down to his sides. We were both silent until he swallowed loudly and then finally blurted, "look, hey … I'm … I'm so sorry, ma'am. I … I didn' mean to grab you like that. Honest."

He looked around nervously.

"Could I just ask you to call me if you find her? Just promise me that."

"Yeah, sure. Absolutely. I can do that, ma'am," he replied quietly, head down.

I stared at him for a moment and then walked quickly away, my hand still stinging.

By August of that year slogans had emerged throughout New Orleans that "Food Will Win the War." Everyone was encouraged to observe such practices as "Meatless Tuesdays" or "Wheatless Wednesdays" since those items could easily be processed within our factories and shipped to war-ravaged parts of Europe, where croplands lay in tattered ruins alongside the carcasses of farm animals long killed off, the result of enemy hands. Americans were urged to eat fresh fruits and vegetables since they weren't easily shipped and many factories changed over towards working on the conservation, distribution and transportation of food items to both soldiers as well as our many starving European allies. Participation was completely voluntary, but everyone I knew certainly complied. At the Exchange we managed to conserve dramatically with everyone's effort on items such as meat, butter and cheese. No one complained. We begged door to door for donations of worn out clothing throughout the town and ripped these up, twisting the fabric to sew blankets and undergarments which we gave to a local factory to ship out with their goods. Even children as young as age three helped with carefully piecing together the edging on the blankets. Since New Orleans was one of the major harbors from which goods were shipped overseas, many of the women in the Exchange managed to find work at the factories manufacturing wartime goods near the shipyards where huge pallets were then quickly loaded for export.

I only had one brief phone call from Ory, who had secured a job during the daytime as a heavy loader at a shipyard as part of his deferment. He said that he hadn't heard from Emma directly. I thanked him abruptly and hung up. I doubt that our conversation had even lasted a full minute.

By October the Department of the Navy had issued an injunction to have all vice districts located within five miles of any American naval base shut down. New Orleans was one of the largest ports for both the shipment of men as well as of goods to Europe. Shocked by how many of its incoming recruits already had syphilis, the Navy ordered that soldiers should not be faced with any temptation exposing themselves to such deadly diseases before heading off to fight. And so, Storyville, one of the largest organized red-light districts in the country, officially closed on the anniversary of its 20th year of existence, and with it establishments such as Lulu White's were shuttered forever. Miss Lulu, however, always a crafty entrepreneur, found ways to keep her better clients' exclusive entertainment needs met … for a hefty price, of which she garnered a hefty percentage, of course. The off-limits, windowless, saloon manager's offices were particularly appealing spaces for such clandestine adventures. And for those exploited saloon owners who remained deeply in debt to the underground thugs who manipulated a large town like New Orleans, they were the easiest of pickings.

Joe's Barroom was doing a brisk business – at least the military still allowed men heading overseas the opportunity to drink themselves to excess, since sexual abandon was no longer on the table. But almost nightly there were fights between men from different regions, different backgrounds and beliefs as they awaited deployment. One marveled that they were somehow expected to arrive on European soil in less than a week's time and suddenly be willing to give their lives for one another, when in many instances they were still fighting the War Between the States back home.

And for those older gentlemen who weren't facing deployment to Europe, but had money to gamble, reinstated horserace betting was now running full tilt as the massive paddleboats continued to bring load after load of gamblers down to New Orleans from the northern states. Many were disappointed that the brothels were now officially closed, but quickly located those saloons at which such liaisons were now illicitly available. The tip off was that those saloons had a pile of the old pocket-sized Blue Books advertising the whore houses and talents of the brothels' occupants of old, "just for show" their bartenders would laugh. On closer inspection, however, one would find several lightly penciled phone numbers on the inside back cover. One of those numbers belonged to Joe's Barroom where a two-drink minimum was sufficient for a prospective client to obtain information. I had long suspected that Joe's saloon was working as an underground brothel and that Joe himself was thoroughly enjoying the talents of these ladies as well. When I had failed to produce anything resembling an heir for him after all of this time, he seemed to have no further use for me other than my willingness to offer him a place to occasionally catch a meal or pass out several times a week in complete exhaustion.

Late one dreary afternoon just a few weeks into February, I was startled to see several police officers looking in our front window, followed by loud knocking at the door. I was in the middle of writing a letter to Alice. Although I'd heard nothing from her for well over two years, I still refused to give up. When

I opened the door I assumed that the officers were looking for Joe, likely regarding his saloon's illicit activities.

"Mrs. Peterson?" asked the one officer, showing his identification, "may we come in? I'm assuming your husband's not here, correct? My name's Lieutenant Granger, by the way."

I stepped aside and four officers walked in, indicating that I should shut the door.

"Yes, I'm Hannah Peterson. And yes, Joe's not here right now. How can I help you?"

Another officer handed me a photograph of a young woman with dark hair. Given the woman's dress and old-fashioned hat it was certainly not a recent picture, although she appeared to be quite pleasant-looking. The other two officers had pulled out small notebooks from their inside jacket pockets.

"Detective Smith, Mrs. Peterson. You recognize this woman?" he asked.

"No, I'm afraid not, although this looks like a rather old picture going by how the woman is attired, officer."

He nodded and handed the picture to one of the other two men.

"But you're certain that you don't recognize her?"

"No, I don't," I repeated.

"Does the name Maudie Spencer mean anything to you?"

I thought for a moment.

"Well, I believe that my husband's first wife's name was Maudie Spencer," I answered slowly. "But they were divorced about seventeen or eighteen years ago." Or were they? Suddenly I had visions of being married once again to a bigamist like I had been with John Barrington. But as our conversation unfolded, it was far worse than that.

"What exactly do you know about your husband before you met him down here, Mrs. Peterson? I'm assuming that you did meet him down here, correct?" asked the lieutenant.

"Yes, that's true. I did. I believe he'd been traveling doing odd jobs of sorts for quite a few years before he settled down here. He mentioned that he was quite upset after his sister died. She was an invalid, you see. Very crippled apparently. I ... I can't remember her name though, I'm afraid."

"Mary Anna," answered Detective Smith.

I frowned. Why on earth were these men here asking about Joe's sister and former wife? I felt extremely uneasy.

"Mary Anna," I repeated slowly. "Yes, I believe you're right, officer. It's not something that Joe and I discuss, well ... routinely."

"Mrs. Peterson, what exactly did your husband tell you about Mary Anna's death?"

"Joe really only went into detail about it once," I replied. "What I remember him saying is that Mary Anna was so badly crippled that she wasn't able to move herself anywhere and she was always just lying on a pallet in front of the fireplace, because that was the only place she was comfortable."

"Yes, go on please," nodded Lt. Granger. "What town did he tell you that he lived in?"

"I think he said near Peoria in Illinois. Joe was at work, I believe. He worked for a bank or something. I can't remember that part."

"That's ok. We don't need to know where he worked," replied the detective. "Continue your story, please, Mrs. Peterson."

"He said that he came home from work and there was a note from Maudie tacked on the front door. She had walked into town to buy a jar of pickles I think he said, because she wanted them for their dinner and didn't realize that she'd already used all of the ones she'd put up. At least I think it was something like that. And when Joe arrived home from work the fire had broken through the grate and Mary Anna had been burned to death."

I paused. This was the part of the story that had always bothered me on the rare times that I thought back on it. The fact that Maudie had seemingly behaved so callously about Mary Anna's death, excited that the woman was gone, fixing Joe's favorite meals and luring him in ways no decent wife should ever attempt, was not normal.

"Yes, go on," urged Lt. Granger, taking notes, looking up briefly. "Please, ma'am."

"Well, he said that Maudie was … not acting the way a decent wife should act, officer. I think he meant acting like a … prostitute towards him, although he never actually used that word. And he left her after that and then divorced her after a few years."

"So you don't know anything about Maudie's whereabouts during any of that time?" asked Detective Smith.

"No sir," I frowned. "I was kind of surprised when I learned that it had actually been almost fifteen years after his divorce when we got married. I had assumed that all of this had taken place just a few years prior to our marriage. Can I ask what this is all about?"

None of the officers came forward with an answer to my question, but when I had mentioned the fifteen-year interval they had all exchanged a knowing look.

"In other words, you had no idea that prior to your marriage that your husband had been in jail for fifteen years?"

My mouth dropped open. "What?" I stammered. "In heaven's name, why?"

"For what was ruled the murder of his sister, Mary Anna Peterson," replied Lt. Granger. "The note your husband claimed to have found on his front door turned out to be in his own handwriting, not Maudie's. And as you'd mentioned, Mary Anna herself wasn't able to move. It was obvious from a faded place on the floor that her pallet had been dragged close in towards the fire, with that fire then stoked extremely hot for mid-summer and the grate left wide open."

"That … that just can't be possible!" I cried, shaking my

head.

"And what's more, no one had seen Maudie Spencer for several weeks before Mary Anna's death," continued Detective Smith. "Rumor had it that she was maybe chasin' around with one of the young bucks in the town, though. Several people interviewed at the time thought maybe she might have run off with the man, because no one had seen either of them for close to a month."

I took a few steps over to the chair at my writing table and sat heavily before my knees buckled beneath me. The officers remained standing.

"And after he hadn't heard anything from her for a few years he could have divorced her even though he was in jail? Or did she divorce him? That would be a reasonable explanation I suppose."

"Well, not exactly," replied Officer Granger looking over at the other men. "After ten years you can remarry without actually obtaining a divorce if your spouse has left and you haven't heard from them for that long. That's known as desertion. So that part was more or less legal."

"More or less?"

"Well, he undoubtedly hadn't heard from her in all of that time. And the house that he'd been living in when all of this happened had then been bought by an older woman who lived there all alone until recently."

I stared at the officer, my breathing shallow.

"That woman died last month and when the place was being cleaned out to put the house up on the market some of the workmen found Maudie's body under a heavy metal plate crushed into the crawl space. They later found the remains of what appears to have been her young man in an eight-foot-deep grave directly behind the shed under an old horse trough."

My hand flew to my mouth but did nothing to stop me from vomiting all over the letter that I had been writing to Alice.

I then began violently coughing, desperately trying to keep from retching again. One of the officers handed me his handkerchief and another walked out to the kitchen and then brought back several wet towels. Hunched over, I tried to clean my face and the mess on the writing table as another officer handed me his handkerchief as well.

"We're here to arrest your husband for the murders of Maudie Spencer Peterson and an as yet unnamed young man. This time he certainly won't be getting out of jail in fifteen years."

> *"They just play anything.*
> *The main idea is to keep the bass going.*
> *That is their thought. By keeping the bass going*
> *it gives 'em a sort of set rhythm.*
> *And by giving 'em a set rhythm they imagine*
> *they're doing the right thing, which is wrong."*
> Ferdinand "Jelly Roll" Morton

# Chapter 11: Joe's Barroom – February 1918

The officers needed my cooperation to isolate Joe from his saloon's patrons in an effort to avoid the possibility of a bloody encounter involving others. They were certain that he was armed, to which I dully had to agree that he undoubtedly would have one of his pistols concealed just inside his jacket for protection as usual. How could I have been so completely fooled by this exceedingly bland, mild-mannered older gentleman when we had first met?

The plan was for me to press one of the bartenders or one of Joe's resident toughs, regarding an urgency to see my husband alone in his office. The officers felt that this would be the safest for everyone concerned. They would wait strategically on either side of the door, out in the hallway. I was to leave the door open unless Joe instructed me to close it. The officers mentioned having been surreptitiously informed that the syndicate thugs running New Orleans' underground were more than wise to the sheer coincidence of Joe's sister's burned corpse and the suspicious disappearance of Maudie Spencer and her young beau, even if the district court in Peoria had ended their investigation at the time. If there were any problems encountered with Joe's cooperation with what they now viewed as one of their own saloons, they could certainly send out a small detail of men to tear apart Joe's former homestead back in Illinois. Basically my husband's goose had been cooked for a long time.

It had been at least nine months since I'd been down to the saloon and when I walked in the door I immediately realized that none of the bartenders looked even remotely familiar. A suffocating cloud of dense, black smoke practically blurred out all of the patrons' faces, all men, like an out-of-focus stereoscopic photo plate from decades back. The dull thump of a piano was only slightly audible in the distance. After several minutes I located the head bartender, introduced myself and said that I needed to speak with Joe immediately – that there had been a death in the family. He gave a half-hearted shrug and told me to follow him down a long, poorly-lit hallway. At least the thick smoke hadn't completely fouled that part of the building. After gently testing the doorknob and finding it locked, he put his ear to the door and then shook his head saying he didn't hear anything, so the boss must be out. Maybe he was across the street at Café Etienne's having an early dinner or running a few errands, he suggested. Since he'd mentioned that he had a key while we'd walked down the hallway, I asked him to kindly unlock the door so I could wait inside. He complied and opened the door.

Joe's desk faced the door. Shirtless, Joe was standing behind it. A nude woman with a cloud of dark yellow hair lay on her back across the desk, her light brown legs straddling Joe's shoulders.

"What the hell?" Joe yelled, moving back from the woman.

The woman propped herself up on her elbows and looked lazily over her shoulder at me.

"Well, mah goodness! A sweet fam'ly reunion, if ah do so declare!" laughed Emma, imitating a Southern Belle's voice in a line that I'd heard her utter countless times in the Mack & Mack shows. "Why Joe, you oughta ask the l'il woman if she'd like tuh join us for a hot l'il *ménage à trois* …"

Using both hands Joe roughly grabbed Emma's arm and threw her off his desk. She landed with a loud thud on the floor. I was completely speechless.

"What the hell are you doing down here?" he demanded, pulling his pants up and angrily snapping his suspenders over his arms, circling around the desk. He still had on his boots. "Sam knows not to ever disturb me!"

He then moved over towards where he had thrown Emma.

"Get your clothes and get out you goddamned bitch! Stupid slut! Now!"

"Now tha's not ver' nice …" Emma purred, smiling at Joe as she slowly stood up from the floor. "C'mon, le's have a drink. You know …a toast! A toast to our whole l'il fam'ly all, y'know, together," she continued, slurring her words. "Now that mommy's here everythin's gonna be real nice, y'know, Joey?"

"What the hell are you talking about?" he roared. "I said get out! You stupid nigger, don't you understand English?" yelled Joe, wrenching her arm behind her back and forcing her towards the doorway.

"Joe stop! You're really hurting me! Stop it! Goddammit, Joe!" shrieked Emma, bending forward in an attempt to reduce the pressure on her arm.

He then viciously kicked her between her legs and she shrieked again like a wounded animal in horrible pain, her knees buckling beneath.

"Joe!" I screamed, finally finding my voice. "Stop it! Let her go! My God, what kind of monster are you?"

At that moment Lt. Granger and his men, guns drawn, moved like lightning through the doorway, grabbing Joe and pinning him to the ground which muffled his voice at first. Emma managed to stagger to the doorway, blood trickling down one leg, clutching her clothing in front of herself and briefly looked back on Joe writhing on the ground as two of the officers attempted to control him.

"No reason you should be all nice 'n happy if I ain't," she snorted, panting hard, glaring at me. She then spat in my face and limped out into the dark hallway.

"Grab that damned whore!" shrieked Joe, finally getting his head turned sideways far enough to speak, even though the policemen were still holding him firmly to the floor while handcuffing his arms behind his back. "What a man does in the privacy of his own office ain't nobody else's concern! That bitch just made off with a huge bankroll of bills she picked up off my desk! Didn't you see her? Dammit, you idiots, grab her! She's the one you want, don't you get it? Lulu's makin' a killin' off those whores robbin' the clients she sets up in here! Arrest all those godammed bitches! The whole lot of 'em!"

"We're not down here about anyone named Lulu," said the detective. "And your private affairs are none of our concern either, although your wife more'n likely would feel different about that."

"You guys are totally missing it! Don't you understand?" exclaimed Joe, his distorted face an angry red as the police jerked him up to his feet.

"We're here to arrest you on a warrant to extradite you immediately to the state of Illinois."

"For what?" yelled Joe, as he futilely struggled against the restraints. "Back taxes?"

"For the murders of Maudie Spencer Peterson and an as yet unidentified man eighteen years ago in Peoria," stated the detective.

"What the hell? Those charges are completely false and you know it! Can't I talk to my wife first?" stated Joe without any visible remorse. "You got the wrong man, officer."

Joe then turned towards me, pleading. "Honey, I'm

completely innocent of all this! I have no idea what these crazy idiots are raving about."

"Not my decision, Mr. Peterson," said Lt. Granger. "That's why you'll be getting a trial back in Peoria. If they'd found those bodies when you went to trial for your questionable role in your sister's death you'd never have gotten out at all ... been swinging at the end of a rope long before now."

I looked away from Joe towards the wall and said nothing, trembling uncontrollably with a rage aimed not only at my husband and at Emma, but at myself ... for having allowed myself to wallow in such utter gullibility during my entire life.

> *"My main thing is tone.*
> *Then knowing what you're doing*
> *and not overplaying your instrument.*
> *It's best to make less notes and make 'em in the right place*
> *than make a whole lot of notes out of line."*
> Edward "Kid" Ory

## Chapter 12: New Orleans 1918-1919

Emma had indeed stolen a large roll of bills off of Joe's desk. An officer not connected with the case interrupted her counting out the cash in the alley behind the saloon shortly thereafter and brought her to the sheriff's office for questioning. Lt. Granger called me regarding the money which he ascertained was undoubtedly procured from illegal gambling and prostitution. Twenty-four hours ago I would never have agreed to take so much as a dime that my daughter might have needed. But now? I didn't even hesitate. I'd already converted Joe's bank account solely to my name and simply deposited the additional funds, as well as setting in motion immediate divorce proceedings. I also now vowed to stop writing Alice. It was a futile endeavor to continue trying to reach out for her forgiveness. What was I expecting after almost three years? That she would suddenly tire of a life of ease, wealth and the absolute latest in fashions and frivolous entertainments and come crawling back to me?

I sold my scant furnishings and moved temporarily back into the Christian Women's Exchange boarding home. They were very shorthanded and had hired me as an interim replacement for an administrative position while that employee was out in California. I had decided to stay in New Orleans until the war in Europe had ended, which the newspapers all agreed would be happening very soon. Now certainly wasn't the time to be exploring the country for new work much less a new life, so I was most grateful to have a decent paying position and a temporary place to live.

Early that spring a brief wave of influenza hit much of the area around Lake Ponchartrain in particular. Many women and their children coming into the Exchange for medical emergencies had experienced bouts of the sometimes deadly disease which seemed to quickly extinguish the lives of the youngest, most fragile babies and elderly, infirm adults within one or two days. But thankfully, the virus soon played itself out with only a very mild threat for most residents. My administrative position had been extended for which I was most appreciative, even though the workload itself had more than tripled as more and more women and their young families in dire need continued to flood the Exchange every week.

One Monday evening several women on the staff invited me to join them for an outing to Economy Hall to hear Kid Ory's Creole Jazz Band. Ory was still renting the place every Monday night same as when Emma and Felicité had attended, however, there was an order from the local government officials that as of July 7 all cabaret music in New Orleans would be banned in deference to our fighting men over in Europe. We certainly should not be amusing ourselves at home while our men were dying for the eternal rights of mankind overseas scolded the local government in defense of the harsh sanction.

There did seem to be quite a bit of confusion as to exactly what constituted cabaret music, however, and in the end, only thirty-five establishments were actually shuttered over and above the Storyville vice district's extensive closures the year prior. It was finally decreed that: "a cabaret was an establishment where there was music, singing and dancing and was frequented by men and women of questionable character." All of the establishments where Ory's group played fell into the music, singing and dancing categories, and more than the occasional audience member was of questionable character.

Respectable women (and many men as well) certainly didn't want their reputations sullied by association with the wrong music houses, yet many folks wanted just a few more chances to hear some great hot jazz music before the ban took effect. I realized that I hadn't even thought of Kid Ory for many months, although I'd certainly seen banners, buntings and other advertisements for his music all over town.

Economy Hall was packed, the sultry summer's heat radiating like an enormous brick oven sizzling through the large room. The band was on a balcony slightly above the crowd, but it was obviously no cooler up there. The bandsmen were sweating profusely, mopping their faces with small towels whenever they had a few bars' break during a tune. I recognized the bass player although I couldn't remember his name, but all of the other musicians were completely new to me. Regardless, Ory's music still had that same excitement and raw drive as when I'd last heard him at the Mack & Mack concerts at Pete Lala's theater. With a subtle hand gesture slicing sideways at waist level, he instantly brought his musicians down to less than half volume and then, usually on a repeat of that same passage, with a quick head nod and small stomp everyone was brought back up to full throttle or even beyond. Others might come close to imitating the man I thought, but there was truly only one Kid Ory in New Orleans. Despite the heat many people were energetically dancing, although how the band or the dancers managed to perform amazed me. I felt so nauseated by the oppressive intensity that I had already decided to leave at the first performance break. I was walking away from the building, liberally fanning myself with a cardboard fan when I heard light footsteps trailing behind me and a man calling my name.

"Hey, Miss Hannah! I saw you down there," said Ory, mopping his face with a towel thrown around his neck, even though the evening air was somewhat cooler than in the Hall.

"Jes' wanted to catch up and uh, say hello."

"You sound great as always, Ed," I replied with a slight nod. "The whole band."

"Yeah, well, even when I end up wrong on a run of notes I try to make everybody think it was the right one, y'know?" he laughed rather nervously. "Just slur over the bass line!"

"I assume you're one of the groups being shut down? Everyone's been grumbling about it."

"Yes ma'am," he shrugged, pulling a cigarette out of his jacket pocket and then lighting it. "I'd rather be over here an' out a few months work than over there an' outta my life permanently, y'know?"

"Goodness Ed, how can you smoke in this heat?" I inquired, baffled, still frantically fanning myself. "I would think that would make you even hotter."

He inhaled deeply and then blew the smoke away from me. "Nah, it's like drinkin' scaldin' hot coffee. Actually cools you off for some reason. An' I need a smoke in between sets to relax. I'm pretty, eh … tense when I play. Kinda nervous, y'know?"

"Stage fright? You?" I laughed in disbelief.

"Yeah, actually, well, that's the truth, Miss Hannah," he stated, flashing his boyish, lopsided smile that I rather suspected broke a lot of female hearts.

I made no comment, but fanned myself even harder, brushing my wet hair back from my forehead with my other arm.

"But, lemme tell you, this really ain' that hot, y'know? You ever hear of Funky Butt Hall?"

"Uh, no. That's an actual place?" I replied quite skeptically.

"Hell yeah! Buddy Bolden used to play there! Believe it or not it was a Baptist church an' the pastor of that church, see, he gets this idea to change it over to a dance hall 'cause the place was kinda on the fringe of the sportin' district anyway. So it wasn't pullin' in much coin, y'know? But, then with dances Saturday and Monday nights, that old preacher? Man! Did he clean up lemme tell you! Place had no decorations or nothin', y'know? Just a shell of a crummy honky tonk if there ever was one. He'd cram in about seven hundred people every Saturday and Monday in that place, and even with that crazy low cover and them dirt cheap drinks he was peddlin', he made at least *six times* what he was makin' just as an ordinary old every-hymn's-gotta-have-blood-in-the-title Baptist church. Now that place was *hot* and I don' jes mean the music, Miss Hannah!"

I was never completely certain if Ory's stories were in fact founded in truth. I'd certainly overheard enough of them when I'd lived with Alice, Emma and Felicité to question their authenticity. He could spin a yarn almost as good as one might read by Mark Twain I'd surmised. And those were only the tales he related in English. Goodness knows what he spun in his native patois! I cleared my throat slightly and looked over towards the crowd.

"So I heard about Old Joe Pete. Man, who would've ever thought that scrawny old goat could've killed three people! Hell, guess you can't tell a helluva lot 'bout someone jes' from his appearance, y'know?"

"Yes, indeed," I replied quietly, still fanning myself. Then I casually asked if he'd seen Emma.

"Well, yeah, I have as a matter of fact," he nodded, removing a bit of tobacco from his tongue and wiping it on the towel.

"And?"

"She's doing some singing again … at least occasionally. Mostly some blues type stuff with a coupla bands here and there. Not such bad engagements, y'know? Those places will for sure stay open during the music ban though, so she's real lucky there. No dancin', y'know? An' she's got a pretty good factory job durin' the day. Steady work too. Least while the war's still on it'll be steady work. She an' that girl Felicité an' a coupla other Creole girls have a place together. Nice place, too. Camelback.

Lucky I got her away from old fat Lulu before things got too far outta hand. Actually Lulu's in jail now. Not sure what they charged her with, but there's a lot to choose from! That could've been real bad if Emma'd stayed around her. She ain' a nice person. Not in the least. Actually, I don't think there's ever been a brothel's madam who was a nice person."

"Actually, that's not entirely true," I replied, quite certain my statement would be something of a shock. "When I lived in Cripple Creek there was a beautiful madam who ran a place called The Old Homestead. She was more like one of those European courtesans that many wealthy men kept outside their marriages – intelligent, gracious, would reach out to help anyone in need."

He stared at me for a moment.

"So, did you know her through Zuma?" he finally asked. "I thought …"

"Yes, something like that."

"Well, I should get back, but I wanted to tell you that, uh, Emma and me, we're … well, sorta back together," he added somewhat sheepishly.

I looked at him, but said nothing.

"But, I'm still livin' with Dort."

"Ah, well I assumed you had some reason for following me other than just to acknowledge a familiar face." And fill me in about your philandering lifestyle I said to myself.

"Yeah, well, I guess. I know the last time you an' Emma saw each other wasn't, eh, so good."

"Yes, one could certainly say that. What she does with her life from here on is her decision, Ed. You've heard of the expression 'the straw that broke the camel's back', I assume?"

"Heck yeah! I was raised a good Catholic boy! Oh no, wait, wait. Wrong camel. That one's 'bout Jesus teachin' us that it's harder for a rich man to enter the kingdom of heaven than a camel to fit through the eye of a needle ain' it?"

Unwilling to be sidetracked into a discussion on Ory's concept of biblical imagery, I continued speaking, despite being faintly amused.

"My husband turned out to be anything but an admirable person as you know. But Emma didn't know that when she went after him. I honestly can't believe for a minute that any of it was your dear friend Lulu White's business dealing, Ed. That was Emma's decision entirely. But I'm finished with interfering in any way. You can tell her that if you'd like."

"What she did was 'cause she was actually real mad at me, y'know."

"Well I must say she certainly has quite a peculiar way of displaying her anger towards you!"

He took one last puff on his cigarette, saying nothing, and then ground it out in the dirt.

"As I said, I'm finished with interfering in any way, Ed. Good luck to you both."

I started to walk away from him when out of the corner of my eye, I saw three men ambling slowly out of the shadows behind me. All three stank of a full night of whiskey and very stale sweat.

"Hey! You!" one man yelled.

I twisted back slightly looking over my shoulder as they sauntered towards Ed.

"Whadda you think yer doin' talkin' with this here pretty white lady, ya coon-ass?" said one of the men, shoving Ed backwards.

Ory said nothing, his face remaining completely passive and expressionless, arms straight down by his sides, eyes straight ahead military style, looking at no one.

"You deaf or sumpin' you ugly coon?" shouted another man. "He's askin' you what yer doin' talkin' with this here nice white lady!" He roughly grabbed Ed by the lapels of his coat and threw him backwards several feet onto the hard ground. Ed's white skimmer had fallen off and the man stomped on it, and then ground it out, as one would a cigarette butt.

"Pick it up!" he ordered Ory, kicking what remained of the hat several feet away.

As Ed slowly stood up still facing the men and walked carefully over to his hat, I spoke cautiously, my mind racing to deflect their scarcely-disguised threats towards Ory.

"Gentlemen, this man's wife cleans for me and she's been quite ill. I simply asked him if she would be at work tomorrow," I smiled, my heart banging in my chest. "There's absolutely no trouble here for you to be worried about. But I do want to thank you. A woman certainly can't be too careful and I do appreciate your concern!"

"Pretty dark out to be havin' a conversation wid some black mule like that," sneered the man who had thrown Ory down. "Put that hat on now, mule! I wanna see that dirt come rainin' down an' muddy up dat nice clean coat you got on there. Ain' no nigguh should have on a nice fittin' light coat like that, right boys? An' look at them nice tight trousers on that boy! Um um. Well, well."

Ory did as the man asked. As dirt fell onto his sweaty face and shoulders from the ruined skimmer the men's raucous laughter rang out. "Well, now that's certainly an improvement doncha say boys?" They continued laughing as Ory, facing the men, still expressionless, carefully took a very slow step backwards.

"Could any of you gentlemen direct me towards ... oh my, how silly of me! Now what's the name of that place?" I began nervously, attempting in as coy a voice as I dared to divert their attention. "I'm supposed to be meeting my husband and several friends there right now for dinner. It's that place over on ... well, you know where I mean ... that place with the best barbeque shrimp and grits in New Orleans. Surely you nice fellas must know the one I mean?"

As I'd hoped, the men got into an argument over which restaurant served up the best barbeque shrimp and grits giving Ory a chance to continue slowly backing away, unnoticed, finally disappearing into the crowds surrounding Economy Hall just as the band's break ended and the audience began filing into the building.

The streetlamps then came on illuminating a small group in the distance, away from the Hall. "Oh, look! I'm in luck!" I exclaimed to the three men. "There're my friends now! I'll just follow them over to the restaurant. Thank you all so much for your help gentlemen. Good evening!"

One of the women turned towards me as I called to them waving. "Lucy? Lucy?" I shouted. "Over here! It's Evelyn! Wait up!"

The woman's name was undoubtedly anything except Lucy, but graciously she and her friends stood waiting for me to join them assuming I had mistaken their party for another. I apologized and then continued walking quickly past them, heading towards the streetcar after verifying that the men weren't following me. Ory was long gone, thankfully. Fear still ran rampant deep within me, however. I thought back to the heated conversation that I'd had with him many months ago outside the Mack & Mack performance when I had slapped him and he'd grabbed my arms. If those two actions had been overseen by men like these tonight, Ory would have never made it back into that theater alive that night. I also kept hearing that horrible thud of leather stinging bare flesh and raw bone and Emma's animal-like shrieks when my husband, boots on, had kicked her between the legs after throwing her off his desk like a sack of garbage. And just a few moments prior to that, he had obviously been fully enjoying the sexual favors of a beautiful sixteen-year-old girl.

I was still shaking long after midnight. This was a world I knew nothing about. When I had been a young girl I'd been mercilessly beaten with a belt by Mrs. Hughes when she thought I was stealing and also savagely raped by a man in payment for my father's debts. But difficult as those moments had been to endure, they had indeed only been moments within a day, not hourly threats surrounding me in constant fear simply because of the color of my skin.

Ory called me the following afternoon at the Exchange to thank me for the diversion. From just inside the building within the crowd he had watched me cross over to the women on the other block, so he knew that I'd had no further confrontations. I hesitantly asked him if that kind of thing happened frequently. "Uh yeah, well, sometimes … it does," he replied slowly. "I just don' really talk about it. But see, here's how I pretty much think about it: when the rabbit bites you the first time, it's his fault, but when he bites you the second time? It's your fault. That's an' old slave sayin' my mama taught me actually. But one that you just gotta keep in mind, y'know?"

*****

In September a shipload of seriously injured soldiers returning from Europe docked in New Orleans. Several men had died during the voyage, which given the circumstances wasn't at all unusual of course. But just before arriving at the port in New Orleans, several dozen additional men suddenly became simultaneously sickened with a respiratory flu-like virus and died within hours after first showing any symptoms. Many of the other soldiers also showed early symptoms of influenza and were immediately rushed from the ship to area hospitals, a tactic which proved to be a very fatal error. In less than a week an epidemic had overtaken the entire city. Scenarios like this were soon found to be exploding all over the United States. Then as *The Times-Picayune* reported in early October, an uncontrollable pandemic of the influenza virus had now taken hold all over the world. The disease typically introduced itself with a high fever, boils, nausea, delirium and paralyzing pains in the back, arms and legs. Then one's skin would turn blue and lungs fill with fluid, causing agonizing suffocation. Although many victims suffered for about three weeks, others were only ill for three days and still others, possibly the luckiest ones, lay in agony only three hours before their deaths. It was not at all unusual for someone to be completely healthy upon rising in the early morning, sickened by mid-afternoon, and dead before nightfall.

Mail delivery, garbage collection, factory employees and farm laborers' services were all curtailed because so many workers had perished. Countless doctors, nurses and associated health workers had fallen ill and subsequently died, resulting in all of their former patients' bodies being laid out in long, snaking rows in temporary makeshift wards of badly understaffed hospitals, with not enough morticians or gravediggers still alive to service them or even the coffins to enclose them. Late at night, special trains were secretly engaged to transport the dead, leaving their cargo in undisclosed locations far from civilization. One newspaper correspondent who had served outside Paris earlier in the war said the situation was far worse than any sight he had ever experienced in France after a major battle.

Citizens were ordered to wear gauze masks. Schools, theaters, churches and all public places were ordered shut down indefinitely. Funerals were limited to fifteen minutes, although some towns refused to allow funerals to be held at all. By the time Armistice Day was proclaimed on November 11 in Europe, the world was facing an even fiercer battle with an enemy that knew absolutely no boundaries. It was widely held that the epidemic may have actually played the largest part in ending the war since so many troops were either badly weakened from the disease or simply lying dead in the trenches.

Saddled on the back of the Spanish flu as it had now been named, rode two other horrific outbreaks – meningitis and bacterial pneumonia. Doctors treated the sore throats that precipitated these illnesses with castor oil thinking at first they were far less serious illnesses than influenza, when in fact they were every bit as deadly although not as inherently contagious. If someone miraculously survived the Spanish flu, their constitution was already so severely weakened that they were easy prey to either pneumonia's lung congestion or meningitis' snare of confusion, seizures and vomiting. Both illnesses resulted almost always in death.

There was yet a fourth insidious illness that silently attacked several million victims across the globe as well, but one where the full impact of the disease wouldn't be completely realized until several decades later. And that was *encephalitis lethargica*. Again, it was simply treated with a few doses of castor oil to calm a high fever and soothe a sore throat, but other than that, the illness was largely forgotten about, the attending physicians' notes buried under those of their more immediately pressing cases of the day.

Publicly, the Women's Exchange was officially shut down. The wealthiest women who contributed to the organization, many of whom surprisingly still volunteered several days each week at the building, insisted that we'd all be dead in no time if we took in every stray dog and cat off the streets as we had in years past. After all, that's what the local hospitals were for they exclaimed *en masse*. The women and children who now qualified for admittance within our doors were always white, quite clean and decently dressed, yet nonetheless cautiously screened, and as a rule had only endured their difficulties for a very short time. Anyone who was coughing or had a runny nose or registered even the slightest of fevers, regardless of race, however, was barred from admittance and immediately dispatched to the local hospital. "We have to look out for our own first," the women agreed among themselves unanimously. I had no choice but to conform. Diligently I wore my mask, avoided crowds and attempted to avoid any place where large block-lettered signs were tacked to walls or fence posts reminding the populace that

"Spitting Spreads Spanish Influenza -- Don't Spit" or "Do Not Spit on Floors or Sidewalks."

I received a notice at the end of the year from Lt. Granger that was almost two months in arriving. Joe's trial was scheduled for February in 1919. However, about a month later I received another notice from the Peoria district courts informing me that Joe had died of the flu as had most of the county's prisoners over the last several months. Like so many other mysteries in my life I realized that this too was now a story that would have no resolution, no ending. One's life is not at all like a book I reasoned. Things are never fully resolved, never fully wrapped up in nice, tidy little stacks and neatly placed in the corner awaiting our leisurely perusal and analysis. We simply do our best to glue together the often shredded pages of our fragmented chapters and arrange them in some kind of meaningful sequence.

With the war finally ended and the worst of the flu definitely easing its iron grip, many restaurants, saloons, cabarets, ice cream parlors and cafés, moving picture houses and large performance spaces slowly came back to life, much like dandelions pushing up through a sidewalk crack. Surprisingly, even the French Opera House re-opened after having been closed for almost six years! I learned that Miss DeWitt was still on their managing staff and left a message asking if they might be in need of any costuming assistance as we always had quite a few women at the Exchange who could certainly hand stitch garments even if they weren't adept with a sewing machine. She was ecstatic to get my call; they were quite far behind with fittings and alterations and hired eight of the women that very afternoon at a very good salary.

Much of my own work now involved the initial screening of the families who sought assistance from the Exchange, making every attempt afterwards to research and verify their stories. Women who had fallen on difficult circumstances due to their own reckless foolishness or indiscreet follies were not considered viable candidates for housing or work assistantships. However, I was not the one entrusted with making the final decision nor was I the only one investigating the background histories. The last resolution was left up to a committee of five women who conferred with one another several times every week.

Most of the women I interviewed were from Louisiana, or occasionally Oklahoma, Tennessee or Texas. Rarely did anyone else in poor financial straits manage to find their way as far south as Louisiana unless they were already living down this way. But shortly after everyone had finally begun relaxing their vigilance regarding the flu and travel, a young mother from Colorado Springs quite surprisingly showed up at the Exchange. Lacking funds, she had left her children behind in Colorado and had used every last dollar to make the long train trip down to New Orleans. Her name was Jane Lawson and she was looking for her husband Jim. Jane was quite small-boned, a very delicate, rather nondescript, soft spoken woman, who looked to be in her very early twenties, if that.

"And you last lived in Colorado Springs?" I inquired, beginning to fill out the usual set of forms.

"Um, yes ... yes ma'am," Jane replied, nervously twisting a handkerchief in her hands. "My husband left Colorado for a teaching post down here. Or, at least that's what he told me. I just don't know what's happened to him, Mrs. Barrington," she said softly, tears starting down her cheeks. "We've been married for almost four years now and he's never just wandered off with no explanation at all like this before. I'm just so afraid to think ... since I haven't heard from him ..."

I lightly squeezed her hand for a moment fully aware of the meaninglessness of such a gesture, nodded and wrote down a few thoughts.

"I just need a bit of information, Mrs. Lawson," I smiled.

"How old are you? And you mentioned that you have two children, correct? How old are they?"

"I'm almost twenty," she replied attempting a smile. "And yes, we have two children. Our little boy Albert just turned three. His daddy's middle name is Albert."

I nodded. Far back in my head rumbled an indistinct memory, but I ignored it.

"And then there's Rosie, that's short for Rosemarie. She's eighteen months next week."

"So I assume you've left the children with family while you've come down here to look for your husband?"

"Well, no, no ma'am. My Pa's long gone – he'd been a preacher, you see -- and my Mama took the flu when it first hit Colorado Springs a few months back and passed within a day. Jim left sometime after Mama's death, but I can't remember the exact date I'm afraid. The job here in New Orleans just came up quite unexpected, so he had to leave real quick. Or ... so he said, anyways."

"That's fine, Mrs. Lawson, I don't need an exact date," I replied gently. "Please go on."

"Well, I'd never had any brothers or sisters or aunts or grandmas or anyone else. We lived with my Mama in her house in the Springs. It was a very nice house. But it wasn't hers. I don't think Jim knew that, however. He was really upset when he found out after Mama passed that the house would now be going back to the church where Papa had been the preacher. You see, the church deacons had been kind enough to let Mama live there all of those years until her death, without her paying any rent."

"And you would have to then move out."

"Yes, ma'am. Since I was married they assumed that my husband would be able to care for me and the children, of course." She started crying again.

"That certainly makes sense. Do you remember the name of

the school that hired him?" I said gently, handing her a clean handkerchief. Her own was already a hopelessly-wadded, soggy ball.

"Well, I thought he said it was a program at St. Andrew's Episcopal High School in Metairie. That's how I wrote it down anyway. He used to be a history and English teacher a long time ago, but then times were hard and he ended up working a lot of other odd type jobs you see, even before we were married to tell you the truth. Most times he'd be gone several months working in different cities in Colorado. I kept asking him why he couldn't find anything in a town as huge as Colorado Springs, but he never really had a good explanation. Sometimes it was Denver or out in Fort Collins or maybe Pueblo. Or sometimes not even in Colorado at all. But certainly never as far away as Louisiana for heaven's sake!"

"I see," I nodded, penning a few quick notes. "And I assume your husband is a bit older than you?"

"He's quite a bit older, actually," she replied, wiping her eyes. "He'd told me he was thirty-eight, but I think he might be even a few years older than that."

"And not that it matters, of course, but why did you think he was older than thirty-eight?"

"I ... I went through some of his well ... personal effects that he'd never allowed me to look at after he didn't call me or write," she swallowed. "I guess you'd call that snooping, which I know isn't a nice thing to do. But I learned that he'd finished high school many years earlier than he'd claimed."

"Sometimes people finish very young, but that's not really the point I assume."

"No. It isn't," she concurred, tears beginning to flow once again. "When I got to New Orleans two days ago I tried to locate this St. Andrew's School and found that no such school exists or has ever existed, Mrs. Barrington!"

I paused for a few moments and wrote all of this down on

the form, keeping my eyes downcast.

"So if your children aren't staying with your family, Jane," I said gently, somehow feeling I needed to address this young woman by her Christian name and desperately hoping to change the subject to something more positive, "are they currently with your husband's relatives?"

"You're going to think I'm the biggest of fools," she sighed, blowing her nose, "but I've never met any of Jim's relatives. He said that he was considered the black sheep of his family and had been disowned by all of them when he was barely out of short pants. Mama never really liked him either I have to admit. She thought he was a bounder."

There was a slight knock on the wall just inside the doorway and one of the other assistants peered around the corner. "There was a call for you from an Edward Ory, Hannah, but I told him that you were taking a history and would have to call him back. I have the number here for you."

"Thanks Ellen," I replied, taking the slip of paper from her. "Would you have a moment to bring us some coffees? I think we're both very much in need of a cup, yes? Milk? Sugar?"

"With milk please," Jane nodded, then adding, "your coffee down here is so … um …"

"Scalding hot, blisteringly bitter and practically undrinkable?" I offered lightly.

Jane nodded with an attempted smile, tears clinging to her pale lashes.

"I've had to place the children in an orphanage of sorts. Temporarily anyway. Well, it's not exactly an orphanage because you can get your children back out once you've proven you're able to provide for them again. For me it's going to be awhile, I'm afraid. I don't know if that makes sense."

I nodded. "It does. Honest. Go on, please."

"It's actually a really nice place. I mean really! First of all, the children there are decently clothed. They're not kept like …

filthy paupers ... like you see so often, which is really reassuring, Mrs. Barrington. There's a school where the older children learn music, drama, dance or sports and the girls learn sewing, in addition to their reading, maths, and such regular studies. And then there's also a farm which the older adults – you see it's also a place for poor elderly citizens as well – and the children tend the crops, gather eggs, milk cows and such. The children are also assigned to the flower gardens and grounds and sometimes help with the cooking. Even little Albert will have his share of chores in the upkeep they said which rather surprised me. Obviously, Rosie's still a bit too young."

"It sounds quite lovly," I replied, indeed surprised by her description. "And this home is in Colorado Springs?"

Ellen brought in a tray with two mugs of coffee and set it on the side table.

"Yes, ma'am. It's called the Myron Stratton Home. It's fairly new. I think it just opened about five years ago or so actually. A multi-millionaire gold miner named Winfield Scott Stratton bequeathed it in his will in 1902. I learned that from this huge bronze statue and plaque of Mr. Stratton overlooking one of the gardens at the cemetery. I guess people didn't think it would ever get built because ..."

"All of the councilmen in Colorado Springs and Denver were after Mr. Stratton's stockpile for what they felt was their own city's rightful share of the inheritance pie," I offered, finishing her sentence.

"Well actually, yes! That's almost exactly what I heard," replied Jane, undoubtedly surprised by the distinct venom in my voice.

"I'm originally from Cripple Creek, Jane," I admitted quietly. "And I knew Win Stratton quite well actually. I'm very grateful that his amazing vision of the home finally made it into a reality."

"You knew Mr. Stratton?" she stared at me. "His statue

seems so huge and well, darkly menacing … and everything. They say he died a raving alcoholic, had a terrible temper and frequented women of the lowest repute in the worst of brothels!"

"I rather think history has not been particularly kind to Mr. Stratton's reputation quite honestly."

"What did he look like?"

I thought for a moment, setting down my pencil on the table.

"Very thick white hair, white mustache, bright blue eyes, rather weather-beaten skin from so many years out prospecting I suppose, with a small but quite muscular frame. Very intelligent and well read. He was a skilled carpenter and much sought after as an architect. Sort of a math genius, but loved all the fine arts as well. In fact, he even had a small collection of women's Impressionist art. He wasn't a very tall man, but he seemed tall the way he carried himself. Long legs, I guess," I smiled. So much like his daughter Emma in so many ways I thought with a momentary pang … except for the white mustache, of course.

"Well," said Jane, "I'm certainly grateful as well that this home managed to get itself built."

"Indeed!" I replied warmly. "So what's next for you, Jane? Do you plan to continue to search throughout the city looking for Jim?"

"You know, Mrs. Barrington," she sighed, "I now actually doubt that Jim ever came down here at all. I think he's just … abandoned us. I'm going to need to work hard down here to make enough money for the train fare back to Colorado and more as well to give us something of a start again. I feel as though I've been away from Albert and Rosie for five years already. Do you have some work that I could help with around here? I don't have too many skills like so many girls in the factories do these days, but I'm fairly good with a needle and thread and those horrible old treadle Singers. Mama had one of those dreadful clatter bang machines!"

"Ah, say no more!" I smiled. "I probably have exactly the job where we can place you for a bit working on costumes at the French Opera House."

Later that night as I lay in bed, I realized that I had forgotten to telephone Ory and wrote myself a note to do so in the afternoon. If he was still working late hours it was highly doubtful that he would be awake before then anyway. Thinking back on my conversation with Jane, I was overjoyed that Win's last horribly troubled months working on the bequest and the subsequent decade of challenges to his will had met with such an amazing success. Mrs. Hughes had mentioned being on some kind of social committee there, but I didn't read very much into that. Her interest had undoubtedly already waned. That it was such an ongoing successful concern warmly surrounded me like a rich silk cocoon as I drifted off to sleep. Then suddenly, I was wide awake. That distant memory triggered by Jane's predicament came roaring to the surface. Practically word for word I vividly remembered the conversation that Abigail Hughes had had with her father Dr. Hughes in our cabin in Cripple Creek about the young man who was the father of the child she was expecting -- Alice.

"I'm sorry, Papa! I'm so sorry," Abigail had cried, gulping for air. "It'll never happen again!"

"No, I seriously doubt that. And just where is this gallant Romeo these days? Do you have any idea?"

"Maybe in Denver? I'm really not completely sure. I think he might have been planning to go back there, but maybe I have that wrong."

"Yes you seem to have a lot of things wrong, that's for certain."

"I remember he said once that you had treated him for a horse bite. On his leg. He showed me ... the scar. Out in Denver."

"Too bad the damned horse didn't bite him any higher,"

her father had snorted.

"Papa! Do you think that maybe you remember him, Papa? In Denver?"

"What the hell's his name again?"

"Jim. James Albert Lawson. He has the same middle name as you!"

"Never heard of him."

Jane Lawson's little Rosie and Albert were quite possibly 'my Alice's' half siblings I realized. Jim Lawson had probably only married Jane because he thought she could provide a free home for them to live in comfortably and he could continue to roam as he pleased, working the odd job here and there if necessary. Maybe he'd died in the influenza epidemic or maybe he'd moved on to yet another sweet, naïve young woman in another state. Did the leopard ever change its spots? Jane would probably never know what had happened to him. We simply do our best to glue together the often shredded pages of our fragmented chapters and arrange them in some kind of meaningful sequence, I thought yet again.

> *"All music is folk music.
> I ain't never heard a horse sing a song."*
> Louis "Satchmo" Armstrong

# Chapter 13: New Orleans - early 1919

Another young mother I'd interviewed had brought in a trove of beautiful wooden toys that she had fashioned, hoping to sell them at a profit far beyond what we could possibly have realized for her. The workmanship was exquisite, but we had many similar items for sale in our two stores and I knew we couldn't possibly list them for what they were truly worth. The woman, now a widow, her husband having died in France during the war, was quite desperate. I told her I would do what I could to price her work for as much as I thought feasible, but I knew she was very disappointed with me. I was still over in the children's store trying to work my way through any reasonable strategies when Ed Ory walked in the door.

"Oh, Ed," I apologized. "Please come in. I'm so sorry. I did get your message yesterday and meant to call you back, but we seem to have so many women desperately in need of help right now. I've been feeling completely useless, unable to help any of them in much meaningful fashion."

He nodded, removing his skimmer as he crossed into the store. Obviously, he had replaced the damaged one I had last seen so ruthlessly ground into the dirt.

"Well, maybe it's better to talk in person than over the telephone anyway," he shrugged. "Contrary device that damn telephone."

I gestured to a chair and he sat wearily. He looked very tired and quite thin. I wondered if he'd been ill. I had also wondered throughout the epidemic if Emma had been ill or Alice up in Colorado Springs. But finding out that someone was healthy on any given day was about as reliable as getting an update regarding the whereabouts of the fox that had just slaughtered your neighbor's chickens.

"Just wanted to relay some news to you, if you got a minute."

"Of course."

"So we played an engagement down at the plantation in Vacherie last weekend. You know, the Claytor place."

I nodded.

"An' I found out while we was there that both Mr. and Mrs. Dawson over at the Godchaux in Reserve had passed durin' the epidemic, an' most of their children. Both Reserve and LaPlace got hit real hard y'know. Person I talked to in Vacherie said they thought two of the little Dawson boys had pulled through an' been sent over to Baton Rouge to live with their great aunt."

I pictured Mrs. Dawson with her flowing diaphanous chiffon gowns, suffering with seemingly endless pregnancies year after year. Now only two of those babies had survived and she herself was gone.

"Poor little tykes," I murmured. "I've heard that something like one out of every three or four people were sick. So many horrible deaths. Everywhere it seems."

"They say that Godchaux's back up on auction. Ol' man Dawson ran the place even further into the pit than when he bought it, from what I heard," stated Ory. "But a lot of their workers died as well, Miss Hannah."

"Such a waste," I whispered, as much to myself as to him.

"Zuma's dead," he continued gently. "Seems she was one of the first deaths when this mess first hit back in November last year. She's been gone 'bout five months. No one even seems to know where all those early folks got buried even. It was so fast and there were so many of 'em. Sick less than a day. Way too many to keep track, I guess."

How many times had I wanted to head out to Godchaux

after Zuma's and my terrible argument that Emma had overheard? What had stopped me exactly? Knowing that she was absolutely right? That if I was too afraid to raise Emma as my own child I should have just let the girl go completely out of my life? My excuse had been an unwillingness to travel on the train during the epidemic. But was that the real excuse?

"Have you told Emma yet?" I asked quietly, feeling a lump forming in my throat.

"Not yet. Actually, uh, Emma's in the hospital right now. She had the flu, pretty bad actually, but she pulled through ok after about a month. I was sick too. My wife's a brick though. Woman never gets sick, y'know? She'll live to be a hundred, I think. She nursed me through the worst of it and somehow I nursed Emma through."

"How ..." I began, but was interrupted by Ory.

"But Emma's been real kinda shaky an' had a coupla seizures or somethin' since she got over the flu. She came down with this real high fever, an' a bad headache an' sore throat that they say has nothin' to do with influenza. Doctor insisted she go into the hospital coupla days ago. I think they're all worried that another epidemic is gonna get started if they ain't more careful, y'know? So I haven' told her 'bout Zuma yet. But I will. And I need to get goin'. Got an engagement startin' pretty early over at Pete Lala's 25 an' I wanna stop by the hospital first."

"Ed ... will you let me know ... how she's doing?" I said quietly. "Please."

"Sure thing."

We both stood up and slowly walked to the door in silence. Somehow a natural impulse brought our arms around each other briefly in a gentle hug. Then he walked out in the chilly afternoon sunshine. I shut the door after him and leaned heavily against it deep in thought. Zuma was gone. For almost half a year already and I hadn't known. I remembered having an odd discussion with her about heaven when I was still a little girl. I had asked her if she thought that after people died that they met up again in heaven. She'd laughed at my question which had surprised me. "Well, y'know, chil' there's yo' black heav'n an' there's yo' white heaven, honey," she had replied with a wink. "Guess we all jes' gotta go where we done gits sent, y'know?"

Now that I was actually fully employed at the Exchange, I could no longer live there. I'd been given a month to find other arrangements, but hadn't had any time whatsoever to devote to such a search and my grace period of a two-week extension had almost ended as well. The Alcion had announced a rare opening and it seemed easiest to take that before someone else grabbed the opportunity. The place was now being managed by a different group and rental rates had actually surprisingly decreased slightly, but the quality of the home's upkeep and services had decreased as well. Something about the inviting huge front porch, which would soon be surrounded by the fragrant scents of blooming lemon and orange trees, the availability of a morning coffee and *beignet*, a prepared evening meal and access to the St. Charles Avenue streetcar mere seconds outside the front door convinced me.

Knowing she would be eager for the additional monies, I asked Jane to help me move my few possessions to the boarding house on her day off from her work at the Opera House. She was one of their best workers Miss DeWitt had proudly remarked to me, exceptionally attentive to the last detail of every garment she touched. After we had finished piling my possessions in my new room, I insisted that we take the streetcar to the French Quarter for a bite of lunch at an outdoor café to enjoy the sunshine since this was the first warmer day of the season. We stopped for her to post a letter back to Colorado Springs. I had given her money for stationery and stamps, something which I really wasn't supposed to offer, but it certainly wasn't the first time and I highly doubted it would be the last I slightly bent the rules to help one of the women. She had been writing one of the caretakers at the Myron Stratton Home several times every week and had received many letters confirming her children's rosy health and general wellbeing: Rosie had recovered from her cold, although she still had a very slight cough occasionally, and Albert had received a small detention of no desserts for five days for throwing sand at another three-year-old while they were playing in the park, Jane had informed me from her latest letter.

"There are two girls working at the Opera House named Adele and Aline who say they worked with you before," said Jane, after we had finished our lunches and were attempting to tame our cups of wild black coffee with numerous splashes of cream.

"Yes, that's quite true!" I smiled. "I actually had no idea what had happened to those two girls!"

"Well, Adele got married, but now she's getting divorced she says," said Jane. "She says her husband is very abusive and takes all of her money that she makes at the Opera House to gamble and buy liquor all of the time. But Aline worked at the same factory during the war as another girl they said you would know named Emma."

"Yes, Emma, of course! And did either of them know what Emma's doing these days?"

"Well, they had a flyer that she's singing with someone named Kid Ory's jazz band next week. I guess he's pretty famous down here. Adele said they used to go over to a hall in Tremé to hear his group on Monday nights. They showed me the flyer and it said that Emma had been a starring *étoile* with a couple of well-known vaudeville touring acts called The Black somethings and Mack & Mack."

"The Black Pattis. Yes, I remember that as well."

"So this Kid Ory is now renting out these various performances places around town the other girls mentioned. Staging his band's own dance programs all the time, they said. But he's a Negro, you see."

"Um, yes ... I think I remember that," I replied slowly.

"Adele said that she'd heard from her husband that Kid Ory's going to get into a lot of trouble with the establishment, you know, the Klan. Or maybe the mob. I don't remember. Are they the same thing?"

"Just for performing at a dance?" I frowned.

"No, for booking them by himself in the first place," Jane replied. "You know, like a white man would do. Said he was kinda uppity. But anyway, Adele and Aline are going next week to hear Emma at the Cooperators Hall. Do you know where that is? Since you know her, would you want to come with us too?"

"Sure," I smiled. "I'll plan to meet all of you girls there after work. That sounds quite lovely."

Emma had on the same wrapped, metallic-blue sheath and wide headscarf tamping down that cloud of long dark yellow hair that she had worn at Margaux Claytor's wedding. I had originally thought the gown might have been borrowed from her days in The Black Pattis and I hoped that it had not been blatantly purloined by my daughter, although that really shouldn't have bothered me. The audience was mixed, but a number of uniformed men surrounded the interior of the hall to make certain that none of the darker-skinned men spoke with any of the white women or approached them to dance. If anything, Jim Crow was slowly tightening its iron grip throughout the entire country, especially here in the South.

Everyone seemed to recognize Ory's newest cornet player, Louis Armstrong, the young musician I remembered Ory talking about with Joe several years ago. He was indeed a remarkably gifted young player. And I finally remembered Ory's bass player's name, Ed Garland, although everyone called him Montudi these days. Emma joined the band about halfway into the first set with three Creole tunes that I definitely remembered: *"Eh la Bas,"* *"Blanche Touquotoux,"* and *"C'est L'autre Can-Can"* followed by her song and dance to *"Ballin' the Jack"* that I'd seen at the wedding, and a couple of slow blues' tunes, "*His Eye Is on the Sparrow*," and "*Mississippi Boll Weevil Blues*". She finished with Ory's own instrumental tune "*Muskrat Ramble*" teaching everyone interested a fast, fun combination of steps from the Black Bottom, Crazy Knees and the Geechie dances that she claimed were of her own invention. Emma's voice was sweeter and more powerful than ever, running through complicated riffs and melodies, rhythms and counter rhythms as though simply a child's game. Years later I realized what a rare gift I'd been given that evening, watching her enchanting performance on stage with the fast-rising supernova Louis Armstrong. Kid Ory's hot music was hotter than ever. Both Ory and Emma seemed to actually be glowing, laughing at each other's comments on stage between songs, with an occasional one-armed hug as well. After one of her dance tunes, Ed pushed back a lock of Emma's hair under her scarf and gently kissed her cheek. Although I knew it was wrong of me, I could only hope that Ory's wife Dort would get fed up with her husband's relationship with Emma … and let him go.

*"The memory of things gone is important to a jazz musician. Things like old folks singing in the moonlight in the backyard on a hot night or something said long ago."*
Louis "Satchmo" Armstrong

# Chapter 14: Octavie Edouard Jackson – 1919

Although I hadn't planned to attend another jazz concert so quickly after the last one, all of that changed with the hysteria surrounding a letter published in *The Times-Picayune* that claimed it had been written by the Axman, a ruthless, ax-wielding mass murderer who had been terrorizing New Orleans' citizens for close to a year. He had attacked over a dozen people, half of whom had died during the exact same time frame as the worst of the Spanish Flu. In his letter, the killer stated that he was a jazz lover and avowed that anyone attending a jazz concert or booking a jazz band into their homes would not suffer the consequences of his merciless wrath on March 19. According to the police, the murderer's usual victims were Italian women, (and occasionally their husbands if they got in the way) however, there seemed no discernible purpose in these attacks. No robberies or accounts of missing or defaced property occurred in conjunction with the grisly slayings, committed using various untraceable straight razors and axes conspicuously left at the scene.

Every music venue in town had quickly booked a jazz band or any cluster of musicians that purported to play jazz, wanting to cash in on what would definitely be a lucrative evening. Ory's band was appearing at Pete Lala's theater and it was a unanimous vote to attend. All of us at the Exchange, employees as well as all of our residents, headed over that evening after stopping on the way for quick paper boats of spicy steamed shrimp. None of us really took this crazed man's letter seriously, but, like everyone else in New Orleans, we were terrified of this ogre. The only description that had surfaced was that he was "dark-skinned, heavy set and wore a turned down hat" which was certainly anything but a detailed account and easily described at least a third of the men in the French Quarter.

The theater was already jammed by the time we arrived, well over an hour before the band was set to begin. Any hope of seating was long gone. That gave testimony to just how frightened the city had become. We somehow managed to squeeze ourselves over towards one side, although we had to split into several groups to accomplish that feat. We were fortunate that only a dozen children were living at the Exchange at the time, the youngest being age six, so everyone attended without the worrisome disruption of howling babies. When the band finally appeared on the raised stage – they were over a half hour late starting -- everyone wildly applauded until Kid Ory raised his hand.

"So, we're gonna keep that devil outta our place tonight, yes?" he exclaimed in a hoarse voice as the crowd cheered. "Here's jazz the way it's supposed to be heard, y'know? We're gonna start out with the *"Wolverine Blues."* Great tune by that one-and-only truly amazin' ragtime piano man himself, Mister Ferdinand Jelly Roll Morton!"

He stomped off the count and the band dove into the tune. An odd sense of relief passed over the entire crowd as they immediately quieted and settled into the music. All now assumed they were safe from the Axman's wrath with New Orleans' top jazz musicians performing right in their very midst. We were quite far back from the stage and the lighting throughout the hall cast rather eerie shadows on the faces of those attending as well as the performers. Ory's face looked darker and swollen around his left eye I thought, but I was so far away I assumed it was simply the erratic lighting. A couple of the Creole tunes that Emma had sung followed, although Ory sang them with a slightly different arrangement that made them more masculine. Several people in the crowd yelled for *"Livery Stable Blues"* so they launched into that tune along with the *"Dixieland Jass Band One-Step"* which, along with the ODJB's newly released *"Clarinet Marmalade,"* were still the hottest-selling jazz tunes captured on shellac all over the country. Finally he said that most of the musicians were going to take a small break, but that the piano and bass players would keep playing so no one would get nervous that the music had stopped. In fact, they would keep switching off like that all evening so the music would be continuous until daybreak. We would all have a chance to hear the band members play various instruments over the course of the evening.

Only a handful of men and women were brave enough to exit the theater for even a few moments. From Ory's days with Mack & Mack I knew exactly his destination to smoke a quick cigarette between sets and I was certain this evening would be no different. I somehow pushed my way through the crowd to one of the side entrances and walked out.

"Ah, Miss Hannah" he nodded, exhaling smoke, glancing nervously over his shoulder. "So you've joined the rest of the crazed citizens of New Orleans on the Axman's big jazz concert night, eh? Didn't see you in there. Chokin' crowd, y'know?"

"It hardly seems a joking matter, Ed," I frowned. Now that I was up close to him, I could see that he definitely had a badly swollen eye that looked even uglier under the starlit night sky.

He shrugged, taking another long drag from his cigarette, looking down at the ground. "So, I really can't be standin' here talkin' with you right now, y'know?"

"Is that the source of the black eye?"

"Eh, no, not really. Not at all actually. Okay, so y'see, I had lined up my own engagement at another hall, already paid for it an' everything, y'know, when this *loup-garou* gets his letter planted smack on the front page of *The Picayune* last week. So then ole Pete Lala insists I cancel out on that contract -- which means I lose my deposit on it, y'know -- and take his 'cause he had some kinda classical string trio or sumpin' lined up for the long-nosed set tonight an' he cancelled them to put me in. Jacked the ticket prices way up too, as I'm sure you noticed. Anyway, I told Lala that we already had an engagement and he could go to hell ... and then he, uh, sent some of his, eh, goons, over to convince me otherwise, y'know? My ribs are really messed up right now. Hurts like hell to play, lemme tell you. Stayed clear of my lips though, y'know ... those boys were real professionals. Knew just exactly how far to go. Nothin' broken, y'know?"

He forcefully blew smoke away from me, scanning the area while doing so.

"Your eye looks really sore, too."

"Yeah, well for all I know ole Lala himself is the Axman. That's my guess, but you'll never hear me squawkin' it since I'd like to stay alive. Lala's ole man was a butcher, in fact, *the* butcher in town, and so was Lala originally. And as we all know, the man loves his jazz music ..."

"That doesn't seem possible," I replied shaking my head. I had never met Pete Lala, only seen him from a distance, but his was a name on everyone's lips. Although not directly involved in politics, Mr. Lala's opinions held sway with the town councilmen on many issues. And I was embarrassed to admit that he was the major contributor to the Christian Women's Exchange where I worked as well. As the saying went: "when money talks, people listen" and people always listened to Pete Lala.

"Well, the police are sayin' they think it's some upright citizen with a violent, eh, alter ego, y'know? Fits ole Lala to a 'T' in my book anyway. But, like I said, I can't be seen talkin' with you right now."

"How's Emma?" I asked. "Just tell me that, please. She seems to be …"

"Oh, yeah. Emma. She's doin' real good. No more convulsions er nothin'. Her doctor thought it was just some crazy fluke from that high fever. You heard her singin' the other night. I saw you there. She's soundin' great now! Beautiful tone, an' nice, warm nuances in her work, y'know. But still a natural, nice big voice. So many of them blues singin' women just screech so's they can get booked into the bigger halls an' make more money like the jazz bands. You ever hear them records those women make? God awful. No tone. Just a lot of loud God awful screechin'. They don't know how to pull it down for any acoustic expression. But Emma's doing great. Thanks for bein' concerned, but I won't mention it, 'course."

He shook his head and crushed out his cigarette on the ground. As I walked past him back towards the theater he made a slight painful bow.

The entire audience stayed until well past dawn. Most of us drifted off into a restless sleep, either draped over a chair seat or curled over one another in small piles on the floor. Every time I woke up however, hot jazz music still pulsed throughout the hall. I have no idea how those musicians maintained that energy. I heard Ory playing banjo, guitar and upright bass at different times. Other musicians took over playing piano, clarinet, cornet or drums as they spelled one another during what should have been their breaks. I never heard anyone else playing trombone, however. And I also realized many hours into the concert that Louis Armstrong hadn't been playing with him tonight at all. However, there was yet another very talented young cornet player working with the band who I didn't remember having seen before. One wondered if Ory found them or the other way around. Probably a little of both.

There were no murders committed that evening; everyone breathed a sigh of relief. However, several more attacks occurred before the end of summer, some resulting in deaths, other victims sustaining horrific injuries from which they would never fully recover. And then, the tirade simply stopped. Much like the fury of a drenching thunderstorm crackling with ferocious tongues of lightning – once spent, it quickly ended. The madman simply disappeared from history without a trace, a mystery never solved.

The summer heat climbed to extreme discomfort very early in the season and unrelentingly continued its hostile blast week after week. Everyone did their shopping and eating either very early in the morning or quite late into the evening long after the sun had set, dealing with the added nocturnal wrath of hungry, swarming mosquitoes. Tempers flared even among the best of friends and many ugly confrontations escalated nightly throughout the city. On two separate occasions all of the members of Ory's band, along with most of the audience, were arrested in raids at dance halls that Ory had booked. After the second arrest, in a drunken fit which he later very much regretted, Ory remarked to a reporter that it was all Pete Lala's doing. Lala was just jealous of Ory's success in managing his own venues without Lala and his thugs' Neanderthal interference. And furthermore Ory alleged, Lala considered himself a jazz lover? The idiot couldn't distinguish a jazz riff from a slice of salami!

By early August Jane Lawson had finally saved enough money for train fare back up to Colorado Springs as well as a decent cushion to house, feed and clothe her two children for several months while she looked for work. Even though she was far closer to Emma's age than mine, we had struck up a warm friendship and promised to write one another every few months. I helped carry her few possessions from the Exchange over to the train station on a drizzling Thursday afternoon, one of those rains that does nothing to freshen the air and in fact, only makes one more miserable in the dense humidity. After a lengthy hug she surprised me when her eyes suddenly flooded with tears and she dramatically exclaimed that she would have been completely lost had I not helped her over these last seven months.

As she boarded the train I waved to her and then began walking back up the steps towards the streetcar. Half a block away an older style cab splashed through a large puddle as it pulled to the curb and a man and woman emerged. Several large suitcases, now copiously dripping, were strapped outside onto the back of the cab. I realized it was Kid Ory and the woman undoubtedly his wife. Ory paid the cabbie and whistled over to a boy with a pushcart, gesturing for the boy to load the baggage. I could have simply crossed the street and not encountered them, but determined it couldn't possibly be inappropriate for me to call over to the man while he was with his wife in the afternoon.

"Mr. Ory!" I shouted, waving. "Please tell me you aren't leaving us!"

He looked over just as the boy had begun loading the suitcases onto the cart and said something briefly to his wife as he walked over to me. She continued to oversee the boy's progress and then began walking with him down a ramp towards the station.

"Yeah, I'm headin' out to California. 'Cause of my, uh … health, y'know?"

"Your health?"

"Yeah, my doctor says the climate here's too damp. Not so good for my lungs. Says I should find a drier place to live, y'know. That's the story I'm goin' with anyway," he shrugged, coughing slightly for emphasis. "But, uh, I'm kinda bein' pushed to leave town by ole Pete Lala's people 'round here too. So Dort an' me, we made a quick decision a few days ago an' we're headin' out to Los Angeles, you know in California, this afternoon. Little Louis, well, guess he ain' so little anymore actually, an' everybody else, they've promised that they'll join me soon's I've lined us up steady work. It's a hot town for jazz out there these days. Livin' costs way more, but the pay's more too they say."

"And Emma?" I whispered. "Did you say anything to her?"

"Well, she's also kinda part of the reason we're leavin' too," he added, clearing his throat. "Dort's puttin' her foot down 'bout my, um, what do they call 'em in the Bible? My, uh, grievous sins, trespassin's, transgressions an' so on and so forth."

"Ah. I see."

"Emma'll be all right. She's got some good singin' jobs lined up. Some really good people here in New Orleans are interested in her now. You, uh, might check in with her at some point though."

"I don't know if she'll want that. Nothing's really ever been resolved about ... well, anything."

"Well, y'see, truth of the matter's this: Emma's pregnant, Miss Hannah. Probably sometime end of November or maybe December. She didn' want me tellin' you, but I feel like I needs to since I'm leavin', y'know."

A woman's voice yelled from just outside the station's doorway. "Ed! Get over here! We only have a few minutes left to get our tickets before the train pulls out!"

"Train's leavin' in twenty-five minutes an' the damn woman acts like it's five," he muttered, and then called loudly over to her, "I'll be there in a minute!"

"Emma's still livin' with that girl Felicité an' I think the other girl's name's Celeste. Yeah, that sounds right. Celeste's even a *fanmsaj* uh, *une sage-femme* ... eh, what'n hell d'you call it in English? Oh yeah, a midwife. An' Felicité claims she's a cousin to some kind of dead voodoo priestess. Tells fortunes, burns herbs an' shit, y'know," he shrugged. "But people pay her real good, so that's all she cares about. Anyway, Emma'll be fine.

Y'see here's one thing that you white women will never quite understand. Black women'll almost always stick together an' help each other out in these situations, y'know? But white women? They'll just throw a Bible in your lap an' walk out in disgust with their snooty noses in the air."

Without question he certainly had that right.

"I gotta go before ole Dort sends out the bloodhounds," laughed Ory. "Tell you what. I'll call you at the Exchange an' give you a number where you can reach me once I got a steady engagement out there. I told Emma the same."

"Edward Ory!" shrieked his wife impatiently, both hands on her hips. "Do I have to come over there an' drag you down here myself?"

"Next thing y'know she'll be countin' to ten," Ory joked. He gave me a kind of salute and ran down the ramp towards the train station. In a flash it occurred to me that the man would never give up his wife for Emma or probably for any other woman either. Elizabeth or "Dort" was unquestionably a replacement for Ory's mother who had passed away when he was quite young. He truly needed that level-headed, mature stability in his chaotic life as a jazz musician -- someone to remember to change the sheets or darn the cigarette burns in a favorite shirt or throw out the tomatoes when they were past the sauce stage.

Over the next few months I caught a glimpse of Emma twice in the French Quarter. She was walking with Felicité and another woman, whom I assumed was Celeste. The second time was in late October and by then she definitely looked and moved as though quite pregnant. I wondered if she would actually make it to November, much less December. I was surprised to receive a torn-off matchbook cover advertising a place called the Cadillac Café which listed the address and phone number on which Ory had simply scrawled on the back: "playing here ~ Ed".

I'd also received a brief note from Jane Lawson. She and her children were now living with a family in a small frame house near Colorado Springs. Things were quite tight, but they all loved being together again. Understandably both Albert and Rosie (who now stubbornly insisted on being called "Rose" and not "Rosie" since that was a baby name she insisted) had grown immensely and picked up some rather rough habits while Jane had been down in New Orleans, but that was of small matter. She still hadn't heard anything from Jim. And if you're lucky, I thought to myself, you never will.

The French Opera House was in the throes of opening a new production of *"Carmen"* and many of the women now living at the Exchange had been hired in the pre-production frenzy to construct, alter and embellish a vast array of new costumes and properties. They were being well paid and were more than willing to work additional hours at extra pay on the weekends. The Opera House had been one of our main employment avenues ever since it had finally reopened. Miss DeWitt was quite strict according to the women who I sent over to help with the sewing, but wages were always exactly as promised with adequate breaks and excellent working conditions.

Then, near midnight in early December, as the orchestra's concertmaster turned the corner back towards the Opera House, after having consumed a few drinks with several wealthy benefactors, the men noticed smoke emanating from the second story windows just above a first floor restaurant. The alarm went out immediately and the fire department was on the scene within minutes. The firefighters valiantly fought the huge blaze, which quickly consumed the wood-framed structure and was voraciously fed by ample painted canvas backdrops, muslin scrims, highly lacquered costumes, shellacked wigs and headpieces, and disconnected, yet still flammable, gas-lighting jets.

The following morning dawned on the smoldering ruins

that had once been the magnificent edifice. *The Times-Picayune* front page stated: *"Gone, all gone. The curtain has fallen for the last time upon Les Huguenots long a favorite with the New Orleans public. The Opera House has gone in a blaze of horror and of glory. There is a pall over the city; eyes are filled with tears and hearts are heavy. Old memories tucked away in the dusty cobwebs of forgotten years have come out like ghosts to dance in the ghastly Walpurgis ballet of flame. The heart of the Old French Quarter has stopped beating."* Optimistically, the headline boldly stated the day afterwards: *"The French Opera House to Rise Again from Ruins"* -- a declaration that sadly never came to pass. The theater had been shuttered from 1913 until finally gloriously reopening early in 1919, but the now-charred ruins would wait in vain for well over a decade hoping for yet another miracle.

I learned a few weeks later that Emma had given birth that same disastrous night to a little girl, Octavie Edouard Jackson, who was called "Tayvie", named after Ory's mother and the original French spelling of Ory's first name.

> *"New Orleans is a place*
> *where we had our own way of doing."*
> Ferdinand "Jelly Roll" Morton

## Chapter 15: New Orleans 1920-21

By the following summer I had moved to a very tiny apartment tucked into a Creole cottage in the French Quarter. Mrs. Trent, the elderly widow renting out the two rooms, was quite infirm, more than slightly muddleheaded, and needed help with everything from getting dressed appropriately each morning to remembering to feed her late husband's poor parrot (oddly named Monsieur Autruche, which was French for 'ostrich') to locking up her doors and jalousies every night. In fact it was at the insistence of her adult son that she had originally decided to acquire a tenant when she had been robbed on three consecutive nights by failing to correctly fasten her windows. After singeing off part of an eyebrow while attempting to light her stove one afternoon, she had also finally hired a woman to do her cooking. Mrs. Trent was quite certain that the cook was stealing part of her money when shopping, however, so I had gratefully offered to do her marketing as well as my own.

This gave me an excuse to be working my way through the various shops for our purchases and on many occasions I glimpsed my beautiful little granddaughter out with Felicité or Celeste. Tayvie had thick straight hair pulled back into two large ponytails that shone like wine-colored ebony, threaded with iridescent gold in the sunshine, a round light cinnamon face, darker than Emma's but not as ruddy as Ory's, and Ory's expressive, dark brown eyes. Celeste's English was only slightly better than Felicité's, but I did manage to learn that Emma was now in Chicago for a few months. She had been working in the kitchen at a big restaurant up there – peeling so many potatoes her hands were often raw and bloody and sometimes horribly shaking explained Celeste with grimacing gestures – while trying to find singing jobs. It was a struggle, but it was a singer's paradise Emma had told them. She had been sending money back for them to care for Tayvie. There had been some promising work, but nothing that had lasted more than a week or two. Everything that the two women said to Tayvie was in patois I noticed. I asked Celeste if they ever spoke to her in English and she had smiled her broad white smile and answered with a slight laugh, "*Eh? Pourquoi*? She get en school, *tôt ou tard, non?*"

I tried my best to mimic Zuma's piewheel recipe, which Emma, Alice and I had all so adored, and came close, although it was definitely lacking some essential ingredient. The treats had disappeared quickly when I'd baked them for the children at the Exchange, but I was far from satisfied with my results. If I could get it right I wanted to offer Tayvie one of the little cookies one day.

Although I never spoke with her, Emma had returned to New Orleans for most of that winter, but most recently had taken the train back up to Chicago after having received a phone call from Kid Ory, according to Celeste. I wondered if he was now in Chicago.

One afternoon I saw Tayvie, now walking, grasping Celeste's index finger, her chubby little brown legs peddling furiously beneath her yellow daisy-print dress and light wool jacket. Félicité crossed over to me, holding a small black notebook.

"Eh, Emma's," she said handing the book to me along with a slip of paper. "*Est-ce que tu posterais ça? Voici son adresse en Chicago. Elle l'a oublié sa livre.*"

The book was Emma's journal. I had no business reading it of course, but I knew as I walked back towards Mrs. Trent's house that I would unquestionably be doing just that. I couldn't help myself. I was so hungry for news about her singing career in Chicago or perhaps when Tayvie had actually cut her first tooth or said her first word or well, news about anything.

I was slightly disappointed that it was a new book with only the first several pages filled in, although her writing was quite tiny, undoubtedly in an attempt to conserve paper. I knew she had starting keeping journals back when she had first joined Sissieretta Jones' Black Pattis; in fact, I had given her that first journal! By now she would have filled quite a few books I guessed. Remembering a few years back when I had made a large pot of tea and settled in to devour Emma's descriptive letters, all of which I'd kept, I set the kettle on to boil after making certain that all of Mrs. Trent's last minute directives, including cleaning up after Monsieur Autruche, now rampantly molting, had been completed. When denuded of his colorful feathers he did indeed remind one of an ostrich!

I was disappointed that Emma's diary was undated. *"Worked with Bill H. again tonight at Elie. Very small crowd. People only come out to hear Lucille so no surprise there. Bill's tired of Lucille changing her show right at curtain. Then she's nasty when he forgets to play the changes. He thinks my voice sounds like hers but, UGH, I don't! Edward always says I should work to be my own voice not somebody else's. He says that's why his band has such a good sound & good reputation because they're just trying to sound like themselves. Make their own music their own way, not somebody else's way. As soon as he has to make his music somebody else's way he'll just refuse to play. That works ok maybe for a band.*

*I'm glad I'm not a musician though. My left hand is doing it again. It's getting worse. 2x this week already. Shaking like crazy. I can't make it stop no matter what until it finally stops by itself after many hours. From peeling those goddamn potatoes at the restaurant. I know it. Crippled my hands. At the Elie tonight I put my arms around my stomach so less obvious. Bill asked if I had a stomach ache & I said yeah. No $ for a doctor. Only colored doctors down at Provident* (the rest was smudged out).

I turned over to the next page and there was a thick diagonal line actually slashing completely through the paper in one spot, snaking from the top left corner all the way down to the bottom right corner. Over that line were long trains of gouged x's and also smudged out parts of the line as if she had attempted to erase it. On the opposite page she had written:

"What SHIT! SHIT SHIT SHIT SHIT! Just happened again! What? What? What? What? What? Missed rehearsal – Luis Russell! Elie next Friday. Fogged out today. Just sitting here. Can't move. Hours & hours. Just sitting here. Can't move. Hours & hours. Just sitting here. I can't move. Hours & hours. Clock ticking, water dripping, old Mrs. Ackerson shrieking in the stairwell - husband's boozed out of his mind <u>again</u>, again, again, again, spent all their $$ <u>again</u>, streetcars, dogs fighting. Dogs fighting. Dogs. Dogs. Dogs. Car klaxons. Klaxons. I can't move. I can't. I can't. I can't. I can't move. Why? Why? Why? Why? Why? Why? Why?"

The next page was covered with the word "Why?" scrawled one over another, hundreds of times and all directions so the page was almost completely black. Then on the last page she continued seamlessly, as though oblivious to all that had preceded it:

"Heard from Luis. Opening at the Plantation! Didn't ask about yesterday. He's so sweet, not like Jelly - no patience with any singer, except when he's screwing us. <u>Then</u> he's Mr. Sweet Talk. He knows I'm Edward's so bonsoir monsieur ravageur. Luis got us in for 2 wks next month! Can't believe it! Bill H wanted it for Lucille. Probably not good enough $$ for Lucille. She demands more & more money. But if she can get it, take it! Hell yes!

E called. His band's to record w/ Roberta Dudley. Four sides for new co. cutting race records in Los A. Still several months off though. He hates her voice, but $$ are $$ he says. He says backers may let his band record 2 sides. Hope so. Hope I can make a record one day. With Edward's band. That would be heaven. No, better than heaven! I need him. *I miss him so bad!*

*Taking early train to N. O. tomorrow. Celeste's message -- Tayvie's stomach is ok now. Hardly recognize her -- looks so different each time. Forget she's there at times. Forget she's mine at times. How can I forget she's mine? Edward thinking about coming to Chicago to work w/ Oliver soon cause Joe keeps asking. Of course Dort says no. But I say yes!*

My pot of tea sat untouched, a cold brown glass globe. I read over Emma's entries at least a dozen times then finally forced myself to wrap the book in waxed brown paper, securing it tightly with string and printing her address on the label, which I pasted on firmly to impede any attempts to read the book yet again. I would post it on my way to the Exchange in the morning. Was she drinking heavily? With prohibition now a federally enforced amendment I had heard that people were mixing together horribly toxic beverages to sell on the underground. Many drinks were often far deadlier mixtures than what had been available before. And with the ruthless crime syndicate in command of Chicago's entertainment establishments, the alcohol was undoubtedly flowing profusely, legal or not. Or maybe she was heavily dependent on some drug like laudanum or opium. It seemed as though two entirely different women had written those pages. Would it make sense for me to try to get in touch with Ory? I decided against that idea. What could he do anyway? For all I knew he might just treat the entire matter as a joke. And maybe as Emma hoped, he was planning on a visit to Chicago anyway. For many hours after wrapping the package I sat quietly on the side of my bed deep in thought, the dark room lit only by a silver-veiled crescent moon.

*****

By some miracle during the next few months I actually convinced Felicité to bring Tayvie, now close to eighteen months, to the courtyard at Mrs. Trent's for a little visit one sunny afternoon. Tayvie was still very shy and rarely spoke to me at all during my occasional encounters with her in the marketplace and I knew that Emma would not have approved of our communication.

The proffered attraction was to meet Monsieur Autruche, who, unlike a talkative magpie sporting a rather blue repertoire back in Cripple Creek many years ago, actually had a relatively innocent vocabulary, or at least what I understood in English and my limited regional patois. The bird started into a little song which I had always assumed was simply nonsense syllables to a tune that rather reminded me of *"Twinkle, Twinkle, Little Star."* But almost immediately Tayvie began excitedly clapping her little hands and singing along! Félicité held Tayvie on her lap and nodded, smiling.

"*Tante Félicité! Il chanté Creole Bobo, lui! L'oiseau chanté Creole Bobo!*" Tayvie exclaimed, laughing. Monsieur Autruche, undoubtedly aware that he had just established a potentially clear pathway regarding the receipt of excellent treats, excitedly hopped sideways along his perch and repeated his performance with Tayvie a number of times. He then launched into another tune and she sank back against Félicité, thumb planted firmly in her little bow mouth, frowning, and bowed her head while kicking the chair rung. Seeing that this tune obviously wasn't eliciting the desired response, the parrot immediately started into yet a third song, "*Eh, la bas.*" Tayvie's little voice chimed in immediately on the echoed part of the chorus each time. Then Tayvie started a tune and the bird tilted his bright green head looking at her quizzically, black eyes riveted on her face as he bounced up and down in time on his perch. She sang it several times and Monsieur Autruche, ever the showman, quietly mimicked certain parts as he learned it, watching Tayvie intently. After several additional visits, the duo had added that tune as well as many others to their charming repertoire.

*****

And well before her last visit some two years later, before

Emma took her up to live in Chicago, Tayvie had also finally given me a name: Maman Chenille, meaning Mama Caterpillar. This came from a game we played where we slithered about on the floor in my hallway, then sprouted wings and turned into magnificent twirling butterflies finally flying out the doorway to skim lightly, dancing over the grass. No longer shy of me, she would cover my face with her huge wet kisses at the end of each visit. I would read books to her in English, but she only conversed in the patois spoken by Felicité, Celeste and her playmates at home.

*****

Before daybreak just a few days before Christmas, I awoke to the telephone's harsh ring out in the hallway. Mrs. Trent expected me to answer any calls, but never had anyone called quite this early.

"Mrs. Barrington?" said the operator's voice.

"Yes," I managed to reply, still groggy with sleep.

"Proceed with your call, sir," the operator continued, followed by a loud click as the connection went through.

"It's Ory," said a raspy voice. Loud static almost obliterated the man's words and then gradually cleared. I wasn't sure if this person was Ed Ory himself or someone looking for him.

"Yes," I answered. "Can I help you, sir?"

"Miss Hannah," the man coughed, his voice shaking. "No, no, it's me. It's Ory."

"What's happened, Ed?" I inquired quietly, shaking as I sat down on the stool next to the phone.

"They're gone!" he replied. "I don't know what ... where to ... oh God ..."

"Who's gone? Are you in Chicago? Are you with Emma in Chicago?"

"I came out here from Los Angeles 'bout a month ago or so. That was after she brought Tayvie up from New Orleans."

"Of course," I answered.

"But now they're gone!"

"When …" I began, but Ory interrupted.

"Y'see, I was workin' with Oliver. Eh, Joe Oliver, y'know? He had a one week band job down in Indianapolis. Paid more'n three times the regular, y'know? An' we had a good room, clean even, free food most the time. I just couldn' turn it down. No way to call an' there ain' no telephone at her place anyways. An' Emma understood that. But I came home an' she ain' here. I'm just prayin' she's down there. That she got mad at me for some reason an' took Tayvie an' left for New Orleans."

"I can go over to Felicité and Celeste's this morning, Ed. See if she's turned up. Can you call me at the Exchange this afternoon?" I had an important meeting with the benefactors of the Exchange later this morning to present our budget needs for the New Year and had intended to review a lot of numbers beforehand, but I erased that concern from my thoughts.

"But y'see, I … I really jes' don' think she's down there, Miss Hannah."

"Why not?"

"She'd been actin' real strange for at least a week before I even left. I mean, truth to tell, she's been actin' kinda strange the whole time I've been out here."

I thought of Emma's frightening diary entries.

"What do you mean by strange," I replied, trying to keep my voice as even as possible. I sat on the stool, shivering both from the chilly wind blowing through the hallway as well as my recollection of those frenetic entries.

"I … I can' say. Just strange. Like she ain' always there or somethin'," he sighed. I could hear that he was fumbling as he struck a match, undoubtedly to light a cigarette. "There're times she just stares at me with her mouth kinda just, I dunno, hangin' open like a … a dead fish or somethin'. Last time I saw her an' she did that I yelled at her an' kinda yanked her arm, y'know? Probably harder than I meant to, I gotta admit. Tayvie started cryin' too. But Emma wasn' even mad that I yanked her arm at all. Naw, in fact, she goes 'n says in this real weird low voice 'thanks that always helps,' but I dunno what in hell that meant now!"

"Is there anything else?" I asked. I wondered if they'd had a serious quarrel and he wasn't being completely honest about the status of their relationship.

"Oh, yeah, yeah, there is," he answered, taking a long drag on his cigarette. "Tayvie's red coat, her hat 'n scarf, mittens an' boots are gone."

Well, that would make sense, I thought to myself. As cold as it was here in New Orleans right now it had to be far worse up in Chicago!

"But y'see, Emma's coat? It's still hanging right over the back of her chair, kinda just slopped over to the side, in a heap. I swear same's when I left for the trip. Her hat's stuffed part way into the pocket an' kinda bulgin' out the top like a ... a bad sausage or somethin'. I dunno why I said that. But her boots are here. An' her thick scarf. An' all of their other things are here too, y'know? Tayvie's favorite bedtime books an' little animals, Emma's hairbrushes and all that black eye stuff, their suitcases. Everything. I think the only thing of Tayvie's that's gone's this toy parrot she insisted I buy her a couple weeks back."

I swallowed hard, momentarily closing my eyes.

"An' there ain' no food in this place either. I mean nothin'. No bread, no coffee, no milk, no cheese, not even a goddamned cube of sugar. Nothin'!" He had started crying.

"Ed, Ed," I finally interjected. "Did you just get back in town? If so, go back to her place to get some sleep. Please. You sound exhausted. I'll get over to Felicité's this morning. Surely one of them will be home. Call me at the Exchange this afternoon, yes? Do you have that phone number with you?"

"Yeah," he replied weakly. "I do. I'll call you then."

Borrowing his usual expression to end a call I said with far more cheerfulness than I felt, "So long. I'm sure there's an explanation."

There was a pause. "Yeah. Yeah. So long." We both hung up.

Celeste was home, but Emma hadn't been there. Neither girl had heard anything from her since she'd taken Tayvie up to Chicago almost two months ago. I tried to rationalize the various possibilities. What if she and Tayvie had only left Chicago within the last day or so? There was nothing to indicate that they had actually been gone the entire week, meaning they might yet turn up down here. But the fact that Tayvie's coat was missing, Emma's was flung over the chair, no suitcases had been packed and not a scrap of food could be found simply didn't add up. During the entire meeting with the benefactors that morning, various ugly scenarios continually played out in my head resulting in more than one of the board members commenting on my decidedly distracted attention.

When Ory called I was reluctant to tell him that Emma hadn't shown up in New Orleans, however, I'd already made up my mind that I was going to take the next available train to help search for them. I had no idea how difficult obtaining a seat might be with Christmas only a few days away. Ory, however, actually laughed at my suggestion which completely threw me off guard.

"What's so funny?" I had replied, frowning.

"An' just how d'you think a white lady can help with lookin' for a colored girl an' her baby up here in Bronzeville, Miss Hannah?" he snorted. "What, you gonna prowl aroun' in blackface? Nobody'd even talk to you. An' people'd know you's white anyway."

"Blackface, yes," I replied, slowly piecing together an idea. "But ... not brown stain."

"What in hell's that?"

"When I worked on costumes for the Opera House, we

used to boil pecan shucks to dye all of the men's vests and hats, other materials too. You had to be very careful not to let your hands get stained because it would take weeks for it to finally wear off. Do you remember Adele and Aline, those two white Creole girls that worked with us?"

"Uh, no. Sorry. What about 'em?"

"One time, on a dare from Emma as I remember, Adele took a wide brush coated with the stain and painted a long streak on the inside of her arm. It took several weeks to fade off. And it looked very normal."

Ory said nothing. Then after clearing his throat, he added authoritatively, "pecans get harvested by October in New Orleans, Miss Hannah. You ain' gonna find no shucks this late in December, y'know."

"Ordinarily no," I agreed. "But we've had a lot of cloudy, real rainy weather in August this year. A lot of the crop is just split open on the ground, ruined. No pecans formed at all, just the shucks. I see mounds of them oozing brown stuff everywhere almost every day."

"Huh," he muttered.

"I have the next ten days off on holiday, Ed. I can help you. I've run away from my responsibilities all of Emma's life. And Tayvie's. I don't intend to let that happen again. Please understand."

"Hannah ... I mean, Miss Hannah," he sighed, "you ain' got no idea how to act like a colored woman. Or more exactly, you don' know how people will act back at you. It's ... very ... different. No respect, y'know what I mean?"

"I guess I'll find out. And you forget that I was practically raised by Zuma."

"Yeah, well, Zuma was different. She was Zuma, what can I say?"

"Agreed. And you know she would've wanted me to go looking for them."

"Hell, Hannah ... Miss Hannah," answered Ory, obviously exasperated with me. "Chicago's really a brutal place. An' Jesus it's cold! It's cold as hell up here right now, man! Not at all like New Orleans, y'know?"

"Probably more like the mountains of Colorado where I grew up I expect," I countered. "I still have my warmest coat mothballed in my trunk in fact."

"You're serious. Oh man. I dunno what you're thinkin' you can do anyway."

"Yes. I'm serious." There was a long pause as he took a long, very audible drag on his cigarette. I was certain he would be continuing with all of the many reasons that I couldn't possibly pull off this entire endeavor. "I can ask questions of neighbors, women that is, local shops, people she's been working with. We probably need to alert the police. Follow up on any leads. Someone out there must have seen them. But I can't just stay here doing absolutely nothing. I just can't!"

"Jes' so you know, lookin' for black women or their kids ain' never been a real high priority for your typical Chicago flatfoot, ma'am."

I made no reply.

After another few seconds pause he began speaking again, sounding something like a scolding parent. "Well, here's a samplin' of what you're gonna be up against if you try this, ma'am. For startin', you know, on the train there's white an' colored sections. Usually different cars although not always. But you may have to move to another car when you cross the various state lines. Every state has its own rules an' such. The conductor might not come through an' tell you, but if everyone else's movin' you moves your ass along too. Don' fall asleep. You might miss it. Get arrested. An' there's no heat in the colored cars. Then, there's different, uh, you know, washrooms at the depots."

"Yes, I'm aware of that." Thank you President Wilson for

your endearing equality decrees.

"All right, an' there's, uh, also separate entrances to the train station, in fact, there's separate entrances to most public buildings, you know, an' separate ticket offices an' waitin' rooms at the station. Sometimes that ain' so well marked or the sign's been torn down. The sign for how to get to that other entrance. They'll take 'em down just as kind of a joke, y'see? So you gotta be real careful 'cause they're tryin' to trip you up, y'see. An' if you end up in the wrong place you could, uh, get arrested an' spend a fair amount of jail time while you're just waitin' for your case to come up. No lawyers to take your case, y'know? A lot to watch for."

"Yes, of course." How had I never been aware of any of this before? Sadly, I knew the answer to that question: ordinarily, it simply wasn't any of my concern.

"An' then, y'know, you can be stopped any time an' be, uh, forced to state your purpose, that is, your reason, for bein' in a certain place at any given time. An' if they don' like your answer, well, you can be arrested for that too. You gotta take all your own food on the train. An' don' forget plenny water. The colored drinkin' fountains are always filthy at train depots. Never get cleaned. Oh, an' don' take a chance at gettin' off after sunset at a train stop even to stretch your legs or nothin'. There's sundown laws all the way up to Chicago these days."

I took a deep breath, hoping to camouflage my increasing anxiety, and finally asked for their address.

"We're at the Mecca Flats, apartment 63, closer to 31st at State," he said. "If you can get here in the daytime you can just walk over to Michigan Avenue. There's a bus heads south, but that wind's somethin' fierce! Wear everythin' warm you got, lemme tell you! Oh, an' the sign's ripped off at the bus stop, but just stand with the other black folks, y'know. But if the train gets here at night don' walk all the way over to Michigan. When you come outta Union Station there's only one black cab stand an' it's a couple blocks down Canal St. Be real careful. Walk with some other women an' their men if at all possible. Nasty stretch. A lot of thugs with knives that would as soon cut ya as kiss ya."

"If you're trying to frighten me you're doing an excellent job of it, Edward Ory," I replied with a strangled attempt at a laugh.

"Here's the most important thing you need to know, Miss Hannah," he stated soberly, just before hanging up. "Bein' white's a helluva lot easier, y'know?"

*"You writin' music?*
*It ain't relaxin' to write it, man, only to play it!"*
~ **Louis "Satchmo" Armstrong ("Paris Blues" 1961)**

# Chapter 16: Tayvie's Coat – Chicago, December 1923

The train ticket prices were almost doubled for the few remaining days until Christmas and there were no seats left in the white section of any train until after the first week of January. Undoubtedly because of the increased pricing, however, there were seats available in the colored section on the northbound train leaving very early the next morning and scheduled to arrive late the following night in Chicago. I had gathered a full basket of the shriveled pecan shucks hoping they would still produce the desired stain, unearthed my camphor-exuding rabbit fur coat as well as assorted dreadfully out-of-fashion woolen garments and undergarments from my trunk, and canvassed my favorite French Quarter markets to purchase cheeses, a salami, a small loaf of bread and three oranges for my trek north.

After Mrs. Trent had retired for the evening, I boiled the shucks for the stain hoping that this idea would actually work. Fortunately, she was expecting her son's arrival on tomorrow afternoon's train from Oklahoma, so my leaving was not in any way an issue. She was a demanding woman and, of course, just supposed to be my landlady and not my employer, although she often seemed a bit muddy on that distinction.

For whatever reason, I began slowly painting myself with the stain lit only by several candles, reflecting mysteriously in the hallway's dark cheval mirror. Up until that moment I hadn't considered this as some kind of bizarre ritual, but it now took on that distinct manifestation. Monsieur Autruche, sadly molting yet again, had curiously elected to join me. He quietly jumped up on the stool near the telephone, tilted his head sideways and watched silently, his beady black eyes scarcely blinking. Shivering, despite the fact that the stain was still warm, I attempted to paint while clad in a short cotton chemise with thin straps, but soon realized that this approach was ridiculous after having painted both legs. I yanked the chemise off over my head and stood completely nude in front of the mirror, my dark gold curls piled up high on my head.

There stood a white woman with two long brown legs. I stared for several minutes and then continued to carefully paint upwards. Months of tedious brush work at the Opera House had long steadied my hand, trusting to the blending of each stroke to its successor. My buttocks, my stomach, my breasts, my chest and as much of my back as I could reach, gradually warmed to a bronzed hue. Ironically, the parts I couldn't reach were the permanently raised welts and scars from Mrs. Hughes' vicious belt that had slashed into my skin all those years ago. I continued painting down my arms, around my neck, careful to get none of the stain on my palms which I knew needed to stay lighter. How well I knew that unusual fine line of demarcation from tracing it along Tayvie's sweet little hand! And finally my face. The woman whose large deep grey eyes were reflecting back from the mirror was unknown to me. She was a shadowy composite, a frighteningly ethereal image of Emma and me.

Monsieur Autruche, who had not sung one note in my presence since Tayvie's departure, began very quietly to sing *"Eh la Bas"*. He then flew to my head, gently kissing my hair, jumped down to the floor and walked silently back out to his perch. As I watched his stately exit, I carefully removed several tiny pearl-like feathers off my cheek and shoulder that seemed almost like tears. He knows, I thought. He knows our Tayvie's in trouble.

*****

I almost failed to even make it out of the train station in New Orleans the next morning. My carpetbag dragging heavily against my hip, my hair pulled tightly back into a twisted knot hidden by a faded wrapped scarf, I had paid for my ticket at the correct office and was waiting in the correct waiting room, which was already quite overcrowded well over an hour in advance. Everyone sat quietly on the splintered, well-worn benches in the waiting room, heads bowed, looking down at their hands except for one young mother, silently nursing her infant, a rag thrown discretely over her breast. I walked over to a small table just inside the door where there were a few tattered train schedules. As I picked up one of the schedules a baton suddenly snapped loudly against my chest from the side. My first impulse was to yell at the guard who stood there, but caught myself just in time as I blinked back tears from the sting.

"Jus' what'n hell you think you're doin'?" the man growled, the baton raised eager to strike again.

I had already carefully replaced the schedule on the table and simply shook my head, staring at the floor.

"You got an answer for me?"

"Noth … nothing …"

"Nothing? Nothing? Nothing what?" he demanded, leering down into my face, his breath stinking of rancid onions.

"Nothing … sir," I replied quietly.

"Fold that paper back up! Way you found it! You didn' find it all messy like that, did you now?"

"No, sir," I said evenly, eyes down, carefully refolding the schedule correctly on the table.

"Sit down!" he ordered. "Over there! There's a seat right there for you, miss high an' mighty. You people is jus' dumb. Dumb! I swear I just do not get it."

Somehow after that unexpected confrontation, I managed the right car sections, right bathrooms and the right waiting rooms at two train transfer points. Unlike the conviviality of the well-lit white train cars, there was absolutely no conversation as everyone sat silently in the completely darkened car, looking out the dingy windows at the rapidly changing landscape. Only the young mother's infant began several small bouts of crying and the woman nervously calmed the child each time. We were almost in Chicago before I attempted to speak to my seatmate, a large dark woman who had clutched a heavy basket on her lap from which I never saw her extract so much as a morsel of bread during our entire journey. I had made a silent offer of a segment of orange and section of cheese to which she had sharply returned her gaze out the window, thoroughly ignoring me.

"I'm wondering if you might be walking down towards Michigan Avenue … to the, uh, streetcar or bus," I asked.

She scowled at me, rubbing her hand over her mouth for a moment.

"Yeah, mebbe," she admitted coldly, squinting sideways. "Who needs tuh know?

"I just need to get there, that's all," I replied, attempting a smile. "Can I walk with you?"

"No laws 'gainst it I knows of," she muttered, looking back out the window.

Ory had been right about the fierce winds. It was certainly far colder than I remembered during any blizzards in Colorado or Missouri! And this was just wind! What would it be like when there was snow stinging our faces as well? Just after we had crossed the river on an icy bridge that maniacally bounced underneath our feet from the traffic, we stopped in the sheltered entrance walkway of a building and hastily put on every sweater and jacket we owned. We than wrapped our wool shawls over our heads and heavy coats as we continued walking, heads bowed into the wind. Later, when she got off the bus, the woman thoroughly surprised me by grunting "Merry Christmas." Up until that point I hadn't even realized it was

Christmas Eve.

I got off at the next stop and walked over to State Street. A crush of very fashionably dressed black people, warm in their thick fur coats and hats, had threaded their arms through one another's against the cold as I passed them in the brightly lit streets. Hot jazz music poured out of the doors of many cafés and restaurants along the block. It truly felt like New Orleans ... except at least 100 degrees colder obviously. I asked for directions to Mecca Flats and was steered there without incident.

The four-story apartment building was luxuriously conceived with two large atriums in the interior wings and large, beautiful though quite dirty, skylights cut high into the ceiling. All of the upper levels sported ornate, wrought-iron balconies very similar to those in the French Quarter. As always when I encountered such architecturally intriguing designs, I wondered what Win Stratton, truly a master architect, would have thought of them. A favorite of newly arriving blues and jazz musicians to Chicago, Mecca Flats was rather sadly showing early strains of serious overcrowding, however. The biggest attraction was its proximity to "The Stroll," an area extending many blocks down to 39th Street where all of the best black or black-and-tan cabarets, cafés, bars, dance halls and music shops were located. One could find jazz headliners like Louis Armstrong, King Oliver, Jimmy Noone, Jelly Roll Morton and countless others on any night of the week at the Dreamland, Royal Gardens, Plantation and Sunset Café. Emma had been working with Luis Russell recently at the DeLuxe Café.

Ory was nowhere to be found, but the landlady, upon the receipt of an outrageously-demanded five dollar tip, reluctantly opened Emma's apartment door for me. I walked into the dark apartment, grateful for the blissfully warm, albeit loud, gurgling and clanking accompaniment of the hot water radiators. I tugged at the pull chain for the overhead light in the kitchen and the bulb slowly warmed to a dull blue haze, bringing into focus a newer style icebox, tiny two-burner stove and a high-backed, white enamel sink with two very rusty spigots and containing only a large spoon. A board straddling a very small second sink held a pile of laundry, washed but simply thrown into a pile, rather than having been hung up to dry on the thin rope serving as a clothesline that was strung in front of the shelves. Tayvie's little dresses, sweaters and leggings had simply molded into one another in that pile. My throat tightened at the sight.

I closed the curtains in the adjacent living area, deposited my carpetbag and shed my outer clothing onto the couch. Just as Ory had described the scene, Emma's coat was still thrown over a chair at the table. I was exhausted, but strangely energized. I sat at the table devouring my one remaining orange, juice dripping through my fingers. If I could find Emma's most current journal, and I had no doubt she was still writing one, I was certain that I would be on the road to finding Emma and Tayvie. Since Emma had left her coat here in this kind of deadly weather, it was extremely doubtful that she would have taken along her journal.

I found the book, pages almost completely filled, on a low closet shelf in the bedroom and flipping through several pages began reading. Yet again, there were no dates, but after skimming through a few paragraphs I discovered an entry coinciding with Emma and Tayvie's trip to Chicago two months ago.

*"So tired, so cold. Bones just ache down inside themselves sometimes. But so happy to see my little Tayvie finally! She looks more like Edward every day. That sweet brown sugar face. But hard to get her to talk. She's so shy. That's the saddest part. I've been away too long my little one, but I will make all of that up to you. With your daddy. With Edward. He's meeting us when we get back to Chicago -- <u>finally</u>! It's not final his being separated from Dort (what kind of name is "Dort"-- donkey snort?), but he's going to give all of us living together in Chicago an honest try he says. Have to trust he means it.*

Know he does. <u>I just know he does.</u> Louis is up here & Joe Oliver & so many others like Johnny Dodds & Jimmie Noone — all these amazing musicians that E had in his bands back in N. O. <u>Made all of those men famous in his own band!</u> Chicago LOVES hot jazz! Just know Edward can put together a band that nobody else can touch! Just know it!"

I skipped through several pages.

"This train is so dark now -- a black velvet curtain. Tayvie scared, whimpering a lot -- can't get her to shut up. Can't make her understand if she doesn't shut up we'll get thrown off. That sweet little brown face & huge bright brown eyes -- like a little puppy. Ma chere petite — je t'aime toujours, toujours! So hard to hear her little voice over & over & over. Maman, j'ai froid, moi again & again, Maman, j'ai froid, moi, Maman, j'ai froid moi. Please, mama! Please mama! J'ai froid, moi! J'ai froid! J'ai froid! S'il te plait, maman! & I know she's cold, I know it. We both are. There's no heat in this cattle car & she has no warm clothes yet. Wrapped her in some of my long shawls & sweaters but keeps sniffling. Tell her to be quiet or will get in trouble. If we're thrown off don't have money to even buy a loaf of bread.

At a depot, maybe Indiana, went outside for better air. My left hand started shaking real bad again & Tayvie asked what's wrong & I told her that I was just cold too. Stopped soon after. Lucky. Usually goes on for hours even days. Awful.

Saw this white girl, few years older than Tayvie, had long blond sausage curls & glittery headband get on the dining car. Had on this burgundy wool coat w/ black velvet bands at collar, cuffs & hem & four huge black buttons in square on front. Tayvie said that was exact coat she wanted -- nice & pretty & so warm. She fell asleep on my shoulder but crying out she was cold & shaking hard.

Sometimes food's left in the dining car at night & the staff forgets to lock up. Maybe sugar cubes or biscuit hidden behind the napkins or cigs have rolled away you can sell. Snuck into the car after midnight — checked no one's guarding behind half wall. Whistle blew -- scared me to death. Maybe deer on tracks. 2 sugar cubes on chair & good teabag. Busted up cigarette. Nasty so let stay.

*Then saw it -- that burgundy coat on floor behind chair. Just left there. Forgotten. Not needed. Thrown down. Picked it up & saw this fancy green label sewn in said **'This is Helen Mason's coat'**. If this white girl Helen Mason could forget her coat in the dining car she must not need it much I decided & hid it under my coat. Also a black knitted hat & mittens tucked into the sleeve. Nice. Put it around my Tayvie when got back to our car & put shawls over to hide it. My baby finally stopped shivering, stopped whimpering, smiled, put her thumb in her mouth & slept into next day. Hardly ever stolen in my life. But didn't think different for 1 sec about taking that stupid Helen girl's coat for my little Tayvie."*

I closed her diary for a moment, rubbing my forehead, wondering if I should continue reading. What if Emma happened to walk in on me right now, snooping in this very private information? In the distance I heard the church bells starting to peal midnight. It was now Christmas Day I realized. I heard a man's voice on the outside stairs and thought it might be Ory's, but the footsteps continued up the stairs past me to one of the apartments on the next level. A door squealed open then slammed shut and the firm steel latch dropped with a small clunk into place. I flipped forward through several more pages, almost to the last page of Emma's entries, now a rambling barely legible scrawl, and continued reading.

*"Here's what happened. Writing now while can remember, WHAT can remember. Sitting on floor. Behind the table. Behind the chair. Against the wall. Know this but can't move. CAN'T MOVE! Can't blink unless work very hard to make eyes blink. Staring and I see but at same time don't see. Don't see. I don't see. How can this possibly happen? My eyes see but my brain doesn't see. How can a brain not see? My arm is reaching out to her. It won't bend. Like a fence post. Won't bend. I know all of this. Remember all of this. Breathing hard inside. Outside not at all & can't speak! Can't speak! Can't speak! Oh dear God help me! Help me! Can't speak except uttering something like uh,uh,uh. She's crying so hard. She's pulling on my arm. Leve-toi,*

*maman! J'ai faim, moi! J'ai soif, moi! Maman! Maman! Leve-toi! S'il te plait! J'ai faim, moi! J'ai soif, moi! J'ai faim, moi! J'ai soif, moi! Maman! Maman! Maman! She's crying harder & harder. Tears running down her sweet little face & she's shaking. So hard. My poor sweet baby! Goes out of sight & then comes back. Has on red coat & hat & boots - & toy parrot E just got. Je vais nous trouver du pain, Maman. Eh, bread, oui? Je vais y aller, Maman! T'inquiete, Mama! & she's kissing me. & she goes out the door! Hear her little boots on steps. Call but only uh, uh, uh! comes out. E says have a big voice but now only stupid brainless monkey uh, uh, uh!*

*Awake now. Writing what remember. Don't know how long she's gone or what day now. E's in Ind. Still. I think. Can't tell him these black trances for day. Tayvie. lost. When legs stand must go. Look find. <u>Still</u> <u>Can't Walk</u>. Hardly hold pencil. Has to be in building. Please, God! Let her be here. Will knock on every door. Every door. She has to be here somewhere.*

*Oh God, what am I going to do if she isn't?"*

Emma's journal ended there.

> *"In the summers I was around*
> *the fields and woods of the plantation…*
> *fishing in the Mississippi River from the banks of the levee*
> *and doing all of the hundred and one things*
> *that any child of that time could and would do."*
> Edward "Kid" Ory

## Chapter 17: The Dunning Institute, Chicago 1923-24

My tears soaked through the page almost obliterating Emma's last sentence as the Christmas church bells continued chiming throughout the city heralding the miraculous birth of our savior. I finally looked over to Emma's coat thrown over the opposite chair. It had simply been forgotten there because as soon as Emma had gotten any feeling back in her legs, she had gone out knocking on all the Mecca Flats' doors looking for Tayvie … sweet little Tayvie who had donned her favorite coat and in desperation, ventured out to look for something to eat. But neither of them had returned, meaning Tayvie hadn't found anyone in the Flats able to give her any food. Since the child spoke so few words in English, that most likely further frustrated her search. If Emma had found her I was convinced that they would have returned to this apartment. She wasn't running from Ory over some possible slight. She was very ill I realized, undoubtedly from some kind of horrible drug she'd gotten hooked on years ago it seemed at this point, and was desperately trying to locate her little girl.

A key turned in the lock and Ory walked in, backlit from a harsh security light on the landing. Wearily, he set down his trombone case and music folder next to the door and started to unbutton his coat before he saw me sitting at the table.

"Emma?" he whispered.

"No, Ed," I replied quietly. "It's Hannah. I had the landlady unlock the door for me a few hours ago." I considered going over to hug him, but an overwhelming inertia kept me rooted to the chair.

He hung up his coat on a peg near the door and walked over towards me, pulling a short stool to the table.

"I honestly didn't recognize you," he shrugged, then adding with a slight cough, "y'know you'd make a damn fine black lady."

I had completely forgotten about the stain I had so carefully applied just a couple nights ago. I slowly pushed Emma's diary over towards him. "Here, Ed," I said gently. "This may tell us something about what's happened."

Ory glanced at the book and then turned his head away slightly to look at the wall.

"I, uh, don' like readin' in English," he stated, clearing his throat. "I'm good with music readin' most times an' French since my daddy taught me French. Unlike Emma I didn' have a great teacher like you. Part way into third grade I was already workin' the water wagon, y'know, takin' water out to the men in the rice an' sugarcane fields. Readin' English was never too important, y'see."

He then looked back over at me with those brown eyes, his sad expression so much like Tayvie's. I walked over to him. Pulling his head gently to my chest I began reading out loud to him as I had done to so many of my beloved brown-skinned babies, Emma's classmates at the Mary Stratton School, for so many years. Ory and I were close to the same age, but he had somehow always seemed like a child to me. I stroked his hair, not with a lover's touch, but with a mother's, as I read. I barely managed to utter Emma's last written line *Oh God, what am I going to do if she isn't?* By then we were both in tears.

"I was sure that they were stayin' with some friend of hers or somethin'. That she was just angry with me about … God knows what," he mumbled hoarsely. "*Qu'est ce que je vais faire?*"

I stepped away from him and shut the journal. "We need to go to police headquarters as soon as it's daylight. Do you know where it is?"

"Yeah, I do know actually," he nodded, rubbing his hands over his face. "What in hell's wrong with her, Hannah?"

"My thought was … drug addiction," I replied quietly. "We don't know what she might have gotten into … even years ago. Maybe at that awful Lulu White's place."

"I doubt nothin' occurred at old fat Lulu's," Ory refuted, shaking his head. "She woulda had those girls' heads skewered backwards on a hog platter chompin' a red apple before she'd let 'em get into any of that kinda shit, y'know? For a brothel, Lulu ran a high-class place."

I made no reply as I walked back over to my chair and wearily sat down again.

"Besides, I've been livin' with her here for almost a month an' I ain' never seen her gettin' into any shit. She don' drink much either. Maybe a glass of red wine or a beer or two every great once in a while, but that's it."

I thought it best to avoid mentioning that she would have been alone on nights that he was working and she was home, maybe after having put Tayvie to bed. And I had seen her very drunk or high on some kind of substance when my husband had been arrested. Somehow I was certain that Ory most likely had seen her in that condition back in New Orleans as well. But that was before she'd gotten pregnant with Tayvie. I wanted to think that once her daughter was born that all of that had ended. But obviously, I was wrong.

"Where did Tayvie stay when Emma was working at night?" I asked. "She didn't take her along, did she?"

"Actually, I think she did most times. Least that's what Luis

Russell said. He said she'd just fall asleep behind him next to the wall while they were workin'. He also says he's never seen Emma gettin' into anythin' when she performs either, not even after her set. Well, before she was fired anyway. She got fired from that DeLuxe Café a couple of weeks ago 'cause she was a no-show too many times Luis said an' he just couldn' cover for her any more. I found that out when I was first lookin' for her a few days ago. Fact she's been fired a lot over the last seven or eight months for bein' a no-show."

Ory paused, shaking his head. "But Luis also said he'd never seen drug fiends or any of that sort hangin' aroun' tryin' to sell her any shit either. An' he can always spot when those boys get their meat hooks into another dame. He's seen enough of them blues sluts half seas over to know when they're high."

Blues sluts. Was that actually what Ory or Luis Russell or Jelly Roll Morton or any other male musician considered these young women singers trying to get ahead in their careers? Suddenly I realized I didn't want to hear any more. I was absolutely exhausted.

"Ed … I'm … going to try to get a few hours of sleep. You maybe should do the same." I curled up in my coat on the coach. Despite my thoughts still chaotically churning, I was asleep within minutes only vaguely aware that Ory remained sitting at the table, watching me, smoking a cigarette in the dark.

Chicago was hit with a deep snowfall overnight. We weren't able to begin our trek to police headquarters until well after noon, once the streetcar tracks had been cleared sufficiently. Ory had insisted that I read as much of Emma's diary entries as possible to him during the morning hours as we waited for the winds to stop howling. He made us coffee and offered to fix up a couple of eggs, but neither of us was hungry. When I read the section that Ory's coming out to Chicago might well be a permanent arrangement and that he was leaving his wife, Ory muttered an expletive under his breath and I stopped reading.

"I told her it was a trial, Hannah," he shook his head, lightly drumming his fingers on the table and then stood up and began pacing, running his fingers through his thick mahogany hair. "I told her that. I really did. I told her that I maybe wasn't gonna be able to stay around too long 'cause I would have to get back to California. I'm just here kinda testin' it out right now. Playin' out here, y'know. Seein' how the money is, y'know? I mean, Dort and me could still move out here. But somethin' *real* good would have to be in the works for me to actually come out here to live!"

I nodded. "You maybe weren't going to be able to stay," I repeated quietly, emphasizing the word 'maybe.'

"She knew that, dammit! She knew that! My band's still back in L.A., y'know? I left 'em with Papa Mutt … eh, you know, Mutt Carey, in charge. Temporary arrangement, y'know? I'm just fillin' in, playin' with people out here right now. A sideman, a total nobody. But she wanted me to finally meet Tayvie. Maybe she thought my bein' a father would mean I would come out here to work an' live with her. I dunno. Tayvie's just as sweet as can be. An' just so shy, poor little thing. She was finally startin' to get used to me, but I don' think she's been around many men in New Orleans an' I think I … well, kinda scared her sometimes. But, even so, hell, if nothin' else, at least the weather's better in California an' Emma knew that without ever havin' been out there! Nobody in their right mind would want to actually live in Chicago if they had a choice!"

"Ed, does your wife even know about Tayvie?" I ventured. "Does she know that Emma's in Chicago? For that matter, does she know about Tayvie or even Emma directly at all?"

"Eh, directly?" replied Ory, scratching his ear self-consciously. "Uh, no. Not, er, directly. Dort knows I was *seein'* somebody back in New Orleans … well, she usually kinda knows when I'm seein' somebody …"

"And is she usually correct?" I inquired boldly,

exasperation fueling my question.

Ory smiled rather sheepishly and looked down at his hands. "There's a lot of temptation out there, Miss Hannah," he finally replied, glancing at me. "I ain' makin' any claim to be better'n most men, especially musicians, given those kinda, er, well, temptations, y'know?"

"But your wife keeps forgiving you."

"I don' ask for forgiveness exactly," he shrugged. "She loves me for who I am. Faults an' all."

"Ed, do you even love my daughter?" I suddenly blurted out. "And your own daughter?"

"Of course!" he replied quickly. "How could anyone not love Emma? She's beautiful, she has a great voice, she's real smart, she's mostly sweet natured … and I'm just gettin' to know Tayvie! *Ma foi,* Miss Hannah! I can't make promises 'bout anything to either of 'em! I've got my music to think about. My work an' so forth and so on, y'know? Emma knows that. She understands all that!"

I closed my eyes, shaking my head slightly. Undoubtedly if Emma ever ended up with Ory she would be in exactly the same position as Dort now: constantly putting up with her husband's endless indiscretions if she wanted to have him in her own bed occasionally. Unless she had changed quite a lot, I really just couldn't see her willingness to agree to such. In many ways, I had been just like Dort I surmised. A naïve, completely ignorant fool, I had desperately tried to please everyone within my own world, clinging to the shreds of perceived respectability without realizing the utter futility of said task. Quite unlike me, however, Elizabeth "Dort" Ory truly loved her consistently philandering husband. Many women simply expected it; many men simply took full advantage of those expectations.

When we arrived at the police headquarters later that day the place was practically deserted. Since it was still Christmas Day, the saloons, gambling joints and dance halls were closed, so police business was blissfully slow. A pale young man, Officer O'Keefe, with an unruly thatch of bright red hair and one of the strongest Irish brogues I'd ever encountered, took down the details of our report. I was reluctant to talk about Emma's shaking spells and prolonged blackouts, but Ory felt it was important that we include that information. Officer O'Keefe wanted to know if we'd looked into any of the hospitals. Well, at least over at Provident since that was the only colored hospital in Chicago he admitted. He asked if we would like to have him place a call over to the city's morgue also. He didn't like asking such things, but since so much time had elapsed since Emma and Tayvie's disappearance he felt it important to do so. Reluctantly we agreed. After several minutes on the telephone located at the back of the investigations room, O'Keefe reappeared with a slip of yellow paper.

"They don't have anyone matching an Emma Jackson's description," he stated. "But, uh, they did take in an unidentified little black girl a couple nights ago and are waiting any further notice. So far no next of kin or such has come forward looking for her. No missing persons filed. Here's the identification number for the morgue clerk. But I should tell you that her skull was bashed in. Pretty bad they said. Somebody hit her with a brick or a rock probably. Poor kid. Won't be pretty to look at."

"How far is the morgue?" asked Ory evenly.

"Just a couple blocks. You can walk it," nodded the officer. "Uh, if it does turn out to be her, I'm real sorry asking, of course, but if you could come back over to let me know that would save me a lot of paperwork I need to fill out. You know since she wouldn't be … uh, missing … anymore."

"Yeah, sure," Ory somehow managed to reply.

The snow, still blowing, had drifted over streets and sidewalks once again, making our walk to the morgue treacherous. I started to walk towards the front door but Ory immediately cautioned me, shaking his head and pulling me back. "This most likely has a back entrance. Seemed odd to me that the police headquarters didn't, I have to admit. But in Chicago ... eh, who knows?"

There was no sign designating that the front entrance was for whites only, but just as Ory had surmised, there was indeed a back entrance with a small battered sign reading 'colored'. We knocked several times before someone finally opened the door. We were led through a large, cold white room lined with long, dark metal basins, with sheets drawn up over most of the basins revealing only the top of a person's head. There was a far more crowded, smaller room further back. Even in death they were segregated I thought bitterly. The clerk checked a couple of tags at the end of the metal basins and then brought us to the end of one row. Dark reddish-black hair was visible above the sheet and part of a wool plaid material, probably a skirt, to the side. I closed my eyes as the clerk moved the sheet from the girl's face, tightening my grip on Ory's arm.

"It's not her, Hannah," Ory relayed gently, putting his arm around my shoulders. "It's not Tayvie. You don't have to look if you don' want to, but it's not her."

I did finally open my eyes. A huge part of the little girl's skull was crushed on the side, her black hair matted with dried blood, her horrified expression frozen in that split second of time her attacker had struck. No, it wasn't Tayvie. But she was someone else's little girl. Someone else's beautiful little girl who would never laugh again or skip to the park crunching through orange and red leaves on a bright autumn day or maybe sing along with her favorite parrot or play butterflies in the meadow with her grandmama. I was sick at the sight and turned my head away. That meant she was still out there. Somewhere. Anywhere. Hopefully still alive. Maybe with Emma. But probably not.

The clerk carefully pulled the sheet back up over the child's face. "Well, I'm glad it's not your little girl," he mumbled, looking back at us as we started retracing our steps towards the larger room. "Don't know if O'Keefe mentioned that you should try the orphan asylums as well. They're always takin' kids in off the street. Kids just get abandoned or lost all the time. Wander all over beggin' for food. Parents sometimes just forget they have 'em. Or mom thinks grandma has 'em an' she thinks an aunt has 'em an' she thinks the stepdad has 'em an' so on and so forth. Hard to understand, but it happens all the time."

"Where would we find the asylums?" asked Ory. "Seems like she couldn've made it too far on foot before someone would've well, maybe helped out, y'know? She's only four years old."

The man nodded. "Well, actually you might be surprised to learn there's quite a few. Some are for white kids only, but most of 'em take in everything luckily. There's your Children's Home and Aid Society. Huge operation. I think they've got places all over the state. They've got boarding houses, foster care for kids who need closer attention and such. Even have private trains running all the time to get the kids out of Chicago to their downstate locations to do a better job with sorting them out for adoption. Then there's your Catholic institutions more or less connected with the different parishes in the outskirts of the city. There are also quite a few forward-thinking Protestant groups -- Baptists mainly, I think --- running these cottages, as they call 'em. But again, most of these institutions aren't actually here in the city itself. Let me think. What else … well, there's also a boys school that occasionally takes in a few girls as well in Glenwood. Oh, and then there's Hedwig's, that a Catholic girls' orphanage, up in Niles. Course there's that Catholic boys' asylum out in Park Ridge as well, but guess you wouldn't be needin' to check that one out."

He gave us a small smile, extending his hand to shake Ory's as we all paused at the back door. "They're trying to make smaller buildings rather than those big institutions those poor kids used to rattle around in all the time too. So wherever she is,

I'm sure it's a good place, so don't worry about that. But, I have to mention that I'm not real sure just how good some of their record keepin' is. Uh, please don' say you heard that complaint from me, however. You mentioned that your little girl doesn't speak much English so that could be mighty tough."

"Thanks," replied Ory.

"And definitely try Provident Hospital, see if they've got any leads for you," added the clerk.

Ory had an early afternoon rehearsal followed by a restaurant gig and then a late night dance hall engagement, all with different bands, the next day. We had agreed on my heading to Provident Hospital over on 36th Street early in the morning while he checked with the only two infant asylums actually within the city limits, both of which were located within a few miles of his band rehearsal. The day dawned bright with sunshine, but unlike the days following a Colorado snowstorm, the sun radiated no warmth whatsoever. Ory was right. No one in their right mind would actually live in Chicago.

The waiting room was filled with dozens of injured and seriously ill patients. One of the nurses finally called me into a staff office saying she would send one of their community volunteers down to help me as soon as possible. None of the hospital employees would have any time to help me she apologized. The volunteer, surprisingly a middle-aged white woman who introduced herself as Mrs. Collier, brought along a cart with the admitting and outpatient treatment folders from the last couple of weeks. Page after page of people being treated for wound infections, ulcers, cancers, knife gashes, ingested poisons or medicinal overdoses, pneumonia … the list of those having been treated and their symptoms seemed endless. The person's age and sex were listed at the top of each new file so I eagerly volunteered my assistance to work through the folders, which seemed to surprise Mrs. Collier. Nothing showed up for Tayvie in the children's files, however, Mrs. Collier mentioned that she would be sending notice immediately to *The Chicago Defender*, the city's black newspaper with excellent circulation to those communities downstate as well. Two little boys who may have been brothers and a family of six children had been given over to the Children's Home and Aid, but unless Tayvie was masquerading as one of those children, nothing fit her description. We were almost at the end of the paperwork for the adult patients when Mrs. Collier pulled one sheet out of a folder.

"Well, this looks like it may be ... promising," she stated, adjusting her glasses.

I held my breath as she continued reading.

"A very light-skinned young black woman, with dark blue eyes, quite thin, thoughts were she might be Jamaican actually it says here. She was found lying on the floor in one of the park's public men's bathrooms. Person who found her thought that she had frozen to death. You see those bathrooms are closed this time of year," she added, looking over the top of her reading glasses at me.

"So she may have been there for awhile, it's difficult to tell," Mrs. Collier continued slowly, shaking her head.

"Go on. Please," I urged her, my hand stretching across the desk towards her.

"Well, according to these entries they brought her in and couldn't get her to wake up, although she was able to swallow a little soft food that they later fed her. The assumption was that she had overdosed on some kind of drug that had paralyzed her, at least temporarily. Ah, then it looks like she awoke later that night and started shrieking and violently throwing herself against the wall. Ended up bruising herself quite badly while the attendants struggled with her. She had to be restrained with harnesses and then like a 'candle was snuffed out' according to a nurse, she became completely inert again, staring into nowhere."

Mrs. Collier paused for a moment then continued. "We have a very small, badly overcrowded hospital here, as I'm sure you've noticed, Mrs. Barrington," she sighed. "The young woman was sent the following morning over to Dunning to see if they could do anything for her since it was obvious we simply weren't ... sufficiently equipped to help."

"Dunning?"

"Well, it was called Dunning until a few years back. Now it's Chicago State Hospital, but everyone still calls it Dunning. It's over on the far northwest side of the city."

"And they ... take ... black patients, I assume?"

"Dunning is an insane asylum, Mrs. Barrington," Mrs. Collier replied, carefully removing her glasses and beginning to polish them with her handkerchief. "The asylum houses all races. Odd that one has to be insane to truly be treated equally don't you think?"

I shook my head slightly but made no reply, stretching my arms out even farther along the top of her desk, my hands folded together, head bowed. Both of us were silent for several moments.

"You know, I might add," she continued, gently placing her hand over my wrist, "you've quite a good disguise. It's certainly none of my business why you are, of course. But it's rather obvious. At least to me, that is. You see if nothing else, a black woman in the presence of a white woman would be far more uncomfortable than you appear to be. Also, she would have kept her hands tightly folded in her lap when not looking at the folders and would have been quite reluctant to look at the folders at all to be quite honest."

"Ah," I replied with a nod, slowly retracting my arms far too late. Ory was right: I would certainly never be convincing at this.

She studied me quietly as she replaced her handkerchief in her jacket pocket and then began speaking again after a long moment.

"I started volunteering here many years ago, Mrs.

Barrington. And do you know why? When I was seventeen I ran away with a black man who worked as a drover for my family. I was desperately in love with Carl. Foolishly, we thought we could get married in the next state. When my father and several of his drunken Klan buddies found us, they lynched Carl right in front of me, throwing gasoline on him and lighting it as he shrieked to God and me for forgiveness. Our son was born less than two months later and I was told that he had been taken to a colored orphanage. But I found a funeral pyre of his little bones, poorly camouflaged with the pig manure my father had spread out in our garden just a few days after his birth. I left that day and have never spoken with anyone back in my hometown again. I have no idea if my parents or siblings or anyone else are even still alive. And I simply don't give a damn."

"I … I can't imagine how you …" I began, but my voice just trailed off.

"I have a very demanding full-time position as a legal researcher with one of Chicago's most prominent defense attorneys, Mrs. Barrington," the woman continued brusquely. "And I volunteer almost as many hours at this hospital. There are plenty of women my age out there making pointless speeches from the backs of trains or handing out badly printed leaflets in the marketplace or waving their pathetic little flags in parades. But you see I feel as though I'm doing far more good smack down here in the squalid trenches of life, Mrs. Barrington," she added.

I nodded with a slight smile.

"I will have to contact Dunning in order to schedule an interview and allow you to see the young woman in question. I'm quite certain the earliest they would be able to do so would be tomorrow morning."

"That would be excellent, Mrs. Collier. Thank you so much for all of your time. This hospital is extremely fortunate to have you. Also, please call me Hannah," I finally managed to utter, slowly pulling up my sleeves to my elbows and placing my arms over her desk once again. "And about the disguise ... the ... staining. It's made from boiled pecan shucks. That's what they call the soft shell surrounding pecans down in New Orleans. I used to work as a costumer for the French Opera House and this was how we dyed men's coats, hats and boots and such. On a dare one of the girls I worked with took a brush to the inside of her arm one day and the stain wore off gradually after a few weeks. That's what gave me the idea. I do have to wear a scarf over my ears though, because I did a dreadful job there and I must confess it's all fading away much faster than I expected."

"Well, I rather doubt you'll find pecan shucks up here," nodded Mrs. Collier, smiling slightly.

"No ma'am, I'm quite sure not."

"Tell me more about your daughter, Hannah," Mrs. Collier continued, sitting further back in her chair. "And your granddaughter."

"There's so much really," I said, slowly pulling my sleeves back down to my wrists. "I've made so many foolish errors throughout Emma's entire life."

"Such as?" she inquired gently. "I assume you were also involved with a black man?"

"No, actually I wasn't," I replied, shaking my head. "Well, not exactly. But he did tell me that his mother was a quadroon, probably an escaped slave in fact. And it never occurred to me ..."

"That having a child by him might result in your bearing a darker-skinned infant," concluded Mrs. Collier, finishing my sentence.

"No," I admitted. "It didn't. In fact he swore that he couldn't father a child at all! Win was quite a bit older, you see, and ... and ... terminally ill. He was a very serious alcoholic. He died two days after Emma was born. I was forced to make a decision whether to try to raise her on my own or marry another man and have my dear friend Zuma -- she was a Creole of color -- raise Emma. I also had another friend's abandoned white child named Alice with me who I ended up claiming as my husband's and mine. He gave me no choice and forced me to let Emma go. It's all just a convoluted mess really."

"Why on earth was this man so determined to marry you if I may ask?"

"Money, what else!" I replied dully. "Emma's father was a multi-millionaire named Winfield Stratton. Win had retained quite a few shares of stock for me in a huge gold mining operation he had sold to a group of London investors. John Barrington, the man I married, ended up acquiring all of those funds when we married, of course, laws on inheritance being what they are. I basically sold myself to Mr. Barrington in a rash attempt to remain respectable in good society. But the joke was on me. Upon Mr. Barrington's untimely death I learned he was actually married to someone else!" I concluded bitterly.

"But you were desperate to stay in Emma's life through all of this, yes?"

"Oh yes, yes, absolutely," I admitted. "I ... I started a colored children's school out in Missouri. She was far and away my brightest pupil, with a beautiful voice as well. I had been studying to be a singer when I was young, although I never had anything resembling the talent that Emma has. Not even close. Alice used to refer to Emma as my 'pet pupil' all of the time ... with considerable malice. Alice of course attended the white school."

"And I'll wager that eventually the two girls somehow figured it all out."

"Yes, ma'am," I replied sadly. "They did. There were several horribly ugly scenes a few years back."

"And might I ask just where's the father of Emma's child in all of this? You mentioned that both of you were searching for Emma and her little girl ... Tayvie, correct?"

"Yes, Tayvie. It's short for Octavie, which was Ed's mother's name. Ed's a musician – a jazz musician," I said. "He's out here from California right now, but it seems rather muddy whether he plans to stay in Chicago or return to Los Angeles sometime soon. The weather here isn't exactly winning that war I suspect."

"A jazz musician? Who does he play with?" she frowned. "If I'm not working my regular job or volunteering at the hospital, one is almost certain to find my husband and me at one of the black and tans, especially wherever King Oliver's Dixie Syncopators are performing."

I stared at her for a moment. "Well, actually, he's been filling in quite a bit with King Oliver's band since he's been out here. He plays trombone – Kid Ory."

"Your granddaughter is Kid Ory's child? *The* Kid Ory?" She stared at me wide-eyed with disbelief.

"Yes, ma'am," I answered slowly, quite surprised that she would know Ory at all. After all, the man had only been in Chicago for a few weeks and not even with his own band!

"My dearest Hannah, in my totally unbiased musical opinion, Kid Ory *is* jazz music. Frank and I thought so the very first time that we heard the man play!"

"I have to confess that the first time I heard him play many years ago I thought he was dreadful!" I admitted sheepishly.

> *"By that time I was gettin' ready,*
> *thinkin' about leaving Chicago.*
> *I didn't like Chicago so much,*
> *they had an influx of the different class of people*
> *that was invadin' Chicago at the time."*
> Ferdinand "Jelly Roll" Morton

## Chapter 18: Chicago 1923-24

It was easily after 3 a.m. when I heard Ory's key in the door. His inquiries at the two orphanages had turned up nothing. Since he didn't have a performance until later in the evening, he had the names of three Catholic asylums located just south or west of the city that he planned to investigate. Mrs. Collier had made an appointment for me at 9:30 a.m. at Dunning, but she had cautioned me that Ory should accompany me if at all possible. Somehow I knew the young woman in question was going to be Emma.

And for better or for worse, I was right.

The elegant stone building of Chicago State Hospital, formerly the Dunning Institute, presented a stately edifice from the exterior, but revealed a crumbling sea of overcrowded inhumanity from within. Mattresses lining the hallways reeked of urine. Ceilings were stained with concentric, modern art motifs where rusted metal pipes had leaked and walls oozed black, moldy daguerreotypes. Patients were either lying on the fetid mattresses or slumped down in large, battered upholstered chairs staring into space, having been given cocktails consisting of various mixtures of chloroform, morphine, opium and alcohol similar to a Mickey Finn. Maybe the outside world was experiencing the restrictions of Prohibition, but that certainly was not the case inside Dunning. For most of these people there was no treatment prescribed whatsoever. They would just be drugged until they finally died and then, long forgotten by remaining relatives, namelessly flung into one of the three unkempt cemeteries surrounding the property.

"*C'est l'enfer*... a fuckin' *pissoir*," muttered Ory under his breath as we followed the attendant down the series of hallways. The attendant opened an office and told us to take a seat, informing us that the assistant director would be along in a few minutes. The stench of disinfectant and formaldehyde burned my lungs and I had to take very small breaths. Large signs throughout the building strictly forbade any smoking materials, undoubtedly with good reason. The place would instantly burst into flames with the strike of a match surmised Ory. It was close to an hour before the director appeared, his frayed, grimy cloth coat flapping about his knees.

"Hell of a morning," he said, sitting down heavily behind his desk. "Why are you people here?"

"We're here to see if a young black woman brought here recently is my daughter," I said. "Mrs. Collier had made an appointment for us yester ..."

"Yes, yes," he interrupted, waving his hand in annoyance. "Those people over at Provident think we have nothing to do here but play guessing games trying to identify our patients."

"I have a copy of their report which I believe came with the girl when she was transferred over here," I replied, handing the folder over to the man who had yet to even introduce himself or ask our names. Although the man was white, I suspected that he treated everyone who showed up in his office exactly the same – his hostility deferring to no particular race.

His small eyes skimmed down the information on the report and he shut the folder, quickly thrusting it back over his desk in my direction. "And?"

"And we'd like to see her, sir," requested Ory firmly, who had been quiet until then. "To see if it's Emma Jackson."

The director picked up his telephone and dialed an extension, muttering about his wasted time while he was waiting for the double ring and a loud buzz following each ring to finally be answered."Yes, it's Dr. Andersson. Do they have all of those patients in ward seven down in the baths right now? Right. Yes. Yes, ward seven. No, not ten, you idiot, seven!"

He rolled his eyes and shook his head, looking down at his desk. "Yes, ward seven. Ok. Good. I'm sending two people over to see if they can identify a woman. I *know* they'll only be able to see her head, thank you, Miss Murphy!" He slammed the phone down and stood up abruptly, seemingly talking to the ceiling. "Morons. I'm completely surrounded by morons in this hell hole. *Hilf mir bitte!*"

Then facing us he stated, "The woman was placed in ward seven. That ward is in the basement in the continuous baths right now. You can look in the hall window to see if you think it's her, but you can't go into the room itself. It's not allowed."

"Could we wait until she's finished her, uh, bath?" asked Ory. We were both surprised to learn that the patients in this place would be getting a bath at all! Certainly those we'd seen lining the hallways had gone for an extended period of time without benefit of so much as a dab of spittle.

"This isn't *that* kind of bath," replied the director brusquely. "Continuous baths go on under a canvas strapped cover overnight or more likely run for several days usually. They're basically locked in up to their necks. It's one of the few ways we have of calming these people down there when they're out of control. Out of their minds, you understand. Ward seven is one of our most violent female wards. We need to isolate all of those women in separate cells."

The continuous baths were housed in a dimly lit basement area that was comprised of four long rows of bathtubs, supported underneath by a heavy metal framework. As the director had mentioned, all but the patients' heads were submerged beneath the canvas material that was boldly strapped down over the entire tub. This was to keep the heat walled in at a constant 98 degrees we were told. It would obviously be impossible for any of the patients to manage to crawl out of the tubs, we realized. In some cases the patient's eyes were hidden by a white blindfold as well. Metal tubes fed in quite low, from the outsides of the tub; no faucets or drains were in a place where a patient might be able to affect any controls by suddenly thrashing his head. Some of the patients had trays on top of the canvas and were being carefully fed by nursing students, who were fearful of being bitten.

Ory spotted Emma first. She was in the third row almost at the end of the tubs to our far right. Her head was wrapped in a thin bluish-white turban but not her eyes. Glassy-eyed, she stared into space scarcely blinking. Something about her skin seemed oddly luminescent, almost a greasy grey. Ory remarked on her odd color as well. One of the nursing students knelt down near her and asked a few questions, but there was no reaction of any kind on Emma's face. Her blue eyes, possibly dulled with some kind of drug, just continued staring straight ahead, her mouth hanging oddly open. The student worked to shut Emma's jaw, but was powerless to do so. The position seemed to be as rigid as a steel trap.

"Even if we can find Tayvie, there ain' no way Emma's gonna be able to take care of her," muttered Ory. "Maybe ever."

"I've already decided that I'm taking Tayvie back with me to New Orleans when we find her," I replied after a moment, glancing at him. "It only makes sense, Ed."

He looked at me with a slight frown, exhaling slowly, then looked down before speaking.

"Dort's really after me to come home Hannah," he said quietly. "So, I'm plannin' to go back home to California. I called her on Christmas, of course, y'know. She was cryin' an' all. I ... I can't stay up here much longer. There's always a chance that we'll come back if there's promise of some good payin' work for me … but, I just dunno …"

At that moment I realized that I would be quitting my position at the Exchange in New Orleans and moving up to Chicago to be with both Emma and Tayvie once we'd found her. Ory was about as dependable as the wind, as Zuma used to say, although I truly believed that he felt guilty in all of this.

Given Emma's diary entries, her descent into her current mental state had taken about three years, possibly longer. How much of this was reversible was anyone's guess. We filled out the paperwork identifying Emma in the Records Office and made an appointment to meet with the staff doctor of ward seven for the following day to discuss currently recommended treatments. The patients lining the halls were deemed completely hopeless we were informed; those in the various wards were younger and possibly treatable, with the emphasis on the word 'possibly'.

Making the most of the feeble daylight, we then walked out into the icy afternoon towards the streetcars, heading in two different directions to visit the three orphanages still remotely within the Chicago city limits. None of them had taken in any children matching Tayvie's description, however.

Later that evening, back along The Stroll after Ory stopped to pick up his trombone, we opted for a quick dinner at what was supposed to be a New Orleans' style restaurant that came up far short in Ory's opinion. How on earth anyone calling himself a chef could mess up a recipe as straightforward as red beans and rice baffled him. He'd already discovered that Chicago palettes were clueless with regard to anything involving seafood, but beans and rice? Unwilling to head back to that chilly, empty apartment, I agreed to go with him to his gig with King Oliver at the Dreamland. At Emma's apartment I knew that I would just continue searching her journals for possibly nonexistent clues regarding her illness. And I needed a break.

Not surprisingly, just before the band began performing, Mrs. Collier showed up. The club was already packed even though it was only a Tuesday night. An unpleasantly loud, grating blues singer accompanied by a questionably talented pianist had just finished their set, opening for the band. Mrs. Collier was pushing a man in a wheelchair, whom I assumed was her husband. I was sitting alone at a table far into the corner and waved at her hoping they might want to join me.

"I don't know how long I'm staying, Mrs. Collier," I said, "but if you're not meeting anyone else it would be lovely to have you join me."

"Frank, this is Hannah Barrington," she said close to his ear and then straightened up and said to me, "yes, that would be nice. And I'm Alma, by the way. Frank's a retired judge. He may seem a little slow, obtuse, and a tad hard of hearing at times, but trust me, little gets past those old white whiskers!"

I smiled as she kissed him affectionately on the cheek.

"And?" Mrs. Collier added, tilting her head looking at me. "How was the Dunning visit?"

"Yes, it's Emma."

She put her arm around me for a quick hug. Her husband now comfortably positioned at the table, his plaid blanket smoothed out over his legs, she pulled out her own chair and sat down. "Somehow I knew it would be and I also thought you might be here tonight. For now just try to listen and enjoy the music, Hannah," she said. "There's nothing more that you can do tonight."

The band started playing a few minutes later. Frank Collier knew the names of all of the selections and filled them in for me whenever Joe Oliver neglected to do so. They started out with several tunes that the band had recorded back in Richmond, Indiana earlier in the year – this was before Ory was out here, Frank informed me. Frank mentioned that he was one of the few people in Chicago who had actually managed to snag a copy of

Ory's recording of his *Creole Trombone* and *Society Blues*, a record that had been released almost exclusively on some obscure race label in California early last year. That's how he knew about Kid Ory in fact. As soon as he'd heard that Ory was going to be in town for a few weeks filling in with Oliver's Dixie Syncopaters, he made sure that Alma cleared everything possible from their schedules so they could get to as many shows as possible while the man was in town! In fact if I listened closely right now, there were those growling trombone parts in Oliver's version of *Snake Rag* that sounded just like those in Ory's own *Creole Trombone* Frank swore, as the band's rendition heated up.

I wondered if the Indianapolis trip that Ory had mentioned was a recording venture and Frank shook his head. Nobody was recording race records in Indianapolis, oddly just in Richmond, he stated. And the company doing those recordings out in Richmond wasn't the best in the business unfortunately. Very mediocre product sadly. Frank doubted it would stand the test of time. The recording industry was missing out on a very lucrative venture he added. The stuff was literally black gold! And whenever those sybaritic fools at the helm realized that and started putting a little cash up front behind those recording endeavors why, they would be struttin' down Easy Street attested Frank.

I had forgotten that Emma had mentioned in the diary I'd mailed back to her that Ory was supposed to be making a record in California. According to Frank, Ory's Creole Band was the first Negro band to release what was now referred to as a jazz music record – there had been several female blues singers backed by various black ensembles, Ory's included, of course, but Ory's record was the first actual instrumental music recording of its kind. Frank was hoping that there was truth to the rumors floating about these days that Jelly Roll Morton and Louis Armstrong were going to pull together some of the best New Orleans men to get that real gritty early jazz sound down on shellac sometime soon. Chicago was definitely the place to make all of that happen, Frank stated. No question there. The money was here, the audience -- black and white -- was here, the better recording equipment was here, and most importantly, the absolute best of all those early jazz musicians were here. New York jazz was ok, but Chicago's version of New Orleans jazz was unquestionably the best. Those guys had all grown up breathing this stuff practically from birth! Must have been in their mother's milk, he exclaimed! You don't just go out and take a couple cornet lessons and play like those New Orleans men!

During the band's first break Ory came over to talk with us. I introduced him to the Colliers and the two men immediately lapsed into an intense music discourse while sipping on excellent whiskey, courtesy of two large dull metal flasks concealed under Frank's plaid blanket. Alma and I joined them for one small glass as well as we listened to part of their conversation. I told her about Ory's and my discussion earlier that day.

"Oh dear Lord," Alma Collier replied, shaking her head as she gestured to the two men. "Whatever you do don't let Frank hear about that! He'll be first in line to buy any recordings that Kid Ory has with anyone in this town – Louis Armstrong, King Oliver, Jelly Roll Morton, Mutt Carey, Johnny Dodds ... I think even the man in the moon if he plays New Orleans jazz with Ory on trombone to tell you the truth! You know he heard Scott Joplin at the Exposition here in Chicago back in '93 and he's been absolutely nuts about ragtime piano and how that's just naturally fed into jazz music ever since. I bet he was the only white man in the audience at the Exposition, but that's my Frank. Didn't bother him in the slightest!"

I laughed lightly.

"Are you still working for the Opera House in New Orleans by the way?"

"No, actually it burned down to the ground just before

Christmas in 1919. In fact, Tayvie was born the night of that awful fire. There've been rumors swirling forever that it's going to be rebuilt, fundraisings and everything, but it's now been so long. I just don't know," I replied. "I've been employed as an administrator for the Christian Women's Exchange in the French Quarter for a number of years. One of their few paying positions and I truly enjoy my work, but …"

"If you end up here in Chicago, we'll find you work, Hannah. Don't worry about that. However, you may have trouble finding pecan shucks to refresh your … um … staining…" she winked at me.

"Yes, well, I would plan to 'reappear' as myself."

"And if so, you'll be staying with us until you've found employment and are settled," added Alma. "I'll absolutely refuse to hear any additional discussion regarding that decision."

Their break over, Ory stood back up still talking to Frank, and I felt his hand lightly on the back of my neck, his thumb gently caressing my collar bone for a few moments. Without explanation a small shiver raced through me, unwanted. He then gave his strange little salute to the three of us and rejoined the other musicians on the stage.

I left with the Colliers around midnight. They had pre-arranged a taxicab and insisted on dropping me at Mecca Flats before they headed home. As I fell asleep I kept hearing Ory's growling trombone slurs and countermelodies in my head while I mentally listed questions to ask at tomorrow's meeting with Dunning's ward seven staff. Alma had given me her law office's telephone number and told me to telephone after the meeting. She had already begun placing calls to the Children's Home and Aid asylums located downstate since there was always the possibility that Tayvie had been sent on one of those trains, as well as contacting *The Chicago Defender* again to list Tayvie as a missing black child. There was always the chance that someone would remember little Tayvie in her burgundy coat quietly singing in French patois to her green and yellow toy parrot.

Far away I heard a clock chiming two a.m., also several irate automobile klaxons, and a brief argument on the stairway somewhere outside the apartment. Afterwards the quieting night seemed to finally dull my thoughts, the music fading out as well as I drifted elsewhere. Then I realized that a murky shadow stood quietly in front of me. A few moments later I felt several tentative, slow kisses, gradually deepening, yet pressing so softly, so tenderly, on my neck then moving to my mouth, pulling me closer to the surface. His fingers lightly brushed through my hair as he whispered, "like gold, just like spun gold." His mouth was now on my breast, teasing, sweetly biting, his thumb then gliding lightly, slowly, delicately drawing a line over my shoulder, then continuing gently over my nipple, his lithe strong legs so warm, now encircling me. Sugared moonlight played over our bodies. How could I have forgotten that this was what lovemaking really felt like I heard myself whispering back.

I sat up, my hand moving quickly to my mouth as I scanned the dark living room. The blanket had fallen off the couch to the floor. I shivered, listening to the radiator gurgling and Ory's soft snoring in the bedroom. I had been fast asleep when Ory had returned to the apartment.

It had just been a dream. But a very disturbing dream. I was almost 38 years old. A grandmother. A young grandmother, but even so, grandmothers certainly didn't dream about encounters like that! And was it Ory in my dream or had it been Win Stratton? I was ashamed to admit that I had absolutely no idea. I wrapped the blanket around me and remained sitting, staring into the dark, still shaking, for at least another hour. My thoughts should be only centered on Emma and Tayvie. Not this kind of nonsense I scolded myself angrily. But I finally guiltily concluded: this was not entirely a dream. Not exactly unwanted.

Not really. For the first time I acknowledged the suppressed loneliness that had haunted me since Win's death.

> *"Kansas City style, Chicago style, New Orleans style -- hell, they're all 'Jelly Roll' style!"*
> Ferdinand "Jelly Roll" Morton

# Chapter 19: Emma – Chicago State Hospital – 1924-26

Ory and I retraced our steps via the streetcar and train to get over to Dunning by 10 a.m. the next morning. I could tell that he was exhausted, but we were both anxious to talk with the ward seven staff to find out what they knew about Emma. We were introduced to Dr. Marcus Johnson, a small unattractive man who somehow reminded me of a lizard, not to be confused with Dr. J.L. Johnson he grunted as he limply shook our hands and then gestured for us to take a seat in his small cramped office. He immediately opened the file on his desk and began reading.

"The woman who you claim to be Emma Jackson was found by a man named Bennett about two weeks ago in the closed men's toilets near Evergreen Park. She was lying naked on a blanket over the floor drain ... sometimes there's some heat from the sewers that comes up through those drains," he remarked glancing up at us, "and was unresponsive. Mr. Bennett assumed that the woman had frozen to death and contacted the police at that time."

"What was Mr. Bennett doing there in the first place since the toilet was supposed to be closed?" interjected Ory.

Dr. Johnson regarded the two of us slowly, taking a deep breath. "Apparently he'd been told by a, uh, good friend, that there was a young woman there who was available for whatever services a man might ..." he replied with a shrug, smirking.

"So then was she originally arrested?" countered Ory.

"No, not arrested," replied Dr. Johnson, shaking his head as he looked down over the notes. "The assumption was that the woman was dead as I mentioned before …"

"And this man Bennett had nothing to do with that?"

"Ed," I whispered quietly, lightly touching his elbow, "please let him give us all the information he has before we start assuming … anything."

Ory looked over at me and exhaled, sitting heavily back in his chair. "Sorry, doctor."

"Miss Jackson, assuming that's who she is, was then taken to Provident Hospital pending any other charges. Her body temperature was so low that she was in shock or possibly in a coma at that time of her transfer according to the medical staff at the scene. Slow pulse and equally slow respiration. Very dilated pupils. She made no response to any questions and was stiff 'like a corpse' according to the police moving her onto a cot and into a transfer van."

Dr. Johnson flipped to the next page and scanned down to the bottom, mumbling to himself.

"Later that night at Provident she awoke, became violent, throwing herself with herculean strength against the walls and bed railings until there was blood everywhere, according to the nurses in charge that evening. She then attacked one nurse along with two other female patients in the ward, injuring one of those patients, who was quite elderly, most severely. In fact, it looks as though that woman, who was white – odd that she was at Provident in the first place actually," he said almost to himself. "Anyway, that woman died a few hours later from injuries she more than likely sustained from Miss Jackson's vicious attack," sighed Dr. Johnson, looking up at us. "At that point, she was immediately transferred up here, to ward seven specifically, since there was no way she was deemed fit with respect to these manic episodes you understand. In fact, the deceased woman's family may well look into pressing charges against Miss Jackson if she's ever released from here."

"And has she had any of these manic episodes since she's been here, Dr. Johnson?" I asked, deliberately sidestepping the possibility of a murder trial. "What drugs, treatments ... what exactly is needed to help her?"

He smiled briefly at me and laughed slightly. "Drugs? Treatments? Surely you're not serious!" he snorted. "We have use of the continuous baths, cold wrap treatments, electrotherapy ... I believe they've tried one or two sessions of strychnine to induce seizures since we believe that she's suffering from some form of schizophrenia. A schizophrenic patient is much calmer for several days after an induced seizure you understand. The best treatment to date that we recommend for all these people is beer laced with a variety of morphine, opium and so forth. Usually calms a schizophrenic patient within a half an hour."

"Has anyone tried to just work with her gently? Talk with her gently," asked Ory. "Maybe she's just ... well, frightened right now."

Dr. Johnson stared at Ory for a moment. "There's truthfully not much to be gained by working gently with this kind of patient when they're absolutely out of control. They respond best to concrete boundaries, rigid structures, isolation, restrictions such as straight jacketing in order to feel safe within the confines of their own badly distorted minds. Only then do we sometimes begin to perceive the slightest modicum of improvement."

Neither Ory nor I had any reply. Dr. Johnson snapped shut the folder and cleared his throat.

"I should also mention that part of the blood from her rampage was from her miscarriage of the child she was carrying. Our staff gynocologist believes her to have been about three months along. Possibly a bit longer. And because she's of childbearing age and a dark prostitute with obviously no mental capability whatsoever to care for herself much less for a child, I should inform you that we've taken the liberty to sterilize her to avoid any such complications while she's in confinement in ward seven. This is standard procedure and completely legal you understand. Far safer than performing an abortion after the fact. We do have men taking care of various jobs, guards for example, other men cleaning the wards, and it's impossible for us to monitor every single moment where they might come in contact with one of these, well, these loose women."

I placed my hand over Ory's forearm to prevent his assaulting this greasy, arrogant little man.

"Three months?" queried Ory, visibly irritated with my restraint, shrugging my hand away. "Your doctor's certain about that?"

"Possibly longer, but yes, he's typically quite accurate."

I swallowed and avoided looking at Ory. He had only been in Chicago for just over a month. The child obviously hadn't been his. Surely he hadn't expected Emma to simply wait several years for him to make a tentative decision to leave his wife and head out to Chicago! On the other hand, I was certainly the first to admit that I had never excelled at grasping any man's expectations.

"We would like to see her today, Dr. Johnson," I stated firmly.

"I haven't had an opportunity to check in with the nurses on that ward yet this morning, but if you'll follow me we'll see if that's a possibility. And we'll have to have one of the guards stay in the room as well."

"Are most of these guards male?" asked Ory.

"Of course," replied the doctor. "With these crazed individuals very few women are strong enough to subdue them if needed, although we do employ a handful in the female wards."

Ory and I exchanged a quick glance, but made no reply.

There were no mattresses or chairs lining the hallways in ward seven, but the stench was every bit as overpowering as the main entrance wings. The director had referred to the rooms yesterday as cells and indeed that was exactly what they were. A chorus of moans punctuated occasionally by deafening shrieks ricocheted off the dank walls as we walked past the line of dark, narrow cells, boasting only a window slat opening to the hallway.

Two narrow, barred windows close to the ceiling admitted a grey light into Emma's almost-bare cell. Emma was sitting on a hard-backed chair that was firmly bolted to the floor. Her arms were crisscrossed over her stomach and tethered to the chair spindles on the sides. A long canvas sheath was wound tightly from her thighs to her ankles like a cocoon and was tied to a large metal ring just in front of the chair. Her head was down, her tangled filthy hair still matted with dried blood and crawling with small white nits that hadn't been visible when she'd worn the turban yesterday during the bath. Ory began caressing her hair for a moment then tried to lift her chin but found it immovable even without any strictures. He knelt in front of her and began murmuring over and over, *"ma petite musquette, que t'ont-ils fait? Eh? Eh, ma petite? Que t'ont-ils fait?"*

"Are you able to even feed her?" I quietly asked the guard, an extremely muscular woman with a deep voice, who had unlocked Emma's cell.

"I don't," retorted the guard, leaning against the pockmarked cement wall, her powerful forearms folded. "Ain't my job. If they's hungry when the food comes along, they eats. If they ain't hungry or they spits it out, then they don't eats. Pretty simple in my book. They learn. Real quick."

"Is she ... always ... bound like this unless she's in that bath thing or ..." I couldn't remember any other possible treatments that had been mentioned.

"I ain't seen her violent, if that's what ya mean, but Dancie did. She's one of the night guards. She said the bitch came bustin' out like a werewolf straight outta hell even without no full moon."

"*Peut être un loup-garou,*" Ory whispered, shaking his head. "*Ma cherie. Ma petite fille. Merde.*"

"Can I at least wash her hair? Or cut it? Or something!" I begged the guard. "That must itch something awful and would drive me completely insane!"

The guard glowered sideways at me. "Scissors? You're not serious! You want me to find scissors? Ain' my job."

"No, I certainly wouldn't expect you to find them," I replied, a sharp edge creeping unexpectedly into my voice. "If you'll be so kind to let me out of the room, I can see if one of the nurses can help me find some soap, water and ... scissors."

"Y'know you sure talks uppity for a nigger. Him too, but his is different. That nonsense ain' even English he's talkin'," she said, eyeing us both suspiciously as she finally unlocked the door.

I was back within a few minutes with a small bucket of warm water, a bottle of Lysol, a discarded newspaper and a very blunt pair of scissors. There was plenty of Lysol on hand since that was used for female douching to thwart possible pregnancies and to treat the patients' rampant vaginal infections stated the nurse who had handed over the large murky brown bottle. Just don't let the patient drink it, she'd warned. A lot of them attempted suicide that way, thus creating a lot of unnecessary paperwork, she'd complained, rolling her eyes. And make sure all that nasty hair gets rolled up in that newspaper ... floors'd been mopped just last month.

Ory had already begun to separate Emma's hair into small sections when I had returned. We wetted down each section, working the Lysol into it, then combing it through with our fingers and gently straightening each piece into long ribbons stretching out for well over two feet. I then cut off most of each ribbon only leaving about six inches of hair that curled back slowly to her reddened, but at least clean, scalp. The guard started complaining after we'd scarcely been working for fifteen minutes that it was almost her lunch hour and we would have to leave soon. Working quickly we finished as best as possible, hoping that Emma would at least be a little more comfortable. Both Ory and I kissed her on her cheek before being forced by the guard to vacate the room. There had been no recognition, no change whatsoever in Emma's face throughout our visit. I wondered if she knew we'd been there at all.

Back outside Dunning an intense, whiteout blizzard had been raging over the last two hours. Buffeted by the winds as we trudged to the train, we stopped briefly at a small market where Ory purchased bread, coffee, eggs, an illegal large bottle of wine made from a wine brick produced from Al Capone's favorite vineyard, according to the shopkeeper with a knowing wink, and the makings for something Ory referred to as 'faux gumbo' since there was no way one would ever find the actual ingredients in this culinary wasteland. Heavy snow now piled up over the train tracks and several telephone lines had snapped, thrashing uselessly in the wind. Huge drifts pushed up against buildings, sidewalks and fences, obliterating roads and automobiles alike, creating a vast churning white sea. Fearlessly, several cars and buses skidded sideways.

The electricity at Mecca Flats was intermittently out, sputtering back on for several minutes, dimmed, and then finally, went out altogether. Ory lit the gas burner and started to cook up the roux for his gumbo while drolly talking me through the recipe. The only other light in the room was an old-style oil lamp that he lit from the stove and brought over to the table where I was sitting.

"Best roux is one made with okra, but even in New Orleans no way you'd find okra this time of year," Ory admitted. "But you can just use flour an' lard, long's it whisks up to a nice bronze, y'know? Gotta just keep stirrin' an' stirrin 'til it's nice an' smooth. Then you adds your onions. Usually some butter as well, an' liquid, chicken broth's best, but whatever's on hand. Supposed to add celery and peppers too, but, then, like I said, this is a faux base! A little smoked pork sausage, canned meat's fine, maybe some other canned items, y'know like tomatoes just so's they ain' too disruptive an' can simmer down quick, y'know? I brought my Creole spices along so that'll work a little magic. Roux needs to simmer for about an hour at least – longer's even better."

I knew he was talking about the gumbo to avoid the subject of Emma and I welcomed this tiny bit of levity. "What exactly makes a tomato 'disruptive'?"

"Eh … you know when you taste it. Just too much. Y'know, tastes like some kinda, eh, y'know, Italian grandma's version of *langue de boeuf.*"

"*Langue de boeuf?*"

"Cow's tongue," he laughed. "Only the French really know how to cook up that one! My father faked a decent version of it. My mother, eh … well, not so good! Tasted more like *langue de la moufette!*"

"*Moufette?* I don't know that word either," I admitted. "Sounds rather tasty though."

"*Moufette's* a skunk, Hannah," he mused, eyebrows lifting slightly. "I'm openin' the Capone special. I'm assumin' you'll join me? I noticed you didn' refuse Mr. Collier's whiskey last night, so …"

I nodded as he poured two glasses of wine and sat down opposite me at the table. The radiators were maintaining a rather weak affront to the invasive cold. I had only just taken off my coat, which Ory had quite graciously hung up on the coat peg, within the last few minutes. I wondered if Emma was warm enough. Or Tayvie, wherever she was. I closed my eyes momentarily and worked to push the two of them from my thoughts. I knew if I dwelt on them constantly I would drive myself insane. Alma had cautioned me last night that I needed to mentally step away if I really wanted to help them.

"I'm sorry?" My thoughts had been absorbed elsewhere and I'd missed Ory's last few words.

"Tell me about Emma. Her uh, real father. About you and Zuma decidin' on Alice an' Emma an' everythin'," he said, as he walked back over to stir the gumbo for a few moments.

I took a long sip of the wine, which was surprisingly excellent. Evidently gangsters had better taste in wine than one might have surmised. "It's all kind of a blur anymore. I don't know exactly how much Emma overhead from Zuma's and my conversation or what she told you."

Ory walked back to his chair, gesturing for me to continue as he sat down.

"Emma's father was Winfield Scott Stratton, known as the Croesus of Cripple Creek, original owner of the Independence gold mine and a millionaire many times over. He supported the artistic pursuits of young women. One of them was me."

I looked up at Ory fully anticipating a crude retort, but his face remained impassive.

"Emma was quite dark when she was born and apparently Zuma didn't believe the infant was Win's daughter at all, although I never knew back then she'd doubted me. I found that out at Reserve that awful day of our argument. I was shocked to learn that Zuma ... well, who cares what I thought at this point! Anyway, Emma's actually gotten much lighter as the years have gone on. Even her hair and so forth ... I really don't know exactly how to talk to you about any of this, Ed."

"Do your best, eh?" Ory encouraged, smiling. "If I don' understand, I'll ask questions, *non*?"

I sighed, looking down into my glass of wine.

"Win had told me that he thought his mother had probably

been an escaped slave … a quadroon. Win was born in southern Indiana, late 1840s. He hated the fact that his mother was basically nothing more …"

"Than a prostitute for his father," Ory filled in for me quietly. "And they couldn't possibly have been legally married. My parents weren't. *Plaçage* arrangements down South are never legally binding."

"Yes," I nodded, frowning. "You're probably right. You know I hadn't ever considered that."

"Not uncommon, Hannah. White men have always had an insatiable desire for black women. The entire black Creole population in New Orleans' the result of rich white men an' their relationships *avec les femmes de coleur*. 'Course, black men have always had an insatiable desire for white women as well, but we're never awarded *une place à cette table*, y'know?" he winked.

I let that go by unacknowledged.

"So what had you originally planned to do once Emma was born?"

"With the money, well, stock certificates actually that Win had set aside for me, I planned on taking Alice, who was actually my friend Abigail's one-year-old child, and my own child once born, to Europe."

Ory nodded while taking another sip of his wine.

"Abigail had simply disappeared. I learned later she was killed in a dynamited mine, a month or so after Alice's birth, Ed. I found Alice in a brothel discarded like an animal in a dresser drawer lined with filthy newspapers. I had helped with her birth, Ed! I couldn't just walk away and leave her!"

"*C'est affreux*," muttered Ory, leaning back in his chair.

I looked down at my hands on the base of the cloudy glass. "I had rash aspirations of becoming an opera singer back in those days if you can believe. There's no way I could have ever made a success of any of it. Youthful folly at its worst."

"I can't believe that," replied Ory gently, touching my

elbow.

"When Emma was born, Win was on his deathbed. His mind was completely gone by then. He died two days later and never even knew that I was pregnant. He was a raging alcoholic. His liver had slowly poisoned him they said. I don't know if I had mentioned that before," I stammered.

I took a long sip of my wine before I was able to continue. "Zuma and John Barrington, who was Win's secretary, convinced me that I couldn't possibly raise a black child, that both of us would have nothing in our futures except a lifetime of desolate prostitution and we would never be accepted into the other's world. Do you understand how frightening that was to hear?"

Ory frowned, but said nothing.

"Also, John claimed he had withheld evidence against Zuma regarding her brother's jailbreak in New Orleans. I know you're aware of all of that mess since you knew Paul. I think Zuma was released from jail based strictly on John's testimony. He could be extremely persuasive and could easily lie in whichever direction best served his needs. He forged a marriage license, Alice's birth certificate naming us as her parents, and another document showing that Zuma was Emma's mother … father unknown. That meant that John legally held all of Win's original stock holdings, of course, and was free to pursue any investments he wished when we moved to Kansas City. But then the real joke? John Barrington's eight-year-old son from his actual marriage is the one who shot and killed him. When you add that to my, less-than-wedded bliss to put it bluntly, with Joe Peterson, you can see my relationships with men have certainly left much to be desired." I concluded bitterly.

I took another long sip of the wine. Admittedly it was contributing to something of a sense of warmth, making it easier for me to talk about those dark days surrounding my daughter's birth and my lover's death. Ory sat silently, studying me intently as he waited for me to continue.

"At least Win's estate was finally carried out as he had willed. I found that out from a woman, Jane Lawson, who showed up at the Women's Exchange a few years back. It's a completely self-sufficient village known as the Myron Stratton Home, all contained on the grounds and even includes an orphanage where both boys and girls are trained in music, cooking and farming, as well as the usual academic fare. I was thoroughly shocked that Win could have thought all of it through! He was so sick, Ed! I was helping Jane as she was heading back to Colorado Springs when I ran into you and your wife at the train depot that day you left for California."

"Ah," replied Ory, nodding his head at the memory. "Tell me more about this home, Hannah."

"Win had worked practically nonstop for that last year of his life drawing up all of the architectural renderings and financial strategies to build and consistently fund this home for orphaned children, but he also intended it to house the infirm, mentally ill or older poor adults who had been born in Teller County. What's so unsettling is that, according to Jane at any rate, only poor white residents of the county are ever admitted. Considering the fact that Win suspected his own mother was a former slave, I find it very hard to believe he intended that kind of racial restriction within his own legacy! More than likely some ... well ... meddling misinterpretation by their admitting committee."

Ory looked at me quietly for a moment, deep in thought, and then spoke. "Miss Hannah, do you still have Alice's birth certificate?"

"Well, not here. It's with my things back in New Orleans, but I'll be bringing everything with me when I return. And, please ... just Hannah," I replied.

"Alice's birth certificate states that as your daughter she was born in Cripple Creek, no? An' I assume that's also part of this, what did you call it, Teller County?"

"Well, yes," I frowned, confused.

"That's where Emma should be. We need to get her admitted there. Get her in a good home for mentally ill adults. Not keep her in this putrid animal cage."

"Ed," I said carefully, "Alice's birth certificate states that she's white."

"That's true. And at that point she will be. You can manage that. She's an odd color ain' black or white anymore. More like a greasy grey. We both seen that for ourselves."

He poured us each another glass of the wine, stirred the gumbo again and then brought his chair next to mine.

"You don't think she's going to recover," I said quietly.

"No. She's been going downhill for years. Trying to hide it. Her diary shows that. Do you?"

I shook my head slowly.

"I didn't think so," he replied, putting his arm around the back of my chair. "An' places like this home you can bet there's a waitin' list as well, y'know? Write your friend, this Jane, for the particulars. We can't leave Emma in this *pissoir* for the rest of her life. An' this is important to understand ... Hannah: anywhere she's transferred as a colored girl, the conditions, the treatment, all that shit's gonna be exactly the same. Or even worse. Mark my words."

"What about Tayvie?"

"That's a different problem, Hannah. We need to deal with Emma's situation first, *non*? Tayvie's somewhere close. I just know it. I know she's all right. Don' ask me how I know that, but I just know. Call it hoodoo voodoo nonsense, but there it is. Someday we'll find her. Ya gotta keep that much of your faith alive."

I sat back, gazing at him in the soft lamplight. He was a handsome man, small and compactly built, just as Win had been I realized. Both men had lost their young black mothers early in their lives and were raised by white fathers. Irrationally, their acceptance in society was based solely on the fact that Stratton had been raised a white man, and Ory, a black man. Both John Barrington and Joe Peterson had been tall men -- men for whom I had never felt any real physical attachment despite years of trying. Men who had always seemed to tower over and somehow crush my spirit without hesitation. I could completely understand why Emma had fallen for Edward Ory, same as I had for Win Stratton.

"Don' you ever wonder why I wasn't interested in you when you first showed up at Reserve that day of the Dawson's harvest picnic?" Ory suddenly asked.

"No, of course not," I replied, rather startled at the question. "I never thought about it. I know I was embarrassed for Emma when she jumped up on you that day, obviously not aware that her dress was soaked through. And you were married. You still are in fact. And now you're the father of my only grandchild."

"An' my being a black Creole wasn' a deterrent?"

"Ed, be sensible," I sighed, weary, but also wary at the turn of this conversation.

We sat in silence looking at one another for a long moment. Then I felt his hand lightly touching my hair, his warm mouth on my cheek, then easily on my lips. This time I wasn't dreaming. At first I tried to move away, but he gently pulled me towards him again. I gave in to his deep kisses and then, shaking, forced myself away, breathing hard.

"We can't do this, Ed. Please. It's just wrong ... immoral!"

"Eh, well, I don' remember any scripture dealin' with, well, this exact situation, y'know? Don' covet your neighbor's wife an' that ... eh, dreck," he smiled, bringing my hand up to his mouth, gently biting my fingers then softly kissing my neck. "You need to live life as you find it, Hannah. That's just how it is, y'know? You defer, you analyze, you criticize, you scrutinize, an' what's that buy you, anyway? Eh? Old age an' emptier dreams. I can' lay claim to that statement, but it's a good one, y'know?"

"Please don't," I whispered. "Please, Ed ..."

And at that point I was lost. Our years of history flashed before me. I saw three drunken white thugs, throwing him onto the ground then ruthlessly challenging him to don his battered skimmer, showering dirt over his sweaty face. I starkly remembered his badly swollen eye and bruised ribs as he was forced to play all night to thwart off a jazz-loving madman. I recalled his genuine warmth as we briefly hugged at the Exchange that one afternoon when he'd told me about Zuma's death and also both of our shocked reactions after I had slapped him when he'd angrily grabbed my arms outside the Mack and Mack concert. I now admitted to myself that while stroking Ory's hair, reading Emma's journal, emotions long dead within me, unbidden, had quietly resurfaced. For the first time I glimpsed an intense insight into now long-silenced novelist Kate Chopin's character Edna Pontellier in *"The Awakening"*.

I was once again that teenage girl back in Cripple Creek, tenderly wrapped in the arms of a man whose sweet, warm caresses, subtle rhythms and instinctive awareness when to alter those rhythms might fully awaken a women's nature from so many years of bleak dormancy. The winds were still howling through the streets several hours later when finally we curled up together and fell asleep, under every blanket to be found, his ruddy brown arms and legs so warm, so gentle, pressing me against him.There was nothing in this moment but the moment itself in both of our lives I fully realized. But oddly, right now, somehow that was enough.

*"Never play anything the same way twice."*
~ Louis "Satchmo" Armstrong

## Chapter 20: "La Piaf Perdu" – 1925

Bright slatted sunlight and the loud abrasive crunching of metal awakened me from a deep sleep as well as a delicious aroma I couldn't place immediately. I was alone in the bed, but could hear Ed on the other side of the wall in the kitchen. Gradually I realized that the aroma was Zuma's pie wheels. Not my detestably poor imitation, but exactly the way I remembered them from so many years ago. I dressed quickly dismissing the immediate walloping headache from my unbridled wine consumption.

"Ahhhh!" commented Ory. "So our lost sparrow has finally chanced to abandon her nest!"

I hadn't remembered telling him last night that Win had always called me his 'sparrow', but most likely that was far from the only thing I had divulged. I definitely remembered his fingering the small roping scars, like long earthworms, that I still retained on my lower back from the horrible beating by Mrs. Hughes and whispering that we had more in common than he'd realized.

"You've made Zuma's pie wheels!" I replied in awe. "I've tried for so many years and could never get the recipe even close. There's just some magic ingredient or something!"

"Almond paste," nodded Ory adding a sly wink. "An' a special kind of almond paste as well. My mama made 'em too. Creole uh, hoodoo specialty, y'know? Pretty amazin', eh? Nothin' like 'em. An' without that almond paste they's just, eh, ordinary, rolled dough with some sugar or molasses. Blah. Put a little *sucre de confiseurs* on top an' they're even better, but *c'est la vie*. No powdered sugar so no such luck. First batch'll be done in a few more minutes. There's coffee. Dark an' no cream just so y'know."

"How long have you been up?" I asked, feeling quite guilty as I sat down at the table. I had been sleeping the sleep of the dead it seemed. Outside the noise of heavy metal street cleaning trucks and the sharp ring out from a chorus of shovels had escalated. I noticed that one of Emma's diaries was on the table.

"Have you been looking at Emma's diary?"

"Nah, just using the paper," he answered. "Actually she gave me that one when I first got here last month. None of her writin's in it. Wanted me to start writin' down my, uh, compositions an' some of my arrangements, y'know? So's nobody else could steal 'em. She's probably right. She mentioned that Mr. Jelly always makes sure he gets his music copywrote right away so's nobody else can steal it an' put their name on it. Emma doesn' like Jelly – he can get real nasty with the girl singers they say, crude language an' uh, too many hands, y'know."

"He sounds quite the charming gentleman."

"But she sure as hell learned a lot from him! Anyway, with regards to writin' out the music, I just never thought 'bout it much. In New Orleans I don' think our musicians steal each other's work, plop a new name on top and lay claim on it for their own like around here. Well, except those ofays like the Original Dixieland Jazz Band down in New Orleans. They used to follow us all around, just writin' down our music ideas, the bastards. That first record they made back in '17? Direct steal from me, Joe Oliver, John Robichaux, Freddie Keppard, Lawrence Duhe. The works. Even stole some of that old Buddy Bolden stuff still floatin' around in the wind."

"But not from Mr. Jelly?"

"Nope. See he's always been one helluva a smart man. A lot of people don' like him, but he knows how to protect his interests, y'know? I worked with him out in California on a few gigs an' he worked us hard, but the music? Always first rate and I mean, real first rate! An' he always paid top dollar – even paid rehearsals. That's almost unheard of, y'know?"

I opened the book. At the top of the first page was written *Muskrat Ramble* and was then lined off into narrow staves, writing out several different parts of the score on each page. I tried to figure out the melody from what he had marked as the cornet line but failed.

"Do you remember it?" he asked.

I shook my head, although something about the name seemed familiar.

"It was that crazy dance that Emma was doin' at some concert or somethin'. I named it after her 'cause all the other kids were followin' what she was doin'. Bunch of new dance steps like uh, snake hips an' flat foot floogie an' black bottom from that Sissieretta Jones' troupe. 'Course, everybody's doin' that stuff nowadays."

He then sang part of the melody to me and it did seem familiar. I definitely remembered Emma dancing to a similar tune at the Claytor wedding.

"You know, Ed, it seems to me that if you can read and write music that you could certainly read English! This stuff is a lot more confusing!" I flipped through several more pages of dense notation and found that he had scribbled out scores for several other original tunes including *"Sweet Little Papa," "Ory's Creole Trombone," "Savoy Blues"* along with his own arrangements of Jelly Roll's *"Wolverine Blues"* and *"Original Jelly Roll Blues"* among others.

"Eh, maybe," he shrugged. "French is easy, but English? My papa taught me French, both readin' and writin', like I told you. See the Creole kids in New Orleans never learn any English 'til they goes to school. Then they got no choice 'cause that's all they teach. That's true even now far's I know. 'Course that's why

Tayvie didn' know much English."

I nodded, a lump suddenly stuck high in my throat at the mention of her name.

"Pie wheels are done, but gotta cool ... poaching some eggs now."

All of this conversation skirted around my facing last night or thinking further about Emma and Tayvie. As he set a mug of coffee in front of me he kissed the top of my head then pulled down my gown slightly to kiss my bared shoulder.

"So what exactly makes New Orleans style jazz music, *jazz music*, Ed? Frank Collier said the other night that 'Kid Ory *is* jazz music'," I asked, self-conconciously pulling my sleeve back up in place.

"If Frank'd ever heard Jelly perform with a top notch band he'd know that *Mister Jelly* is jazz music," Ory chuckled. "Man's got this outta-the-ballpark ego to go with all that talent, which is why so many musicians an' audiences don' like him, but he's one of the best musically in my book. Writes absolutely first rate tunes an' then goes an' tops that off with first rate arrangements, y'know?"

He set two plates down in front of us and then sat down opposite me at the table.

"An' don' let them Original Dixieland Jazz boys hear Collier say that either! They still think they are the, uh, what did I hear the other day? Oh yeah, they think their music is *le sommet absolu de jazz*."

I began blowing on my coffee while Ory, a true Creole, immediately consumed at least half of the scalding beverage without the slightest hesitation then sat back thoughtfully.

"But in answer to your uh, question, what makes jazz music, jazz music, I'd say jazz is kinda improvised, but then each instrument can only improvise in a particular way, y'see. So there's a kind of chaos, kind of a raw freedom y'know, but there's also strict rules inside that chaos if that makes any sense.

Ain' just roamin' all over the place *comme une chienne en chaleur*."

I frowned. "A what?"

"Eh, a female dog, y'know, in heat, yes?"

I nodded as Ory continued.

"Your cornet plays your main melody, an' then your clarinet kind of improvises a nice obligato line above the cornet melody. Uh, obligato means he's playin' fills, a melody circlin' aroun' that original melody, y'know? Rhythm section gives you a march feel underneath everything, keepin' us all together so we have some idea where in the hell we are. You know when you play with a lot of other musicians, even just four, five, six guys, you really can't hear what anybody else is playin'. You just hope it's soundin' something like music out there in the audience! Hell, it's almost impossible to even hear yourself if you've got some gas pipe clarinet shriekin' in one ear an' Oliver or Armstrong or Papa Mutt blowin' it up like Gabriel chokin' his horn in the other!"

"And the trombone?" I asked, thoroughly intrigued with his explanation. "Where's the trombone's place?"

"Eh, well, the trombone sorta goes anywhere an' everywhere, but you needs to keep your ear tuned in best ya can to what's goin' on with the ensemble all around you while you're playin'. An' that's tricky! There's slurs an' purrs an' growls, sometimes a simple melody or countermelody that's under the chord progressions an' such. Harmonies to a coupla melodies gotta be simple an' just thread it all together. You don' think twice about it when it works an' you just steer clear of blowin' any clams! *Trouve ton 'x'*, eh, find your center, you follow?"

I nodded, smiling, but knew that no, I didn't really follow at all. When you watched these guys on stage it all seemed so completely effortless. I was astounded to find out that they couldn't even hear what their own music sounded like!

"But when it's bad? *Merde*! *Epave de train*! Eh, train wreck, yes? I have to confess, I'm havin' a hard time findin' my place at times in Oliver's band. Not used to skirtin' aroun' so many other players like he's got in his lineup. With that many men you can' have it so nice an' free feelin', y'know? Gotta stay in line, read the chart. I'm managin', but it sure ain' my best work."

I finally managed to take a small sip of the coffee, treasuring as well my first bite of the delicious pie wheel as Ory continued talking while he poured another cup of the scalding hot coffee for himself.

"Now you take Buddy Bolden. He was the actual King of Jazz, y'know. Even Mr. Jelly would agree with that! Man that cat could be heard blowin' that cornet for miles an' miles! His family made him practice out on the front stoop 'cause otherwise the house shuddered so bad they thought the damned roof would fly off an' the windows'd shatter to bits! Blew his brains mad they say. He's in the madhouse y'know. I ain' makin' that up. Somewhere in New Orleans, I think. Anyway, he wanted me in his band, y'know. Did I ever tell you 'bout that?"

My mouth full I simply shook my head.

"Yeah, King Bolden heard me blowin' a few notes on my first real trombone back when I was just a kid an' wanted me in his band. But my older sister said no sir, no way, I was much too young. An' she was right. I needed way too much work, y'know? But here's the really crazy part. Jelly Roll's even younger than I am! Can you believe that? He'd lied about his age for years so's he could play piano in them honky tonk brothels like Lulu White's in Storyville an' then all them vaudeville troupes he went aroun' with. Jelly was just born amazin'. Rest of us took years an' years of hard work!"

"Ed," I began tentatively, the mention of Storyville prompting me to speak, "about last night…"

"Nah, we ain't gonna talk 'bout that, Miss Hannah! You an' me? We've been through hell with all this mess. An' it ain't over yet an' we both know it. My daddy's old Catholic Bible says even God rested on the seventh day, eh? Although, admittedly yesterday wasn't Sunday, but then again, maybe the damn calendar's wrong, who's to say, eh? Who come up with 28 days in February or 31 days in December in the first place, eh? An' then every once in awhile they gotta ante up an' give February 29 days! Just 'cause them days by then are all messed up! *Merde*!"

I shook my head slightly and started to protest but Ory continued speaking.

"An' here's another thing. Just exactly what was God doin' with His Sundays off, anyways? Eh? Think about that, eh? You think He's just sittin' around countin' the stars or clouds or gold coins or worryin' about them weeds in His back lot in the Kingdom? Yeah? You tell me, huh? I'll tell ya what he was doin' an' it wasn' countin' no damned weeds, let me tell ya!"

I laughed in spite of myself. Ory grinned, finished his coffee and not surprisingly, in true Ory fashion, completely changed the subject.

"I don' think the trains are gonna be up an' runnin' to get out to see Emma even by tomorrow, but in a few more hours if they got the streetcar runnin' again I'm headin' down to the Dreamland tonight. Place is right along The Stroll so you know people'll be walkin' over after bein' pent up all last night an' today!"

"I want to try to read through Emma's journals again. See if I can find anything that maybe I missed before. I keep thinking there's got to be some clue I've overlooked … something that will help me understand what's happened to her. And maybe why."

"That 'why' part, Hannah? Doubtful y'know?" He brushed my hair lightly away from my shoulder. "I remember when they put her in the hospital 'cause she was havin' convulsions an' that real high fever. The doctors were afraid there was another epidemic startin'. That was what, five or six years ago? Before she got pregnant with Tayvie anyway."

I had completely forgotten about that.

"Ed, do you remember anything about those seizures? Did the doctors ever have any idea what caused them?"

"Uh, claimed it was somethin' called *encephalitis*," Ory remarked. "I'd never heard of it, but I remember that was the name. I thought they meant it was somethin' like ... well, uh, *syphilis*, y'know, which had me kinda worried, of course. Word sounded kinda like that. But no, it ain' the same thing. Doctors said a lot of people who'd survived that flu were real weak an' gettin' it."

"But what is it?" I frowned. "I've never heard of it either."

"Brain infection they said. A lot of people died right away. But a lot of other people were never completely, well, you know, normal after havin' it either. Dort had this friend in Los Angeles, a Francis somebody or other, who was paralyzed a coupla years after we moved there. Couldn' move at all. She was takin' in sewin' for awhile, same as Dort. Nice lady. Anyways, Dort said Francis' doctors called it the sleepin' sickness, but claimed it was that *encephalitis* disease that brought it all on a couple years later. Like she was never cured an' it came back, they said. But that seems real different from what Emma's got. Dort's friend didn' have any shakin' stuff or wild rages or nothin'. It was just like one day she an' her husband were sittin' there with us drinkin' some amazin' whiskey at a local blind pig an' a couple days later she was completely frozen like a stone statue. Husband thought it was maybe bad booze at first, but the rest of us was fine."

"How's she now?"

Ory looked steadily at me, gnawing on his thumb for a few moments before answering.

"Eh, well ... she died maybe six, seven months after she was paralyzed. It got to where she couldn' even swallow food no more so that was, y'know, uh, the end."

I closed my eyes and vowed to contact the hospital in New

Orleans when I returned in the next several days. I had never heard of anything called sleeping sickness or *encephalitis*. Curiously I hadn't seen anything in Emma's journals about her time in the hospital, although I now remembered Ory telling me about it back then. But Emma had also never mentioned any romantic relationships with men other than Ory in her journals either, so obviously she was extremely selective regarding her entries.

"Maybe Emma was seeing that one pianist, you know, Luis Russell. She seemed to be very fond of him as opposed to Mr. Jelly," I threw out, even though we hadn't been discussing anything about her recent pregnancy. "Obviously she was seeing someone …"

"Eh, well, maybe," shrugged Ory, tugging at his ear. "Tough to say who exactly. When she first got out here she was working with a New Orleans pianist named Tony Jackson. Since their last names were the same people kinda connected them for awhile which was pretty amusin'. Tony was the only piano player that Jelly Roll claimed was better than he was, so he was damned amazin' y'know? He died a few years back though. Real young, too. Most people blamed his death on his, uh, light nature."

I shook my head, frowning. "Light nature?"

"Eh, goes a different direction? Not into the ladies so tuh speak? But to each his own, I say."

"Ah," I nodded. "Okay. I see."

"Does that bother you?"

"Does what bother me? The fact that Emma was in bed with different men or that Mr. Jackson is not … normal … at least as I see it -- forgive me if I'm offending you since he's a fellow musician."

"Eh, people get too mucked up over who's havin' sex with who, y'know? Nobody's business 'cept their own. D'you ever hear 'bout a singer named Adah Menken at the Opera House?"

"No. Was he also, um, 'light' as you put it?"

"No, no, not at all. Adah was a female -- this beautiful, extravagant lighter-skinned Creole in New Orleans, right aroun' the Civil War. My father tol' me 'bout her, claimed that *his* father was even one of Adah's many lovers, in fact! They say Adah had four different husbands, an' she only lived to be 32 or 33 or something! Divorced every one of 'em an' bedded countless others. Just for the hell an' enjoyment of it! They say she never took a dime from any man ... at least, not for, uh, any sex favors. So that she couldn' be considered a whore, y'know? But every performance she booked was a sellout y'know so she made a lotta money even though her singin' an' actin' was pretty *atroce* they say!"

"All attended exclusively by men undoubtedly. And?" I bristled. Was this supposed to be some crass reflection on Emma's talent or my own recent behavior?

"Eh, just a thought. See, I think that women, well, you white women anyways, are so pent up 'bout who knows what nonsense 'bout 'em that they miss out on all the fun in life."

"The 'fun in life' meaning bedding as many men as we can possibly cram beneath our sheets in our lifetimes?" I retorted icily. "What about children, Ed? What about families? Who moves us along as a society into the coming decades if women don't maintain some reasonable respectability or ... moral barriers, I guess you could say? My behavior last night certainly wasn't me at ..."

"Well, y'see, that's where the church really gets you ladies comin' an' going, *non*?" interrupted Ory, chuckling.

I made no reply. Ory had the uncanny ability to thoroughly alienate me with his vagrant viewpoints as well as so lovingly draw me in close at other times. So much like Win I realized, acknowledging the raw exasperating comparison.

"How about Victoria Woodhull or Margaret Sanger – you familiar with those ladies?"

"Yes, and Tennessee Claflin, Miss Woodhull's free love advocating and birth control-peddling sister, Edward," I countered. "I'm not as backwards a female as you must think. Not anymore I'm happy to admit. Not with the situations I hear from the desperate women I attempt to help at the Exchange every week!"

"You ever hand out Miss Woodhull's or Mrs. Sanger's pamphlets to your uh, lady clients, at the Exchange?"

"Of course not, Ed! It's against the law. I'd end up in jail for God knows how long! But what exactly is your point with bringing all of this up right now? To cast a blight on Emma's behavior or on my own for failing to deflect your obviously meaningless amorous interest in me last night? In fact my having foolishly encouraged it, I'm embarrassed to admit!"

"Whoa, whoa! Where the hell did that accusation fall from? *Zut!*" he whistled softly, moving closer to me. "Nothin' further from the truth, Miss Hannah Barrington. Not a thing!"

Angry with myself I felt tears forming as he pulled me into his arms, kissing my eyes, then slowly moving to my mouth, his hands tenderly moving over me, relaxing, exhilarating, loving.

"We need each other right now," he whispered. "That's all I was tryin' to say. An' that's reason enough, ain' it? I'm sorry if that seemed rough in talkin'. Just makin' love in the winter sunshine is a gift. An' with you it's very nice. Just relax *ma petite piaf*. Did I mention that in Paris they call a cabaret singer a little sparrow? *Non? C'est vrai.*"

When Ory returned very late, easily close to 3 a.m., I was still re-reading parts of Emma's diaries, absorbed by my daughter's dreams and wondering if, like a sleeping beauty she might suddenly awaken and miraculously start her life once again. There had been a phone message from Alma Collier that Ory had followed up with from the club earlier in the evening. She may have found Tayvie. There was a little girl closely matching Tayvie's description who had been taken downstate to an orphanage near St. Louis within the last several weeks. The information had come Alma's way from her unrelenting quest through *The Chicago Defender*'s in-depth grapevine. Train service was still unreliable she had told Ory, but if I waited until the following day, which was New Year's Day, at least all the tracks should be completely cleared even though the service might be somewhat eclipsed it being a holiday. I went with Ory to The Dreamland that night and called Alma who had already booked a seat for me on the earliest train from Union Station that following morning. It's in the white section, she cautioned, but Ory had told her that I was very rapidly fading back to my natural white skin tone and thus receiving very questioning looks from everyone at Mecca Flats as well as the local police, whose job it remained to keep black men from socializing in any way with white women along The Stroll.

The Dreamland was a dark, rather cavernous place, completely filled despite the effects of the blizzard, and we sat at a table in the deepest shadows when Ory wasn't on stage performing. Early into the second set though, he surprised me by coming back offstage, taking my hand and moving quietly, still in the shadows, to dance to an unpublished Fats Waller tune someone had just snuck in called "*Black and Blue*".

"The sax player can do a decent job doubling on my part," he murmured in my ear. "Only time I'll ever get to dance with you in this lifetime ... well, unless you show back up in more shoe polish. Great tune, don't ya think? In fact, whenever you hear me playin' that song from this day until forever, I'm playin' it for you, *ma petite piaf perdu*. You remember that, yes? You know, you're the only white lady I ever, uh, been with. "

I pulled away from him slightly and frowned.

"Now don' get mad 'cause I said that. Please." His fingertips lightly traced the wormlike scars along my lower back as we continued dancing.

"We're all workin' hard to be something in this world, I

think. But somebody's always gonna be knockin' ya down, tryin' to put their big foot in your face, y'know? If you're gonna get anywhere you just gotta push that foot aside, stand back up an' keep movin'. That's the same no matter what color's your skin." He kissed me as a wish for the New Year then; the band would have to keep playing when the actual hour struck of course. By the time I returned from New Orleans, he would be on his way back to his wife in California. But as Ory had said, 'we need each other right now … that's reason enough, ain' it'?

\*\*\*

The train was several hours late leaving Chicago. By the time it finally puffed its way into the last station in Illinois before crossing over into Missouri, I had thoroughly convinced myself that the little girl in question absolutely had to be Tayvie. I would sign whatever papers were needed, take her down to New Orleans to gather up all of our things as well as any of Emma's remaining belongings, and attempt to get back up to Chicago within the next three weeks I reasoned. I hoped that Tayvie would be able to stay with Felicité and Celeste for the two weeks I would be required to work after I'd given notice at the Exchange. I had a lengthy list that included sending Alma's address out to Jane in Colorado Springs, notifying Alma when we might be returning, retrieving any notes available from the hospital in New Orleans that had treated Emma during her hospital stay, and giving final notice to my landlady Mrs. Trent, hoping that Tayvie would understand that we would have to bid the real M. Autruche farewell. Countless other essential tasks loomed in front of me such as shopping for favorite foods to take along as well as the daunting task of purchasing whatever warm outer clothing I might possibly locate in a deep southern state! But joyfully, I constantly daydreamed of bringing Tayvie to see Emma and watching Emma, somehow miraculously reawaken, rush over to hug her little girl, covering her daughter's tiny face with teary kisses … and that after so many years, I might finally have a real family.

> *"I think one reason why these records were so good was that the OKEH guys left us alone and didn't try to play the experts with us."*
> Edward "Kid" Ory

## Chapter 21: Chicago 1925

But it wasn't Tayvie. The little girl was probably a year younger than Tayvie and outfitted in a very ragged, badly stained coat of indeterminate color. She wasn't able to speak very well and also seemed to have great difficulty understanding anyone speaking to her, squinting intensely as she desperately tried to make sense of what was being said. The orphanage thought most likely she had simply been abandoned by her family since her problems were so extensive. I think they hoped that I would be interested in adopting her anyway, but I simply could not. I had to walk away. Disheartened, I sent a short telegram to Alma from town and asked her to please call Ory at the Dreamland to let him know as well.

Once in New Orleans, welcoming the refreshing breath of balmier days, I collected all of Emma's, Tayvie's and my own belongings and had two trunks sent to Alma's house in Oak Park. My superiors at the Exchange balked at allowing my departure without my assistance in training my replacement, but begrudgingly agreed following much negotiation. Mrs. Trent was decidedly unhappy that I would be breaking my lease and M. Autruche, having finally sprouted a few wispy feathers upon his elongated neck, muttered his own colorful concoction of Creole explectives as he aimlessly puttered about, as though he too disagreed with my plans.

Alma called me several times, warning me that the family accusing Emma of that fatal beating would be pressing charges against her, the ambulance team, and the hospital itself within the next few weeks. The deceased, Mrs. Georgina Havenstock, had been inadvertently transported that night to Provident and placed in a holding area with Emma. The family claimed she was merely suffering from congestion due to a very bad cold and that her doctor had advised strict hospital rest and medications for a few days.

Paraphrasing from recent news releases, Alma said that they certainly hadn't expected their mother to be transported to a colored hospital down in a godforsaken pigsty like Bronzeville of all places! And then, even worse, to be placed in a room with this filthy heathen who completely unprovoked had clawed huge gashes on their mother's face and then strangled her while tearing off their mother's antique pearl choker necklace! Frank was making calls to several former contacts looking for a good legal representative, since, unfortunately, none of the lawyers in her own firm would be able to add Emma's lawsuit to their already overburdened files.

She also mentioned that Ory had dropped off everything from Mecca Flats at their home and then taken a train out to Los Angeles. Surprisingly, however, he and Dort would be coming back to Chicago within the next several months to live! Ory had agreed to again perform nightly with Joe Oliver's Dixie Syncopaters when they opened at The Plantation, which was another club near The Stroll, and had also agreed to record with Jelly Roll's, Oliver's, Louis Armstrong's and several other ensembles starting that Fall. Needless to say Frank was ecstatic admitted Alma, although he expressed some concern about The Plantation since it was a well known Al Capone hangout. With the ongoing war between Capone's men and Hymie Weiss's, it was a sure-fire power keg according to Frank. Louis Armstrong's band was now working steadily at the Sunset Café these days, however, which had an even worse reputation in Frank's opinion. "Satchmo" as he was now usually called, had a thriving reputation and a lot of talent to offer up to the jazz world, said Frank. He just hoped that the Sunset wouldn't ultimately be "the sunset" for the musician.

I finally returned to Chicago a month later, during what was considered a winter thaw, which really meant the temperature registered about 20° for a few moments in the afternoon. After quickly dropping my suitcases at Alma and Frank's beautiful home in Oak Park, I raced out in the same cab to Dunning to see Emma.

She was still confined to ward seven, but no longer subjected to the severe arm and leg restraints. One of the young nurses was slowly feeding an oddly pale, skeletal, almost completely motionless Emma as the guard admitted me into her room. I asked if I might be able to take over the task and the nurse hastily handed me the bowl of oatmeal and a small spoon, warning me not to give her more than a small, half teaspoonful at a time and quickly left. Emma's unfocused eyes stared past me, scarcely blinking, her face a complete blank as she opened her mouth slightly whenever I lightly touched her lips with the spoon. Then, she very slowly mashed the food around in her mouth, finally swallowing with great difficulty. Each small bite seemed to take almost five minutes. One could feed her for twenty-four hours straight and she would scarcely have consumed enough to keep a snow rabbit alive, I despaired.

The guard said I would have to leave shortly since he needed to open another cell. I begged him to let me stay with Emma – he could certainly lock me in with her I pleaded.

"If she turns violent ain't no way anyone could get back here fast enough to subdue her, lady," grumbled the guard. "You heard what had happened to that Mrs. Havenstock? It's been in the papers all over again now that the case was coming up to trial soon. That poor woman had been torn to pieces by Emma, raging like a she-wolf they said, in the matter of just a few minutes, with no one even observing its happening! No way they'll ever prove she's anything but totally insane. And if somehow they claim she ain't? She'll be locked up for that brutal murder anyways for the rest of her life, thank God. You can't ever be too careful with this kind of animal. Oh no! Let me tell you!"

I asked the guard if there had been any more violent episodes with Emma.

He didn't know of any, but that didn't mean nothin', he'd spat out. "Sometimes they just, you know, lie in wait, for days and days, even weeks or months on end, just for that chance at your gullet in the middle of the night," he snorted. "It's happened to me more'n I care to mention. Other guards, too."

When I returned to the Colliers' home, Frank was sitting in a large armchair in front of a roaring fire in their comfortably furnished living room. His assistant, James, had left him there as Alma was expected home sometime within the half hour. The rich aroma of dinner being prepared by what Alma had laughingly claimed was the "best cook in Cook County" combined with the drowsy warmth of the fire.

"Well, well!" chuckled Frank as I entered the room. "You're looking a bit different these days! Although, let me see ... is that just the bit of shoe polish I detect behind your left ear?"

I gave him a long hug in his chair and then, after accepting his offer of a glass of red wine – from yet another bottle supposedly produced from a wine brick fashioned out at Al Capone's favorite winery in California – sat on the adjacent sofa. Evidently Capone's tastes evoked widely held endorsements.

"So, how was Emma?" he asked gently, his white eyebrows knitted with concern. "I'm assuming that's where you've been since your arrival earlier this afternoon."

"She's so thin, Frank ... like a gaunt statue," I shuddered. "A cadaver. I took over feeding her for a short while and she's scarcely able to swallow even thinned-out oatmeal. She may not even make it to this trial."

"Do you have any information regarding evaluations of her

medical condition? Or for what she's been accused to date?" questioned Frank. "Any new evidence?"

"A lot of horror stories, that's all, Frank. And every story gets worse with the retelling. Not very much in the way of facts it seems to me. When I first heard about Mrs. Havenstock's death, no one even mentioned that woman's name! They just said that Emma had struggled with an elderly woman and the woman had died several hours later. It sounded to me as though she had succumbed to whatever illness had first brought her into the hospital and there was probably nothing to be really concerned over."

"Ummm," nodded Frank. "And of course, the wrong hospital on top of all of that. Well, the family is after the ambulance drivers that brought her to that place as well."

I exhaled and shook my head. "Alma said you were contacting some lawyers you thought might be willing to represent Emma?"

"Yes, I've lined up a couple men to talk with you either tomorrow or the day after, Hannah," he nodded. "But if she's proven not guilty by reason of insanity she'll be kept at Dunning, or a similar facility, until she dies you understand. And if by chance they determine that in fact she was actually sane at the time of the incident …"

"She'll be in jail for life anyway," I concluded morosely.

"Uh, well … actually the Havenstock family is in this for full retribution, Hannah. They won't stop until Emma's hung for Georgina Havenstock's murder," he said quietly. "I'm afraid that a black woman murdering a white woman isn't a situation that's going to be simply swept under the rug, even here in Chicago."

I closed my eyes. Frank leaned towards me, gently placing his hand on my arm. "You need to determine if she's still violent, Hannah. I might be able to help you, ultimately get her transferred to a slightly better facility a little west of the city in a couple of years. Also, I've been doing some research at the

Chicago library about *encephalitis* and this *sleeping sickness* that you and Kid Ory both mentioned to us. My assistant James checked out several books for me and I marked passages I think you should read. I had James take them up to your room with your other things."

"Thank you, Frank," I mumbled, nodding slightly. "I don't know where I would be in any of this if it weren't for you and Alma."

"Well, you've got Alma on the hunt throughout the entire state determined to locate Tayvie and me battling for Emma's future. We usually make a damn good team if I do say so myself," conceded Frank, as he settled back further into his armchair. "As for tonight, my lovely wife's ordered up my favorite meal for dinner and she'll be home in the next few minutes. Relax with us this evening and enjoy a fantastic repast and what I guarantee is the best wine available anywhere in the city of Chicago, maybe in the entire Midwest! Hell, maybe even the entire country! Please wait to start your journey unraveling Emma's illness until tomorrow ... yes?"

The following morning I was awakened by a light, tentative knock on my door. James, Mr. Collier's assistant, wanted to let me know that the first of the lawyers that Mr. Collier had summoned was due to arrive in about an hour. Mr. Collier wanted me to have enough time to get dressed and have a bit of breakfast. Mrs. Collier had already left for her office he mentioned as well.

Had it not been for Frank's calm, quiet interventions, I would have simply crumbled under the lawyers' brutal questioning. The Havenstocks had been coerced to drop charges against Provident Hospital apparently, not that this helped Emma's case in any way, of course. It just gave some limited proof that the family might be malleable from its original unyielding stance in the broad sweeping brush of their accusations, Frank informed me. Frank was most impressed with the last lawyer, Thomas White, who was newer to the Chicago bar than the other two men, but had quite a bit of experience in New York City defending unusual medical cases similar to this one. In fact, Mr. White had recently very successfully defended two almost identical cases for patients in a mental hospital located in the Bronx. We agreed to meet again with Mr. White in two days after I'd had a chance to digest some of the material that Frank had brought over from the libraries.

I was far later catching a train out to Dunning than I had hoped and was only able to observe Emma from the hall window in the continuous baths in the basement area. Something about her thin face seemed slightly more alert, yet at the same time oddly calmer I thought. As I stood watching her I realized that I could hear very remote strains of music. Was there a gramophone playing in the bath area? This was definitely something new. I was certain that at no point in my prior visits had I heard any music throughout the entire building.

After a few more minutes I determined that I was indeed listening to a gramophone. As the record ended each time, there was the loud identifying, trail-off static for several moments until one of the nurse aides on the floor walked behind a partition to either restart the record or change to another. To my complete surprise after listening to the same operatic aria several times, I heard the Original Dixieland Jazz Band's recording of *"Livery Stable Blues."* As I watched Emma, I was certain that I saw a ghost of a smile play at the corners of her mouth. Her large blue eyes closed for a moment and then reopened, almost seeming to sparkle, her focus lightly on the nurse's aide walking past her tub, following the young woman until she had disappeared from Emma's range of sight. That record was turned over and *"Dixie Jass Band One-Step"* began and was restarted twice. I watched Emma carefully. She was definitely listening, intent, absorbed, her eyes focusing yet again on a nurse aide walking up to her, the aide noticeably startled when Emma actually whispered something. Very cautiously, understandably afraid, the young woman bent down closer to Emma's lips. She then nodded, moved out of my sightlines and returned with a small glass of water.

*Emma had asked for a drink of water.*

The Victrola was silenced after the last record had finished. Like an old-fashioned music box automaton, I watched Emma's expression slowly retreat to her rigidly fixed stare, her lips resealing once again. Another aide passed behind me in the hallway and I asked her if she knew the name of the young nurse in the continuous bath area.

"I think that's Mary Simpson," the girl replied, squinting. "Hard to tell from up here though, ma'am. She just fills in sometimes though, if that's her. She ain't a regular girl far's I know."

When I returned to their home I learned that Alma and Frank had eaten a very early dinner and headed out to hear Joe Oliver's band at the Dreamland. The Plantation gig wouldn't be starting until right around the time of Ory's return in a month or so, according to Frank. I devoured a small plate of yesterday's leftovers, complete with profuse apologies from their cook Maisie, who had apparently misunderstood that she was to keep a dinner on the warmer for me. I was anxious to begin my search through the books that Frank had so carefully researched and were piled in my bedroom; a hot dinner was the furthest concern from my thoughts.

Two large very tattered, medical tomes mentioned nothing about any condition called *sleeping sickness*. However, they both offered up an almost identical diagnosis of *encephalitis* as an "intense headache brought about by a brain infection, usually accompanied by a high fever, stiff neck, intense confusion, needing several days rest and fluids." But the medical dictionaries went further to state that the condition very rarely proved to be fatal, as in Dort's friend's case, and there was no allusion whatsoever of its provoking any kind of violent episode, as in Emma's situation. There was mention in the newer of the two books that there had been many verified cases of *encephalitis* after the Spanish Flu epidemic of 1918. This was thought to have occurred because of those patients' weakened constitutions after the flu epidemic. Ory had mentioned to me that he'd been told the same thing during the brief time Emma had been hospitalized.

But another book researching the many early 20th Century medical mysteries that Frank had unearthed and bookmarked for me yielded this remarkable paragraph:

"Manifestations of the *sleeping sickness* (an epidemic virus-borne illness known as the *'sleepy' sickness* in Great Britain) are so varied that no two patients ever seem to present exactly the same complications or symptoms. As reported first in *The Lancet*, a globally respected medical journal, 'a plethora of diagnoses such as *epidemic delirium, epidemic schizophrenia, epidemic Parkinsonism, epidemic disseminated sclerosis, atypical rabies, atypical poliomyelitis, atypical schizophrenia, atypical delirium, atypical hysteria*, among many others, are newly and profoundly confusing illnesses utterly littering the pages of every physician's notebook both in Europe and the United States'."

The author went further to declare: "it seemed at first as though a thousand new diseases had suddenly broken loose upon society and it was only through the profound clinical analyses of pathologist Dr. Constantin von Economo, based on his studies of the brains of deceased patients and his demonstrations that there existed a unique pattern of damage, containing a sub-microscopic, filter-passing agent, or virus as it were, which could transmit the disease to monkeys. This unquestionably identified this protean disease which was named *encephalitis lethargica* – truly a menacing Hydra of a thousand heads." There also followed a brief, very rough, but certainly understandable translation of Dr. von Economo's recent lecture regarding this topic, "*Cellular Structure of the Human Cerebral Cortex,*" that had just been published within the last several months.

Nothing about violence other than the possible mention of *atypical schizophrenia*, whatever that meant, I thought with a sinking feeling. Just sleeping disorders such as *epidemic delirium* or *atypical delirium* stood out to my eyes. None of these disorders gave any credible explanation whatsoever for Emma's disease, if in fact it was even a disease at all.

But then I was drawn to another bookmark of Frank's in the middle of that same book. "You are the music, while the music lasts," was a quote used by T.S. Eliot centered at the top of the chapter. One patient had described herself as 'helpless, completely stationary until the music came'. Then, she said, 'songs, tunes I knew from years ago, catchy tunes, rhythmic tunes, the sort I loved to dance to' would immediately remove her from her catatonic abyss.

And then, further along on that same page by yet another author: "Equally striking was the power of touch. At times, when there was no music surrounding the patient and she would be frozen absolutely motionless in the hospital corridor, the simplest human contact would come to the rescue. One had only to take her hand, or touch her in the lightest possible way for her to seemingly 'awaken;' one had only to walk with her, perhaps shuffling, at her own speed, in her own direction, in her own way. But at the moment one stopped walking, the patient stopped as well and was totally unable to move unassisted. 'I can do nothing alone' stated one patient. 'I cannot initiate, but I can fully share. The moment you go away I am nothing again.' These words, continued the author, were of course taken from those few patients who still maintained some limited vocal communication ability with family members or hospital staff."

Yet another section that Frank had identified with a bookmark, (on which he had scribbled and twice underlined, *read with caution*) detailed the often unpredictable behaviors of these patients. Some expressed such bizarre compulsions as to tear off their clothes in freezing temperatures, engage in horrifically wanton sexual acts often involving animals, pull out all of their teeth or toenails, apparently registering no pain whatsoever, tie themselves with strictures so taut as to completely cut off their circulation to various limbs, resulting in the subsequent amputation of those limbs, or oddities such as strangling cats or lustily devouring nests of live baby mice or cockroaches. These conditions were understandably first referred to psychiatrists until symptoms progressed beyond that of the occasional psychiatric appointment and necessitated hospital admittance with strict dietary and morphine interventions. Typically the diagnoses ranged from that of epilepsy, intoxication, a severe drug reaction, very advanced venereal disease or complete madness.

Quite close to the end in the last book, Frank had marked off a passage with two question marks on another bookmark, reiterating the earlier observance that some patients responded remarkably to music. That passage also alluded to the horrific possibility that these patients were being shuttled into a madhouse, "completely shut off from real life" and that many of them might well have recovered with consistent, disciplined medical intervention.

The more that I read the more I became convinced that Emma suffered from this *encephalitis lethargica*. But given the multiple manifestations of the disorder, this so-called Hydra with many heads as it were, there was absolutely no way for that to be proven and it provided nothing in the way of a defense for her having strangled Mrs. Havenstock anyway. Ultimately, she was probably better off just being considered insane, although how she could be expected to live out her days in that dank medieval hellhole thoroughly paralyzed me.

There was a light knock on my door followed by Alma's

soft voice asking if I wanted some company. "Somehow I knew you would be hard at it," she smiled, glancing over at my disarray of notes and several opened books. "Frank was rather tired, so we didn't even make it through the first set, unfortunately. Just not the same without Kid Ory, of course, Frank complains. How he loves that growling trombone! But luckily, he's a patient man. So what have you found so far?" She sat down on the edge of the bed.

"There's so much here, Alma. Frank's done an incredible amount of the digging to find everything, however. This *encephalitis lethargica* ... I just don't know how he's managed to unearth all he ..." my voice trailed off.

"Ah, yes, well that's our Frank!" Alma smiled. "A true bloodhound of a judge back in his day as you can well imagine, Hannah. That disease was originally known as *neurasthenia* about thirty-five or forty years ago Frank told me. The cause back then was pinned on the early installation of electricity in wealthy homes. It was one of the first cases he tried in fact, right after he'd passed the bar. You can imagine all of that frowsty old money becoming frantic with that scare!"

"But sadly, I don't think there's anything to be gained at all by a doctor stating that Emma has that disease, Alma."

"No," Alma replied softly. "You're probably right. Frank came to the same conclusion, but he wanted for you to do your own research, although, admittedly, he did select the only medical books in the Chicago library that address the illness. Most of them simply dismiss it as a brief minor ailment with various symptoms that simply followed shallowly in the footsteps of the 1918 flu."

"So in other words, there's really nothing to be done."

She put her arm around my shoulders. "We can always appeal after a passage of time for her to be relocated to a better hospital."

"Prison cell from hell you mean."

Alma sidestepped my remark. "Who exactly have you told at Dunning that Emma is your daughter, Hannah?"

I frowned as I thought back for a moment. "Well, I believe the only person was that doctor that Ed and I spoke with originally after we'd seen Emma down in the continuous bath area. I don't remember that he even introduced himself and I don't think he asked for our names come to think of it."

"Good," Alma nodded, her lips pressed tightly together. "Keep it that way."

"Meaning?"

"I'm not entirely sure to be honest with you. Just that it might be easiest to have her transferred at some time if she has no family. The law works in very strange ways sometimes, you realize. Frank mentioned that Tom White won't be coming back to speak with you again until Wednesday, so that gives you time for a long observation of Emma tomorrow now that you've read more about what may be contributing to her illness, Hannah."

After Alma had left I realized that I hadn't mentioned my distinct observation of the effect that the jazz music record had had on Emma. I determined that tomorrow I would try to get her to take a few steps.

> *"Yeah I knew him, knew Al [Capone].*
> *Knew all his boys, yeah.*
> *He used to come in the club, the Plantation all the time.*
> *The guys, they were very nice to me.*
> *Prohibition time, they used to have the best liquor,*
> *better than we're drinking now.*
> *They gave me a fifth."*
> Edward "Kid" Ory

## Chapter 22: Chicago 1925-26

On Tuesdays the fewest number of guards were employed unfortunately. I had to wait for several hours to see Emma, who by then was fast asleep having been given a hefty morphine concoction shortly before my arrival. I tried to get her to sit up slightly, but she was in a complete daze from the drug. No way could I attempt walking with her other than a few weak steps. Nothing was reaching her. The one nurse said she would probably be unresponsive for the rest of the afternoon and probably most of the evening as well. They didn't even have orders to try to feed her until late tonight. I asked why she had been given the cocktail – had she suddenly become violent and they needed to subdue her? The nurse simply shook her head. That was the usual routine unless she was headed for the bath treatment. The patients didn't need to be heavily drugged if they were going to the baths; the staff would just take the usual precautions. I left only an hour after having first been admitted to see Emma, feeling very discouraged as I returned to the Colliers' empty house.

My dinner with Alma and Frank that evening was also fairly subdued. I knew that Frank was easing me into my inevitable conversation with the lawyer tomorrow, but a wave of discouragement thoroughly swamped me.

"For what it's worth, Hannah, I share many of your impressions about the *encephalitis* outbreak. I've come to many of the exact same conclusions that you've had from researching those medical texts," prompted Frank, sipping a small glass of sherry after our dinner. We had all seated ourselves around the fireplace. "However, there's absolutely no way that it can conclusively be proven that Emma isn't suffering from schizophrenia or delirium or some other mental illness. I think that White is going to try to convince you to go with an insanity defense and resist, let's call it the temptation, to delve into any possible other alternatives."

"Which means she's a prisoner in that ... *place* until she dies, Frank!" I cried. "How can I do that to her? My own daughter!"

Alma walked over and sat on the arm of my chair, resting her arm above me on the chair back. "Remember, Hannah," she said quietly. "This is Chicago. Nothing is exactly final in this immense, scattered city of thousands. Sometimes names are scrambled about or they're lost in transition from one set of official records to another, and frequently no one follows up on said records anyway. I wouldn't look at Dunning as the last place she might be held ... there's still the chance of her being moved to another type facility outside the city."

Frank frowned slightly at Alma, shaking his head.

"Let the court proceed as we've suggested tonight," Frank continued. "In fact, Tom White's hoping to get the family to agree to a bench trial based on the fact that Dunning's doctors insist Emma's insane. And then most importantly, you need to work with Emma as you've mentioned. You thought even though she was so monstrously drugged earlier today she was at least attempting to walk with your help, correct?"

I gave a small shrug. Truthfully, I was so determined she would be able to stand up and take a few steps with my assistance that I wasn't certain.

"And then there was also her reaction to the gramophone

music that you mentioned tonight when she was in the bath treatment," added Alma reassuringly. "That's an extremely important observation, you know. So fortunate that you discovered that link after having just read about it! Or even the nurse's aide bringing her a glass of water that Emma apparently requested. There've been many studies in the last decade or so about just how important music is to our inner being, our eternal soul in religious parlance if you will. I think even Sigmund Freud recently touched on something to that effect in a paper he presented last year in Austria, didn't he Frank? But at any rate, studies all the way from the practices of religious crackpots to the care of those suffering in horrible pain upon their deathbeds and everything in between have shown music's amazing healing benefits." Alma moved towards the fireplace, grabbed the iron tongs, and began moving several logs, sending up a brief shower of fiery blue sparks.

"You know, I've been a little reluctant to mention to you that I actually heard Emma sing one time, Hannah, probably, oh, two years ago or so now," said Frank, slightly clearing his throat. "I had met with a friend, another former judge actually, for a late lunch at some lounge just a few blocks off The Stroll – can't remember the name of the place. It's changed names several times since then anyway. We thought that Lucille Hegamin was supposed to be performing, but turned out she had just left for California with Eubie Blake's musical revue '*Shuffle Along*'. Apparently Lucille and her husband Bill's marriage had finally just blown up for good that week as well. Anyway, Bill Hegamin was still playing piano at that lounge and they had several girls filling in for Lucille. Your Emma was one of them. Please understand that at first, when Alma brought your situation to my attention, I didn't put the two things together. Then, once I'd made the connection, well, as I said, I was a bit reluctant to let you know."

"How did she sound, Frank? Please!" I begged. I definitely

remembered both of those names from Emma's journals.

"Beautiful girl, with an absolutely gorgeous, huge voice," admitted Frank quietly. "So different from any of those other blues singers' voices out there. Amazing. My friend George and I were truly stunned. She was infinitely superior to Lucille in our opinions. Neither of us had ever heard any of those lounge singers sound anything like that. George thought that her voice reminded him of ... can't think of the woman's name now ... she had her own very high class black vaudeville act up until about ten years ago or so ..."

"Sissieretta Jones," I offered.

"Yes! Exactly!" Frank exclaimed. "The uh ..."

"The Black Patti," I continued. "You might be surprised to learn that Emma actually was a member of The Black Pattis for that last year before it went under. She learned to mimic Mrs. Jones' extraordinary singing voice very well apparently."

Frank frowned slightly, shaking his head in disagreement. "That can't possibly be, Hannah! Emma would have only been what, maybe 12 or 13 back then!"

"No, it's true. Kid Ory got her that job in fact. He'd filled in with Mrs. Jones' orchestra several times when they'd played in New Orleans or up in St. Louis. He challenged me that Emma didn't sing like a black girl, attacked my interference in her education. In retrospect, he was right of course. He said the only place for her to get a professional start would be with The Black Pattis."

"That's truly remarkable!" replied Frank, sitting back in his chair staring at me. "I remember when George and I saw her she was wearing this unusual wrapped dark blue and silver dress with a long matching scarf wound about in her hair."

"Yes, I think she may have ... um ... permanently borrowed that from Mrs. Jones' review," I admitted with a sad smile. I wondered what had happened to that dress; I realized it hadn't been with Emma's things back in her apartment.

"Ah! Well, regardless, she seemed like some extraordinary figure out of Greek mythology – Aphrodite came to my mind at the time in fact! I don't usually remember what women are wearing – ask Alma! I'm an utter Neanderthal in that regard! Anyway, she was an extremely light-skinned black girl with this ... Medusa-like golden hair. In fact even up close, unless she held her face a certain way, she could have easily passed for white I thought at the time." He took another long sip of wine, staring into the fire. I desperately wanted him to continue with his recollection of her concert.

"Please go on, Frank," I asked, a lump in my throat. "What else? Did you speak with her afterwards?"

"No, unfortunately we didn't. We stayed through her whole set and spoke briefly with Bill Hegamin wanting to know when she might be appearing again. She was also working in some restaurant kitchen and had left immediately after walking off stage Bill told us. She had only been introduced as 'Emma' by the lounge, but Bill mentioned that her last name was Jackson and that he'd now worked with her several times. In fact at first some folks thought she was a cousin of Tony Jackson's since they were both from New Orleans. Bill definitely thought the management wanted to hire her on to replace Lucille for the remainder of the run, although there was considerable concern that the girl was a habitual drug user apparently. She'd been fired from several other lounges when she'd failed to show up for work."

Failed to show up for work. As though that was her choice!

"No, not drugs," I whispered, shaking my head staring into the fire. "You know it wasn't drugs or alcohol either, Frank. This damn disease. This God-damned disease. Eating away at her like a cancer week after week, month after month. And now ... probably forever."

Frank and Alma exchanged a long glance, then Alma began speaking again.

"Frank and I want you to have the chance to work with Emma and continue your search for Tayvie. You're free to stay here – no, no, we insist! The guest room you're in was just sitting there fomenting slut's wool. We're now both of us quite involved in all of this, as I'm sure you're aware."

I started to protest, but Alma waved me off.

"When you and I first met at Provident Hospital, back when you were looking for both girls, I felt a draw to you that I've never experienced with another woman before. Not that kind of draw, don't be afraid!" she added with a chuckle, then continued soberly. "You're the only person other than Frank that I've ever told about my relationship with Carl or my father's having brutally murdered both Carl and my baby and simply walking away scot free without the smallest speck of remorse. Seeing a white woman so desperate to find a young colored woman and her child that she would go so far as to stain herself brown so that she might be free to move around in black society for her search was quite remarkable."

"Alma, she's my daughter … my granddaughter … and without Ory's help …" I began limply, then trailing off again.

"Well, she was Ory's lover, at least for awhile," smiled Alma. "And it would appear as though Emma was hoping that once Ory was around Tayvie here in Chicago that both their personal and music lives would somehow magically blend and make everything fall into place from what you've told me from her journals. A fairy tale that I honestly don't think either of them would have been able to have made a reality, if I may be so bold. Ory's an incredibly handsome, rather devilishly charming man and tends to move fairly quickly from one lady to the next according to most gossip. Something that his wife undoubtedly grumbles about, but continues to stand by him it would seem. They say Louis Armstrong's wife Lil Hardin faces the exact same dilemma with Mr. 'Lady's Man Louis' and they've only just recently gotten married! I'm not sure someone as spirited as your Emma would have been quite so forgiving. In fact, you probably encountered some of Mr. Ory's later-than-ordinary-without-explanation nights while you were both staying at Mecca Flats."

I felt my face burning. Incredibly handsome. Devilishly charming. Oh yes, that was certainly an excellent description of Edward "Kid" Ory! Somehow I felt she knew about my brief relationship with him, but surmised that she would never speak directly of it, even to Frank, and certainly not to me. I made no reply to her remark. I had almost convinced myself that I had dreamed up the entire affair and regardless, I had firmly ceased chastising myself over my behavior.

"Well, tonight I'm the exhausted one," yawned Frank. "That sherry was quite nice, Alma, but nothing comparable to those delicious Al Capone dark reds ... you don't suppose ..."

"Frank ..." chided Alma playfully, winking at her husband as she shook her head.

"Tom White's appointment with us is at 9 a.m. tomorrow, correct, Hannah?"

"Yes, I believe that's right," I replied, grateful that the conversation had moved past Kid Ory's lascivious reputation.

"Well, best to adjourn until then," he remarked, punctuated by another yawn.

*******

Over the next nine months, I managed to adhere to a simple schedule at Dunning. Three days each week I arrived no later than 8:15 a.m., well before any medications, baths or experimental treatments were initiated on ward seven. Dunning's newest, malevolent medical arrival, the electrotherapy treatment, was now utilizing a far stronger, more dangerous, untested current than in the original Tesla violet ray machines. These electric currents initiated convulsions supposedly to help reduce the severity of possible seizures and were said to help clear brainwaves from abnormal function.

There were many glass adapters that could be fitted into the metal fixture, some soothing like the various-sized, blown-glass rakes that mimicked the stroking of fingers, but other larger adapters, when used at higher frequencies, caused horrible blistering at the contact points. A prisoner, Emma had absolutely no rights to refuse any type of experimental treatment I was informed. In later years when I first learned of the horrific experimentation to which the Holocaust victims were subjected in concentration camps across Europe during the war, I always thought back on Dunning's unfettered exploits with Emma and so many others like her. I was certain that this treatment alone did the most damage to her brain, extinguishing any small hope of recovery.

Working as diligently as I was allowed each day, I would typically finish feeding Emma and then, fully supporting her weight against me, her arms bound rigidly down at her sides, get her to shuffle along beside me, aiding her every step, within the small confines of her room at first, and then later, under the constant watchful eye of a guard, in the corridor outside her room.

Alma continued making phone calls, running ads in *The Chicago Defender* and I visited facilities, contacted police departments and social welfare agencies throughout the state looking for any clues about Tayvie, everywhere there were towns along the incredibly expansive tangle of railroad tracks in Illinois, but without success. Tayvie had to be somewhere safe I constantly reassured myself, although I frequently awoke drenched in sweat from renewed nightmares about Joe's wife Maudie Spencer Peterson, being beaten to death and then shoved behind a furnace to be forgotten for almost two decades.

The case against Emma by Mrs. Havenstock's family had been proven in the deceased woman's favor as was expected, but it was brought out during the proceedings that Mrs. Havenstock was far more ill than originally claimed and that in fact, it was because her face was such a bloated, dark grey gargoyle, so oddly distorted in appearance when first loaded into the ambulance, that the drivers assumed that she was a colored woman and had thereupon driven her to what they assumed was the appropriate hospital. Tom White's claim that Mrs. Havenstock had more than likely suffered a massive stroke long before her tragic encounter with Emma was ordered struck from the testimony as an invalid unsubstantiated assumption by the officiating judge and not allowed to appear within the court records. But, that potential variance was most likely noted by the judge both Tom White and Frank later concurred. When the court reached a final decision in the case, it was judged to be one of unintentional homicide by an insane woman, resulting in a final judgment of not guilty due to insanity. This meant that the family could not press further for Emma's execution for having unknowingly committed the crime. It also meant Emma was a prisoner on ward seven at Dunning until she died.

A number of almost imperceptible changes in Emma took place over that time frame, but none quite as dramatic as during the continuous baths. There was no way that I could transport the Collier's heavy Victrola from their home to Dunning every day and it would have disappeared immediately had I ever attempted to leave it in Emma's room. But once Kid Ory arrived back in Chicago, he began his recordings with King Oliver's Dixie Syncopators and Louis Armstrong's Hot Fives, along with a handful of other bands. As each double-sided record first appeared in the various 'race record' shops along The Stroll -- several weeks after having been recorded in Chicago, rushed to New York for processing and duplicating, and then rushed back to Chicago -- Frank, his assistant James and I eagerly snapped up two copies of each instrumental recording. We bought one record for me to entrust to the Victrola album sleeves on the basement shelf of the Dunning continuous baths and the other for Frank's burgeoning jazz music collection. Both Oliver's band

and the Hot Fives occasionally included female singers, but we purposely avoided any of the well-known female blues records made by Bessie Smith or Ma Rainey.

The basement rooms of the continuous baths were off limits to everyone other than staff members, doctors and patients, and one could only observe from the windows in the suspended hallway above. But I was always encouraged when watching Emma's reactions to the records, which I could just barely hear through the thick panes of glass. From listening closely to the same recordings at the Collier's home, I knew exactly when Ory's famous trombone growls would begin and eagerly watched for that slight softening on Emma's face every time. She wasn't always placed in the same tub, but on the occasions when she was actually facing me, her lips appeared to be moving very slightly, perhaps singing lyrics or possibly keeping time to the music. Physically and emotionally she had gained a little strength from our small walks each week, as well as a very slightly increased appetite.

Early in 1926, Ory recorded his tune "*Muskrat Ramble*" and shortly thereafter "*Sweet Little Papa*" with Louis Armstrong's Hot Fives. I distinctly remembered seeing both of these tunes written out in Ory's notebook back at Emma's place in Mecca Flats. These were now two of the most popular tunes being played nightly along The Stroll, and undoubtedly elsewhere throughout the country. It took Frank several months before we were able to obtain two copies of those sides and then, only through a shrewd black market deal that Ory himself pulled off for us. I was fairly certain that much of the upfront money for these recordings was obtained from the Chicago mob. Other than Capone himself, who, much like Pete Lala back in the Storyville days down in New Orleans, was known to be a big jazz music lover, my guess was most of these guys wouldn't have known a trombone from a tambourine. But Capone's music saturation was truly surprising. Ory insisted that the man had an impressive collection not only of jazz records, but of classical symphonies and operas as well and that even more surprisingly, Capone actually wrote music and was an incredible banjo player!

Oddly, Ory never had any interest in listening to any of his own records. In fact, he claimed that none of the musicians cared to listen to themselves on shellac. "Puts down in time a lot of miss-cues, muffed chords, clams, too much bass end at times, an' always real tinny soundin', y'know?" he had shrugged, looking very tired, inhaling on his usual cigarette smoked during a concert break one night. "We all know we sound a lot better than that eh, mess you're hearin'. An' if we don't? *Merde!*" He was now alternating nights playing with Louis Armstrong at the Dreamland and King Oliver at the Plantation.

Ory did have great admiration for the actual *process* of recording and pressing the records, however. And the money for a recording session was pretty damn decent too, he willingly admitted. During one of the Colliers' and my many treks to hear him play once Oliver's band had opened at the Plantation, he had explained the old acoustic horn recording process and the new electric process that would be used to record Jelly Roll Morton's band, known as the Red Hot Peppers, on the Victor label. Even with having every man in his own cubicle with the huge acoustic horns the way that Armstrong or Oliver had been recording, the wax disks were sometimes badly distorted or the recording needle would start maniacally flailing and jump the track. Other times even though the recording session had gone extremely well, the entire day's work had to be thrown out after the wax disks had been carefully sent out for preservation, processing and electroplating and when finally played back at the factory were found to have mysteriously melted within the interior grooves and were absolute garbage.

The new electric microphone recording apparatus still recorded on wax disks, but it wasn't nearly as sensitive to the needle jumping the tracks or distorting the high or low ends Ory told us. There were several symphony orchestras and opera stars recording classical repertoire now using this new technique and they were very enthusiastic about the results. That Jelly Roll, a black jazz musician, was able to capture the attention of bigger money for this very expensive new process said something about Morton's reputation and the man's sheer talent, stated Ory. Like any other enterprise, unless backers knew up front that they would be making a fast, sizeable profit from the goods, they weren't about to go out on a speculative deal, especially one involving a black musician – even Capone wasn't willing to take on that kind of expensive risk without guaranteed results!

Interestingly also, neither the Hot Fives nor the Red Hot Peppers actually existed outside of the recording studio Ory told us when Frank inquired about the various bands. All the musicians played all night with completely different groups and just met in the early morning to record for the OKEH label (Armstrong) or Vocalion label (Oliver), frequently then going to rehearse for another upcoming recording date before heading back out to their regular all-night gig. Ory was pretty exhausted and had been for months on end he admitted, but the money was real good everywhere, so he sure as hell couldn't complain. Dort, truly a pessimist of the first order and an unrelenting miser at heart Ory mused, was making him save practically every penny he groaned frequently. Tired out from her work as a housemaid and seamstress, she never accompanied him to gigs.

"Chicago's a goddamn jazz musician's gold mine!" Ory stated on many occasions. But despite that optimism, Ory also mentioned that there were those who felt the old style New Orleans players were now *passé*, too clunky, too gritty and all of that hokey vaudeville stuff was just too damned corny for the newer, more sophisticated smooth jazz music scene developing among the younger, trendsetting white audiences. Armstrong's possibly biggest rival, a white cornet player named Bix

Beiderbecke from Iowa of all places, was sanitizing jazz with Paul Whiteman's popular dance orchestra out in New York City. "Long's that ole whitewashed shit stays out in New York we're ok here in Chicago!" Ory commented wryly, lifting his glass in a toast.

"Do you think you see something like, well, writing on the wall maybe?" Frank had asked, as always providing top grade whiskey in the large flask concealed under his plaid lap blanket. He topped off Ory's glass as he asked the question.

"Eh, I dunno," shrugged Ory. "You ever seen that guy play?"

"Beiderbecke?"

"Yeah."

"No."

"Well, he just kinda stares at his feet when he's playin', y'know? Never even looks out to the audience. An' I mean never! Very weird. I mean, you gotta look out there at 'em sometime durin' the night, even if they ain' applaudin' anything you play, y'know? Beats me why he's so popular. No real brass wizardry like Satchmo or Oliver or even Papa Mutt for that matter. Just dry, dry, dry. Eh, to each his own I guess," replied Ory. "Great whiskey as always, Frank! *Toujours une fête magnifique* when the Colliers are in the audience!"

And then, one scorching hot September night, the Plantation, though air cooled, was unquestionably losing its battle against the humidity. Ory had joined the Colliers' and my table as usual for a cigarette during the band's break. Oddly though, instead of immediately lighting up when he joined us, he was tapping the end of his unlit cigarette on the table several times, then flipping it around and tapping the other end, continually repeating the process. The cigarette was finally so badly mangled, spilling out tobacco from multiple rents, that he simply threw it under the table and extracting another, began the same ritual. He had brought his own glass over to the table, accepted Frank's offer of whiskey, but then oddly sat quite mute, again mutilating the second cigarette and looking out over the crowd, not engaged in any way with Frank's attempts at conversation. Frank knew that Ory had just completed the first Jelly Roll recordings earlier that week and was understandably eager to hear about the session with the new electric recording equipment.

Ory suddenly stood up and turned towards me. "Sorry Frank, I'll have to talk to you later," he said brusquely. Then, his hand on my back, his voice urgent in my ear, he stated: "meet me during our next break. I'll be in the hallway behind the kitchen. You can get directions from one of the waiters." Then, obviously extremely distracted, he thanked Frank for the drink and said he needed to attend to a problem and walked quickly away. Ory had engaged me many times in small bantering conversations at the Plantation and had shown up quite often at Dunning when I had been working with Emma, as well as frequent visits with her completely on his own. But I was thoroughly unprepared for what followed.

The next set seemed endless to me. I told the Colliers that I would simply take a cab back to their home and insisted they not wait for me. I knew Frank was tired and Alma had mentioned she would be volunteering at Provident Hospital before heading into work the following morning. When I asked one of the wait staff about the kitchen hallway, he directed me through a pair of narrow doors and told me to follow the darkly-tiled tunnel as far as I could and then just wait. Someone would probably be joining me in a few moments, he had shrugged. I stood nervously at the end of the tunnel lit only by a dim, single light bulb, its spindly cord dangling from the low, blistered ceiling. It was definitely much cooler down here I realized, but that lent very small comfort. After several long minutes I heard voices. A section that had appeared to be a supporting partition was then pushed back to admit three very rough-looking men alongside

Ory. As they walked over towards me he mouthed the words "it's ok," but the dark expression on his face was not at all convincing. Trembling, I took several steps backwards, now supporting myself against the greasy tiled wall.

"She'll show you which one," stated Ory tensely.

"Which one?" I whispered, glaring at Ory. I had only caught occasional glimpses of Al Capone's thugs at the Plantation Café and unquestionably, these three were full members of that regime.

One of the men grabbed me, turned me around and quickly tied a blindfold over my eyes while another man tied my hands in front. "Don't say nothin' an' you'll be fine," he grunted. "Otherwise I tape up your mouth."

"Do you have to do that?" I heard Ory ask.

With one man on each side rigidly holding my elbows, I was buffeted along through the tunnel, which seemed to be running under noisy street gratings and then somewhere near water I thought. A few times I stumbled, my legs buckling underneath, but the men immediately jerked me back to my feet. We got to what might have been a loading dock; I could now definitely smell water nearby. Although I was still blindfolded, the men untied my hands and roughly pushed me into the backseat of a car, one man seated on each side. There seemed to be a large pillow on the floor under my feet. The third man had gotten in front. As the doors slammed the driver made a sharp turn grinding the gears with a hideous screech, the wheels bouncing over some kind of barrier as we began the drive. The men next to me laughed and said something in what I guessed was Italian to the driver. After one or two more sentences none of the men spoke again for the rest of the trip. I had already guessed that we had left Ory back in the tunnel, but continued listening for his voice in the vague hope that I was mistaken.

The car had been winding over what seemed to be a long gravel drive for several minutes when it abruptly came to a stop.

Removing my blindfold, the men yanked me out of the car, rigidly grasping my elbows on each side and we started down a set of very dimly lit, steep stone stairs, pausing at the bottom. The building looming up in front of me finally began to take some kind of shape. It was the basement entrance at Dunning. The other two men had caught up to us and I was pushed through the door, walking down a narrow corridor towards what I was certain would be the continuous baths. Though that entrance was not visible from the suspended hallway where I'd watched for almost a year now, I knew it had to exist. There were no guards, nurses or nurses' aides anywhere in the baths area.

"Which one's Emma?" demanded the man on my left.

I looked over the four long rows of heads zipped into their wet cocoons, soaking in the gurgling metal tubs. The dizzying smell of antiseptic surrounded us with a swamp-like miasma. Emma was all the way down at the end of one row. "There," I pointed half-heartedly. "At the end near that sink." What could they possibly want with her? And what could Ory possibly have done for these thugs to come after Ory's paralyzed, former girlfriend? I felt sick inside.

As we started walking towards Emma I noticed that the two men behind me were carrying a rolled blanket and I wondered if this had been the pillow under my feet in the car. Within seconds the men had unzipped Emma's cocoon and pulled her from the tub, tearing off her turban and then roughly laying her out nude on the cold grey concrete floor. There was a series of circular burns, almost as large as cigarette burns, dotting up her arm and onto her chest from the electrotherapy contact ends I noticed angrily. The men then unrolled the blanket revealing a dead young white woman, eyes still wide open, with short curly brown hair. I inhaled sharply, but made no other sound.

They quickly stripped off the girl's clothes, threw them over to me and told me to dress Emma. While I dressed her, like a large doll spread out on the floor, the three men quickly wound the turban around the dead girl's hair, dumped her into the cocoon, and zipped her up into the tub.

"C'mon, not much time. Dunno for how long they paid them two guards," one of the men remarked gruffly as they attempted to jerk Emma up on her feet.

"She ... she really can't walk at all," I pleaded. The man then threw Emma over his shoulder like a sack of grain and we moved swiftly out of the baths area. I doubted that we had been down there for longer than five minutes. Obviously we were taking her with us, but where exactly? And why? What role Ory had played in all of this remained a mammoth question. His nervous preoccupation during the break tonight haunted me, as I remembered his battering those two cigarettes into tobacco oblivion.

Once back in the car, the men again blindfolded me as the car roared into reverse, gears grinding, and then sharply turned around. As they were doing so I asked that they not blindfold Emma since I thought it would be too frightening for her. I didn't know if they respected my request or not; all I received was a low grunt in the way of a reply as we were jolted along the gravel drive. I kept telling myself it only made sense that the dead girl had been substituted for Emma, so that it would look as though it were Emma who had died and the other girl would simply disappear with no questions asked. And that Emma and I were safe. That Ory wouldn't have intentionally put the two of us in any danger.

But I was also certain that he wouldn't be so foolish as to believe that some unintentional outcome might not befall us. He could quite easily be informed that some unforeseen tragedy had unfolded. Assuming you could believe what you read in the daily papers, these thugs were ruthlessly non-discriminating. That's why Ory had been nervous I realized. When this situation had blown up tonight, whatever that situation must had been, he had seen what might well be the only possibility ever to get Emma permanently out of that hell hole and had rashly acted on a huge gamble. I desperately wanted to believe that he'd been given assurance regarding this entire plan, but the fact that I had been blindfolded once again was a very chilling omen.

We had stopped for a few moments, for gasoline it seemed. The man on my left had pulled my head over to his shoulder -- my nose was now buried deep in his armpit, where his shirt was thoroughly soaked in rancid sweat. As we started again the roads were getting bumpier and the driver had slowed down considerably. I heard no traffic. Wherever we were headed, it was not back into the city I realized numbly.

We had probably been driving for well over an hour when I became aware that there was another car ahead of us. A duplicate set of gears audibly downshifted before our car's echo of the same, as we jounced over huge ruts, plowing through thick brush that scraped viciously against both sides of the car in an obviously narrowing path. Suddenly we stopped. All the car doors opened at once and the men exited simultaneously – a practiced precision. The man on my left ripped the blindfold from my eyes. At first everything was coated in a deeply velveted darkness until my sight readjusted. Standing just outside the car he yanked me forward in the seat, then quickly roped my hands to the window handle. All four doors then slammed simultaneously. I could barely make out that Emma's hands had also been roped to the opposite door. Her head was tilted against the window sash, eyes wide open, unblinking, staring up into the night. The man from the other car had now joined in and all of them began running alongside the car, propelling it forward until one of them uttered *"ora! va bene!"* as they jettisoned it forward. I heard the gurgling rush of water coming up all around us, the car slowing as it began its swim out into the darkened waters, beginning a slow descent. Car doors slammed as the men piled back into the other car, followed by the now familiar screech of gears as they pulled away. I kept my eyes focused on Emma, dimly outlined, as I felt the car's steady slow decline, pitching further forward. But then we stopped. Tongues of black water lapped briskly outside the car, but we were no longer sinking. I stared out into the dark. Waiting. Simply waiting.

I awoke in the same position, rain splattering in the early dawn. I didn't think that the car had sunk any lower. Because I was roped to the window handle, I could move the window down slightly, at least enough to bring some air into the car. We were both sweating profusely in the dense humidity. Emma seemed to be in the exact same position that I'd seen her a few hours ago – head against the window sash simply staring into space, blinking only very rarely.

Gradually as a weak, greasy daylight surrounded us, I could only see tall grasses extending high above us on either side. The windshield was mired in grey mud, tangled in an enormous net of kudzu vines. Those vines were exactly what kept us from sinking any further I guessed. Once they gave way nothing would impede further descent. Fighting the lump in my throat I suddenly started singing softly. Ory's *"Eh, la bah."* I had no idea why it came to me. I knew that I had never gotten the pronunciation of the lyrics correct even way back when I'd first learned the tune from Zuma when I was a little girl – in fact, she used to laugh at me trying to approximate her patois. But that sure as hell didn't matter now. I knew without question Ory would have sung it to Emma during his visits at Dunning and Tayvie had even taught it to Monsieur Autruche down in New Orleans: *"Mo che kouzen, mo che kouzin, mo lenme la kizin! Mo manje plen, mo bwa diven, e sa pa kout ariyen! Eh, la bah! Eh, la bah! Eh, la bah! Eh shel la bah! Ye tchwe kochon, ye tchwe lapen, e mo manje plen. Ye fe gonmbo, mo manje tro, e sa fem on malad. Eh, la bah! Eh, la bah! Eh, la bah! Eh shel la bah!"*

It was a silly song – hey over there, cousins! I'm making a gumbo in my wonderful kitchen, eating too much pig and rabbit and getting a stomachache was the full extent of the song. There was at least one more verse possibly, but this was all that I could remember. Emma's eyes stopped staring out of the window and, her head still resting on the door, her focus very slowly shifted towards me. A tiny smile graced her lips. She might even have been moving her lips slightly, singing along at times, although I probably imagined that. I sang the song over and over again, just above a whisper, finally stopping when I realized I was getting very thirsty, becoming quite hoarse. The rain outside had increased in intensity, now drumming hypnotically on the car's roof.

"Maybe I shouldn't sing about food," I sighed. Like a child, I put my tongue on the window to catch a rivulet of rainwater trickling on the inside and was surprised how good it tasted. Suddenly, the car gave a shudder and downward heave as we moved a few inches forward and listed heavily to the right side. I wondered how long the front windshield could hold before completely giving way from the weight of the water and then wondered why on earth I wanted to speculate about it. Water had very gradually begun seeping in over the floor of the car, definitely deepening more quickly on Emma's side.

I'm going to sit here and watch my daughter drown I realized dully. That will be the last thing I see before I leave this earth. My father had been a psalm singer, that is, someone who wailed psalms at any occasion without any true religious provocation whatsoever. Wailings that had no depth, no reason, and certainly no meaning other than a jumble of syllables, uttered by a deceitful, destructive, self-centered bastard. Suddenly, unrequested, one of those psalms, one I had forgotten about after so many years, came vividly to mind:

*I am like a pelican of the wilderness*
*I am like an owl of the desert.*

*I watch, and am as a sparrow alone*
*Upon the house top.*

"There's nothing I can do to save you, Emma," I mumbled, tears streaming down my face. "From your birth I've destroyed every shred of happiness you should have claimed for your own. I'm as useless as my father with his worthless psalms." I prayed for the vines to just give way quickly, drown us both together. Immediately. "Please God," I begged, "don't make me suffer watching her die first."

I drifted in and out of consciousness. Sometimes it was dark, other times daylight, but I had no idea if those awakenings belonged within the same span of hours. Time was lost to me as any reliable measure. The rain had finally stopped however. The murky grey water was now lapping over Emma's waist, the bottom of her dress spread out like a dark water lily from her thighs. My knees were no longer visible beneath a veil of thick, cloudy mud.

*"Well, of course, my theory is to never discard the melody.*
*Always have the melody going some kind of a way.*
*And of course, your background*
*would always be perfect harmony.*
*With what is known today as riffs,*
*meaning figures, musically speaking."*
Ferdinand "Jelly Roll" Morton

## Chapter 23: "Alice made the train ok."

A pair of gangly beanpole-thin boys stumbled upon us, out early that morning with their poles, hoping to find good fishing back in the swampier areas after all the rain. The one boy stayed with us while his friend went to find help, talking to me from the closest spot where he could stand, astride what might have been a beaver dam at one time. I knew that I made no sense answering his questions, but thankfully, he just kept talking. We were on his family's land, he told me. Almost all the way back where they dumped rotten crops, trees, weeds, brambles and such near this sort of ravine, he explained further. Nobody ever came back to this stretch. Used to a long time ago when they would cut ice blocks for the cold cellar, but not too many people needed big chunks of ice like that anymore, he'd shrugged. Water was up really high on all of the other areas along the lake after days and days of rain and he and his friend both preferred wading in to fish, so that's why they'd thought to come back here.

His friend "Mouse" had run to get his dad since their farmhouse was the closer of the two. They thought his dad could hitch up the drays and maybe pull the car far enough back for us to get out before completely flooding the vehicle. He didn't think there was much left of the car to salvage though. Looked pretty dented and mighty banged up the boy remarked. He wanted to know how we'd ended up there in the first place and I said I didn't know. I hadn't mentioned that both Emma and I were both still roped to the doors inside either. The muddy water was now swirling high underneath Emma's arms and over my waist. When the boys had first appeared I thought I was imagining them, dreamed them up in one final desperate hallucination. I still wasn't certain they were real.

Mouse and his dad returned within minutes, driving a team of four enormous dray horses hitched to log-pulling chains. His dad roped the chains over the back bumper and carefully guided the drays as they eased the car backwards a couple of feet so that we were enough clear of the water for my door to be opened. However it was still locked. My arms completely numb, I worked to roll down the window as far as possible so that Mouse's dad could reach in and unlock the door. Water had immediately swamped the car, rushing in with his added weight. He pulled a switchblade from his back pocket and sliced quickly through the rope, freeing my wrists.

"Help her!" I sobbed. "Now! Please! Please! She's paralyzed!" Emma was now completely submerged, her hair floating out under the foul water like muskrat fur.

He pushed me out of the car into the water and I landed spread eagled, but Mouse grabbed my arm, putting his arm around my back to steady me, and we swam in a clumsy formation towards firmer ground. Mouse's dad pulled Emma out of the same door since the car had now capsized completely onto its right side into the water. Cradling her in his arms, he maneuvered towards the sky from the rapidly swamping car, first landing on his back then turning, holding her in front of himself, awkwardly swimming towards us. The bumper suddenly gave way and broke free of the horses' chains and the entire car rapidly disappeared, gurgling down into the murky lake. The two front horses were almost submerged as well, but somehow the team managed to work themselves sideways, pulling away from the quickly sinking automobile.

The boys and I managed to hoist Emma up to Mouse's dad who was now astride one of the dray horses. Mouse pulled me up to ride with him. The other boy had unhitched the two remaining drays and followed along behind us. A loud chorus of what I assumed were birds suddenly increased in intensity with the sun's strengthening rays, but Mouse smiled and informed me that "naw, them's jes' frogs -- thousands of 'em in point oh fact!" Birds. Frogs. A dragonfly's darting dance just overhead. Tall sawgrasses gracefully undulating as we cut our way along the muddied path. The blistering hot sun scorching the top of my head. These were small gifts I swore I would never again take for granted.

Once at their farmhouse, Mouse's dad, a rather taciturn fellow named Clem, quickly started boiling up water for hot baths. My arms, upper back and legs were completely numb from having been riveted to the door for so long; I doubted that Emma had much feeling throughout her limbs anyway. We were both coated in a slimy, greenish-grey tar. I washed Emma first, but I was so weak I had to ask Clem for assistance getting her in and out of the tub and washing her hair. She had gained a little weight these last few months, but was still tragically emaciated. Clem frowned when he saw the snaking pattern of burn marks along her body, but asked no questions. As I got her dried off and dressed in some of Clem's late wife's clothing, Mouse added several more buckets of scalding hot water to the tub for me.

While we were getting cleaned up, Clem had scrambled up some eggs and potato pancakes for us. Ravenous, I fed both Emma and myself, tears rolling down my face at times. Food had never tasted so magnificent to me. Clem helped me get Emma put down in bed before starting to ask any questions. He was already quite certain that the car had been stolen and fairly confident it smacked of the syndicate's calling cards. I replied it was plainly a case of mistaken identity, but that the men wouldn't listen to my explanations. I had no idea why they had grabbed Emma and me and, needless to say, they offered no clarification.

Clem had nodded his head slowly, chewing on the end of his pipe. He believed that it was a mistake, but even so, he certainly didn't want us staying at his family's place for more than a night or so, "get out earliest we could possibly travel," he'd stated. "Too risky otherwise." He'd be more than happy to give me the fares; the train depot at Janesville was only about ten miles down the road, just over the line, and either he or Mouse could certainly take us down there. I fully understood Clem's concern. One of those men would certainly be coming back to check on the car we were all certain. If for some reason it wasn't totally invisible beneath the bracken, neighbors might well be questioned, houses searched and the like.

Clem continued speaking. "Did you know there was a massive hit on Al Capone by that Northsiders gang a coupla days back? Led by that big gangster down there -- Hymie Weiss," he muttered.

He then showed me the newspaper article. Al Capone's headquarters at the Hawthorne Inn in Cicero, Illinois was sprayed with 1,000 rounds of machine gun fire in broad daylight through the windows of the Inn's first floor restaurant as Capone was eating there. Surprisingly, Capone himself was not injured, although some of his men had been slightly wounded stated the article.

"Sure don' know why anybody would wanna live in Chicago, tell you the truth," Clem added, shaking his head as he methodically relit the tobacco in his pipe. "Helluva godforsaken place to raise a family. Entire place is a chronic den of political hypocrisy, shamelessly wallowing in every sin imaginable. Shamelessly wallowing I tell you. If my granddaddy hadn' already owned this land an' passed it down to my daddy an' my daddy down to me, I'd be even farther away from that place, lemme tell you! Even with Prohibition now the law of the land, they say there's people drunk all over them streets, day or night, night or day! Then you got your gangs everywhere shootin' each other up, gamblin' their money foolishly to all kinds of sport, horse racin', dog racin', car racin', boxin' matches! What hooey! And that's not to mention them loose color'd women, half dressed nigger sluts, singin' all that nonsense, draggin' down the good name of womankind, an' even worse, them color'd boys playin' that awful jazz music all night every night! I tell you, we've got our own Sodom and Gomorrah right here in the State of Illinois! Utter travesty, I tell you, ma'am!"

I gave a quick smile and nodded nervously in agreement. I was obviously far more decadent in my beliefs than I realized and discreetly chose not to reply. Not that she could have responded, but I was grateful that Emma was already asleep in the back room.

Clem drove us to the train station, thankfully after a full day's rest (and rain), handing along a well-apportioned basket of food and some money, as well as kindly having purchased our tickets. I'd managed to get some oatmeal down Emma and we were both clad in rather large, slightly wrinkled, but at least clean dresses, looking like a pair of weather-beaten farm wives boarding the train to head out to Colorado Springs.

I had no idea how long it might take me to obtain one of the cottages at the Myron Stratton Home in Colorado Springs, but I was now determined for us to end up there. Win Stratton certainly couldn't have foreseen that he and I would have a daughter who would be so desperately in need of the very services his endowment of this Home could provide. I would have to leave the search for Tayvie to Alma, Frank and Kid Ory at this point. I could never go back to Illinois or New Orleans or even Kansas City again – anywhere that the Chicago-style gangster scene thrived was now far too dangerous. I now looked at Colorado Springs almost as a mecca. I wrote down Alma's

Chicago law office phone number for Clem and asked him to reverse the charges to call once our train had departed. Knowing that Alma would not actually be answering the phone, I asked him to please just relay this exact message: "Alice made the train ok. She'll call when home."

We checked into the ground floor room of a very cheap hotel upon our arrival in Colorado Springs. I had begun to call Emma "Alice" all of the time for us both to get used to the idea. I truly didn't know exactly how much Emma understood when I spoke to her, but for some reason, I thought that she comprehended at least some of it. Most of the time, however, she appeared to be in a deep sleep, even when her eyes were wide open, rarely focusing on anything, her breathing often frighteningly shallow. Dealing with her needs all alone was very difficult at first, I will admit. Feeding her was always an extremely slow process and I only attempted an actual bath for her every few weeks, having to obtain another woman's assistance to lift her safely in and out of the tub. Every morning she needed to be thoroughly sponged with warm water, however, since her skin continued to be oddly covered with a thick, greasy gray film, almost like a luminescent cold cream.

I had rented an ancient wheelchair from a local hospital so that we could go outside whenever the weather permitted. Other times, holding her tightly against me, we slowly shuffled in our hotel room, or occasionally, on her better days, down one of the halls. It was something of a trial and error experience for us both, but after several weeks we had managed to get ourselves into a reasonable routine. Once we were settled at the Myron Stratton Home I vowed that my first purchase would be a newer style Victrola! Finding any of Ory's records would be almost impossible however; there was not one music store selling 'race records' to be found anywhere in Colorado Springs, Denver or anywhere else in the entire state I learned immediately. That kind of thing would only be available in more decadent cities like Chicago or New York City I was informed rather icily. Cities where "those" people would want to purchase such an item. There aren't any colored people in Colorado Springs claimed all of the business owners near our hotel, which even from my own small observance was not remotely true. They were even more discounted and invisible here than in Kansas City, Missouri all those years back I reflected sadly. These last twenty years we'd made no progress whatsoever in this country I thought bitterly.

Two weeks after we'd arrived in Colorado Springs I finally felt brave enough to contact Alma at her office, calling from the hotel's lobby, reversing the charges. After a long wait, Alma finally came on the line and I learned what had taken place earlier on that pivotal night.

One of the musicians in King Oliver's band had been dealing heroin for quite some time and was seriously hooked himself. Despite multiple attempts to get off the stuff, as well as Oliver's threats to fire him on many occasions if he persisted in the habit, he continued to perform at the club. Young, smart, very talented and very handsome, he was especially charming with the white girls, often lavish spenders from the well-to-do suburbs, who frequented the club. One of the girls he'd been seeing was a very wealthy Irish girl from the North side and he'd almost immediately gotten her hooked on the stuff. She'd quickly developed an unquenchable addiction and the two of them were rumored to throw intimate impromptu parties, usually numbering no more than three or four people, in the upstairs back rooms that this girl had rented out in the Plantation's expansive building.

That night, however, the girl's luck had run out, said Alma. Everyone had panicked looking for the fastest solution. Not just because she was a rich white girl who'd overdosed shooting up heroin while having a wild sexual orgy with two very black men, but because she was Hymie Weiss' only niece. The same Hymie Weiss who ran the largest rival gang to Al Capone's organization and had put out the hit on Capone that following night. Disappearing in plain sight was one of the most efficient techniques employed by these gangs stated Alma. And someone had craftily left a fake note at the girl's parents' front door saying that the young woman and her new beau, a man her parents had never met the note claimed, had decided to elope that evening. She was now of legal age and no one could stop her. As a complete aside, when the nurses checked into the continuous baths at Dunning Institute they would discover that a woman named Emma Jackson had passed away over night.

"And, what then happened to ... Emma Jackson?" I replied slowly.

"She was cremated two days later, since there were no immediate relatives. Someone did mention yours and Ory's visits with her, but none of that could ever be verified. Mental hospital records are typically a jumbled trail leading nowhere as you've probably guessed."

"So you really have no idea about anything that happened after that do you," I inquired quietly.

"I will say that I thought Ory took something of a chance with this idea, but he was informed at the end of the night that everything had gone fine. He said that you and Emma had been put on a train that night, destination undisclosed, and that eventually you would contact him, although it probably wouldn't be for several months. So I'm really glad to hear from you this soon, actually."

I then explained all that occurred that night. The car ride, the lake, the water seeping into the capsized car for days, being rescued miraculously by Mouse, Clem's team of dray horses, followed by Emma's and my blind train excursion to Colorado Springs. I spoke quietly into the telephone, located quite openly in the center of the hotel lobby. I feared anyone who might be within listening distance; other than Alma, Frank and Ory, I knew that no ears could be trusted with this story.

"Oh dear God," whispered Alma, at first speechless, finally replying in a choked voice. I could tell she was horribly shaken. "Does … does Ory know about any of this?"

"No. I haven't spoken with him."

We were both quiet for several moments. It was rare that Alma was at a loss for words.

"Did you hear the recent news though?" said Alma, finally finding her voice.

"No."

"Hymie Weiss was gunned down, murdered, yesterday outside the O'Banion Flower Shop at the Northsiders headquarters."

I exhaled, shaking my head. I did not miss Chicago. Clem had been right in many ways.

"Kid Ory joked last night he'd recorded *'Dead Man Blues'* with Oliver and then recorded it again only four days later with Jelly Roll just before Weiss was killed … oh Hannah, I'm just blabbering to disguise the fact that I'm just shaking ..."

"Is Ed still playing at the Plantation?" I quietly interrupted.

"Yes. He'll be happy to know that I've heard from you. That you're both … safe."

"Yes," I replied slowly. "I'm sure he will be. You need to be extremely careful obviously when you speak with him, Alma. All our lives now hang in a delicate balance."

"Yes. Understandably. Frank and I will head out over to the club tonight, Hannah. I'll have him talk with Ory while I keep stray ears away. Is there any way Ory can contact you? Or me?"

"No. Absolutely not. It's far too dangerous. For the time being, I'll have to just call you."

"What else do you need right now?"

"Could you send Emma's and my trunks out to the train depot? I can claim them once they've arrived. Send them to Alice E. Miller. That's the name I've registered under at this hotel."

"And who is Alice Miller?"

"No one, I sure hope!" I replied, affecting a small laugh.

"Of course. I'll have James take care of it first thing tomorrow. He'll be good to keep this under wraps as well, Hannah. Please don't worry about that. I'll pack out everything in your room. Now, money. What do you need immediately?"

"I've looked into piece work at a hat shop here – have already started working for them actually. There appears to be a fevered market for trimming-out plain felt cloche hats with beads, velvet and such out here presently. My guess is that it can't possibly last though. Women seem to be very frugally tightening their purse strings bit by bit here. At least that's my observation. But, I can work from home and be with Emma almost all the time ... 'Alice' that is. But ..."

"I'll wire you a modest money transfer at the depot tomorrow so not to rouse any kind of suspicion. Anything else?" inquired Alma.

"Records. Whenever Frank has a chance to buy any of Ory's new records and send them once we're settled. Any of the sides that he just did with Jelly Roll Morton and King Oliver when they're available would be a godsend ... I'm sure he won't be able to find any of the old ones anymore. I know once they've run all the original copies they never do so again. Ed says that he thinks one day that will all change, but who knows. Emma would love to hear them, I'm absolutely certain. I don't have a Victrola yet, but that's earmarked as one of my first major purchases – along with a sturdy wheelchair. Certainly someone's got to be selling an old wheelchair and a decent, used Victrola around here in the next few months! I've rented a wheelchair for the time being and our room at this hotel is on the first floor. Very noisy overhead day and night, but at least we're able to get out most days into the fresh air for much-needed walks. Somehow, I'm managing."

"I'm just wondering Hannah, whatever happened to the first ... Alice?" questioned Alma. "Did you ever hear from her, or, what was her name again, Mrs. Hughes? Do you want me to, well, look into that? Since she was also in Colorado Springs she might turn up somewhere. That could be, well, ugly."

"I've no idea," I replied with a small laugh, sounding far more bitter than I'd intended. "But after almost twelve years I'm sure I'll never hear from either of them again, so please don't waste your time, Alma! I remember Mrs. Hughes telling me that she had briefly been on the hospitality board for the orphanage at the Stratton Home, but do you remember my mentioning Jane Lawson, who was one of my clients at the Women's Exchange in New Orleans?"

"Yes, I think so."

"When I mentioned Mrs. Hughes to Jane, she'd never heard of her. Jane's two children were in that orphanage for almost a year while Jane was trying to earn enough money to prove that she could support them. If Mrs. Hughes was no longer there at that time, I seriously doubt she's suddenly found it deep within her heart to become involved again. And this hotel is definitely located in a less desirable section of the city. I'd say there's next to no chance I'll run into the woman dashing out of a cheap confectionery just as they're closing, spiriting away colorful tissue-lined boxes of bonbons for her poor neglected orphans!"

Ironically, the question of both Alice's and Mrs. Hughes' whereabouts inadvertently answered itself several weeks later in an article in the society pages of *The Gazette*, Colorado Springs' leading newspaper: *"Word has just been received of the recent marriage of Alice Elizabeth Hughes, granddaughter of the late Mrs. Margaret Hughes, to Chester Alan Fiske, Jr., held at the Grand Ballroom in New York City on September 5. The former Miss Hughes recently completed her graduate studies in mathematics and the sciences at Mount Holyoke College in South Hadley, Mass. She also has been internationally recognized for her golf acumen, having won multiple trophies while at Mount Holyoke. Mr. Fiske, heir to the Fiske fortunes in Philadelphia, Penn., holds a graduate degree in engineering from Yale University. After honeymooning throughout Europe, the couple will reside in Philadelphia at the Fiske family enclave.*

*Colorado Springs' residents will remember the late Mrs. Margaret Hughes as the owner of the beautiful McAllister House, perhaps The Springs' best-known representative of the Winfield Scott Stratton architectural style. Mr. Fiske's nephew, who owns a transit business in the City, and his wife, will occupy that home according to the new Mrs. Chester Fiske. Information about Mrs. Chester Fiske's wedding dress, apparently an exclusively-designed Madeleine Vionnet gown, along with her Jean Patou trousseau, which sports an entire new line of professional women's golf wear also designed exclusively for Mrs. Chester Fiske, will be published when that information becomes available."*

There was also a rather grainy picture of Alice and her new husband waving at the camera, liberally showered by well-wishers' rose petals. Her blond head was tossed back, the veil flowing back over her shoulder as she smiled brightly at her adoring crowd. She was as beautiful as ever, obviously successful and I would assume, happy with her new marriage. I thought back on that squalling infant Alice, whom I had rescued from a urine-soaked dresser drawer, lined with torn newspapers like an animal's cage, in a brothel when her mother Abigail Hughes had failed to return. I had played an immense part in Alice's getting to where she was today, even though I knew she would never concede to that fact.

---

Once my trunks had been delivered from Chicago and I had Alice's birth certificate and my marriage certificate to John Barrington, I contacted the admitting superintendent, Miss Lucille Lloyd, at the Myron Stratton Home. As Ory had feared, there was indeed a sizeable waiting list to obtain a cottage at the Stratton residences I was informed by Miss Lloyd when I first telephoned. This wait could easily take a year or more, but typically admission was possible within six to eight months, likely even less when there was an invalid adult involved stated Miss Lloyd. Mr. Stratton, that is, Mr. *Winfield* Stratton, had been adamant in the precise wording of his endowment for the Home in order to reach out quickly in situations such as Alice's, especially since she had been born in the county.

As they were always looking for qualified teachers for the orphanage, Miss Lloyd was also quite interested in the fact that I had taught grade school age children in Kansas City for many years. I told her that I still had my letter of introduction from one of the school's lawyers, which I hoped would suffice as a reference. My school had ironically been named by me as the Mary Stratton School for Colored Children. But fortunately, the school lawyer, Mr. Reedy, had simply attested to my having been an exceptionally qualified teacher in the district and neither to the school's appellation nor the race of the many children who had occupied my classroom over those six years. And, as so often happens with life's ironies, Mary Stratton had been none other than Myron Stratton's wife and Winfield Stratton's mother ... whom Win had loved so dearly before her death as yet a very young woman ... yet so oddly forgotten by Win upon establishing his endowment. Mary and Myron Stratton were therefore my Emma's – now forever to be known as "Alice" -- grandparents.

As a possible date came closer, we would also have to be evaluated as upstanding potential tenants by Mr. David Strickler, the Home's legal representative, along with that of a small assessment committee stated Miss Lloyd. Before we hung up from our conversation, Miss Lloyd again reiterated that it was imperative that I have in hand all the necessary documents including my teaching letter of introduction, since our appraisal would undoubtedly come about with rather short notice.

According to her birth certificate, stamped in a hazy blue-inked "official duplicate of documents lost in the Great Fires", Alice Elizabeth Barrington, a white female, had been born in

July ? 1901 in Teller County, Cripple Creek, Colorado to Hannah Owens Barrington (born in Teller County in July ? 1886?), married to John Daniel Barrington (born January ? 1875) in Teller County, marriage performed in July ? 1901. By virtue of our Teller County birth and marriage affiliations, current poverty designation and Alice's illness, I had been assured that we were both excellent candidates for admission.

Neither document was authentic, however. Both had been artfully crafted by the man to whom I had thought myself married for over six years, shot by his then eight-year-old son from his actual marriage. I'd often wondered when I saw those rope-muscled, slick-talking, narrow-eyed young thugs hanging around the Plantation every night if any of them knew Dannie Barrington. I naturally assumed that Dannie would have continued in his father's footsteps as a high stakes roller in some large city's crime syndicate. I never did find out though.

I tied together Emma's journals with several wide, dark blue ribbons, placing them at the bottom of our trunk, vowing to read them again sometime in the future. Right now, looking at the shadow of that once-promising young life, it was far too difficult for me to read about her dreams ... dreams that would never be realized.

As I continued digging through our trunks, I found many of Tayvie's little items as well – wood rattles, a leather drum, a cloth book with pictures of animals, stained bibs and jumpers. She would now be almost eight years old -- the exact same age as Dannie Barrington when he'd shot his father, I thought soberly. That seemed utterly impossible. We'd never uncovered any other clues about her disappearance, although I knew Alma continued searching for her out in Chicago. My concern day to day was for "Alice" now. I worked hard to keep Tayvie from haunting me, although she often invaded my frantic dreams, sometimes happily singing along with Monsieur Autruche or munching on pie wheels. I constantly told myself that she was in good hands, that she was safe. But of course, I really didn't know that.

Also in my trunk I rediscovered the novel *"The Awakening"* inscribed so long ago by Kate Chopin for Win down in New Orleans. As Mrs. Chopin had feared in her inscription, the book had indeed been out-of-print since its tiny first publication run back in 1899, harpooned by every reviewer in the country for displaying such hideously derelict themes. Though I could now far better understand her motivations, I would certainly never publically defend Mrs. Chopin's main character, Emma Pontellier. An upper-class white woman, sensitive, highly intelligent and extremely bored, who dismisses what should have been her unwavering obligation to her demanding husband and children and instead scandalously initiates intimacies with various men, seemingly just for idle amusement. Curiously, I wondered if there would ever come a time when such behavior might be considered even remotely justifiable in our society. I highly doubted it.

Ory was never far from my thoughts -- the man himself certainly, but more importantly, his music. Jazz music, played exclusively by white bands, had unquestionably wended its way to Colorado Springs, one of the wealthiest cities in the country. A wealth easily explained by the dozens of infrastructure grants subsidized so many years ago by Win Stratton's millions. On several occasions I hired a nurse to stay with Alice for a few hours while I walked down to a club only a block from our hotel. I always made certain to enter the establishment with a small group of men and women to avoid any hint of impropriety. Kate Chopin, or her fictional counterpart, Emma Pontellier, I definitely was not.

The bands that were playing at any of my visits were comprised of at least a dozen white men, including two or three saxophones, several clarinets and trumpets, and two or sometimes, even three trombones. The music was much tamer, "eh, y'know, just on script" as I'd heard Ory remark with disdain about other bands or jazz orchestras as they were frequently known. Despite the ever present, unenthusiastic though certainly skillful trumpet, clarinet, sax and piano solos, the music just seemed to occupy the room, but never quite fill it with any real electricity, any vibrant excitement. Each tune seemed more refined than the last, as did the dancers, again all white, moving colorlessly en masse over the huge wooden dance floor. There was no such thing as a black and tan establishment in Colorado Springs. Never had been and more than likely, never would be, I surmised. How sad to miss out on that wild, free expression of melodies, countermelodies and rhythms, swirling together, evolving to create the very essence, the nectar, the heartbeat of this music. How on earth when I had originally heard Ory's band all those years ago at the plantation at Reserve had I thought his music, and in particular his trombone playing, utterly hideous? For some reason after each of these lackluster renditions, I would often think back to Ed's funny departing gesture when his own band had played in New Orleans. He would spread his fingers out like a fan, and with a part salute, part wave and broad smile, bow slightly and then say affectionately to the audience: "Good luck and good night everybody!"

I would never have guessed that it would be two years before I would see Kid Ory again. Or that it would be our last meeting, ever.

> *"When money got to be twenty a week*
> *– and I had to fight to get that –*
> *man, I was through!"*
> Edward "Kid" Ory

## Chapter 24: Fall 1929

Late that following Spring, Alice and I moved into a very cozy cottage at the Stratton residences, boasting a kitchen freshly wallpapered with checkered black-and-white Scottie dogs sporting jaunty red-and-green plaid tams, beautifully honed cabinetry, a small stone and brick fireplace that drew well and burned wonderfully hot, and brand new steel and enamel appliances. It also possessed what was to become my lifeline to the world -- my own telephone -- even though I shared the use of the line with four other cottages.

Before his discovery of the Independence gold mine had made him a multi-millionaire, Win Stratton had been a highly regarded architect in Colorado Springs and many homes still boasted his late 19th century original designs or additions. He had left detailed instructions in his will regarding the design of the entire Myron Stratton complex. Win had been schooled in cabinetry and architectural crafting under the strict eye of Myron, a superb cabinet maker and shipbuilder in his own right. The fact that Win had not spoken to his father for twenty-five years following a vicious fight, during which he had almost killed the man, yet had left his entire endowment in his father's name only, remained a thoroughly puzzling, head-scratching gesture in everyone's eyes almost three decades later.

Although the public was grateful for the man's self-perpetuating endowment, Win Stratton himself retained the sordid reputation as a raving alcoholic, scandalous womanizer and thoroughly disagreeable, nasty-tempered man. He was indeed all of those things to be sure, but he was also a charming, extremely well-read and diversely informed man at the turn of the century, who when he believed in something ... or some*one*, as in my case ... did absolutely everything possible to nurture that cause.

There was a huge bronze statue originally commissioned by the Colorado Springs' councilmen in 1906 that was later moved to the Myron Stratton Home's elaborate garden, leading into the cemetery, and labeled with a large dedication plaque that read: "Winfield Scott Stratton – 1848-1902". I didn't think the statue actually resembled Win at all. For one thing, there seemed to be taut ironed creases in the front of his pants, and as anyone who knew Win was aware, he thoroughly detested creased trousers! He preferred an unstructured yet modestly fitted coat and overcoat; the ones on the statue seemed a bit too large, flapping about, which would have made his small stature even more noticeable. He was extremely sensitive about his height, which brought up the fact that his personally-constructed Swiss leather boots would most likely have been far more built up in both the sole and heel to give him just a bit more height. So often, while I gently pushed Alice in her wheelchair, we would stop for several minutes and I would stare at the expression molded for eternity on his face. He was a complete recluse from the eye of the camera and almost no pictures had survived of him, so the artist certainly had very limited resources from which to do much detailing. But despite the intervening years slightly muting my memories, I could never forget his thick, silvery-white hair and mustache, those vivid, sparkling blue eyes deeply set into his weathered skin, and that intelligent, humorous quick wit, which could just as quickly devolve into an angry retort with frighteningly minor provocation.

Alma had written me that the Plantation nightclub had been closed down for repairs mid-winter and then just as it was preparing to reopen by early April, an explosion and massive fire had swept through the entire structure razing it to the ground. Most newspapers alluded to gang interference yet again, which had now become a daily situation. King Oliver had managed to obtain very temporary work for his band, including Ory, at a few other clubs along The Stroll, but by early May he'd decided to take up what on the surface appeared to be a very lucrative offer in New York City. Much to Frank's disappointment, Ory had followed along, although as it turned out, the entire trip only lasted a few months. Joe Oliver's teeth had begun to bother him so badly that he could rarely play at all and he had to be replaced most nights in his own band. To make matters worse, there were all kinds of payout shortfalls from poorly written or mysteriously lost contracts, and within a few months, financially wiped out, Oliver abandoned the entire enterprise.

Ory had returned to Chicago working with many different bands, none of which, according to Frank, really showcased Ory's or any of the better musicians' talents. The Kid looked to have aged a decade and was very discouraged, wrote Alma. She and Frank had seen him perform over the last few weeks with some ensemble at the Sunset Café when Louis Armstrong's band, still the Sunset's regular group, was playing an engagement elsewhere. Alma confessed that she couldn't even remember the names of any of the other players. Nothing about the program had been particularly memorable. And Frank was even more disappointed since Ory had missed out on quite a few excellent recording opportunities with Jelly Roll Morton's Red Hot Peppers and Satchmo's new group, called the Hot Sevens, while he'd been out in New York City with Oliver's ill-fated orchestra.

Frank had added his own two pages with Alma's letter which was extremely unusual. He wrote that he was uneasy about the whole economic situation in Chicago and what he perceived as happening possibly everywhere in the country right now. Things just didn't seem to be adding up in his eyes.

The amount of money loaned out by banks was far more than the entire amount of currency circulating in the country, he wrote. Just employing the simplest math of debt to ratio showed that the country was literally teetering on the abyss of catastrophic failure Frank had begun warning his close friends, hence his cautionary words to me. So many businesses, small and large alike, were now selling fewer goods, but were simultaneously increasing their loan amounts to ramp up production, convinced that by doing so the stream of prosperity would miraculously once again flow in their direction. Adding up all of these numbers we were looking at a deep dark hole which America had never before experienced, he warned. He advised me to be extremely frugal with all of my expenditures and save every cent.

Feeling far less constricted, I wrote back about my new position at the Stratton Home; I had been hired to teach three grades this August. This was an extraordinary bit of good luck because the hat-embellishing business had quite abruptly stalled to a complete halt. The haberdashery, along with at least a half dozen shops lining that same block, had quietly closed their doors within the last few weeks.

The recent tsunami of closures on every front made the entire enterprise of the Stratton Home thoroughly amazing, I wrote. We were definitely living in an extraordinarily constructed, self-governing cocoon. The complex was a beehive of a city contained within itself, including a generating plant located right on the grounds, an abundant water supply, windmills, rotated animal feed crops, vegetable gardens within mammoth greenhouses and orchards exploding with well-nurtured fruit. Produce was either enjoyed fresh or quickly canned to be consumed during the exceptionally lengthy winters. Herds of cows, goats, geese, chickens and two very feisty roosters roamed the fields as well. (I had smiled when writing this remembering how much Win had hated roosters, refusing to raise them, and had instructed his cook to take a few plump hens over "to visit" at a neighbor's farm whenever necessary to add to the flock.) Almost all of the work was completed by residents at the Home with very limited skilled labor hired-on from the outside. Children from as young as age three had their daily chores; very rarely was it necessary to issue a reminder or reprimand. How all of this was accomplished gave testimony to the marvel of detailed organization by the staff as well as Win's overall vision. Jane Lawson, who had now remarried and moved to Georgia, had written me about the incredible precision of the Home back in New Orleans several years ago. But until I was actually able to experience the entire enterprise in action, I had failed to appreciate the scope of its magnitude.

In addition to the usual subjects of spelling, reading, arithmetic and science, I taught cooking, canning, jarring and sewing to the girls and was encouraged to organize both a boys' and a girls' choir, each group performing at a Christmas and also late Spring program. During the day while I was teaching the younger children, several of the older girls in the orphanage rotated turns taking care of Alice, carefully feeding her lunch, helping her walk, reading to her and playing her favorite records. Each time she heard Ory play on one of those records, her face would slightly soften. As I constantly reiterated in my letters to Alma, there was no question in my mind that she knew these were his records.

Interestingly, these records quickly became the favorites of the entire Stratton Home, although I kept quiet the fact that they were actually 'race records'. Wherever "negro" or "race" appeared on a record label, I had carefully scratched out those words. This was wonderful music -- music that made everyone in the orphanage and residences happy, made them sing, dance, laugh together, have fun and forget whatever harsh memories or current physical or mental suffering they were enduring. Why shouldn't it be played for all ears I wrote rather angrily to Alma?

What on earth difference did the color of the musicians' skin make in appreciating this incredible music for heaven's sake? Needless to say, Alma wholeheartedly agreed.

And then quite late one night, I had a very brief telephone call from Alma. Her voice was thick as though she had been crying, but she refused to say anything further when I had expressed concern. Frank was sending out all of his record collection to me within the next several days with a special courier. The train was expected to arrive in Colorado Springs sometime in the evening on Friday. She apologized that she wasn't able to talk any longer at the moment, said good-bye quickly and hung up.

A light sparkling snow had begun falling just at dusk that Friday, pretty, but a reminder that it was now almost October, already dark very early in the afternoon. Alice had been unusually tired and not been interested in eating very much, dangerously falling asleep with each mouthful. Although she could only move very soft foods in her mouth until finally making the effort to swallow, tonight seemed to be even slower than usual. Maybe the girls who had been with her this afternoon had taken her on a longer walk than usual or possibly given her something fun to eat thus spoiling her limited appetite. I was fine with that as long as it didn't occur too often. Routine was, well, routine. Something to be followed, but also occasionally to be deviated from I willingly admitted. I had her cleaned up and in bed quite early, made myself a cup of cocoa, added several small twigs to reignite the heat in the fireplace, and once again felt an utter stalemate when attempting to get into the incredibly colorless book I'd recently borrowed from the Home's lending library. I heard a car door slam and something very heavy then being dragged towards our cottage. Looking out the window I saw a man pulling a small cart with a metal crate strapped to it. When I opened the door there stood Ed Ory -- the courier bringing Frank's jazz record collection.

"Ed!" I exclaimed, thoroughly dumbfounded.

"I was in the neighborhood, so …" he grinned as I helped him unhook the straps around the trunk and haul it inside, followed by a long hug. He hung his hat and coat on the coat rack and then nodding, looked around at Alice's and my little home. "Very nice place, Miss Hannah. Very nice."

"Have you eaten? I have a little leftover meat, also some rather dull, boiled noodle casserole I fix for Alice maybe … nothing like your cooking of course …" I began.

"No, no," he answered. "I ate at the train depot when I picked up the car. You know, eh, driver for The Honorable Mr. Frank Collier."

I nodded. Of course. No way would any company just rent out a car to him.

"Hot cocoa?"

"I brought my own, eh, more inspirational … libations, actually. Quite a few bottles in fact. Care to join me? Some of our dear Frank's finest whiskey in fact."

I nodded as he walked over to my kitchen cabinets and surprisingly opened the correct door containing my few glasses. I'd forgotten how he walked, his small, almost graceful, yet definitely very masculine stride. Something about him seemed rather odd, almost subdued, however. He poured out two large glasses and brought them back. I had sat down again by the fireplace. He handed me one glass and added as a toast *"a ta santé,"* with a light click of our glasses, taking a large swallow to my small sip.

"May I?" he inquired, gesturing towards the sofa.

"Oh, of course!" I stammered. "I didn't mean to keep you standing. It's just that I'm so, well, just so completely surprised to see you Ed! I never thought that I'd …"

"See me again?" he said, giving me a rather tired smile. Alma was right. He did seem to have aged almost a decade.

"Well, quite honestly, I guess I hadn't thought about it.

What exactly brings you out here?"

"Well, to start, Dort's kinda, er, counted to ten, if y'know my meanin'," he shrugged.

I shook my head slightly, taking a slight sip of the whiskey. "Counted to ten about …?"

"Mainly she's refusin' to stay in Chicago for another winter, eh … among other things, I suppose."

"Well, I can completely understand that! As brutal as Colorado winters are at least we typically have warmer sunny days in between snowstorms. And the mountains are always beautiful any time of year. But Chicago always just seems cold and grey. And dirty. I can't say as I blame her one bit."

"Yeah, well in Los Angeles, we never get snow at all, y'know? Dort's already back there in fact. I handed in my notice to the coupla bands I was still workin' in Chicago an' am headin' out to California on tomorrow mornin's train."

"I see," I answered, having another sip of the whiskey. I hadn't had anything alcoholic now for over two years and felt a golden relaxing heat spread throughout my entire body within mere minutes.

"Emma's here I assume?" he asked.

"Yes, she's asleep. I think the afternoon girls who look after her wore her out today. But, if you're still here tomorrow … she might be a little more awake, and you know she's 'Alice' now."

"Right, right, of course. 'Alice'," he nodded, taking another slow swallow of the whiskey. "I probably can' smoke in this place, right?"

"Afraid not, at least not in these cottages," I replied. Then, in an attempt to change the subject I asked, "so how are Alma and Frank? I really haven't talked with Alma for more than just two quick telephone calls or even gotten a decent letter from her now these past couple of months, which is so odd for her. I know she mentioned that they hadn't seen you too often at any of the clubs. It sounded as though they never exactly know where you're playing … or something like that," my voice trailed off as I tried to read the odd, darkening look on his face.

Ory was silent, staring into the fire for several minutes, then finally turned towards me.

"Frank's had an advanced, uh, stomach cancer, last few months now, Hannah," he began softly. "Been in horrible pain. Even morphine can' begin to touch it no more."

"Somehow I was afraid you were going to say something like that, Ed, although I don't know why exactly."

"So, two days ago I go to pick up this crate. Frank's assistant, James … you remember James?"

"Of course," I nodded.

"He'd called me, so I went to pick it up. I'd tol' Alma the week prior I was headin' back out to California. Dort an' all that nonsense. Well, y'know, like I said. Alma'd come out to hear me at the Sunset Café. The last coupla times I'd seen her she was there with James, but not Frank. That's when I found he was so terrible sick. He was insistin' though, tha' she come hear me play, report back, y'know."

I took a large sip of the whiskey and tried to breathe evenly.

"And? You're going to tell me that Frank's now dead and that you've brought his jazz record collection for Emma," I answered, as steadily as I could muster.

"Eh, not exactly, Hannah," replied Ory, looking at me for a long moment before he continued. "When I picked the case up from the Collier's place a coupla days ago, James tol' me that they'd both taken an overdose of morphine. Said they were lyin' upstairs in their bed, arms wrapped 'round one another, Frank's head on Alma's shoulder, a note left on the bedside table written by Alma that this was their choice to leave the world together. She knew that there's no way you'd get these records unless I brought 'em to you, an' Frank was adamant that Emma have 'em. I'm the only other person who knows about … well, y'know, all that shit. He's got all kinds of original recordin's in there. Early

Jelly Roll solo stuff, some terrific piano rolls of Scott Joplin's an' Tony Jackson's. James said Frank had everything I put down on wax. I'd actually forgot 'bout some of 'em."

Alma and Frank. Dead. For the last four days.

"You know, it was said that my mother died from ingesting morphine," I finally commented. "And another friend, Pearl DeVere, as well. So many, many years ago. It's certainly a final way out, but so hard on us left behind, Ed. I mean, what could I have done? Have written? Have said? Could I have prevented …?"

Ory was quiet for another few moments finishing off his glass of whiskey then poured himself another hefty glass.

"There ain' no shame in determinin' your own destiny, Hannah," Ory shrugged. "None whatsoever, *ma petite piaf*. We do it durin' our lives, why not our deaths as well if called to?"

"Is that some kind of, I don't know, Creole belief? Determining your own destiny even in death?" I asked wearily.

"Nah, it's just kinda, well …" Ory replied, rubbing his ear lobe. "Y'see, the Church don' tell ya that, but well, jes' livin' in this world does. Experience, y'know? Your own or watchin' someone else. If the pain's too great, whatever that pain may be, y'know, physical, mental eh, maybe some of both, an' leavin' it all behind looks to be the best choice, maybe the *only* choice in fact, then jes' go ahead an' make that choice. Long's it all's thought out. That's all I'm sayin'. An' don' wish any evil on those who've gone that direction, made that choice for themselves or beat up on yourself for not keepin' 'em from, well, y'know, carryin' it all out."

I made no reply. Neither of us spoke for several minutes.

"Emma over in that room?"

I nodded slightly, staring into my glass of whiskey.

He walked over and carefully opened the door looking in at her for a long moment. The moonlight glimmered over her marble-like face as he kissed her lightly on the cheek, then gently smoothed back a lock of her hair before walking out of the room and quietly shutting the door.

"I'm hangin' up my horn when I get out to L.A.," he commented quietly, as he moved back to the sofa. "Dort's got me a full-time janitor's job. Y'know, sweepin' up at some Men's Union buildin' and, uh, cleanin' out the commodes and such. Steady wages and all that. Decent union job. Dunno what's goin' on out there in the big bad world these days, but it's damned ugly an' gettin' uglier every stinkin' day. Musician's salary can' even keep a rat alive now."

"Kid Ory cleaning toilets? Sweeping up cigarette butts?" I exclaimed, horrified. "Ed, you just can't be serious … you're far too talented for such rot!"

"Says who?" Ory shrugged with a slightly mocking laugh as I sat down next to him. "Who says I'm talented, eh? Them l'il green an' orange hot stick men wigglin' them juiced-up purple eyeballs on the moon? Day of my music is over, man. Sad to say, but it's long gone. Poof. An' I don' know how to play much anythin' else, y'know? No, that ain't completely the truth, Hannah. Y'see, I don' really *wanna* play this newer stuff, this closely shaved, eh, dead, sterile stuff, y'know? I kin play the notes, but I don' really have a place in tha' music. If I can't play my own music, the music I love, then I don' wanna play anybody's music at this point. Ain' no heart in it. An' I've decided that if I don' have a heart in my music then I might as well just clean the goddamn toilets. Not sure that makes sense to you exactly, but well, there it is."

"That's your way of dealing with this … well, this pain, isn't it?" I replied softly, my hand folding over his. "Just give up."

He smiled and wove his fingers lightly through mine. "Jes' bein' realistic, Hannah, that's all. When a black man's havin' trouble gettin' hired on even as a janitor, then times is *really* bad, lemme tell you! At least I still have tha' option, y'know? Should be grateful for that, eh?"

We looked at one another for several moments, our fingers still laced.

If anyone had seen Ory arrive at my door, walk in and not depart within those several respectable minutes immediately thereafter, I would have been completely damned for the rest of my life. If anyone looking through my front curtains, not quite drawn all the way shut, had seen me then take this man's beautiful brown face in my hands and kiss him so slowly, so deeply, again and again, I would have been completely damned for the rest of my life. If anyone had seen me then passionately pulling him down on top of me in front of my fireplace, I would have been completely damned for the rest of my life. But no one did. And I spent that night with this extraordinary man, occasionally crying into each other's arms, our slow lovemaking continuing long after the last red ember in the fireplace gave out its final little puff of smoke plunging us into total darkness.

> *"Always figure a horn is just like a voice.*
> *Person have no voice they can't sing.*
> *They can jive a little bit,*
> *but you can't call them a singer."*
> Edward "Kid" Ory

## Chapter 25: The Depression 1929-1944

The entire country plunged into darkness a mere three weeks later when, much as Frank Collier had direly predicted prior to his death, Wall Street suddenly turned upside down on Oct. 29, 1929. With that crash the many businesses that had still obliviously been riding along on Easy Street suddenly found the very concrete foundations of their livelihoods crumbling back into wet sand without any warning, often within a matter of only a few desperate hours. Photos of men jumping off skyscrapers in New York City or diving in front of trains in Chicago and Kansas City flooded *The Colorado Springs Gazette*. The repeal of the Silver Act in 1893, at which juncture the country commenced recognizing gold as the only standard trading currency, was nothing compared to this current disaster.

Unknown to most of the populace the unlimited creation of goods by so many diverse companies, funded by seemingly bottomless, drastically over-extended loans based on non-existent capital, had created an incredible glut of cars, stoves, ice boxes, boilers, farm machinery, home furnishings, cooking vessels -- in fact, practically every item being manufactured in the United States. Long freight trains crammed to the limit were tasked with the goods' clandestine nocturnal dumping further and further from civilization, so that the harsh reality of the situation was completely undetectable until far too late.

The Stratton Home had to seriously modify its admittance

standards since there were so many desperate people now seeking asylum within its walls. An adult had to have lived for a minimum of ten consecutive years as a resident of the county prior to admittance and a child for five years in order to even be considered for housing, and the wait list now extended indefinitely. That Emma and I were already safely within the bubble was truly a miracle. Stratton couldn't possibly have predicted these dismal days when he had established his endowment, but I felt that if this place could somehow weather the current situation, it might well continue its existence even into the next century. Each week my classrooms were always brimming with students, eager learners in most cases, the older girls still helpful with my daughter while I taught their younger siblings. Rarely was any one day distinguishable from the next. But I was eternally grateful to know where we would sleep each night, that food would be available, and that there might even be a few pennies left for extras like a stick of candy.

Prohibition was finally repealed in the nation four years later in December 1933, but it had no real impact on the economy by then. If people were drinking – and in reality, they'd never really stopped – they were doing it as cheaply as possible at home, either clandestinely manufacturing it themselves or illegally buying it very cheaply through neighbors or long-established connections. No one could afford to go out. And what's more, other than mob-connected amusements, there was almost no place for the regular working-class person to go anyway.

In addition to Ory's janitorial job he also became a letter sorter at the local post office a few months after his return to California. This at least prompted him to write infrequently and gave me a way to communicate with him about Alice, although I almost always carelessly referred to her as Emma in my letters. Somehow I had no problem calling her Alice with everyone on a daily basis, but simply couldn't do so with him. All the performance venues and the recording business for the old New Orleans style music had ground to a screeching halt, even if he'd still been out there actively trying to "earn a living off my horn" he wrote. Not just for the race record companies, but for much of the industry from what he'd been told, although there were definitely a handful of exceptions. The three music stores in Colorado Springs that had carried phonograph records, not that they had carried race records anyway, had long ago succumbed to the Depression and closed shop I'd written Ory. Still heeding Frank Collier's advice from so many years ago, I religiously changed the needles on the phonograph, thoroughly cleaned each record before play, and always set down the tone arm very gently to spare whatever records that I selected to play from Frank's collection for Alice (and the absolute horde of enthusiastic music lovers who eagerly gathered in her room each day). But even with my extreme diligence, the pops, scratches and occasional repeats or skips, sadly found their way onto every record after several years of use. Many records were completely ruined beyond play, the needle simply skittering across the shellac surface despite my painstaking efforts.

As month extended into month and year into year, I morosely began to compile a list of musicians' names and their fates culled from Ory's letters and various newspaper articles:

**Scott Joplin** – considered by musicians and audiences alike to be the "King of Ragtime" died in a mental institution in 1917 at age 48 of dementia resulting from syphilis. Although his many ragtime compositions were well received throughout his life, he desperately wanted to be recognized as a legitimate composer of classical work. His first opera was lost when his apartment was ransacked by his landlord for nonpayment of rent. His second opera, *Treemonisha*, had received only one partially staged concert in 1915 garnering very paltry reviews, very likely precipitating the onset of his dementia.

**Tony Jackson** – New Orleans jazz pianist said to be even

better than Jelly Roll Morton (according to everyone who had ever heard him play, including Morton himself), also a very talented singer and composer – died in 1921 at age 38, of liver disease and issues surrounding epilepsy. Other than a handful of nondescript piano rolls, he never did any recording.

**Buddy Bolden** – the true originator of jazz blowing on his trumpet like Gabriel, according to Ory and many others – had lapsed into an alcoholic psychosis and been committed to a madhouse in 1907 and died, penniless, practically an unknown, in that institution in 1931. I could only hope that his twenty-four years locked in that place had offered better care than had Emma's incarceration at Dunning.

**George "Little Mitch" Mitchell** – incredible cornet player with Jelly Roll Morton's Hot Peppers and many other bands, stopped playing in 1931, decided he was done with the extremes of that harsh, unpredictable life and worked as a bank messenger for the remainder of his life, died an unknown.

**Sissieretta Jones** – the extraordinary Black Patti, who was a black opera singer with no place to truly showcase her incredible operatic abilities in the U.S., with whom Emma had worked during the last year of Mrs. Jones' vaudeville show – had stopped performing altogether by 1918 to take care of her invalid mother. Sissieretta died in complete poverty, basically an unknown, and was buried in an unmarked pauper's grave in New York in June 1933.

**Freddie Keppard** – cornetist, said to have sounded just like Buddy Bolden, worked in the early days with many jazz bands – died in 1933 at age 44, an alcoholic, never receiving the recognition he deserved as a musician in Ory's and many other musicians' opinions.

**Honoré Dutrey** – another tailgate-style trombonist whose style was very similar to Ory's, died in agony in 1935 at age 41 from the severe asthma he had contracted during his days of military service while overseas during World War I.

*Joe "King" Oliver* – cornet, trumpet player and band leader died in 1938 at age 57 – he had lost everything he owned in the Depression and died in complete poverty, an unknown.

*John Robichaux* – composer, violinist, and early New Orleans' jazz music inspiration for a young Kid Ory, died in complete obscurity in 1939.

*Johnny Dodds* – died in 1940 at age 48, clarinetist with some of the best working and recording bands of the day, ended his days working as a cabdriver, completely broke and unknown at the time of his death.

*Jelly Roll Morton* – died in 1941 at age 51. Jelly Roll had been badly knifed while playing piano at a dive in a very rough section of town in Washington, D.C. in 1939. Taken to a black hospital, which was much farther away than the white hospital, located only a few blocks from where he'd been attacked, Jelly Roll lay on ice in agony for hours before he was finally seen by a physician. By that time he had developed a deadly infection that was never successfully eradicated. Suffering one infection after another, he finally died from complications of that attack slightly over a year later. Ory wrote me that he, Ed Garland, and Mutt Carey were three of the pallbearers at Jelly's funeral in Los Angeles.

Then there were stories like famed New Orleans' trumpeter Bunk Johnson who stopped playing in 1931 because he had been in a brawl and lost his front teeth. He could no longer play until 1942 when he finally was able to afford a set of dentures. Unable to blow even a single note for well over a decade, Bunk managed to play a few gigs and then died basically an unknown a year or two later.

There were of course those few jazz musicians who managed to emerge as heroes whether dead or alive. Louis Armstrong continued as the star attraction at various venues in New York, Chicago, New Orleans, and L.A. although some blacks and whites as well disliked his shufflin' Jim Crow personae both in person, on radio, and later in film. Despite, or possibly because of his popularity, Satchmo was perpetually hounded by the Italian mob and, fearing for his life, finally made his way over to Europe for an extended stay by the mid '30s, very cautiously keeping his toe in the waters of the American popular music scene.

And curiously, fellow cornetist Bix Beiderbecke, whose playing style Ory deemed about as exciting as a piece of stale white bread, died of alcoholism in 1931 at the tender age of 28 creating a legendary jazz figure, rising like a phoenix, a martyr for the sake of his art. The fun-filled antics of vaudeville's overtones had been completely eradicated from Beiderbecke's sanitized jazz concerts. Ory claimed it was only because he was a promising young white kid and white people typically like to endow the early deaths of their own with religious pronouncements. However, I wisely stayed clear of that discussion having never heard the man perform even on a recording.

Why I seemed to obsess in writing down these often lurid details escaped me. I'm sure at first it had something to do with reading an extensive article about the 10th anniversary of the New Orleans' French Opera House's fire on Dec. 4, 1929, which would also have been Tayvie's 10th birthday. That's when my list began quite honestly. And then a decade later Emma's death on that last day of August, 1939, followed by what would become known as World War II when on Sept. 1 Germany invaded Poland.

Those seemingly carefree early days of the 1920s seemed like a dream to almost everyone. Had women really spent their hard-earned money to have their hair crimped before a dance, where they hoped to meet a special beau, wondered those now gray-haired women often dressed in poorly re-worked, faded slub-cotton fabrics? Or imagine frivolously plunking down a quarter (or even more!) merely to attend a new vaudeville or talking picture show. And fashion! Who hadn't paid good money to have a favorite dress shortened in the latest style or new matching beads or dyed feathers woven into one's hat or purse or shelled out for a new set of faux silver pearls and dancing slippers? And how many had gleefully jumped on board a friend's motor car for a jaunt out to the lake or a wealthy friend's country estate, laughing as they bounced joyfully over ditches, waving at well-dressed young men and women with their picnic baskets swinging over their arms as they walked alongside the road?

In my letters to Ory I referred to the Stratton Home as Win's Cocoon. Although each day uneventfully continued to flow into the next, I cherished that simple monotony. The outside world which crept into the Cocoon via newspaper articles, magazine editorials, newly published literature, and the ubiquitously unreliable gossipmongers, truly reinforced my desire to remain isolated within my Cocoon on the outskirts of the town. Although the many girls who helped out with Emma on a daily basis were continually graduating and leaving their duties to younger replacements as one year dissolved into the next and that one dissolved yet into its successor, Emma didn't visibly seem to age at all. I almost began to wonder if the greasy cold cream-like substance that continued to form on her skin every night might not be some miraculous youth preservative. I continued to play the few remaining records from Frank's collection, albeit very sparingly these days, and still thought I detected that slight spark of life in Emma's eyes each time. Other than that, there were no real changes.

About a year prior to Emma's death, however, while I was carefully feeding her some Jell-O, her hand suddenly began moving very slowly up onto my wrist as I held the spoon to her mouth. She then looked into my eyes, blinking as though awakening to a strong light, a slight smile curling at the corners of her mouth and whispered, "ma…ma." Tears in my eyes, I put my head down on her chest as I felt her raised hand move down onto my hair. She then whispered, almost inaudibly, very slowly, "I ... love ... you. Mama. Mama." When I looked up at her again, tears now streaming down my face, she had once again fallen asleep. She never spoke or moved on her own again after that moment. For thirty-six years I had so desperately wanted to hear those words from her. And finally, I had.

I had Emma buried in the Evergreen Cemetery as close as I could arrange to Win's statue. Her small white granite headstone undoubtedly seemed oddly inscribed to those strolling by: *Alice Elizabeth Barrington 1902-1939 ~ always our Emma*

*****

Commencing in 1933 just a few days after his inauguration, President Franklin D. Roosevelt began what became quickly known as his "fireside chats," a total of thirty radio broadcasts averaging a half hour for each program which were presented until 1944. Reaching over sixty million people, the President's first program detailed his initiation of the Emergency Banking Act, aimed to calm newly emerging fears about yet another banking crisis, potentially plunging the nation back into recession. The Stratton Home had now purchased two radios with far larger sound projection than prior models, one for the main community building and the other for a smaller meeting room at Winfield House, available for those who were hospitalized. The nation now depended on radio broadcasts for more critically up-to-date national and international information, including FDR's terse announcement of our Declaration of War on Japan in 1941 and the chaotic labyrinth of our progress throughout World War II. Everyone nervously traced the advancement or defeat of the Allies on kitchen wall-mounted world maps or large atlases conspicuously displayed within their front parlors.

Radios were now being produced very cheaply in an effort to provide direct marketing of goods and services to a far broader audience. They had become so popular that any home that could possibly afford one now had it accessibly positioned in the parlor for the entire family to enjoy after dinner and chores were completed each evening. There were now many weekly radio broadcasts each vying for the attention of listeners throughout the country. One of these was the Orson Welles Almanac, a half hour show on Wednesday nights broadcast out of San Francisco that had been running under one name or another since 1938. Welles' program was usually quite entertaining and many of us at the Stratton Home would regularly head over to our community building on Wednesday nights to listen to his show.

Welles had occasionally sought out various popular music groups and just as a lark, he asked some of his staff members to see if they could dredge up a few original New Orleans style jazz musicians in the area, if any of those old guys were still alive, thinking it would be fun to have them open one of his broadcasts. Rather amazingly, several of those top names from that bygone era were not only still alive, occasionally being hired as subs to play a "swing" or "bebop" orchestra gig, but were actually residing within a few miles from the radio station – Jimmy Noone, Mutt Carey, Ed Garland, Minor Hall, Buster Wilson … and of course, the tailgate trombone master himself, Edward "Kid" Ory.

In mid-March 1944 Welles simply asked the group, which at the time had no band name or leader, to play a couple of those old tunes live over the airwaves to lead off his program that evening. Unannounced, as soon as they started into "*Muskrat Ramble*" I knew immediately of course that it was Ory's music, with Ory himself performing, along with many of his former musicians, and held my breath awaiting the comments of the dozens of people sitting with me in the community room. Their reaction, along with that of the entire listening radio audience, was instantaneously wild with enthusiasm. Welles was inundated with thousands of phone calls, letters, telegrams and money wires – in fact, the station's lobby was continually mobbed with music lovers of all ages, races and economic backgrounds, begging the show host to "bring back those New Orleans jazz boys" for every Wednesday night's show! No one had ever realized what this music actually sounded like, unless they'd been fortunate enough to hear one of these bands perform live in New Orleans, Chicago or New York City all those many years ago. And in a world already bored with swing and bebop music, this solid infusion of old New Orleans jazz into the younger crowd's musical veins was exactly what society needed.

By the program's third broadcast the group was introduced as the All Star Jazz Group. By the fourth, Kid Ory was announced as the band leader. And within five weeks, Ory's prior decade and a half of janitorial, chicken farming and letter sorting duties had now been enthusiastically relegated to a very dim memory. Now age fifty-eight, Kid Ory experienced a miraculous revival of his music career, along with those few of his colleagues who had also weathered the lean times of the Depression. Records from Jelly Roll Morton's Red Hot Peppers, Louis Armstrong's Hot Fives and Hot Sevens, King Oliver's Dixie Syncopators and many more groups, including those bands led by Johnny Dodds and Mutt Carey, were reissued and available at record stores everywhere throughout the country.

The term 'race record' had fortuitously ceased to exist even if racism itself, unfortunately, had not. But as I'd remarked in my letters to Alma so many years ago, music knows no color. Just like breathing. The air is simply out there for us all. Although it had been about five years since my students had gathered around Emma's chair to listen to Kid Ory's records, the older ones still remembered many of those delightful tunes. From the moment I entered the community building with my newly-purchased phonograph and a handful of reissued Creole Jazz Band records, a small crowd followed me as though I were the

Pied Piper of Jazz Music, sometimes forgetting chores while dancing with their sweethearts or asking me questions about that era. I was surprised by their intense interest, but also quite embarrassed to admit how much I had actually forgotten!

Many of my earliest students, now quite grown-up young women, invited me to their weddings in Colorado Springs, Leadville and Denver. Every time one of those wedding reception bands launched into *"Muskrat Ramble," "Blackbottom Stomp," "Wolverine Blues," "Wa Wa Wa"* or *"Weary Blues,"* all of which were consistently met with a sea of happily sweating bodies out on the dance floor, I broke into a smile imagining Frank Collier all those years ago, sitting back in his wheelchair, enjoying a seemingly bottomless glass of whiskey as he listened to Kid Ory, eager to share a glass of his exquisitely purloined hooch and "talk shop" as soon as Ory's men took a well-deserved break.

> *"As the old men die you have to break in the new men. I've had a lot of trouble breakin' in the young guys ... gettin' them fitted to the style."*
> Edward "Kid" Ory

# Chapter 26: Helen Mason Campbell - Paris, 1956

My own health over that next decade didn't fare particularly well, however. Although I enthusiastically continued teaching and somehow managed to hold onto my little cottage, albeit with a badly-yellowing linoleum kitchen floor, chipped bathroom tiles and multiple cellophane strips over the fragile rips in my Scottie dog wallpaper, the deep beatings that I had sustained from Mrs. Hughes' belt decades ago had gradually begun unraveling the nerve ends in my lower back, leaving me in severe pain much of the time. Various medications helped to dull the pain, but sadly, the best recourse was to cautiously restrict all regular activities before the pain became intolerable. Even a half mile walk was now a treacherous excursion more often than not. My long daily visits out to Emma's grave and Win's statue had by necessity now dwindled to once per week, or if the weather was bad, even fewer outings. I stalwartly continued teaching but realized that my ability to work with these wonderful youngsters was now being calculated in days rather than in years.

By contrast, Edward Ory seemed to have miraculously pole-vaulted atop the fountain of youth. Excellent new records were being released, showing not only his ability to maintain the purity of that old-time jazz style, but to very successfully re-create that style with contemporary tunes, breathing a completely different essence into those newer works. Ory's best known tune, *"Muskrat Ramble"* was now pulling in excellent royalty payments every quarter, so much so that it afforded Ory the opportunity to purchase a beautiful new home in San Francisco, thus maintaining easy access to the many West Coast nightclubs in the area that regularly booked his band.

His extraordinary rebirth had definitely been achieved at a rather steep personal price, however. I knew that somewhere in literature there existed an ancient fairy tale to this end, but I could never remember the precise story. The older style jazz legends were currently keeping pace with the newer, younger, cool jazz and swing musicians such as Benny Goodman, Woody Herman and Harry James among countless others, but as the years continued, finding musicians willing to bend their style to that "older cornball stuff" became increasingly difficult for Ory and other remaining early jazz band leaders.

To make matters worse, Ory had begun alienating many of his longtime loyal fellow musicians, some of whom he'd worked with for over fifty years, once he became romantically involved with his sharp-tongued business manager, a white woman named Barbara GaNung. GaNung was married with a couple of kids, but when she became pregnant with Ory's child, her husband, a U.S. serviceman, understandably sought a divorce. Ed Ory's stalwart wife of forty-four years, Elizabeth "Dort" Ory, having forgiven countless prior infidelities, finally took the philandering Ory to divorce court as well, only to shockingly discover that her husband had originally lied to her back in 1911 and that they weren't even legally married! She'd never sought a divorce from her first husband because Ory had insisted that the man had died back in 1910. When John Wallace walked into the courtroom, albeit forty-four years older, but certainly fit as a fiddle and very much alive, that eradicated any claims she had to Ory's now substantial financial empire. Despite her steadfast loyalty contributing to their financial support throughout their many lean decades as a couple, she walked out of her sham marriage practically empty handed.

Shortly after she had given birth, Barbara GaNung married Ory, much to the disgust of his band mates who now downright despised the nasty woman. According to the news scandal sheets, Ory's longtime bassist Ed "Montudie" Garland and Ory got into a fist fight arguing about the woman while performing on stage one night, during which Garland pushed Ory into the adjacent bar, breaking several of the man's ribs and seriously injuring his back. Additionally, a rumor persisted that two of Ory's musicians cut the brake lines in Ory's new Buick causing the car to swerve out of control down a steep hill, resulting in additional minor injuries for the tailgate trombonist. The new Mrs. Ory, still working as The Kid's general manager and publicist, schemed to completely re-invent her husband's early background, giving such absurd accounts that Ory's father had originally immigrated to the U.S. from Paris at age seventeen and had been a wealthy New Orleans area plantation landowner, and that Kid Ory had been educated in Paris as a teenager and was actually a white man with somewhat darker skin from prolonged sun exposure. She attempted to completely banish all of his decades-old acquaintances, musicians and friends alike, brazenly spent his income practically before he had even cashed the checks, and by many accounts emotionally tortured the poor man in his own home. In all of the years that he'd been a musician, Ory had always adroitly avoided the race issue when asked by simply stating that he was French Creole and leaving the matter at that. Now, assuming what was printed in the papers was true, I wondered if he knew who he was at all. The so-called scandal sheets were incredibly relentless, with one outrageous fabrication seeming to beget yet another. Fame could indeed be an ugly mantle. Sadly, as a result, the real Kid Ory's story, his creativity, his extraordinary influence, charming wit and incredible raw talent simply became lost, little by little, in a shuffling din of early jazz music history.

Ory's Creole Jazz Band was broadcast on radio station KCBS from the famous Club Hangover in San Francisco starting at 11 p.m. for a half hour almost every Saturday night in the mid '50s. I now had my own radio and since the nighttime typically allowed for very clear reception in the mountains, I was usually able to pick up the show. The Kid opened the broadcast each night with *"Without You for an Inspiration."* In one of Emma's diaries she'd mentioned that he'd always played that song for her. Were these same *bon mots* whispered by Ory into many women's ears during all of those years? I sometimes wondered if his womanizing reputation wasn't really more of a façade. Because in reality, the Ed Ory I knew from many decades ago was actually a very considerate, surprisingly shy man. Maybe that shyness had actually led him into the current abyss in which he wallowed. I certainly couldn't condone his having lied to Dort Ory all of those years, but I also felt he'd been swallowed whole by this treacherous white shark.

I was always surprised to get a phone call from him, long distance calling a hefty expense even for the well-to-do, but since his rediscovery on the Welles' program he had begun calling me occasionally. I hadn't heard from him since his marriage to Barbara GaNung though and quite frankly, rather assumed that I wouldn't. But late one Saturday night, my phone rang just after midnight. He knew that I typically listened to the show coming from Club Hangover and apparently that was the band's first break after the end of the radio broadcast.

"Well, hello! I must say this is an unexpected surprise! You know you've just played some of my favorite tunes tonight. And I think I've found me a new favorite … *"I've Found Me a New Baby."* As some of the kids around here would say, 'it's quite the bomb,' Ed!"

He chuckled, although nervously, pulling hard on a cigarette then very audibly blowing out the smoke. Some things never changed from decade to decade apparently.

"The bomb, eh? Hard to believe that stuffy ol' Lady Barrington would use that term!"

"Well, I guess I just did, Ed. How are you? And, well, congratulations. I don't believe I've spoken with you since your ... uh, marriage."

"Nah, I'm sure not," Ory replied somewhat tersely. "Tonight's my first night off the tether, y'know? Baby's sick. Croup or colic or consumption or cholera or one of those damn diseases where babies throw up an' shriek the whole damn night. Anyway, rare night that Barbara ain' here. Eh, she don' trust the babysitter, y'know."

"Understandable. Well, I hope she ... you have a daughter, right?"

"Yeah."

"Yes, well I hope that she gets better soon. There's nothing more frustrating than standing by listening to your child gasping for every breath when they're so sick. I don't know if you remember my mentioning that Zuma and Emma used to live with us when Emma and Alice were babies. Both girls would invariably come down sick at the exact same moment ..."

"So which one d'you worry 'bout first, eh? Your pretend daughter Alice or Emma your forgotten daughter?" Ory interrupted with a snort, a sharp snick from his lighter obviously igniting another cigarette. A sharply taunting malice underscored his words and I wondered why he'd called. I had no desire to fight with him. From what I'd read recently, he'd pick an argument with just about anyone over absolutely the smallest concern these days.

"Ed, I'm so glad that you've called, but I'm ... I'm really very tired. This new doctor's put me on a medication for the pain in my back that I swear really saps every ounce of energy that I have each day. If there's something in particular you wanted to talk about ..."

"So we're goin' to Europe this fall," Ory broke in. "The

band y'know? Three-month tour. Eh, y'know, Paris, a couple of stops in Germany, London. I, er, just thought I'd let you know, although it'll be in the papers an' such like everythin' else I do these days whether I want it or not. Louis's been over there I don' even know how many times. Fletcher Henderson. Benny Goodman. Duke Ellington. Eh, y'know, everybody important! Guess it's time even the unimportant people like me got their day, eh?"

"Why Ed, that's terrific! Congratulations!"

"Yeah, well something positive for a change, y'know?"

"Well, yes, I heard about that, uh … mess with Ed Garland," I replied very cautiously.

"You're on his side on all that goddamn crap, aren't you?" he barked vehemently into the phone.

"I only know what I've read … the newspapers …" I began, shocked at his nasty retort.

"See the press is always gonna be 'gainst me on account of Barbara!" he exploded. "People don' like her. Don' understand her. She's got her extremes, y'know? Kinda like a man in some ways an' that just causes a lotta problems for a lotta people. Rubs 'em the wrong way 'cause she just speaks her mind! Not like a woman deals with shit at all, man, runnin' frantically on tiptoe aroun' a problem like a scared mouse instead of dealin' direct with it, y'know? She's always tellin' me I need to stand up for myself, not just let everybody push me around!"

I took a deep breath. I knew he was not going to remotely embrace what I had to say.

"Ed, all I know is what I've read. There's got to be at least a glimmer of truth in those articles. You're a celebrity! You're in the entertainment section of the newspapers constantly, even all the way out here in Colorado Springs! But you seem to be alienating all of your friends. And why? I mean, this ridiculous fight with Ed Garland, for example. And last week firing several men … for what? They asked for an advance that you had promised them? And then rehiring them two days later! Or not paying out the bonuses that you've been paid by the club and the band takes you to court to collect their just due? That's just not who you are!" As soon as the words were out of my mouth I regretted having spoken them at all.

"So you're 'gainst me now too? Jes' like everybody else, eh? Without all of the goddamn facts!" He then yelled something in patois that I didn't exactly understand, but knew was an extremely nasty expletive. "You know why I called? Tell you 'bout the tour. I thought maybe you'd find that pretty amazin'. Maybe even be happy for me 'bout it, y'know? I mean, after all these years I'm finally playin' Europe. Ain' that where you was headed before Emma was born? I swear that's what you told me!"

"Yes, it is," I answered quietly. "Then once she was born everything ... changed ... as you know."

"Yeah, 'cause you was too damned afraid to raise your own goddamned kid when she came out with dark skin!" he yelled hoarsely. "Don' you talk to me 'bout any shit I've done wrong with my life miss high and mighty!"

"Why on earth are you being so hateful? Why now? What the ..."

"Why? Why bother to spell it out to you! I expect you of all people will understand how the world can turn vicious on you ... but, oh shit ... jes' forget I called. Never mind any of it!"

He slammed the phone down. I stood in my kitchen listening to the buzzing tone on the dead line mourning the loss of our longtime friendship, our secrets, respect and yes, our love for one another.

I continued to listen to the Club Hangover broadcasts for the next several months and was still absorbed by Ory's music, but there were times I agreed with many critics that his work seemed an uncomfortable caricature of itself. That innate sense of when to be the rhythm man, when to push forward with a countermelody or when to lay back with a series of smoothly blended harmonies, now seemed elusive at times. He was always revered as an ensemble player, envisioning every band he directed as a tight unit, not a backup group behind a soloist or two. And to be absolutely fair, that never changed. Let the Tommy Dorseys and the Glenn Millers and the Benny Goodmans and the Woody Hermans and the Satchmo Armstrongs dominate their bands by their namesake's spectacular soloing he'd been quoted in numerous news articles. Ory never considered himself as a soloist, and oddly when I thought back, I actually felt that the boastful Jelly Roll Morton was the only other bandleader in the original jazz days who sought to accomplish the same. That's really what made that old Creole jazz music of New Orleans "the bomb" – that tight ensemble of a half dozen musicians offering up their unique creations either from a roughly sketched lead sheet or more than likely from memory, night after night, to a world thirsty for that hot, extemporaneous diversion.

    I followed much of Ory's European band tour. France had always thoroughly loved American jazz and welcomed Ory, the supreme papa in many opinions, with open arms. The French newspapers couldn't begin to understand what had taken one of their most revered recording stars, Kid Ory, so long to finally make his way across the Atlantic. But, the harsher American press followed Ory overseas as well. Ugly news hit the U.S. tabloids when Ory's longtime drummer Minor Hall became seriously ill and was abandoned in one city without any money whatsoever, forced to fend his own way back to the States for treatment. Bassist Wellman Braud, who had taken over for Ed Garland, ultimately had to sue the Orys through the musician's union to recoup back wages from the tour. Barbara was also on the tour and unless the interview was in French, which Ory could understand, but thankfully, Barbara could not, she was constantly adding her remarks and incorrect back stories which embarrassingly often needed to be further clarified by Ory himself.

I went with several neighbors to see the movie "*Around the World in Eighty Days*" when it first opened at a theater in Colorado Springs and was quite surprised to see a two-minute short of Ory's French tour featured on one of the opening newsreels. Despite the silvering hair and craggy face, he still moved gracefully, truly dancing with that trombone at age seventy as the band played an excellent version of "*Muskrat Ramble.*" I tried to read his face during that larger-than-life newsreel up on the screen. Was he happy? Had the tour been going well? Somehow I perceived tension between Ory and several of his musicians even in that news short, something completely foreign to the easy ambience within his bands of years gone by. Ory's band had played in brief cameo segments in several movies that I'd seen prior to that as well, "*New Orleans*" in 1947, "*Mahogany Music*" in 1950 and "*The Benny Goodman Story*" in 1955. At least by the time of the newsreel, producers had given up smearing what looked like a bucket of rancid tar all over his straight, thin silvery hair!

A couple of months later I received a large envelope postmarked New York City, apparently sent by Ory when their ship had landed, just prior to his having boarded a train out for the west coast. I pulled out two glossy, colorized newspaper photographs of Kid Ory and a very attractive young woman. Well, that certainly didn't take long I muttered in disgust, wondering why on earth he felt it necessary to send this to me. I looked at the back of one photo and saw written: '*Le Kid' Edouard Ory avec la chanteuse extraordinaire Helen Mason Campbell – dans la Salle Pleyel, 17 Octobre 1956.*" A hastily scribbled note in Ory's handwriting was taped on the back of the other photo: "*Came up after show. Singer from the States. Knew "Eh la Bas" et "C'est l'autre Can-Can" but didn't know how. Said she'd never learned any Creole patois.*" I glanced at the photos quickly again and had started to replace them in the envelope, then stopped and took a harder look at the picture. Ory and the young woman were smiling directly at the camera. I stared at the young woman again. Then I saw it. They shared almost identical cinnamon complexions and height. Ory's dark eyes. Ory's arched eyebrows. Ory's slicked back thick straight hair … Emma's beautiful smile.

Shaking, I pulled out a three-page magazine article, written in French, but Ory had circled a large portion in red and then written out a page in translation: *"They said I crawled into Mama's car when we stopped for petrol in Milwaukee, Wisconsin. That's where they found me, under the fur wraps on the floor when they got home. They lived further north. The police took a photo, but no one ever came forward, so my Mama and Papa, the Campbells, adopted me. My Papa died a few years later and Mama and I moved to Memphis, Tennessee to be near her family. I was one of the children from my church in Memphis who sang in a film made there called "Hallelujah."A very pretty girl named Nina Mae McKinney was the star. She told me I should go to Paris if I wanted to be a real singer or an actress, so that's what Mama and I did when I was a little older. Paris was a good place to be for my race even during the Nazi occupation. We have a little girl, Deidre. She loves to sing and has this huge voice, huge range! But she's much more serious even though she's only 5! She imitates opera singers all the time! I must have some moldy relative dangling from the family tree somewhere out there who loved opera!"*

I looked on the second page of the article and saw the police file's grainy photo of a frightened little girl with huge brown eyes, clad in a dark coat with large square black buttons and black velvet bandings on the cuffs, collar and hem, clutching a little toy parrot in front of her shoulder. Inside of that coat was the label on which I could visualize the line exactly as Emma had written it out in her diary: *"This is Helen Mason's coat."*

Helen Mason Campbell was our Tayvie.

I looked back at the glossy photos of Ory and Tayvie. I now realized that she had to be older than she appeared in the photograph; Tayvie would now be in her late thirties. And her little girl Deidre would be my great-granddaughter. I began to laugh, hiccupping with tears at the same time. Oh yes, there are indeed a couple of moldy opera singers in your past, Helen Mason Campbell! And also, my sweet little Tayvie, you crawled into that car in Chicago, not Milwaukee, probably quietly singing those two songs to your little parrot! We'd never thought to look anywhere north because none of the orphan asylums were located north of Chicago. But Milwaukee was only ninety miles away! Even back in those days the roads were good enough that a car could have made that trip in a few hours with a full gas tank. We'd just never considered such an obvious possibility as a four-year-old child hitchhiking!

Given all of Ory's recent turmoil with the press, his marriage, his new daughter and constant problems that he now faced with his musicians, venues, recordings and copyrights, I knew that he would never admit to this young woman known as Helen Mason Campbell that he was her father, would never announce it to the world. But I also knew that secretly he would follow her career in France as well as that of little Deidre. And I also knew that his having sent me this information was to give me that same opportunity. He knew that I would never intrude on Tayvie's life either. What could I possibly offer this successful young woman or her young daughter at this point? But for me, finally, there was closure. There was a family whose dreams I would now be able to follow, to hold dear within my heart. The most important pull in the universe. An even greater pull than music, as even Edward Ory now knew.

*"If it hadn't been for jazz,*
*There wouldn't be no rock & roll"*
Louis "Satchmo" Armstrong

## Chapter 27: The Road Home

Somewhere in the early 1960s I was moved from my little cottage over to Winfield House since I was no longer able to care for myself. My room was quite small, but after all, how much space did I really need? Most importantly, it was one of the few that actually looked out over the mountains. Watching the snowcaps slowly creep downward as winter approached or regress in the late spring were everyday joys even if my own infrequent journeys out to Win's statue and Emma's gravesite were now always in a wheelchair and restricted to warm weather.

These days whenever I played my Ory records the young girls who were assigned to help me in the afternoons simply rolled their eyes and politely asked if they might play their own music instead. Most jazz music had now drifted off into its own non-danceable direction, along with performance irregularities such as Miles Davis playing with his back to the audience, and the younger trendsetters had begun to worship artists like Buddy Holly and Elvis Presley, followed a few years later by Chubby Checker, The Beatles, The Rolling Stones and an entire so-called British invasion. To me there seemed to be a lot of painfully loud rhythms and jarring guitar chords, but very little substance beyond that.

For several years I had subscribed to two French music magazines hoping to hear more about Tayvie, but her name gradually appeared less frequently. She had recorded two long-playing records or LPs as they'd now become known, and after a long wait, I finally managed to obtain one of those. The afternoon girls who cared for me knew that if my eyes were closed while listening to *"Le Jazz Chaud! Musique de Helen!"* that meant I was deep into listening and *not* asleep. My tongue had taken on a sharpness all its own at times; I had now gained that ugly reputation awarded to so many elderly women of being "difficult." Years ago I would have been horrified at such an appellation, but now I actually relished it as one of my few accomplishments!

Kid Ory had made another European tour in 1959 and afterwards ran his own nightclub in San Francisco for a few years. But then shortly after my having moved to Winfield House, he stopped performing on any regular basis and he and his family quietly moved to Hawaii. As one of several honored guests, Ory was invited to perform at the New Orleans Jazz Festival in 1971 which was his first trip back in that city since 1919. He was not in the best of health, playing very little, but did manage to sing a few songs according to a shortened reprint from a *New Orleans Times-Picayune* article in *The Colorado Springs Gazette*. Jazz musicians rarely garnered much print space these days. Louis Armstrong was also invited to perform at the Jazz Festival, but was in far too frail of health to attend according to the article. I was excited to see a picture of Ory with Ed Garland. They had finally patched up their feud and were interviewed by a couple of reporters about their sixty-plus year working relationship.

A doctor named Oliver Sacks at the Bronx Hospital in New York City in 1969 had been experimenting with a new drug called L-Dopa on *encephalitis lethargica* patients who had been frozen, mindless statues since the 1920s. Emma had of course been diagnosed with that same disease. Some patients responded well to the treatment, others became violently ill from it, but all eventually lapsed back into their prior, inert state of being. I was so grateful that Emma's suffering was long over.

I had received one last short article from Ory stating that Deidre Campbell, daughter of French jazz *étoile* Helen Mason Campbell, had just been hired as an apprentice at the Metropolitan Opera in New York City. According to the article, Marian Anderson had been the first Negro soloist to ever appear on the Met stage in 1955, although no permanent colored singers were in residence at the Met since problems with travel and housing for them still remained a complex issue in the 1950s and '60s. But despite those problems, Deidre Campbell had now been hired, and was also one of the youngest to have ever been made full apprentice according to the article. She had a long road of expensive training ahead to fully realize her gifts, the reporter added, and hoped some wealthy benefactors might consider donations towards her sponsorship.

Who could remember the importance of Charles Lindburgh's first transatlantic flight when we now had built a rocket ship that had propelled a man to the moon? Or the heroism of men such as Abraham Lincoln when as a nation we had now experienced firsthand our president's being mowed down right in front of us? Or the importance of our country's earlier world wars as we watched in horror live television coverage of a questionable war being fought for unknown reasons on the other side of the world? Or those with darker skins finally being recognized as citizens and given the right to vote? Or any woman finally being recognized as a citizen and given the right to vote or even allowed to keep her own property after marriage or divorce? There were times that I spent several hours mulling over all of these fascinating decades of history, but then afterwards, overwhelmed, simply crawled gratefully back into my withered cocoon and the rather narrowed outlook typically shared by my elderly cohorts.

Some things were now definitely worse in my opinion, however. For example, I would have loved to still possess my original nice heavy, black dial phone instead of this ugly pink cylinder with fat push buttons that glowed in the dark at night and slid off my side table while unleashing a puny ring like a strangled goat. I complained about it to just about everyone within earshot. Fortunately for me, the thing very rarely emitted its annoying bleat signaling the need for any attention.

One January afternoon, one of my young caretakers (I had long ago given up attempting to learn any of these girls' names) had left me parked in front of a nice warm fire burning in the huge new fireplace in the remodeled community room at Winfield House. Quite often I would re-read Emma's old journals before nodding off, but today I had been reading Kate Chopin's *"The Awakening"* yet again. As I woke up I became aware of a blond woman in a tight, pink knit skirt and white leather boots sitting next to me. Why women these days wanted to wear constricted tubes that shoved out their thighs like sausages beneath the hem thoroughly baffled me.

"Yes?" I said, blinking. My memory was not always very reliable, but I didn't think I'd ever seen her before. "I'm sure you have better things to do than sit there and listen to me snore."

"They told me at the front desk that you were Mrs. Hannah Barrington," said the woman rather crisply. "Is that correct?"

"Yes, that's correct," I replied, staring at her. She reminded me of someone, but I couldn't place it. There was something about that insincere way of smiling with just her mouth and not her eyes. "Are you going to tell me *your* name or is this your idea of *"What's My Line?"*

"My name's Muriel Fiske," she nodded, firmly shaking my limp hand.

"And what did you want of me, Mrs. Muriel Fiske?"

"Ms, actually," she replied, flashing that insincere smile again. "I'm actually a senior editor for the new *Ms* magazine. You've heard of it, I assume?"

"I don't read magazines, especially with made up words like *Ms* Muriel whatever-you-said-your-name-was-again. So if you're looking to sell me a subscription or contribute to some charity or other for six months of free magazines, I'm poorer than a church mouse and just plain not interested."

I picked up my book and started to flip to the page where I last remembered reading, hoping she would simply go away.

"No, I'm not looking to sell you a subscription," she replied with a rather contrived laugh. "Editors don't sell magazines, Mrs. Barrington!"

"So what *do* you want? Is it five yet? I think today's tomato soup and grilled cheese. That's my favorite supper you know …"

"No, it's not even three o'clock yet, Mrs. Barrington. Don't worry, I won't keep you from your favorite supper."

I sighed. The Muriel woman wiggled her sausages back into her chair. I appeared to be cornered for the time being.

"My mother recently passed away," she finally began.

"Sorry," I replied, still hoping to find a way to rid myself of this woman. "Can't help you there."

"Well, actually, maybe you can," she continued. "Her name was Alice Fiske."

"Eh, well, that's nice." The name meant nothing to me.

"While cleaning out many of Mother's things that had been left in a relative's attic out here in Colorado Springs long before she'd gotten married, I was shocked to come across a reissued birth certificate changing her name to Alice Elizabeth Hughes. Apparently her original name had been Alice Elizabeth Barrington, daughter of a John and Hannah Barrington, same date of birth. Mother had always said that my great-grandmother, whose name was Margaret Hughes, had raised her, but it looks as though that wasn't true until Mother was maybe age thirteen or so."

I squinted looking at her. Yes, this woman was definitely Alice's daughter. I could see the resemblance now. She was quite attractive though rather full of figure, with those same thin lips that smiled without the slightest warmth reflected within her light blue eyes.

"And why on earth do you think that I'm this same Hannah Barrington?" I retorted.

"Well, I wouldn't have at first! But when I mentioned it to the current house owners, the woman said that you had been one of her teachers here at the Myron Stratton Home many years ago and that she distinctly remembered helping take care of your invalid daughter named Alice Barrington. She also mentioned that she had been with you when your daughter passed away and thought you still lived here. In fact, she informed me about the headstone in the garden which I observed before coming in here to find you just now."

"A magazine editor and a master detective to boot, my, my," I snorted. "And? So?"

"Obviously that can't be my mother who is buried out there with that name, Mrs. Barrington, and I looked up the official birth and death records at the courthouse. The Alice Elizabeth Barrington in that grave is shown as having Mother's exact birth date with you listed as her mother," she replied conclusively, a lawyer smugly summing up her defense.

"Is it five yet?"

"No, it's only a few minutes after three," stated Muriel. "Well? I'm just curious to know your side of the story, that's all."

"My side of the story, eh? Well, I forgot."

"Somehow I really doubt that. I truly think you're as sharp as a tack when you want to be, Mrs. Barrington."

Tilting my head slightly, I pursed my lips for a moment and then replied, "Ok, well how's this for an explanation. You're right. The girl was an invalid, but had committed a murder and we were running from Al Capone in Chicago so I had to change her name."

Muriel frowned. "So that's your explanation?"

"Well, you asked, so there's the story."

"Ok, ok," she answered, shaking her head. "I guess I'm not going to find out anything right now. What are you reading? That's such a wonderfully old-fashioned cover. You rarely see anything like that anymore. May I?"

Reluctantly, I handed over the book. She carefully fingered along the tangled, dark-green vines and red berries printed on the light green cloth cover before opening it.

"*The Awakening*? Where on earth did you get this?" exclaimed Muriel, eyes wide. "This is one of the rare books from its first print run! And it's been banned for something like sixty years at least! Every bookstore in the country is now clamoring to keep it in stock right now, it sells out so fast! I mean, absolutely everyone's reading it right now! And, my God! Mrs. Barrington! It even has a front inscription signed by Kate Chopin herself!

*"To my dearest Win ~ so much of me has poured itself*
*into this creation*
*but I fear the bounds of propriety will soon stopper the bottle.*
*I wanted you to have a copy before it disappears*
*from the face of the earth*
*~ fondly as always, Katie O'Flaherty Chopin."*

"Do you have any idea what this book is worth?" Muriel continued.

No, but I bet you do or you'll make it your business to find out, I thought to myself.

"Do you know who this inscription is made out to? How on earth did you get hold of it?"

"That's two questions. I can only handle one at a time," I commented, as I thrust my hand out to take back my book.

"Oh, sorry. Who is it made out to?"

"Winfield Stratton. He's the man whose statue you saw out in the garden. It's his endowment that built this entire place and keeps it running."

"And how do you happen to have it?"

"Well, if you didn't believe my story about Al Capone you sure as heck won't believe my story about Win Stratton," I muttered.

Muriel shrugged away my retort. "In so many ways this book represents the beginning, the first real exploration from a woman's perspective into exactly the new freedom for women that *Ms* magazine explores, Mrs. Barrington! All of these past years of oppression for women, being kept from knowing our own minds, our career aspirations, our innermost physical desires! I mean, can you imagine when you were a young woman allowing yourself to have sex with a man you were drawn to, like Edna Pontellier did in *The Awakening*? Of course not! No woman can! It was unknown back then! Only a woman of ill repute would have done such a reckless thing! "

She hadn't given me a chance to answer her question, but of course, given my own history, I would have disagreed. She certainly would have been shocked to hear of my affair with Win Stratton resulting in our daughter Emma or my brief, but intense relationship with the man who not only had been my daughter Emma's lover, Kid Ory, but was also the father of Emma's own illegitimate daughter. What kind of women did those things, Ms. Muriel whatever-your-name-is? Well, ones like me apparently. Women who didn't see the need to subscribe to renegade magazines to dictate their actions.

She wanted to take the book to have it appraised and I told her no. She promised to come by again early the following week with that information before she had to fly back out to New York City. Why she thought I wanted to see her again was beyond me. But she did at least push me over to the dining room in time to queue up for the tomato soup and grilled cheese, so I begrudgingly had to agree to her next visit. If you didn't get there early, sometimes they ran out of the soup.

My pink goat phone gave out its strangled bleat the

following Tuesday, an excitable Muriel Fiske on the other end. First off, she apologized that she wouldn't be able to come back to visit today after all. I was scarcely heartbroken, but kept that opinion to myself. Had I heard that the Roe vs. Wade decision had actually just passed in the Supreme Court this morning?

"Roe what?" I replied. "That's fish eggs or something isn't it?"

"Roe vs. Wade, Mrs. Barrington. You know. The abortion bill? It's now passed into law! That means it's now legal for any woman to seek an abortion! Legal and safe! No more back alley butchering. You have no idea how hard today's women have worked to make this a reality!"

"Ah, I see," I slowly replied, nodding my head. "Well, good thing that wasn't around a long time ago or you probably wouldn't even be here."

There was a pause on the other end.

"What on earth are you talking about, Mrs. Barrington?" laughed Muriel.

Well, if you don't get it there's nothing much I can do to spell it out to you, I mumbled to myself, shaking my head.

"Anyway, as I'm sure you must be aware, this has been one of the biggest items that *Ms* magazine has been following, so I have to get back to New York immediately which is why I can't come by today," Muriel continued.

"Well, have a good trip," I replied, poised to hang up before the goat phone slid off my side table.

"Oh, one other thing before I ring off. I asked a rare books dealer here in Colorado Springs about your copy of *The Awakening* and he said it would easily be worth, are you sitting down … six or even seven thousand dollars! My next time out I'll come by and take it in for his actual appraisal. He said it might even fetch ten thousand or even more if the book was in mint condition, which I told him it was! You could sell it and maybe do some traveling! Maybe see some relatives you haven't seen in a long time!"

"Well, well, that's mighty nice to hear," I replied flatly. "Imagine that."

"Yes, indeed! Imagine that!" she laughed. "Well, the airport cab I'd called earlier is here, so I'm going to have to hang up. I'll talk with you in a week or so, Mrs. Barrington. Bye!"

"So long."

I picked up the book off my tiny bookshelf and buzzed for my nurse, asking her to take me immediately down to the mail room in the adjacent building. Once there I had the girl on duty call New York City's directory assistance to get the address of The Metropolitan Opera House. Then I carefully wrapped the book in a cushion of wax sheeting and brown paper, secured with layers of string, addressing it to Miss Deidre Campbell. Inside the front cover I had enclosed a short note which read: *Deidre ~ may your voice always soar out high above the treetops – with all our love, Win, Hannah, Edouard, Emma & Octavie.*

I was exhausted, shaking, once I'd gotten back upstairs to my room. Dinner was tomato soup and grilled cheese, still my favorite, but I had no appetite which concerned my nurse. She thought I might be coming down with a cold and wanted to order a tonic and a hot plaster, but I told her I just wanted to be left alone. I slept fitfully – several hours asleep then suddenly jarred awake, staring out into the cold, dark room, sometimes seeing oddly dancing shadows or hearing distant voices. I heard the newspaper thudding against my door very early and called out, asking that the boy hand it in to me.

The front pages were nothing but coverage of the Roe vs. Wade decision. Some articles euphorically in favor of the decision alongside others claiming that as a nation the United States had now sunk to a moral depravity unlike anything in modern history, jockeyed for space throughout in *The Gazette*. "January 22, 1973 would be a date to forever live in infamy" was the title of one of those articles. Wearily, I turned to the last page of an inside section and quite surprised, saw a small picture of Kid Ory as a young man, displaying his tailgate trombone with that charming gleam in his eye I remembered so well from those early days. He had died very early that morning, January 23, at age 86, in Hawaii after a lengthy illness.

The wind was blowing icy pebbles of sleet, a rapid staccato against the windows in my room. I thought that I'd read of a predicted blizzard somewhere in the newspaper – which was now strewn everywhere in dozens of piles, both on the bed and scattered about on the floor.

The morning nurse came in to check on me.

"They say you didn't eat nothin' at all yesterday, Mrs. Barrington," she began, her hand gently rubbing my shoulder. "I can bring you some oatmeal or maybe some toast. Would you like a poached egg? What sounds good this mornin'?"

"Nothing right … now," I replied, my voice very faint even to my own ears. "But maybe you could put a record on the phonograph for me. Not up too loud."

"Of course," she said, walking over to my bookshelf. "Which one did you want, ma'am?"

"You choose. Please. Anything of …"

"Kid Ory, yes ma'am. That much I do know! Not much else in here anyways!"

I smiled, nodding weakly. I heard her carefully place the needle on the record, felt her warm touch as she smoothed back my hair from my forehead in the light blue mist that had now begun swirling over me, and was only vaguely aware of her quiet footsteps as she walked out of the room.

Suddenly I realized that Win was next to me, his white shirt sleeves rolled up to his elbows, his strong weather-beaten arm so warm around my shoulders, as we slowly walked together down a wide dirt path. We came to a park where people were lying about on blankets or sitting along a mosaic of live oak tree branches that spread out over the area like elongated benches. I asked Win what had happened to the snow. Or the mountains. He smiled, those bright blue eyes looking deeply into mine, hugging me even tighter under a majestically undulating, navy blue sky on this lush evening. The spicy scent of steaming Creole-style shrimp lingered, along with the sight of bluebottles darting high in the air. Down in front of us, I recognized Kid Ory, Mutt Carey, Jimmie Noone, Wellman Braud and Jelly Roll Morton on a wide-plank pier that extended several feet out into a lazy river. Emma was on the pier as well, laughing with Ory, clad in her dark blue wrapped dress with the silver stars, her wild dark-blond hair wound into the matching chiffon scarf.

Win pointed over to our left. There sat Zuma and two men -- her brother, husband and her little girl, fast asleep, nestled next to her in the grass. Just to the right of the stage as we continued walking were Frank and Alma Collier, Frank laughing heartily as he filled another man's glass from his metal flask.

"I saved us a place a little further over to the right, down by the stage, my little sparrow. Looks like the concert's ready to begin," he whispered in my ear, just as Ory stomped off the count.

*Although this novel may not ever manage to actually find its way into print, I think it's somehow pertinent to mention that I finished writing it tonight on Kid Ory's 132$^{nd}$ birthday, Dec. 25, 2018.*

# About the Author

A graduate from the Jordan College of Music at Butler University, in Indianapolis, Indiana, Mim Eichmann has found that her creative journey has taken her down many exciting, interwoven pathways. For well over two decades she was known in the Chicago area primarily as the artistic director/choreographer for Midwest Ballet Theatre, bringing full-length professional ballet performances to thousands of dance lovers annually. A desire to become involved again in the folk music world brought about the creation of her acoustic quartet Trillium, now in its 15th year, which performs throughout the Midwest and has released four cds. Among many varied music avenues she's written the lyrics and music for two award-winning original children's cds. Several of her short stories have either won or been finalists in international competitions during the last few years. Her debut historical fiction novel *"A Sparrow Alone"* was published by Living Springs Publishers in April 2020 and was a semi-finalist in the Illinois Library Association's 2020 Soon-to-be-Famous Project Competition. *"Muskrat Ramble"* is the highly anticipated sequel to *"A Sparrow Alone."*

Please take a moment to visit her author website at www.mimeichmann.com.

## Source Materials

**Books:**

Abbott, Karen – "Sin in the Second City: Madams, Ministers, Playboys and the Battle for America's Soul"

Antippas, Andy Peter – "A Guide to the Historic French Quarter"

Bechet, Sidney – "Treat it Gentle – an autobiography"

Bolcom, William and Robert Kimball – "Reminiscing with Noble Sissle and Eubie Blake"

Cahill, Susan – "Women & Fiction – Short Stories by and About Women"

Chopin, Kate – "The Awakening and Selected Stories"

Dwight, Eleanor – "Edith Wharton – an Extraordinary Life"

Holley, James Stokes – "The Invisible People of the Pikes Peak Region"

Lee, Hermione – "Edith Wharton – a biography"

Lee, Maureen – "Sissieretta Jones: "The Greatest Singer of Her Race"

McCusker, John – "Creole Trombone – Kid Ory and the Early Years of Jazz"

Miller, Donald L. – "City of the Century – The Epic of Chicago and the Making of America"

Reminisce Books – From Flappers to Flivvers ... There's Never Been a Decade Like It!"

Sacks, Dr. Oliver – "Awakenings"

Schuller, Gunther – "Early Jazz – "Its Roots and Musical Development"

Strasser, Susan – "Never Done – A History of American Housework"

Taylor, Troy – **"Wicked New Orleans – The Dark Side of the Big Easy"**
Toth, Emily – **"Unveiling Kate Chopin"**
Traxel, David – **"1898 – The Birth of the American Century"**
Waters, Frank – **"Midas of the Rockies – Biography of Winfield Scott Stratton, Croesus of Cripple Creek"**
Wharton, Edith – **"A Backward Glance – The Autobiography of Edith Wharton"**
Wolff, Cynthia Griffin – **"A Feast of Words – The Triumph of Edith Wharton"**

**Other:**

Kidory.com
Interviews taped by Alan Lomax with Jelly Roll Morton in 1939 – Library of Congress
*"L'homme de la Nouvelle-Orleans: Kid Ory et son Creole Jazz Band"* (short documentary)
Dr. James Dapogny, early jazz music professor at the University of Michigan-Ann Arbor
John McCusker's *"Creole of Jazz Music Tour"* in New Orleans
Laura Plantation – Vacherie, Louisiana
Oak Alley Plantation – Vacherie, Louisiana
Smithsonian Institute, Washington D.C. – catalog of Jelly Roll Morton's works

CPSIA information can be obtained
at www.ICGtesting.com
Printed in the USA
LVHW012009150922
728490LV00002B/253

9 781734 459371